THE EMPIRE OF THE BLACK SUNS: VOLUME II

CODE OF CONNECTIONS

Acknowledgements

It has taken a little while to get this book ready for shelves, and it always was the longest to write – both for the draft and then the re-writes. The Code of Connections is dedicated to personal growth, and the pursuit of the better self.

I once again must thank Johanna Gogos, for her wonderful editing skills in getting this book up to scratch. I would also like to extend a thanks and shout-out to my friend Henry Neilson, a fellow aspiring author, who has encouraged me to reach for the quality of writing and publication that I should be aspiring for. If you're here and you haven't seen his content, I know that you'll enjoy it.

Thanks also go to the keen readers who motivated me to release this. Amongst these are Stephanie Siomos, the sole purchaser of the ebook, and Patty Miller, to whom I hope this book finds well and answers the questions she had for me.

"Us, of course." I said before I knew *exactly* why. "Because..." then the answer came to me, I grinned. "Think of how many connections that guy has. If we want to expand our connections to other Suneva, he's the guy to talk to. Somebody who he knows would have to know at least *one* Legendary."

Chad hummed, frowning. "I don't know about that plan, man." He said. "Seems kind of counter-productive to everything else happening in our lives. We're trying to protect Celeste from Argol's and Hesslik's Suneva, after all. And I don't think Mr Argol, nor other Argols, have a positive opinion of me either."

Chad had been Hesslik's personal agent before abandoning his post to join us. Hesslik had often required him to capture Argol gang members and disrupt their activities. This, to me, seemed only a benefit.

"Then you must know some Argols too!" I beamed. "It's perfect. We've got so many ins."

"It's risky." Chad crossed his arms. "The Argols are unpredictable, and that makes them dangerous to deal with."

"What makes them dangerous at all?" I asked. "I've only ever seen them interrogate a man once, and whilst they were rough, Hesslik's agents have done much worse to me."

"It's their ideology, not their methods." Chad noted. "They see themselves as freedom fighters, fighting to be Suneva in the world that either doesn't know we exist, or feels threatened by our existence. Really, though, the freedom-fighting ended a decade ago. Now they're just a gang racquet extorting Suneva for protections against communities and law enforcement. All they're doing is dragging the Suneva image through the mud. Not the best pack of Suneva, really. Their modern lack of direction makes them unpredictable, and prone to murdering to assert dominance in edge communities."

"That's...not great." I slumped. "I can see why you're cautious."

"Your plan isn't all that bad, James, we just have to be careful." Chad warned. "It might be the best idea we'll get."

"You'd have to hope that we can stay on their good side." I mused, although I was conflicted. Would I want to be an ally of such people? "Hesslik is a common enemy, at least."

"I think with everything we've done to Hesslik's Empire between the four of us, we'd have to be liked by Argols just fine." Chad patted my shoulder. "We should look deeper into this plan."

A muffled voice interrupted, yelling from the kitchen. "James, where on Earth did you get all of this pita?" Mum called. "I like the gesture, but Jesus, James, there's enough here to feed an army."

"I better go handle this." I said to Chad, and he nodded, falling onto the bed and covering it whole. I rounded my room to the kitchen, where Mum stood before the mountain of pita bread I'd been given earlier. She was already eating a piece of it, and her face was trying its hardest to be stern and displeased.

"Mountain of pita?" I heard Simone call from the computer room. Soon, her steps came down the hall, too.

"It's from Natalie's Grandma." I said to Mum. "I didn't tell you about this?" How had I forgotten to tell Mum about the pile of pita bread that was a gift to her? She was home when I walked in with the pile, for *Omercronius'* sake.

"Would I be asking if you told me?" Mum asked flatly.

"Well, no." I hummed. "It was a gift for you, anyway. Which seemed weird at the time. Do we *know* Natalie's Grandma? I've never met her before?"

"What's the name?" Simone asked as she skidded around the corner. Her hand dove for the plate, pulling the biggest piece. "I wouldn't forget a name."

There's a lot that you hold on to, Simone. I shuddered, thinking of her hatred for Suneva. "Tess Floros is her name. She said that she knew Dad, and that she wished she visited before he died."

"Tess Floros?" Mum's face went white.

"Doesn't sound like anybody I know." Simone hummed. "Did you try to have them killed or something, Mum? You've gone white."

"Simone!" Mum grumbled. "No, she was a good friend of your dad's. She's been '*living in Greece*' since about 1982. Clearly she's been hiding a few blocks *that* way this whole time." She pointed off in the wrong direction. I shrugged.

"He never wanted to introduce us?" I asked. "He never talked about her?"

"Well he probably would have introduced you if he knew she lived in the country." Mum said. "Plus, she's an old woman. Not much to about her to tell the two of you, really."

4

"Weird though, isn't it?" Simone asked, looking at me. "That you end up making friends with her granddaughter and reuniting some old, long-lost relation after all this time? It's almost like it was staged."

"Yes, a weird *coincidence*." I avoided the use of the word *destiny* around Simone. "I guess she'd like to catch up again, then?" I pointed to the bread. Mum sighed.

"She was John's friend, not mine." Mum said. "It'd be nice to see her, but I don't know that I care either way. Bit of a strange way to announce her return, anyway."

"I guess." I nodded, and stole a piece of pita for both Chad and I before leaving.

Mum didn't seem at all concerned by my meeting Tess Floros, and neither did Simone, which only meant one thing; neither of them know that Tess was a Suneva, let alone a powerful one. This worked in my favour a few ways. Firstly, Simone wouldn't start fearing for my life and investigating my activities, leading to her inevitably ostracising me. Secondly, Mum wouldn't get angry at me for getting deeper into this 'Suneva stuff' without telling her. And thirdly, nobody knew that Dad knew Suneva, which meant he could have been personally connected to countless more. I could see my plan coming to life.

***

The following day, I invited everybody to my attic to discuss my revelations.

I pushed Natalie, Celeste, and Chad up the dusty, groaning ladder into the roof space of my house. I left the ladder down, giving us greater light, but also stopping it from locking us up in the roof. Here, the light died as it entered the window, and shadows danced and waved just out of sight. The tense expressions strewn across the faces in the dark room indicated that the attic's creepiness was not solely my own machination. I crawled past my friends, over to the chest of my dad's stuff. I drug the crate into the centre of the space, and worked it open. The strange collectibles of his life remained where I'd last left them – when I'd come looking for Kuvalik's book.

Opening the chest, I had a moment of guilt. Mum had taken a leap of faith in trusting me to guard my own safety in all things Suneva. I'd been avoiding telling her everything, until it all exploded out just a week ago, and now here I was doing more secret investigation. Moreso, this was an investigation that I was *hoping* could lead me to a man known by most to be dangerous. What was I thinking? I knew this was wrong, too, because I'd waited until both Mum and Simone were out of the house to conduct this research. I saw Mum's happy, oblivious face in my head, and my disgust at myself gnawed at my arms, almost forcing me to close the chest.

Almost.

I started to pull the mundane items out.

"What's your plan, James?" Natalie asked. "You still haven't really explained it."

"I'm worried you won't like it." I said shyly. *And I'm worried that I shouldn't suggest it, too.* "Because it's daring."

"Can't be more daring than anything else we've done." Celeste chuffed. I turned up to her, her beautiful, deep eyes and red lips so compelling. I still hadn't asked her about our kiss, and what it *really* meant. I had expected some kid of fairy-tale out of the moment, as if the curtain would close and that would be it, she liked me. But instead she brushed aside the moment's significance to hurry me out of the holding cell. I'd have to build the courage to ask her.

"James?" She asked. I realised I'd been staring, and coughed loudly.

"It will be." I said. "I want to use my dad's connections to find Mr Argol."

I continued rummaging, but silence had fallen behind me. Then, Celeste burst into laughter.

"You think Argol can help?" Celeste cackled. "Come on, not even a week after I accused you all of trying to sell me to Hesslik, and your new idea is Argol? Should I believe my thoughts here?"

"Please don't be like that, Celeste. I'm being serious." I was but a whisper to her tone. "I know it might be scary for you, but you're *not* Iva Argol. You'll be fine."

"And why Argol, of all people?" Natalie asked. "I mean, come on, James. That's a terrible suggestion."

"Because he has the most Suneva connections in the world next to Hesslik." I said. "I mean, look, we don't *have* to chase Argol, but the web of the

Argols is huge, and worth considering. Plus, I think my dad will have connections. Either way, he's bound to lead us to *some* Suneva."

"Are you so sure?" Natalie asked, coming to kneel by me. "Why do you think your dad is involved in any of this?"

"Your Yamitse told me that he was involved with Suneva communities here. Plus, he was a police officer working against Argols. He'd have to know Suneva."

"And you think the answers are in this box?"

"We kept a lot of weirder stuff." I said, pulling out his old tracksuit pants. "There's got to be a hint in here."

"I still think it's crazy." Celeste said. "You can't just go walking into Argol's arms."

"If it's any consolation, we probably won't make it." I hummed. "But we'll find a lot of Suneva on the way."

"We've got to be careful on that path." Celeste sighed. "We're not low profile."

"We can lay low." Chad piped up. "I've historically been good at sneaking around and dealing with Argols." He now came over to the box too, leaving Celeste by herself.

Celeste huffed, and noisily came to join. We spread the items across the attic floor, to give ourselves a good look at what we had to work with. Dad's clothes and trophies had gravitated together in a pile, useless to our efforts. Next to it, a pile of interest had emerged, full of books and videos. My eye, however, was caught by another item. His briefcase.

I could see it hanging from his arm, a cold night in winter, as the chill winds blasted through the door behind him. Brimming with papers, he placed it down on the kitchen bench as he knelt to the ground to greet a young Errol. The briefcase was forbidden, it's contents weren't for anybody else's eyes. From it, he pulled his little, leather-bound book, and his police-branch pen.

"His diary should be in here." I broke from the trance. "That could have some connections."

I grappled it in my hands. It was too light, and I realised that Mum would have emptied it before putting it up here. Still, I reached for the zips and whirred them open, letting its familiar smell thrust into my face. I dove my hand into the bag.

I felt around, trying to grab onto something but there wasn't anything big in here. There were a few cards, what felt like some money and some pieces of paper.

"Damn," I quietly cussed and pulled my hand out, "Maybe in the bigger pocket..." I unzipped the main part of the satchel and dove my hand in. Now I was onto something, it was definitely a book. I grabbed onto it and yanked it from the leather casing.

Don Bradman: The record Cricketer.

"Double damn!" I said and put the book gently onto the floor, next to the other sports biographies.

"Still got his bookmark in it." Chad smiled. "I wonder what he was up to..."

"I wouldn't worry," I noted, "He's read that one many times before." I shifted my attention back to the leather satchel and groped it in all positions. There had to be something useful inside.

"Let me have a go." Natalie said, holding out her hand. "You're taking a boy look."

I sighed, and handed her the case. She practically leaped into the thing, thrusting her hand and eye into each orifice, before emerging with some paper and cards.

"Here." She said, laying them on the floor. "I'm not sure how you missed these."

I didn't. I grumbled to myself. "It's no diary. That's a little disappointing."

"Nothing disappointing about somebody's cards." Chad noted. "Any trash is useful when you're trying to understand somebody."

"Exactly." Natalie agreed. She turned the cards over, giving us a look at their back sides. Chad's hand went for the piece of paper.

"See, James, this is a receipt. Maybe what your dad was buying could give us a lead...somehow." Chad huffed, and examined the purchase. "Looks like a fancy dinner."

"Let me see that." Celeste stole the list from Chad, scrutinising it. "This seems like a real feast."

My eye was drawn to a business card. Its edge was bone-white, unassuming, but it drew me in regardless. I picked it from the pile.

A deeply familiar symbol was printed on the front face – the mark of the black suns, backed by an interconnected hexagon. This was the symbol of the Code of Connections, and under it, on a blue wedge in the corner of the card, was the name *Alexis LeGrand*.

"Ha, look at this." I showed the card to the group. In turning it to show off, I now saw its backside. It was printed white, but had a handwritten message cursively penned across it. It was my dad's handwriting.

"The Code of Connections." Natalie nodded. "Who is Alexis LeGrand?"

"There's a message, too." I noted, and pulled it back in to read. Natalie came closer, but Celeste and Chad were still looking through the other refuse.

Dinner with Capo LeGrand. 6.00pm, 22ⁿᵈ of February. Whiteman Street tower penthouse. Bring salad and gift.

"Dinner party?" Natalie hummed, reading from over my shoulder.

"What was on that receipt, Celeste?" I asked.

"Some ingredients for what I imagine was a *great* salad." She said with cheer. "Grains, pomegranate, at least five herbs, yogurt. It sounds like your dad had good taste."

"What's the date on the receipt?"

"22ⁿᵈ of February, 1996." Celeste read. "Why?"

"Matches with this." I said, handing the card to Chad to pass to her. "Dad had a meeting with somebody."

"Somebody who was clearly a Suneva." Chad added. "That's *Na Kitos Keroseva*, the Code of Connections."

Celeste examined the card, both the symbol and the handwritten sides. Her face went white, before she sighed. "Oh, damn." She shook her head.

"What?" I asked.

"Capo LeGrand." She grumbled. "Did it have to be him?"

"Who are they?" Natalie asked.

"*Capo* LeGrand?" Chad sparked up. "That's the Argol leader in Melbourne. He was Vestas' worst enemy."

"Dinner with an Argol head?" I hummed.

"Are you sure that your dad was working against the Argols?" Natalie asked. "Seems weird that he'd be invited to dinner at their house."

"I don't know." I took the card back, and flipped it in my hand. Was my dad a corrupt officer? Why else would he be meeting with crime lords?

"Clearly the dinner happened, he brought a salad along." Natalie added.

"It could be a dinner for any reason." I asserted. Whatever the reason, it worked in my favour. My plan was coming together seamlessly.

"LeGrand will be a great lead, as long as he doesn't recognise me without the helmet." Chad smiled. "He's basically only one or two steps under Argol himself. He'd have to report *directly* to the Green Dragon."

"That's awfully convenient." Natalie hummed.

"And awfully risky." Celeste grumbled. "And for what? If Argol knew the location of a Legendary, why would he tell us? What does finding him through this web achieve, really?"

"In codes and mysteries, the journey is often more important than the destination." Chad smiled. This sentiment did not impress Celeste, who folded her arms. "I think that finding Argol is a good idea, even though it might be dangerous. If we're against Hesslik, Argol and his followers would be our biggest ally. Shouldn't he know what Hesslik is planning? Failing to find the Legendaries, isn't Argol the next best option?"

"That's better than my idea." I nodded along. Natalie hummed and nodded, too, but Celeste remained hard to convince.

"If I go along with this, what is our first step?" She asked.

"I suppose we'll have to talk to this Mr LeGrand." I said, pointing to the card which she still held. "And ask him where we can find Argol."

"And when he turns us back?"

"We bring the card, we explain that I'm John Grey's son, and maybe that changes things. We don't know what my father did, yet. Maybe being his son gets me an advantage. There's more to this that we don't know."

"Exactly. Maybe he hated your father." Celeste raised an eyebrow.

In my head, for the sake of my father's image, I was hoping on that outcome. Celeste smirked, having beaten me, and behind her, I saw a head rising into the attic.

My heart froze, dropping into my stomach. Mum or Simone, this was bad. I shuffled to ram the cards back into the case, much to everybody's confusion, until I locked eyes with Simone.

Four Suneva in an attic, loudly discussing our magical quests, right in the face of a vocal dissenter. Panic rushed me, and I had to stop my soul reaching for its connections. Celeste registered my panic, and went to flick her wrist to summon her Suneva weapon – her *shath*.

"Hi Simone." I squeaked the first word in, and Celeste held her breath, forcing her hand down.

"James, what the hell is this?" Simone growled, wrenching herself onto the trapdoor frame.

"What's what?" I asked – my intellectual and gripping response.

"James, why did you bring people up here to rifle through *that* chest?"

"These *people* are my friends." I defended. My brain struggled to think of a lie – it was hard to think of anything but the truth. I couldn't tell Simone why I was here, though. I had to tick over my thoughts.

"And?" Simone huffed. "You don't see the issue with just anybody trifling through Dad's stuff? Have some respect for the dead."

Everybody wore awkward expressions, ready to scuttle away and roll into the darkness. I should have felt as awkward as my friends, but a strange hotness came to me, and I chose my words flippantly.

"And what, you've got the monopoly on which of Dad's stuff I choose to share with whom?" I asked, a worse sentence coming to my tongue without any sense to stop it. "Last I remember, all you did was argue with the man. Did you even like him? Who are you to guard his grave?"

Simone snapped a sharp breath, her eyes flaring with scorn as they opened wide.

"James, how *dare* you." She rasped, pulling herself fully into the attic. I stumbled to her advance, her fists locked tight. "Get out of here, *now*, all of you."

"That's not fair, we're not even…"

"*Out!*" She demanded. Her voice reigned with such force that even the struggling light was squashed at the window, the room becoming darker. I tried to stand, and tried to move, but I couldn't make myself twitch a muscle. By body had locked in fear, only just jittering itself off the floor. A breeze blew across my face,

11

one that I wasn't aware I was controlling. How else had it kicked up in an attic? Dust stirred into the room.

"I said *move*." She ordered to me. Celeste, Natalie, and Chad were waiting on my move, unsure of what to do. I clawed at the floor, trying to raise myself, when suddenly I moved all at once, as if released from a hook. I fell towards the ladder's opening, and latched a lazy hand onto it.

"Come on, guys. Let's go." I whined.

Chapter 2
Come Dine With Me

Standing before the penthouse, I understood how brash my idea was. It was Sunday of the next week, the sun was out and reflecting off the great glass tower. There was a man up there, Alexis LeGrand, who was likely settled for a restful afternoon and who was not expecting guests. Then there was us, a group of teenagers who had sought him out on no greater invitation than a receipt for a salad made two years ago by my dad. Celeste had clearly seen the logical fallacy in my reasoning. Natalie no longer looked so sure for trusting Chad and me.

"This is stupid, isn't it?" I uttered.

"It's a *step*." Chad said. "It's always worth doing."

Natalie hummed, and marched forward into the driveway of the tower and its lobby. We followed into the grand paved entranceway, laden with luxury cars and attended by a tall, uptight valet. He eyed us pensively as we stepped a wide berth around the elaborate vehicles. We passed the man to the gold-polished rotating door, which flung us into the tower's grand entrance lobby. It was a high-ceilinged spectacle of white marble, black tiled floors, framed about a central chandelier.

Natalie had, at least, taken the forethought to plan our trip here, and had reported the class of the lobby to us. Today, we wore what Chad called *date wear* – the kind of done-up clothes you'd expect to don to a dinner when impressing your love interest's parents. Chad seemed to struggle in his attire, his shoulders too bulky for the hem of his jacket. He subsequently waddled into the lobby behind Natalie, Celeste, and I. It didn't seem like we needed to dress up, though. The lobby was full of regular people, standing about and lounging on its couches, all in casual dress.

Natalie twirled in her long skirt, striding across the dark tiled floor to the lobby centre. She halted underneath the chandelier to survey the area.

"So, what's the plan?" I asked her.

"Let's get inside the elevator first." She said, "I only got this far the other day. Once we're in the elevator, we'll see what we can do."

"An elevator never has a penthouse button," Celeste noted. "And from the *decoration*, this place should be much more secure than a regular tower. We really should have just sent this LeGrand guy a letter or something. Would have been much safer."

"Huh…" I stroked my chin. That *was* a terrific idea.

"I've scaled more fortified towers chasing Argols." Chad lowered his voice. "All you've got to do is get the elevator as high as it goes and climb from there. With four macro-elements and four micro-elements, we don't have many limits."

Celeste rolled her eyes. "And using the elevator? Wouldn't there be a key?"

"Let's find out." Chad smiled, nodding at Natalie, who led us to the hallway where the elevators sat. Celeste trudged behind.

We inspected the elevators buttons when we reached the doors. No key was required to push the 'up' button, so Chad went ahead and pressed it with his palm.

"It's not going to be *that* easy." Celeste whispered.

The doors chimed, and opened to reveal a family dressed in their best. They bustled out quickly, barely giving us room to squish aside and make space. Natalie stumbled as the father, a thick and stout man, barged through her shoulder. She regained, and joined Celeste, Chad and I in the elevator. Chad spammed the 'close doors' button to prevent any stragglers entering behind, and the doors shut just as Natalie strode in. Now we were shown the full array of controls, and the security camera which jutted obviously from them.

"What do we have here." Chad analysed the lit board.

"You need a card." Celeste pointed at the reader smugly. "Shall we climb the whole shaft?"

"No need." Natalie stepped between them, swiping a card at the controls. She pushed the largest number on the array.

"Where'd you get that?" I whispered, away that the camera was listening.

13

"Took it from that dad's jacket – easy pick. I guess he 'left' it in here. Clumsy him." She whispered back, dropping it to the floor.

The elevator lurched, driving up the shaft. I turned to Celeste, who had turned pale now, and leaned against the back wall.

"I'm sure we'll be fine." I said to her, leaning close. My hand dangled near hers, and I was hoping that she would reach out and take it. "Hopefully this will all run as smooth as it has been."

She sighed, and squirmed away from my advance, pulling into the very corner. Maybe her kiss *had* really been nothing but a 'thank you'. *Maybe a stressful, claustrophobic situation isn't the greatest time or place to make a move to validate yourself,* the other part of my conscious mind added in, forcing me to slink towards Natalie a Chad in shame.

The great metal box began to slow, and wound itself to a stop. With a chime, the doors hissed open, revealing a crème wall opposite us. I poked my head outside the doors to see that we were in a shared hallway. Somebody walked our way.

"What now?" I asked. "Someone's coming."

"Just look out at the hallway." Natalie instructed, closing the doors. She zipped her purse and uncapped a vial, charming out a snake of its liquid contents. I made a great effort to look away, even as the circuitry buzzed and fried. The lights flickered out, leaving us in total darkness.

Then there was light.

"We should be fine, now." Natalie said, shining her torch at the floor.

"Very smart." I nodded.

"Or dumb. Good luck getting back down, now." Celeste huffed.

"But how do we get up to the next floor?" Natalie ignored the French girl, pondering.

"Well, most of this elevator should be steel, right?" I extended my soul's grasp to the world around me. Like a heat vision map, my mind's eye was littered with hot-spots of carbon, glowing yellow hot against a cool blue. Above, I could detect carbon in the shape of ropes. "Even the cables are steel. If we work together, Chad..."

"Way ahead of you." He winked, and rammed his hands to the roof, gripping to tear it apart.

"No!" I shrieked, and he halted dead. "Not that! I mean, we can pull the cables to bring us up."

"Oh…" He laughed.

"Two boys hoisting an elevator?" Celeste chuffed. "Unlikely."

"You know, James, I can put the roof back together afterwards." Chad tapped his temple. Then there was a hiss and a flooding of red light into the room. We turned to it, to see Natalie below an escape hatch.

"Isn't this everybody's first thought? Come on." She gestured me up. Blasting off a jet of air, I launched myself through the gap, and squatted over the hatch. I extended my hands down and hoisted Natalie up. Chad made his own way, and lifted Celeste after him.

We were in a dark shaft. There was a dim red light drifting down from above. There were two more storeys above us, dictated by two sets of elevator doors floating up the shaft wall. Next to them ran an access ladder. I hummed at the sight.

"Not so fast, dude." Chad remarked, and thrust his palm to the concrete wall of the shaft. The sound clapped through the space, echoing downwards forever. "And it's hard to read this concrete for sounds. Both levels are occupied."

"Can't you sense Suneva in the quatra field?" I asked. Chad gave me a confused expression, and Celeste spoke.

"Through walls like this and a whole storey of space? The field isn't *that* easy to read. Quatra sensing isn't that strong…"

"Top door." Natalie cut Celeste off, her eyes closed and her palms by her side in the peace-sign pose. "There are threads up there."

"Well, it *shouldn't* be that easy." Chad smiled.

"No, it *shouldn't*." Celeste agreed.

"Let's go." Natalie ignored the praise, and latched onto the ladder. Celeste and Chad followed, but I chose to leap onto the shaft, using my control of air to vault between its walls, and to finally land on the short ledge before the door. I palmed at the metal, but there didn't seem to be a way to make it budge.

"Let me have a look at that." Chad said, stepping precariously onto the ledge. He pawed at the door.

"It's not steel." I told him. To me this truth was obvious, no carbon was present here.

"It's probably aluminum, but that doesn't matter." He flicked his wrist, summoning his massive *shath* – his Suneva weapon. In his hand appeared a red grip from which extended a rod. Two huge axe faces flung from its top edge, creating his battle axe. I had not seen Chad's weapon until recently – when he'd fought against us, he'd always used a chain.

He rammed the face of his weapon into the gap in the metal door, and levered it with all of his might. After a mighty shove, the mechanism hissed and gave way, flinging the doors into their frame. Chad fell into the portal.

A short hallway was revealed, flanked on the left by a zen rock garden and on the right by a Koi pool. At its end, a carved wooden door guarded by a man with an egg-like head and meaty arms. At the sight of us, he stood to his full height of at least seven feet, towering over everything in the room.

"I'd take it you haven't got an appointment." He said in a gravelly groan.

"No, but we'd like to talk to Mr LeGrand about..."

"Oh, stand back, I'll handle this." Celeste pushed Chad aside, coming to the front. "I didn't think we'd get this far, but I'm not going to let us kill ourselves after making it." She turned to Natalie, extending her hand. "Have you got that candle I gave you?"

"I'm keen to see why you wanted me to bring it." Natalie hummed, handing it to Celeste. It was a small, red candle in a glass jar. I hadn't seen it before this moment, and if I had, I would have questioned the worth of bringing it here. The French girl marched towards the egg-like man, who had now flicked his wrist to draw his weapon – a dagger. Chad dissolved his own weapon, realising that he'd walked in carrying a massive axe. His face went red.

Celeste clicked her fingers, forming a small blue flame to ignite the candle. She placed it gently by the man's feet, and stood sweetly before him. The air immediately smelled sweet. Somehow, I knew that whatever Celeste was going to try would work. Any nerves I had were fading quickly.

"We're uninvited, but here to speak with LeGrand." Celeste said calmly. The bouncer cracked a frown, and huffed, leaning down to the candle. He picked it up, and inspected it, before blowing it out.

"Okay." Celeste nodded, "Will this convince you?" She held her upwards-facing palm in the man's line of sight, and it in lit a red flame. Its licks kicked and swarmed brightly, then grew sharp as the flame transitioned. First to orange, then to yellow, green, white, and finally it shifted into its usual, hot blue. The man froze in the sight, dropping the candle and shattering its glass casing.

"The candle is genuine." He said, peering down to its shards.

"Absolutely."

"Right." He nodded. "I'll…I'll clean this. Please, go in." He palmed for the knob, and flung the door open.

"Visitors." He called into the room beyond. Beyond the man, as he stepped aside, was blinding natural light. We followed Celeste into the space.

A wall of windows looked across the river, over the whole skyline of Melbourne city. To the left, a bar of obsidian black tiles shimmered in the view. Towards the gaping window, the floor stepped down into a lounge area, with two large leather sofas before a massive television. A tall, slender man shot up from the couch, talking on a mobile phone. He wore a crimson, pinstriped suit.

"…of course it's important to me Nikki…" He said in a thick, Parisian accent. He flung his hands about as he talked. "No, Nikki, it's not like that. Look, I'm going to have to call you back." He threw the phone over his shoulder, onto the couch, and eyed the four of us with distain. His moustache twitched.

"I told the guard no visitors." He said, sternly.

"And we showed him a candle and he let us in because of it." Chad said, stepping forward in the group. "I know, I'm confused too."

LeGrand huffed, slicking over to the bar. "Who are you and what do you want?" He asked, finally observing us. He glanced past me, and his face shot to recognition.

"Is that?"

"John Grey's son." Chad spoke, although the man was staring past me. I turned to follow his gaze, but Chad threw me forward to present.

"We don't know what he thinks of my dad!" I whispered to Chad, but it was too late.

"John Grey's son?" LeGrand caught my eye, and chuckled. "My, my. You're stepping in big footsteps if you're here on your father's business." LeGrand said, pouring wine into a decanter on the bar. "His death might have been the worst thing to happen to Suneva in this city. I'm sorry for your loss."

"You liked my dad?" I asked, my heart sinking. "I always thought that he worked *against* the Argols."

17

Alexis LeGrand chuckled, and gave his wine a hearty sip.

"Justice is fair, boy." He said calmly, "When we did wrong, your father would apprehend us, but that was his job. He didn't dislike us. We're not the enemy, like the Empire of the Black Suns would have young Suneva believe."

"Yes, but you invited my dad over for dinner." I said, and fished my pocket for the business card. I held it before me. "That's a certain level of friendship."

"That's a certain level of gratitude." LeGrand remarked, and turned away. He pondered into his glass of wine. "Your father might have given me trouble, but he saved me from a lot of it too. He was fair to us when other officers would have presumed our guilt and died to prove it. He helped me find the *man* who murdered my son, and for that I was in his debt." He looked back to me, "Your father was patient, kind, and sympathetic through my struggles. That's why I invited him to dinner."

"I see." I nodded, and it was all I could manage to say. I felt as if I'd never known my dad at all.

"Is that all you came to figure out?" LeGrand asked, still confused by our entrance.

"We're here for other business." Natalie said. LeGrand diverted his attention to her.

"Another favour to the name of John Grey?" He sipped his wine.

"We were wondering where to find Argol, or if you could direct us to him." Chad asked, although seeing LeGrand's face drop halfway through his sentence, Chad let the request fall dead on the floor.

"You want me to give you a map to Argol?" He stammered. "Four random kids. Your dad mentioned nothing about you being a Suneva, I don't even know who you are." He laughed, and twirled to face the outside view. "The gratitude that I owe John Grey doesn't extend that ludicrously far."

"Wouldn't people regularly meet with Argol?" Chad asked. "How else do you do deals?"

"Not a bunch of kids! Look, seeing Naxaer Argol, the *Green Dragon* himself, isn't something I can arrange for you, and it's *not* the answer to your question." LeGrand huffed. "What are you *actually* trying to achieve here?"

"We're looking for the Legendaries." I spoke up. LeGrand paused and squinted, then let out a breathy chuckle and tried to restrain himself. His grin grew condescending.

"You know, maybe Argol would be easier, then." He chuffed. "Legendaries? *Na Nafaroisos?* There's no evidence that they *ever* existed, really. Vinavek probably made them up. And you're searching for them?" He hugged his glass of wine. "And you came to *me* searching for them? What phone book has my assistant been putting me in?"

"Whether or not you believe in them doesn't matter." I defied him, "Hesslik is trying to find them right now, and…"

"Well Hesslik is just as deluded as he seems." LeGrand scoffed.

"But he is a very powerful Suneva." I said, "And if there's even a chance of him finding those Legendaries first, we have to stop it."

LeGrand groaned and turned to face the city again. "What do four unheard of kids know of Hesslik's plans?" He asked sincerely. Chad spoke immediately.

"I'm…I used to work for Hesslik." Chad blurted. "I left Hesslik to stop his plans."

"Terrible plans to end the Suneva." I added. "I saw it in a vision. We're trying to use the Code of Connections to find the Legendaries and stop him."

LeGrand slowly worked himself back around to face me. He was intrigued. "The Code of Connections? Aren't you all a little bit young to achieve realisation?"

"Maybe," Natalie answered, "But we want to use it to find the Legendaries. We think that if we follow our connection to other Suneva, we'll find our way to who we're looking for."

LeGrand rubbed his chin and swished his wine. "That's not an awful plan." He noted, "But where does Naxaer Argol fit into it?"

"He's the connections." Chad said, "Argol has got to have the largest Suneva social web in existence, after Hesslik. He's our *Keroseva.*"

LeGrand cracked a grin. "Very interesting." He said, "But I see two problems. I think you've misunderstood the code – although don't get me wrong, it's a good misinterpretation; and secondly, how will you make Mr. Argol cooperate any more than I have?"

I spoke, to disguise the flaws in my plan. "Well, I figured along the way we'd gain a precedence, and…"

"What's the right way to interpret the code?" Natalie interrupted to ask.

"Can't say," LeGrand grinned. "Ruining the secret destroys the journey. But I can give you one hint. If you're looking to connect with Suneva, don't just attempt to find Mr. Argol. Go to where the Suneva are."

"So where are the Suneva?" I asked, "Melbourne seems pretty pumping."

"That's because Melbourne has the biggest Greek population outside of Athens. You need to go back to the homelands – the Peloponnese and the Mediterranean shores."

"The Peleponnese?...Mediterranean shores?" I pondered, and obvious connections, all mundane coincidences, aligned in my head. Natalie was Greek; Celeste was from Marseille, a city in France formerly a Greek colony, Olomb referred to Mount Olympus as the centre of his Lightning Kingdom; Tess was *definitely* a little, old Greek lady. My dad's family is Macedonian and my mum's is from Southern Italy. The immediate group of Suneva that I could think of all shared Mediterranean ethnicities.

Well, except for Chad.

"Strange." I said aloud. "I thought I'd have realised that by now."

"I didn't make the connection either." Natalie frowned. "Didn't seem important, really."

"This isn't new information." Celeste huffed. "I could have told you guys that."

"New to me." Chad nodded.

"And another hint." LeGrand continued, "Hesslik might not be the best source of unbiased information, but his website is very informative. If you keep up on the Suneva news, you'll find your way around." LeGrand took a card out of his jacket pocket and walked into his kitchen the fetch something.

It suddenly dawned on me that finding these Legendary Suneva would mean travelling across the world.

"I think we'll have to go on a holiday…" I hummed. "When will we have time for that? We're still in school."

"We've got till next June, remember." Chad smiled. "We'll be able to do it."

"I've got family in Sparta, too." Natalie said. "We could stay with them if we needed."

"Knowing your thread and your Yamiste, Natalie, that family is probably Suneva themselves." Celeste added.

"And we could even see your mother, if we were heading that way." Natalie smiled to Celeste, who suddenly turned white.

"Yes, of course we could." Celeste hummed.

LeGrand's footsteps clacked across the black tiles. He came to us with a business card, just like the one he'd given my father those years ago, with the Code of Connections symbol on the front. On the back of the card was a website address.

"Thanks," I said. He then turned to Natalie and gave her something from his other hand. It was a yellowish candle in a glass jar, like the one we'd brought with us.

"What's with the scented candles?" I asked. "We gave your guard one, too, and he let us in."

"They're traditional gifts, they get used a bit like tickets." He said. "If you give this one to Argol – *if* you find him on your own – he'll know that I sent you."

"Ha, *scent*." Chad chuckled. LeGrand rolled his eyes.

"Thank you for the gift, and your help, Mister LeGrand." Natalie cut off the awful joke. "We appreciate your time."

"Yes, well, it's good to see some ambitious young Suneva." He nodded. "Let me know if you find any Legendaries, or Naxaer Argol. I'd like to be surprised."

"Of course." Natalie nodded back.

"And I never did catch the names of my guests." He eyed us each. "You're John Grey's son…"

"James." I said.

"And I'm Chad Rogers." Chad held his hand for the shake, but was ignored.

"Natalie Athanas." Natalie smiled.

"And you, Mademoiselle, in the back?" LeGrand set his sights on Celeste. She sighed, and stepped forward.

"Celeste *Bouvé*." She hummed, unenthusiastically.

21

"An *Ivaer* of great skill, no doubt, to have sapphire earrings like those." He craned his head in close, grabbing the piece between his finger and thumb. Celeste wore her usual blue ankhs. I'd never thought them unusual. "From a prestigious lineage, no doubt."

"I stole them." She said, stone cold. "They belonged to my father. But he was killed by Naxaer."

LeGrand recoiled, but preserved his grin.

"Unfortunate. Sorry to prod, Mademoiselle." He bowed. "Good day, and good luck." He said to us all, and gestured towards the door. It wasn't the warmest goodbye, but it was a clear signal. Celeste marched first towards the exit, and we followed.

"Goodbye." I called to the man as I rounded the door, but he was already on his couch, phone back to his ear. The guard closed the door behind us, and Celeste raced ahead to call the elevator – if it still worked.

Surprisingly, I could feel the carbon in the cables run.

"Where did we get our candle?" Natalie asked Celeste. "How did you know to bring it?"

"I grew up in a strong Ivaer household." Celeste grumbled. "I know these things."

"And you've been carrying that around? How did you know it would work?" I asked.

"It was in *your* attic." She said. "Your dad must have been given it."

"The candle for his meeting with LeGrand?" I asked.

"No, actually." Celeste said. "The guard wouldn't have recoiled like he did if the candle was intended for LeGrand."

"Then who was it for?" I asked.

"Naxaer Argol."

Chapter 3
Good Book Hunting

The doorbell rang, echoing into the busy hall of the house. Light bathed the hallway tonight as Simone and Mum bustled about. I skidded into the hallway, sliding on my socks, and raced Errol to the door. He barked and whined as he ran after me, then slid to a halt, dancing on the doormat. I opened the door.

Celeste was on the other side, her chestnut bob hanging over her face. In the yellow lamplight, the peak of her nose hung so innocently. Her deep, brown eyes caught mine, and her red lips smiled. I felt my heart race. I caught the glint of those blue earrings under her hair, too. I'd have to add those to the list of things to ask this woman.

"Hi Celeste, come in." I smiled, and she stepped through the door frame to embrace me and give a kiss on the cheek. I melted into it, stomach turning giddy. As she stepped back, she chuckled. Her smile was beautiful – I was entranced.

"I think I left that kiss on your face," she said. "Let me get that." Celeste licked her finger, and grasping my jaw in her other hand, rubbed her thumb into my cheek. Her face was close to mine, her breath on my neck. All blood rushed from my brain.

"That's better." She smiled. "Now, thank you for inviting me to dinner." She said, and handed me a container I'd barely noticed in her hand. "I made these for later." The tub was full of dark, rich brownies. I chuckled in delight, still giddy.

"Thank *you*." I managed to think of words, and gestured her inside.

I still hadn't asked her about our kiss on the night she'd rescued me. I needed to bring that up. I hadn't seen her with Rhys Cameron at school since, and if the kiss meant anything more to her than gratitude, I had to know.

I doubt it. A voice spoke in my head. One not like my own. Strangely, with a *kiwi* accent.

"Huh?" I hummed aloud, and Celeste turned to me.

"What?" She asked.

"Hi Celeste." My mum called from the kitchen, diverting the attention. "Not quite ready yet, but we will be soon."

"Hi Maria." Celeste waved down the hallway. "Thanks for putting it on."

"Never mind." I said softly, as if Celeste could hear it, and led her to my room.

Kuvalik had tasked us with a mission, and Celeste and I had taken it. The ghost was attempting to teach Natalie and I *Liktan*, the Suneva tongue, before we went to visit the Suneva homelands. It had only been a week since we'd decided to go, and Natalie was already planning what we'd need to get done.

Kuvalik's mission to us was to retrieve a book from Hesslik's library here in Melbourne – the base that Vestas had operated out of. It was from the library he owned in physical life, all of which was taken by Hesslik during the *Suneva Cultural Reinvigoration* a few years ago, whereby he gathered texts of customary significance.

As Kuvalik described it, the book was thick and leather bound. It would have a 'delightful' illustration of him on the front cover, and have the name *Nafari nas Suneva* – Legends of the Suneva. The author on the spine should be listed as *Salak Nolver*.

Kuvalik couldn't retrieve the tome himself, as he was afraid of getting caught and having his soul neutralised. Natalie advised that she'd be the wrong person for the job, as her fat, orange quatra trail would give her away. Any of Hesslik's cronies would know Chad's quatra scent, too, so Celeste and I were left as the best choices. Celeste reluctantly accepted the job with me, so I was surprised to see her so energetic tonight.

I led Celeste into my room whilst dinner was being finished. She slumped across my bed, and I joined her at a considerable, socially safe distance. She sighed into the covers and lay there silent. Her earrings glimmered in the lamplight of my room.

"What's with the earrings?" I asked, awkwardly. Celeste shifted her head to give me a pointed look.

"What do you mean?" She asked, "I always wear them."

"Yes, but, LeGrand thought they made you important."

"It's an *Ivaer* thing, like the candles." She said. "Lots of *Ivaer* traditions. We've got a distinct culture."

"Right."

Sounds like she's hiding something. The voice said again.

Maybe...

"Plus, I think he was accusing me of stealing his grandmother's earrings." She said, then let her face fall back onto the bed. "I'm still wandering how your father got a candle to meet with Naxaer Argol."

"At least he wasn't aiding corruption." I mused. "I thought that's what a meeting with LeGrand would have symbolised. But LeGrand was just thankful that somebody looked past his Sunevahood to help him out. That's probably why he got a meeting with Argol..." I justified it to myself. My dad was a good guy.

There's probably more about him that you don't know. Think of how much you've learned. The voice told me.

"Maybe." Celeste rolled over, facing up. My door then opened without so much as a knock, and Simone rolled in and planted herself on my chair.

"How are we, Celeste?" She asked, slumping over my desk.

"Hi Simone," Celeste sang. "I'm doing well, thank you."

"Good to hear." Simone hummed, then sat up. "You're not still with that Rhys Cameron boy, are you?"

"I...why do you ask?"

"I saw him at the shops today. He gave me a real greasy eye."

"You went outside?" I chuffed. "Sure you didn't just see a picture of him on the computer?"

Nice call. The voice congratulated.

"Oh, shut it, James." Simone grumbled, flicking her blonde hair aside.

"To answer your question, I don't know." Celeste frowned, clicking her fingers. "I asked for a bit of space last week, and he got all defensive. I don't know that I'll go back to him."

My eye twitched, my heart beating alight. Rhys Cameron was out of the picture? Had I, James Grey, a *chance*? Simone paled to the news, her face flushing white. She stood quickly.

"Don't go back. Boys are trash." Simone instructed, then darted off, closing the door behind her.

"She didn't look too good." Celeste hummed.

"Yeah." I forced a mumble, trying to make my mouth run. Butterflies churned, so close to her on my bed. All I had to do was ask her if she liked me.

I'm going to do it, right now. I told myself, preparing to move my mouth.

And I couldn't.

You knew you couldn't. The voice told me. *If you were meant to have asked it, you would have done it by now. Destiny.*

"Let's check on dinner." I said. "Maybe Mum needs a hand."

***

Mum *tolerated* hosting my friends. She liked to see that my social life was alive and well, and she liked the validation of people other than Simone and I complimenting her food and cooking abilities, but she hated the hassle of being presentable. To have guests over, in the widow house, was all about maintaining the appearances of perfection. Dad was always the perfectionist, causing an argument over crumbs on the day of his death, but Mum had, to an extent, absorbed his perfectionism in his absence. And she hated it.

And her guest sat, not saying a word.

I could feel Mum's irritation building, bubbling into rage as Celeste looked down at her plate, barely responding, barely engaging.

I nudged the girl a few times to get her to speak, but her responses were so drab, so uninspired. Mum was already suspicious enough of the Suneva. I smiled awkwardly throughout the dinner, but had nothing to save the situation. Why the hell had Celeste suddenly become so unresponsive.

Rude. The voice in my head grumbled. *And embarrassing for you.*

I totally agreed with them, letting my own irritation take hold.

After dinner, Celeste and I went into my room to pack my bag. We would be wearing all black tonight, with black masks I'd picked up during the week. It would be a relatively light mission, needing only some torches apart from the disguises. The bag would mostly be used for transporting the book.

"Are you doing alright?" I asked her as she lay face down again on my bed. "You weren't saying much before."

You're being awfully nice for how she behaved. The voice growled, egging me on. My desire for her overrode my anger, forcing my demeanour placid.

"I'm fine James, really." She sighed.

You're going to take that for an answer? The voice asked.

The voice was right, I wanted an answer. Celeste had been rude, she'd pissed off my mother, whose love wasn't so easily earned. I wanted an answer.

But I didn't want to push Celeste away. Not when I wanted her to like me.

Do you ever just...turn your dick off? The voice grumbled.

"Really, Celeste." I smiled. "If there's something bothering you, you can talk to me about it. I'm your friend."

"It's really nothing, James." She insisted, rolling away.

"Something is clearly wrong." I said. "Please, just..."

26

"James, seriously. I don't want to talk to you about it." She snapped.

"Oh…" I cringed and stood off the bed.

"We've got to get to work, anyway." She pulled herself upright, tossing her hair to one side. "Let's get moving."

So much for 'friend'. The voice hummed. *She wants nothing to do with you.*

I nodded along, slinging my bag over my shoulder. We moved on.

***

Celeste and I rode our bikes from my house towards the city, cutting through the back streets and down the bike path. We finally reached the alley leading to Hesslik's compound. We parked our bikes at its mouth, stunned again by the structure. Its warehouse end bathed in bright white light, setting it as a star in the night.

"Surely that's a violation of local light pollution." I grumbled.

"Mask, please." Celeste ignored my thought, holding out a hand. I reached into my bag and tossed a mask to her. She strapped it on, and tucked her clothes around it. I donned mine, feeling stuffy already.

"This better be the best *damn* book I've ever read." Celeste huffed. "Jumping back into Hesslik's compound so soon after we just escaped it has got to be one of the silliest ideas I've ever heard. If the book is to teach you and Natalie *Liktan*, why aren't the two of you here to get it."

"Because Natalie's trail is too obvious. And the book apparently has good lessons for all of us." I said. "I'm sure Natalie would be here if she could."

"Sure." Celeste frowned, reaching into my bag and pulling out the binoculars. She examined the entrances. "Still as risky as ever."

"If you want, I can go in whilst you stay out here." I said, putting a hand on her shoulder. "If I'm distressed I can yell *really* loudly. You won't even need to come in."

"I don't need pity, James." Celeste snapped, shifting away. "Do you really believe I'd not go in there? I *trust* Kuvalik that this book is important."

"What pity?" I asked, "That wasn't pity, it's…"

"What then? You thought I was too weak?"

"No, Jesus…" I rubbed my fingers on the bridge of my nose. "I was just trying to be a good person. You seemed uncomfortable, I wanted to help."

"Well how about you just…don't." She huffed, "I don't need pity and I don't need help."

"Okay, fine." I exasperated. "But Celeste, I really didn't…"

"Don't bother." She growled, taking the binoculars from her face and clipping them to her belt.

She doesn't need you. The voice echoed in my skull. *She doesn't trust you and she doesn't need you.*

"I see my entrance." Celeste said, and strode towards the gate, sleuthing in the shadows.

"Hey, wait!" I called after her, stumbling behind. "Don't be like this. We need each other here."

"Actually, James. I think I'll go in and you can stand guard. You know, because you look scared."

"Oh, seriously?" I huffed.

She put a finger to her masked lips, signalling me to be quiet. "You can find your own way in, if you think you could do it all alone."

There's no way I could do this alone. I thought.

You don't need her. The voice said. *You can do this alone.*

Can I? I whined. *I'm not a skilled Suneva like Celeste.*

Trust yourself. The voice demanded. *You're a Suneva all the same.*

I nodded, watching Celeste slink off into the night. She chose a path to the right of the warehouse, so I looked left, down into the blackness of the unlit section. I didn't think there were any entrances along the left face of the building, at least, that's what Chad had told us.

"Why the hell didn't Chad do this?" I huffed, knowing Chad's justification for not coming. "He worked here. He'd know the place inside out."

Does it matter? The voice asked. *Everybody left you alone. Time to prove what you can do.*

What can I do? I pondered, and the answer came to me: jump. My sight snapped to the roof, and I saw a good point of entry. A door sat atop the roof on the far left of the structure, likely above the offices and labs. Squinting hard through the darkness, I could see an awning at the building's far end which I could use as a platform to reach the roof. Even better, the awning abutted the property's fence, jutting right up to a house on the far left, whose roof came nearly to the fence line. I grinned, and slipped through the shadows towards it.

I jumped the alley's fence before reaching the carpark, using the first two neighbouring backyards to clear the compound's gate. I then climbed back onto the warehouse facility, sneaking through the darkness to the far left of the building. A pile of crates and a forklift sat before the awning, and I jumped off a blast of air to clear the forklift cab, vaulting from that vantage up onto the awning. I dug my claws into the sheet metal, dragging my body over and up onto the steel roof. I then sized up the distance to the roof proper.

That's a big leap. I gawked.

And look at how far you've come. The voice encouraged. *Believe.*

Believe. That word was powerful. The possibilities were endless, so long as you knew your limits could be broken.

Expanding my soul through my fingertips, I meditated on my connection to the world. I amassed air in my reach, and threw it down to the ground. My leap was the most powerful I'd ever done. I soared high in the air, vaulting past the line of the roof, and landing upon a cloud of dust. I coughed in surprise.

I did it. I puffed.

I told you to believe. The voice said.

Standing, I toed over to the maintenance door. I fiddled with the handle first, and it wouldn't budge. I flicked my wrist to draw my weapon.

Gives you away, doesn't it? The voice asked. *Do you need the publicity right now?*

No, not really. I budged. I let the weapon's handle dissolve back, instead feeling for carbon in the door's bolt. Indeed, the lock was made of steel, so I ripped its carbon free and bashed into the door. The locking bolt snapped, letting me fall into the room. The door led directly to a staircase, lit in the green glow of an exit sign. Carefully, I descended the stairway which led to the butt of a hallway at its landing.

I could hear footsteps and a voice coming from somewhere in the complex – they didn't sound like they were coming from Celeste.

Now comes the hard part, I thought. *Where would I keep a little, leather book?* I scaled the hallway, sticking my ear to doors, then checking behind them. The first was a toilet, the second was a small kitchen, the third was a utility closet. I couldn't open the fourth.

It's not here. The voice told me. *I know where the book will be.*

How? I asked, but the voice didn't reply. *Then where?*

Keep going straight. They instructed, so I did. I traversed the left edge of the hallway, turning a corner to come into a living area of sorts. Like the parts of the warehouse I'd seen before, the walls were of the cold, metal, futuristic aesthetic. The room had two couches before a television, with a dining area on the far side. There was an exit to my left with a set of ascending stairs, and another, dark exit opposite.

Up the stairs. The voice instructed. I didn't need their command though – I could *feel* that familiar pull calling me up the stairs. The book was stringing me along, it wanted to be found.

I know. I told the voice.

As I prepared to run across the gap, a light came on in the opposite corridor, and footsteps could be heard. I scuffled back to the bend in the hall, gluing myself to the near wall and out of sight.

The footsteps were metallic and heavy. They clanked into the room, throwing torchlight around the space. They hummed, shifting towards the room's centre.

"Must have imagined it." They grumbled, and turned. Their light left the space, and I spied around the corner to see that they were gone. I threw myself back into the space, and darted to the other set of stairs.

I found myself in a grand study. A brass chandelier, covered in ornate, hanging glass pieces was strung from the high ceiling. To my right, the floor of the room stepped down to make a larger wall space for the massive bookshelf. Directly in front was an antique study desk, as long as a dining table, with a relatively new wheelie chair parked under it. There was a new computer on the desk, maybe running *Windows 98* on it, if Vestas was savvy. On the left wall was a large painting, depicting some Suneva battle I had not heard of nor read about.

I sleuthed over to the library of books. The one I was looking for was thick, made of burgundy stained leather, and written by a *Salak Nolver*. Kuvalik explained to us that the name *Salak* was not a Suneva name. It was the title of a *Sunesca*.

A *Sunecsa*, as he put it, were people who were absolutely and truly destined to receive a thread, but did not. Destiny is usually always fulfilled, so pure Sunesca are inconceivably rare, but sometimes the Black Holes could fail to aim their radiation properly.

A *Sunesca* is otherwise known as an *Energy Transformer* because of their abilities. It is said that they are so destined to manipulate the world around them, that they can steal energy from other sources and convert it into soul energy. They can even rob people of their energy to move, speak, or function. In Liktas traditions, these abilities cast the *Sunesca* as thieves, and their disconnect from destiny titled them as forsaken, even evil. Despite this, some other Suneva societies have been known to revere them as Gods.

I trawled through the books. Admittedly, I was never one to spend too much time in a library. Natalie would have found the book straight away. Luckily, Vestas catalogued his books, and I quickly found my way to authors starting with *S*. Kuvalik's book wasn't there.

Libraries catalogue by last *names*. The voice reminded me.

Oh, right. I coughed. I then went to *N*, but was stopped in my tracks as I skimmed over *O*. There it was, with the authors name misspelled on the card as *Olo* instead of *Nol*.

Odd mistake to make. I thought.

Odd indeed. The voice agreed, *But look, you did it on your own. You believed in yourself.*

Yeah, I did. I nodded. I swung my backpack around my body and placed the book inside. It was remarkably heavy, and the bag sagged down on my back.

I felt a pang tear across my consciousness. My body shivered in a strange distress, but I knew the issue – Celeste was in trouble. Not bad trouble, *yet*, but she was about to be.

Do you know where she is? I asked the voice.

No. It said. *Why should we care? She didn't care about you.*

I grumbled, slipping down the staircase, I peeked around into the living room.

She cares, she's just stressed or angry…or something. I pushed her past her edge.
And she won't open-up to you about it. Does she even consider you a friend?

31

What, of course she does? I defended. *She came to help me when I was stuck in here. If she didn't trust me, or wasn't my friend, she wouldn't have risked herself for me. Hell, she wouldn't have even come* here.

Things change. The voice cracked. *She was going to leave you defenceless here.*

And I let her split us up. We're a team.

Are you? The voice growled.

I stepped into the shadows around the room. I could feel the pull of Celeste's distress, it was coming from the hallway where the guard had been. I peered down the dark passageway. The coast was clear, but the end door was closed. I'd have to rely on my senses to find her.

Yes, we're a team, and we're friends. She needs me right now. I need her. I argued with the voice.

You're only saying these things because you think she's hot. The voice spat. That surface level of truth was the final straw.

That's it buddy. I said, *You're clearly not some level of my subconscious. Who the hell are you?*

I am the one of knows all. The voice grinned. *I am the Finder of Secrets.*

The implication of the name made me *shiver.* I felt ill, suddenly, and knew that I'd been deceived. This voice delivered me to what I wanted, but at what price.

That's it, I'm not listening to you anymore. I told the voice.

Well that's okay. It said smugly, *Because they'll have her before you can save her, and you'll never find your way out of here without me. Believe in yourself, Maiki.*

I could feel my skull become lighter. The presence, whatever it was, fell out of my head with the same feeling of water dripping from my ear. They were a Kidin after all – a mind reader – how had I not expected that? How much had they seen?

There was scuffling behind the closed door at the end of the hallway. I peered around to the roof access staircase, gaining my bearings. *I can get out of here without them.* I resolved.

The scuffle escalated, muffled bolts of quatra being thrown and dissipating, feet racing, wood breaking. The closed door at the halls' end burst open, blasting the light of blue flames all the way onto my face. A Suneva had run out, and now leaned up against the wall to catch their breath. They peered into the room.

I ran towards them.

The figure at the hall's end turned to the sound of my footsteps. Their eyes glowed blood red, their armour gleamed against the smattering of colours behind them. They raised their weapon and a red bolt of quatra sailed towards me.

I held my arm out and took it through my hand. The bolt raced towards my neck, and I summoned my own quatra to flush it out and through my other arm. The marbled, toxicated bolt flew back towards the red-eyed Suneva.

The bolt, accelerated by my sprint, flew low and slammed into the Suneva's leg. Taken by the speed of the strike, they stumbled to react, and the toxicated bolt obscured his thread. Their armour shattered off their body, and they fell unconscious to the floor.

Celeste was still masked and in her black clothes, kneeling behind an office cubicle. We'd found ourselves back in the office room of Vestas' compound. The two other exits were closed off, and the corporate plastic plants burned with blue flames. Three Suneva stood off in this room against Celeste, quatra bolts whizzing through the air. A silver Suneva took up the far side, a blue armoured crouched closer to me, and an orange peeked around a cubicle in the centre. As I barged into the space, all eyes turned to me.

"There's *two* of them?" The furthest Suneva in the room whined.

The scene, strangely, failed to intimidate me. I felt confident, even. Celeste stood from cover and shot three bolts in succession. One was redirected by the orange Suneva, the other two missed and were quickly countered. The silver Suneva fired on me. I extended my arm, toxicated the bolt, and redirected. The orange Suneva stood, sprinting on Celeste's position. I rolled for cover, launching towards my friend.

"Watch your flank!" I shouted to Celeste. I blasted off the ground out of my roll, pouncing high to fire a two quatra bolts onto the orange Suneva. Celeste fired at him at the same time, overwhelming him. He swatted the first two bolts away, but succumbed to the third, slumping down in his shattered armour.

I came back to Earth, parking myself next to Celeste.

"I've got the book." I said, "Let's get out of here."

"Okay." She said flatly. We both peeked around cover to see bolts flying towards us. We let them sail past, then stood tall.

Celeste and I fired two bolts each. My two missed, one of Celeste's hit a computer, causing the tower to glow hot before exploding. Celeste and I fell behind the cubical wall as light enveloped the room.

"I've got an idea." Celeste said. "You fire the bolts. Cover me." She stood tall, and I shot up to meet her. Bolts soared our way immediately. I vaulted the cubical wall, blasting up to meet one of the bolts halfway, and redirected it to the other Suneva in the room. Celeste reached to the far end of the room, gripping deep into her soul connections. The two Suneva took their opportunity to charge.

I flinched, stumbling back into a cubical wall. Two white lumps formed behind the two Suneva, and suddenly they were lifted off their feet, flung backwards into the wall. I could feel the massive pressure gradient in my palms, enough to suck in two huge Suneva.

"Now!" Celeste urged, and I fired my bolts. I hit each man – such an aim was a feat from my hands – and their armour shattered to the floor under them.

"What was that?" I turned to Celeste.

"Oxygen." She said. "That's what happens when you condense a quarter of the air."

"I see." I hummed.

"Come on." She grabbed my arm. "Let's go."

We ran down the hall that I came from. I took the lead, pouncing off the right wall to spring left, up into the staircase. We burst out of the broken rooftop door. Running to the ledge, I scooped Celeste up in my arms and leaped down to the awning, then from the awning into a neighbouring back yard. I landed on a blast of air, setting Celeste down and running off around the block and towards our bikes.

We finally had a moment to catch our breath. As far as we could tell, there were no Suneva on our tail.

"Thank you...James." She rasped between breaths, taking off her mask. I did the same. "Really...I appreciate it."

"Well, you told me to stand guard. I think I did a pretty good job of rushing in to the rescue." I smiled. She turned away.

"I guess you did." She said. "You didn't have to, though."

"What was I going to do, just leave you behind?" I quizzed.

"I've been rude all night." She huffed, turning back towards me. "I just never expect you to keep coming back. I'm sorry."

"Look, I…" She was searching for something in my eyes, her head leaning in closer. A bit of consolation right now could have been condescending. I swallowed my next sentence, instead staying quiet. "That's what friends do." I squeaked out. "And I'm sorry for pushing help onto you, too." I said. "I didn't mean to come off as pitying. That would have been annoying." I chuckled, and she laughed with me.

"Thank you for being so understanding." She said, and wrapped her arms around me. She squeezed hard, then pulled away to kiss me on the cheek.

"That's alright." I said as she pulled away again. Her hands over my shoulders, mine on her waist, her breath ran hot from her red lips over my skin. I could feel it, both in my palms and on my lips. Adrenaline rocked me as we held each other in place. I could feel her heart beating, thumping against my chest. I could feel her leaning in.

But she didn't. She lowered herself onto her heels, throwing aside the embrace. Her face red, she turned away, and stepped over to her bike. I could picture her riding off, me accepting my fate to never ask her how she felt, what anything *meant* with her. I peered down to my useless hands, and caught the glimmer of my golden ring. That ring belonging to my dad, John Grey. Dad would have been brave enough to ask, he could take a risk.

I couldn't let him down, not whilst wearing his ring.

"Wait!" I called, and maybe a bit loudly, because her eyes shot with concern as she craned back to me. I had to ask her about our kiss, and this had to be the worst time to do it, but the only time I'd ever muster the courage for it. Even then, we both waited on my next words. I had to force them. "What did our kiss mean to you, Celeste?" I asked bluntly, letting the question flow. "I need to know."

Celeste sighed, rubbing her brow. "When I rescued you?"

"Yes."

"I don't know." Her gaze met mine. "It just felt right in the moment. I felt like I wanted to do it. That's all."

"And what about just now?" I asked, pointing to the ground with two hands. "That wasn't just *nothing*."

35

"That's…" She mashed her fingers across her brow. "James, you catch me in very emotional moments. I trust you, James, where I haven't been able to trust many people before. It's refreshing."

"That means a lot to me."

"It's why I followed you here, despite this being a terrible idea, and why I trusted you on visiting LeGrand, and the whole crazy idea of searching for Argol in general. I can see the honesty in your soul, and that's rare. Sometimes a kiss feels natural when you have to express that to somebody – when the emotion just tips out. I'm sorry, I didn't want you to put that much weight on it."

"I…" I wasn't sure how to respond. She hadn't *necessarily* rejected me. I didn't quite know what her stance was. I suspected that she didn't know, either. "Okay." I found myself nodding.

"It was a nice moment though." She smiled, her eyes staring past mine, into my soul. That made me giddy on instinct, and stopped me from enquiring further. It was then that she stepped away, onto her bike, and we rode back to mine in the peaceful silence of night.

Chapter 4
Dancing Streamers

Simone found her vision faltering in strange ways. Not that her vision wasn't weird enough – Simone had always had the ability to see quatra energy, despite *not* being a Suneva. That, Simone was sure of. She had no soul connections, nor had she other symptoms, such as self-determined righteousness, stubbornness, or general incompatibility with society and life.

But recently, Simone had found herself seeing some new phenomena, something that didn't quite fit into her worldview of herself.

Ribbons.

Not the kind that hung from signs at fairs, or the kind that you glued to your macaroni art to present to a parent who was condescendingly enthused about your creative skills. These ribbons were strange, throwing themselves into existence in different lengths and colours, and only when she concentrated on something would they appear around it, wriggling with an object's *intensity*. It was

36

as if they were the fibres that made experiences, something to the backstage of the world that you weren't meant to see. A strange expression of creation, maybe?

She'd first noticed them when out to brunch with her university friend Kate. Simone had ordered a vanilla milkshake and an eggs Benedict, and despite the flavours being some of the best she'd tasted in any example of these dishes, that wasn't what was memorable about the occasion.

Kate's mouth ran like a motor.

The girl could talk, God damnit, and Simone sat nodding her head. What had initially started as a catch up to talk about anything *other* than school work whilst the stress of it crushed Simone's head through a brick wall, had cascaded into the juicy details about Kate's friends. Some insane stream of gossip, a void of unfamiliar names and associations, broke the dam and flooded the table, leaving Simone lost in a sea of missed connections. A pure wall of sound buffeted her face, tearing a layer off her skin. She could do no more than comprehend that it was happening, zoning out, watching Kate's mouth move and the sound spew out.

And that's when something strange happened. The air escaping Kate's droning gob seemed to shimmer, and with it, the girl sprayed dribble radially. Simone squirmed back into her chair, avoiding the rain, until she noticed the little grey specs of spit sizzling out of existence like hot embers from a midnight fire. They burst and crackled similarly, coming from splits in the air itself, born from the shimmering.

Then, as Kate reached the climax of her tale, her hands working a whirlwind of signs, Simone saw the specs for what they were. Streamers. They shot from the mouth excitedly, anchored to Kate's words, and danced about in the breeze of her voice before springing back to their origin and terminating. A dozen little grey ribbons dancing in Kate's voice.

The girl then clicked her fingers in front of Simone's face, waking her.

"Hello?" She rocked Simone from her trance. The ribbons were gone from her voice now, as if they never existed.

"Sorry." Simone apologised, chugging her vanilla milkshake. "I don't think I slept enough last night."

"Then stop doing assignments and get yourself a coffee. *Girl*, I swear." Kate rolled her eyes, and signalled for assistance.

Simone had only caught glimpses of the ribbons since. They were captivating, yet frightening to witness. What exactly *was* she seeing? She got many replies to her almost daily, anonymous threads on *Fairysmog.org*, telling her a whole plethora of possible explanations. Most suggested remnants of ghostly activity, such as ectoplasm, ghost trails, demon hands, or personal auras, but none of those fit. Kate's words weren't haunted, and neither were the other random locations she'd come across the streamers.

Well, except for one place. Simone had gone to check out noises in the attic to find me and my friends up in the dark place, sorting through Dad's belongings. Her mind shot with panic when she saw me fiddling with his briefcase. Would I notice that the police files were missing from it? She'd read and stashed them elsewhere, the certain evidence of Suneva corruption in our government system. And who was I to show a dead man's stuff to my friends for some sick amusement, had I no sense of respect?

As she flew into a rage, and my friends and I started to shuffle, she saw red ribbons rising, writhing off our skin. They tangled and wafted in the dead, dark air of the attic, simmering closer to her, reaching out.

And in the height of her rage, ribbons attacked her.

They flung themselves onto her skin, stretching, writhing around her forearm and digging into her palms. They tunnelled into her skin, wriggling beneath. Despite the initial shock, this hallucination was incredibly *empowering*. It fuelled her convictions, scorched her anger, and set her dominance.

Then, after the fact, it freaked her all the way out.

She was still human. Simone *was* still human. No doubt about it. She was hallucinating. She searched for further information, and found one possible cause – synaesthesia. A condition which created a melding of senses, in some cases leading to people who could see sounds as colours. To most holders of the ability, it occurred as a projection from their minds eye. Simone was fine to ignore her physical evidence of interacting with the ribbons to call them synaesthetic hallucinations. The only thing that ran odd was the limited array of colours she saw compared to a synaesthete. So far, she'd only seen ribbons in red, orange, grey, and white. The world was meant to be colourful and vibrant with this sense fusion. This probably wasn't her explanation.

Maybe there *were* ghosts in everything...

38

The predicament lingered with Simone, as she kept having sightings of the strange, reality-breaking streamers, popping up in fields of colour, wriggling without a breeze to back them. The thought of it had almost left her mind by the night that Celeste came over for dinner. Simone was fetching herself a glass of water from the kitchen sink, when she turned on the tap. Grey ribbons streamed from the tap nozzle, with red ribbons bobbing and swimming with the water's stream. The little streamers rose slowly towards her, reaching for her. Simone, frazzled, shut off the water and sculled her glass. She needed a distraction, and she had something to ask Celeste anyway, so she came to my room.

She opened the door without even a knock, still worked up, and stumbled into the room. Therein she found Celeste and I sprawled across my bed. She recoiled, until it was obvious that nothing was going on.

"How are we, Celeste." Simone buzzed, her head spinning. She leant onto the table to get her bearings.

"I'm doing well, Thank you." The French girl replied. No grey streamers buzzed at her lips, setting Simone a little more at ease.

"Good to hear." She hummed, then stood up. "You're not still with that Rhys Cameron boy, are you?" Simone asked her question.

"I…why do you ask?" Celeste said. Simone could have sworn there was a grey speck on the girl's breath.

"I saw him at the shops today. He gave me a real greasy eye." Simone remembered, although the event was a few days ago now.

"You went outside?" I chuffed. "Sure you didn't just see a picture of him on the computer?"

"Oh, shut it, James." Simone moaned. She wasn't feeling jovial at all, her mind was racing.

"To answer your question, I don't know." Celeste frowned, clicking her fingers. A black ribbon danced from her palm.

Black Ribbon? Simone hummed, staring. Simone hadn't seen a black ribbon before. It slicked in the air, short and fat, bouncing back and forth. It persisted. And it did not come towards her like the others did.

Simone had had enough. She needed to get away from this madness, to clear her head. "Don't go back. Boys are trash." The words slipped from her mouth, and she darted off, flinging herself into the study, in front of the computer.

39

Tom had helped her buy a new processor for the machine. He'd given her instructions for how to install it, and Simone had been putting it off for a week now. She needed something to concentrate on, something to let her mind wander before she went to bed, to keep her away from these damned ribbons. She could only hope that this strange peering into the backstage of reality wasn't chronic. When could she have her normality back?

She'd never been normal, though.

Simone pulled the chip out of its box. It was huge and bulky, like a miniature city soldered onto a green road. She flipped it about, analysing it, identifying the ports Tom had told her about. She found her mind easing. Software was her specialty, not hardware, but it was relaxing to learn a new skill. She sighed, admiring this piece of technology in her hand. There was nothing here to upset her.

The dog burst into the room, the door flying open, smacking into the wall. Simone jolted with surprise, eyes darting to Errol. Following him, stapled to his tail and flicking in his wake was a fat, long, lustrous red ribbon. It slicked close to her skin, and in her fright, she must have gripped it, because it tunnelled into her palm.

That euphoria hit her again, lifting her emotions, setting her alight. The chip melted in her hand, melding to her fingers' touch.

She had to hold her mouth to keep from screaming.

Chapter 5
Shake the Shiverman

"*Na orecos nas Ocras Quatrona a Shiverman*" – The Story of the White Witch and the Shiverman, Kuvalik began reading from his book. We all sat in the living room of the abandoned house as the ghost attempted to give us a lesson in the Suneva language – *Liktan*. He read a story from the book that Celeste and I had collected well over a month ago. This story was pertinent to our search, apparently, but it was also useful for teaching Natalie and I the language which Celeste and Chad already spoke.

"*Ocra*, for *white*." The black, incorporeal mass smiled. "The *s* makes it an adjective. And *Quatrona* is a Witch – a Suneva who practices soul manipulation

40

internally, instead of on external soul connections. A *Quatrano* is a male Witch, in the same way that *Tona* means *Lady* and *Tano* means *Man.*"

As we sat in his living room, the light of day no longer shining down through a massive, gaping hole in the roof. Chad and I had spent weekends patching the house up with diamonds, iron, and steel, so that he could live in it with the ghost. Celeste had moved in too, as her time with David's family had expired, and Chad's local part time job, paid under the counter in cash, allowed him to pay some bills and have water and electricity in the home once again.

We were all saving our money. We'd bought our tickets to Athens for the days after our final exams. Only a few meagre months they were away now, and then we could chase answers in the Code of Connections around the apparent Suneva homeland. Natalie had planned a road-trip to her family in Sparta, and from there we would drive to Celeste's mother in Marseille, using connections as stepping stones to finding the elusive Naxaer Argol. Whether we'd actually need his help or not, we didn't yet know.

"*Shiverman*," Kuvalik continued. "Is also a *Liktan* word. From *Shiv* – to find, and *Erman*, secrets. The finder of Secrets. So begins *Na Orecos nas Ocras Quatrona a Shiverman.*"

'In the century before the Christian Calendar, the Roman Empire held Southern Greece under its grip. Groups of Suneva dotted the landscape of the Empire's holdings, forming their own social circles in their villages and towns. The Suneva society of the past had dissolved long ago. It's teachings, established by Zeus - a legendary *Liktas* amongst the first known Suneva – were still in fashion. They prophesised the existence of four Gods: Amasos, Veritas, Omercronius and Nerios. Zeus guided the Suneva from his throne on Mount Olympus, ironically becoming revered as a God himself through his amazing actions.

"The other *Liktas* in the land were seen as demi-Gods, until they became too abundant. They lost claim to their position in the Pantheon, and with Zeus long dead and his myth replaced by that of Jupiter by the invading Romans, there was nobody to support Suneva claims of goodness and holiness. The Suneva fell into outcast and their society crumbled.

"Suneva powers at this time were not what they are today. With a limited level of scientific understanding, and a limited understanding of the soul

41

connections, most Suneva were simple Witches, using their powers internally to heal. This made them a hearty people, and perfect candidates for slavery.

"Their level of ability made them good fighters, too. Suneva were marched across the Mediterranean shores in droves, pushed into servitude and combat for the hungry empire, broken as a people. Those who escaped slavery created settlements in the hills to act as bandits. Those who fared luckier retained their farms, but faced being racially ostracised from the community.

"Under the city of Thebes lived a Suneva named Masalik Vinavek, a young woman from a family of humble, struggling farmers. The aristocracy of her city, their lives powered by Suneva slaves, propagated the mistreatment of Suneva by refusing them access to markets, then buying their crops at the bare cost. Suneva, separated by culture and distance, had become weak and their future looked bleak. Vinavek searched for meaning in her life. Young and hopeful, she knew that something could be done.

"Within the Roman Pomerium lived the politician who represented a group of Greek-colonising aristocrats near Thebes city. Vibius Caecina Curiosus less commonly known as *Toskidin*, was a man who defined politics by trading secrets. He built his name and power slowly by planting rumours into the heads of others. He tore down rich and powerful men through his lies to pave the pathway for his influence. He embraced corruption and power struggles.

"The *Kidin* of Italy mostly operated like this. Men could become powerful by transmitting their grandeur into the minds which surrounded them. Thought manipulation always paid off, but over time, people became wary to the tricks of a suave gentleman or woman. Curiosus, however, was a step above the rest.

"He had come back from a military pursuit through North Africa when he was promoted to the representative for Thebes. In his battles, he led a charge into a group of Egyptian soldiers who either soiled themselves with fear or surrendered on sight. He had spoken in all of their heads at once, the entire army worth of men, and told them of how he would ruthlessly dismember their bodies whilst they lived.

A true *Kidin* would never reveal their tricks, and Vibius Caecina wanted to conceal his abilities, so he pinned the talented mind-trick on a *Kidin* soldier who fought by his side. For the act, the solider was awarded the title of *Shiverman*, the most powerful *Kidin* alive.

Curiosus was otherwise a simple man. Where there was money to be earned, he manipulated somebody to fill his pockets with it. As far as governing was concerned, the rich and powerful men kept him rich, so it was into their demands that he leaned.

Masalik Vinavek schemed. She watched the planted Italian nobility grow fatter, and heard tales through *kidin* tongues about the mistreatment of hearty Suneva slaves. The story of a *Liktas* shocking their master was common, and always ended in a sharp blade through the gut. If only Suneva knew more about themselves – if only there was a community to rediscover the old truths about their abilities, then they could escape this oppression. Only through unity they'd been deprived of for so long could they be free.

So Vinavek searched for answers, and read the stories of Zeus and of the old Suneva greatness. She knew that if united under a single culture, if strengthened as a people under old philosophers' teachings and the old Suneva religion, the Suneva could prevail above their oppression. They could regrow their identity as a people.

After much thought and learning, Vinavek left her home. She snuck out, under the guilt of a poor harvest, to follow the compulsions of destiny of which old Suneva had spoken and written in *Liktan*.

Over the next year of travelling between Suneva communities in central Greece, the young Vinavek compiled the Suneva beliefs of hundreds of isolated communities, and would go on to redefine the Suneva belief system. Feeling the pull of destiny around her, she acted as the Gods would have her act, as she believed their path to be righteous. Through listening to the world, she learned to strengthen her connections to others, herself, and the universe around her, essentially creating the backbone for her *Code of Connections*.

In order to change the Suneva's place in this Roman Empire, she had to go beyond a cultural renaissance. She had to confront those men who pulled the strings of Suneva lives – the politicians. Her first target was Vibius Caecina Curiosus, who represented the Roman-ethnic nobility from her family's city in the senate. Vinavek's march towards him was a long journey, as she felt the black hole Nerios draw her through a pilgrimage in the Peleponese. It was on the beaches in the town of Kalamata where Masalik Vinavek achieved realisation, and channelled

43

the first ever instance of white quatra. Rumours of her power circulated immediately – spreading the story of the White Witch.

In her journey through the Peloponnese and Western Greece, Vinavek spread her revelations to all Suneva. Some received her with awe, some were more sceptical, deeming her powers evil. Most Suneva had simply lost hope in a greater path for the Suneva people.

She marched on, housed by her supporters during her journey. Her persistence to the call of destiny, and to realisation through her code of connections, led her to finding the three Suneva of the powers considered Legendary by Zeus; *zirran* – time, *vectis* – gravity, and *kida* – teleportation.

The four most revered Suneva in the known world marched on to Venice, where they would confront Vibius Caecina Curiosus, the most powerful *Kidin* of the age. *Salkida*, the Legendary of Teleportation, made the journey to Curiosus's Venetian mansion instantaneous. Masalik Vinavek, *Salkida*, *Ranka* of Time, and *Veccan* of Gravity, warped onto the steps of the house which hung over the waterfront.

Being the White Witch, Vinavek had the supreme ability to sense quatra. She led the three Legendaries up three flights of stairs and burst through the door to Vibius Caecina's office. He was in relations with a man on top of his study desk, with such intimacy that he initially didn't notice the four Suneva enter.

"Have you never heard of knocking?" He famously asked as he pushed the man aside. A woman appeared from under the desk and shrieked. Both partners ran off into a room past the bookshelves, robes in hand. Curiosus took minimal effort to cover up, as he slowly strutted his way towards the four, armoured Suneva.

"You know," he said. "I'm not sure that a government official's office is any place for a Suneva. You'd better run along before people start thinking I engage in questionable deals." He drew his staff, a single pole with an orb at its end, and pushed it into Vinavek's armour.

Vinavek didn't cede to the hollow threat.

"We know of your corruption." She said, "I have bought the three Legendary Suneva, told by Zeus to exist, into your house to end this."

"End what?" He chuckled. "End my relations?"

"The suppression and ostracization of our people. Your policies hurt the Suneva in Thebes, and many likeminded politicians have caused similar despair across the empire. Suneva division has weakened the community further, but you can help us solve it."

"I think you came to the wrong office." Curiosus shook his head, slumping on his desk. "How do you expect me to help? I'm only a small time influence here. Your problems go beyond my control."

"You are the Shiverman" The White Witch stated. "And whilst you use your power to spread fear, lies and rumours, I know you could use it to spread other ideologies. I know you could change the minds of politicians and Suneva. Your people need you."

"I'm not the Shiverman." He sighed. "Haven't you heard? It was that general who…"

"I'm the White Witch, Tano Toskidin." Vinavek grinned. "I can see your future in your eyes. Together, with your people, you will make changes."

Vibius initially dismissed the party from his office, but couldn't fight the strange feeling of loss it gave him. Curious, he searched for Vinavek's mind, and he experienced her struggles, and through them, the struggles of disenfranchised Suneva across the empire. In her hear, he experienced his moment of realisation, the turn to white. He knew that Vinavek was a truly great Suneva, and a great leader. She was the person he'd always wanted to be.

So Vibius tracked her across the city, and he accepted her terms. He housed Vinavek and the three Legendaries in his mansion, and he got to work. Toskidin traversed the minds of the populace, spreading the seeds of ideologies into the minds of those who could affect change. Talking into sleepers' dreams, he implanted into politicians that the rich were manipulating them, and would seize power if they were supported in their amassing of wealth. To the layman he impersonated the God Jupiter, and condemned the mistreatment of Suneva.

The rumours and tricks of the mind he spread festered, growing and mutating over a year. Soon, there was a lingering conscious of the power of Suneva – fear rising to the eyes of politicians and aristocrats. Rates of Suneva slavery dissipated as anxieties over such investments spiked. Those who traded unfairly with Suneva were met with contempt, many of their ventures failing.

With culture slowly subverting, Vinevek knew it was time to gather the Suneva. She zipped through the Roman Empire, jumping from village to village with her Legendaries, spreading the ideology of power through community, peace, and enlightenment. She spoke of the pull of destiny, and the connections one should feel to others, themselves, and the world around them.

The Shiverman aided by questing for the troubles of Suneva in each town they visited. He drafted lists of the Suneva worries and doubts, and had Vinavek weave these concerns into her speeches. He compiled the information, holding the concerns so that their new Suneva religion could craft policies to solve them. As payment for their worries, the Shiverman left impressions of hope and worth in those he visited, and encouragement for the new Suneva revolution.

After two years of campaigning around the Roman Empire, the dream for Vinavek, the Legendaries, and Toskidin was realised. Vibius Caecina Curiosus came out of hiding to become *Faraku* – right hand man to Vinavek's *Fara*. Suneva were united under the new Suneva teachings, known simply as Sunevic, and under the old language of *Liktan*."

Kuvalik let the book rest on the couch, sighing deeply. "For the thousands of years which followed there existed a strong centre of community for Suneva. Whilst nations and teachings rose and fell around, the nation started by Vinavek was the inspiration for all, and the ancestor to my Liktas Nation of Greece."

"I think I heard Hesslik mention parts of that story before." Chad hummed. "Why would so few people believe in the Legendaries if they follow the Code of Connections?"

"Just because it's written in a book doesn't make it true. Especially when it's a book of very old, translated stories." Celeste chimed. "Although for the effort we went to get that book, I'd like it to be true…"

"Should we be concerned about the *Ocras Quatrona* or the *Shiverman*?" Natalie asked. "The Legendaries might be important, but the White Witch and her *Finder of Secrets* seem like the biggest influences in that tale."

"This is true." Kuvalik nodded. "If Hesslik's mission was only to find the Legendaries, he may already have the other two pieces which he needs."

Natalie hummed, stroking her chin.

46

Finder of Secrets – the name bounced in my head. I had heard that title before, hadn't I? There was an accent to it, a strange inflection about the *e*, but who had it been?

"Oh *cheese.*" I gasped, brain rushing. The voice, the one whom had fed me doubt and appraisal. The mystery guest on my night with Celeste. "If it makes you feel any better, Natalie, I think I've already talked to the Shiverman, and I don't know what he was looking for nor how much he's seen."

Chapter 6
Return to the Homelands

The *Shiverman*'s voice had intermittently come to me as I crammed for exams – the only time I'd heard it after my operation with Celeste. Natalie was the last person I told about the Shiverman's new intrusions, as our lives were stressful enough. Each day she found herself deep in an organised, colour coded stack of books, writing sticky notes to line her bedroom wall with facts. I awed her technique whenever I had the chance to study with her. Most of my efforts to remember things were in vain, spent doodling strange characters onto the backs of class handouts.

She and Celeste sat next to me now, as we crammed notes on the dining table of the ghost Kuvalik's house. After so many months of restoration by Chad and me, it had now become his and Celeste's home, and our usual group hangout whenever we weren't busy. Kuvaik idled in the shadows, always ready to throw tidbits of wisdom and boil the water for tea. He sometimes read to us from the book of Suneva Tales, but we'd heard each story a few times now. It made Celeste and I wish that we'd stolen more books.

Celeste nestled close to me, her elbow knocking mine as she dove into her books.

Don't even notice her. The voice of the Shiverman warned, an infrequent intrusion. *Also, you forgot to carry the negative, be more careful.* The voice addressed my math work. I'd struggled to ignore him over the past week. If he knew my fear, I wasn't sure what he would do. However, it was easy to forget the Shiverman's voice when Celeste's accidental touch sent me strangely giddy. I knew it shouldn't have, because I had no clue what was happening between us, and the ignorance proved bliss. It had been months now since I'd seen her talking to Rhys Cameron or any of his friends. The dirty looks I received from the bulky footballer would have been enough to satisfy me, but Celeste had even started hanging out with me more at school. She would steal me away from Tom and David at odd lunchtimes to chat and lie under the shade of the boundary trees. I wasn't even sure how she was still at school. With her exchange running out, and her time with David up, it seemed almost as if she'd slipped under the system's radar by continually rocking up and expecting to be taught. She'd only told me that she'd talked with the principal and 'made an agreement,' although she was tight lipped as to what strings she was pulling.

We'd grown closer during our time together, and she did her best to guide me through my Suneva connections when she could. Our closeness made my feelings for her feel selfish. I was certain by now that she couldn't have reciprocated them, but I could never be sure. Rogue hints kept appearing when I'd least expected them, and I was becoming convinced that I had no idea what a hint even was. She felt comfortable enough around me to rest a head on my shoulder or chest, or to make an innuendo at my expense. I didn't know what to feel, but her cheeky, lip-bit smile always kept the butterflies churning. I let her arm touch mine as we did work.

Over the past few months, this schoolwork had taken priority to direct action in Suneva duties. Life seemed to take a turn for the normal as we each started to practice working at our connections in the background. Between bouts of schoolwork and early mornings, Natalie was spending whole days with her Yamitse working on the connection she had to herself, and to quatra. Much more than practicing her quatran abilities of water and hydrogen, Natalie was learning about the quatra field, auras, senses, tracking, and the soul. It was this *witchcraft* that she was becoming proficient in. Celeste and Chad were practicing their own abilities – Celeste's flames glowing even bluer, and Chad standing in mud for more hours of the day. I'd been practicing too, with Kuvalik and Celeste, and had managed to create diamonds. I couldn't shape them yet, as trying to alter the structure caused it to crumble in my hands, but I would get there… eventually.

I had perfected my gliding technique also, by jumping off bridges and buildings in the dead of night when I really should have been in bed. The real skies teased me though – I still had that sensation that if I leaped, I might *never* fall.

Kuvalik urged that flight, that beacon of mastery for all *Kiin*, was not actually attainable for all. Some great *Kiin*, the late *Muhrakiin* included, could never fly. He told me that my progress was strong, but that flying really was a *kiin* art reserved for those who had attained realisation.

Over these passing months there was no shortage of celebration. Tom had hosted a birthday party like nobody else before him, creating a night that would be forgotten in hours but remembered in stories for years. Natalie had her birthday in August, turning eighteen and celebrating with a small Sunday brunch at her house, food supplied by her Yamitse. I had had my own eighteenth, trying to match the grand scale and vibe of those before. In the end, there were cheese-rings and dancing, which is all I could have asked for.

And now we studied for exams, our trip to the Suneva homeland looming just weeks away. The side door to Kuvalik's hallway screeched open, and Chad threw himself into the living area.

"Come have a look at this, guys." He panted. "Big news on Hesslik's channels."

I wonder what that is. The Shiverman hummed into my skull.

Chad ran back down the side corridor, leaving Natalie, Celeste and I to follow. We slouched into the room, drowsy from our studies, to find Chad buzzing by his computer's screen. He scooted his chair aside, making a clear view to the monitor.

"I think we found your Shiverman, James." Chad said, gesturing to the screen. I could feel the voice in my head prick up, keen. Chad had loaded Hesslik's Empire Website, a domain we'd been frequently analysing the chatter of. We hadn't changed our main plan yet – to find Argol through our connection to others – but this website could give us more leads. So far, it had given us none.

We gathered closer to the screen. On it was an announcement from Hesslik himself. It read:

Hi all,

After years of searching for a new Shiverman, one kidin has stood tall as the most ingenious and creative in their abilities and understanding of kidin concepts.

The annual kidin contest, held on the 29th of October this year, was won by none other than the right-hand man to my Empire, Boekidin.

49

*We join to congratulate Boekidin on his success, and hope that he may lead the Suneva
into as new world as previous Shiverman before him have done.*
Fara Hesslik.

"Boekidin…" I mused. I'd only met Boekidin once before, when I had
met Hesslik. They wore black and silver, raven-like armour, with beady, pink eyes.
"He's the bird-guy, right?"

"Yep, the big bird." Chad nodded. "The first time I saw his wings I think
I fell over. He's an alright guy. I did a lot of jobs for him."

"Wings?" I stammered.

Don't worry, they don't do much. The voice chuckled.

"If he's been listening to any of your thoughts and conversations, this
could be dangerous." Celeste frowned. "He could know exactly what we're
planning, and he'd be telling it straight to Hesslik. Hesslik could know *everything*.
What has he heard?"

My stomach dropped, burning hot. Anxiety hit. "I don't know what he
knows, but don't say anything now." I warned, "because he's here."

Don't ruin the fun.

"Right now?" Celeste huffed. "James, you could have mentioned that."

"I didn't know it was Boekidin until right now." I defended, pointing to
the screen. "It wasn't *that* dangerous until a moment ago."

"Don't *Kidin* have a range?" Natalie asked the group. "This says that he
was in Greece a few days ago. He can't *also* be here, close enough to read thoughts.
He'd become *Natasvoul*, a *wandering soul*, too far from his body to return."

"He *is* the Shiverman." Chad said, his tone changing sharply. "He could
talk to me at a distance when I worked for him, although he himself said that you
had to be within a few hundred metres to read the mind, not just communicate."

And he's giving away my surface secrets. I worked hard to keep those. The voice
joked.

"He's not around, I'd be able to sense him in the field." Natalie added.
"I'm not sure we've got too much to worry about."

She could be wrong on that. The Shiverman said, before I felt the water drip
from my ear, announcing his leave.

Chad, Celeste, Natalie, and I dropped our bags onto the stewardess' conveyer, ready for the plane's belly. Exams done, and the school year over, we were finally heading on our secret journey. Natalie's family and mine had come to see as off, as well as Tom, who tagged along with Simone, Mum, and I in our car. Our plans were becoming real now, and there was the sharp tether of apprehension strung between us. Celeste, most of all, had been tense.

"I know I'll see my mother," she said when I asked what was wrong. "And maybe that's the frightening part for me, past even the *possibility* of running into Argol, I'll have to explain to her what I did. Her husband died and I left her."

Argol had killed Celeste's father, and as an odd coincidence, had lost his own daughters within that week. Celeste's misidentification by hunters following her father's murder had caused her to run from home in the first place. I'd never considered the other side of this coin – that she'd abandoned her Mother without warning.

"I guess you've got all of us to lean on." I said. "But that's rough, anyway."

"It is." She sighed. "I don't know what I'll say when I see my family again. I know why I chose to run, but I was nine years old when I did it. My reason won't make sense anymore."

Less advice was always good, or so Simone had coached me, so I chose to let Celeste simmer on the feeling. There was a tap on my shoulder, and I turned to find Tom. He pulled me aside and out of earshot of my friends.

"Thanks for coming, man." I said to him. "It means a lot that you're here."

"I just wanted to make sure that you leave alright." He said, a hand on my shoulder. "I hope it goes well."

I could feel some resentment in him – either an emotion that I'd imagined, or something I read on his body. I hadn't invited him on this trip, and I knew that it wouldn't have seemed right to him. Why wouldn't he get to come on a holiday with one of his best mates, and Natalie and Celeste, who he'd become close with over the year? I couldn't tell him about our Suneva abilities, either, because he was too sceptical of anything supernatural, and wasn't the kind of man to use a quiet voice. That said, he'd also seen *The Umbrella Lady* and Genive in the alley, and I had no idea how he would react if I told him that we were like those mechanical creatures he saw.

"I'm sure it will." I said. "I'll send you postcards, anyway. I'll probably get back before they do, though."

"Maybe." Tom brewed, then finally continued. "I don't trust this Chad guy." He said, glaring over my shoulder at the tall, broad boy. "He organises a holiday for the four of you? Why?"

"Look, I'm sorry he's been a dickhead about who can come and who can't." I said. "I didn't organise it."

"I know." Tom grumbled. "I just always thought it would be me, you, and David taking on the world."

"We'll get time." I said. "There's plenty of travelling to be done in university. Sit tight."

"Alright, man." He nodded, dropping his hand from my shoulder. "But keep safe, and don't get sucked into weird shit."

"Keep safe?" I chuffed. "Come on man, you know me."

"Yes, yes." He smiled. "I *am* talking to James Grey. The same James Grey who dobbed on me when we were six because I climbed a two-foot shrub."

"That's the James Grey you know." I smiled. Tom laughed along, but his face fell blank, turning serious.

"Still, there's weird stuff happening around." He said, hushed.

"Weird stuff?" I hummed. "What do you mean?"

"I don't know that I ever told you this…but the night of Christy Nanos' party, when you were searching for your ring. I saw something in an alleyway."

Oh, sweet cheese…

"And I thought I was crazy, but then I found the weird forums on Penny's computer when I was cleaning it out, and I dusted it all off at the time as crazy…"

"I remember." I interrupted him.

"But it's not. The world's become dangerous. There are these people called *Suneva*, James."

"I know all about Suneva, Tom." I tried to remain straight faced, although the fear in my eyes was surely deceiving me.

"You do?" Tom was surprised – offended, even. "Well they're all over Europe, man. It seems like a bad time to be going…but if you're in the know."

52

"I'll be fine, I promise you that." I slapped a hand on his shoulder. "It's nothing to worry about."

"It *is*." He insisted. "I've been talking to your sister about it, actually."

Rats. "She's the one who told me." I withheld a lot of the truth. "I'm informed, I'm all good. Don't worry a muscle. You, on the other hand, are always getting into trouble. Don't make too much of a mess for me to clean up when I'm back." I deflected the conversation, and immediately the young man lit up, his golden-orange locks shining to his smile.

"Mate, a bomb will have hit when you get back, don't you worry."

"Good. Make it big." I smiled and hugged him for our final goodbye. Tom then stepped past me, off to say his final words to Natalie and Celeste, leaving me shaken.

Tom hates the Suneva too... I cursed, drifting towards my family. *And he's talked to Simone about it. How didn't I find out about that?*

But how had I waited so long to tell him about my abilities? It wasn't like they needed to be kept secret, except from Simone. Maybe I could have swayed him against her views early on. Now it was risky to bring it up. I grumbled, dragging my family and friends over to the customs. I let Celeste and Chad through first, and I said my farewells to Mum and Simone.

"Be good." Mum said, and I knew what she meant by it. Mum knew that these were my Suneva friends. I'm sure that she figured we would be getting up to *something.*

"You can count on me, Mum." I said. "I know what I'm doing."

"... be good." She repeated, tearing up. She stole me from Simone, hugging me so tight that my bag melded into my spine. When she finally let go, I got to say bye to Simone.

"Don't find anything too interesting whilst I'm gone." I said to her. "Remember to leave the study once in a while. I'll try to email you if I find a computer." Simone could not be allowed to know the purpose of this trip. I'd already had to think of my most intricate lies to tell her about what I was doing. The immensity of which had caused me to write them down and rehearse the delivery, or else I'd have given myself away.

"You'll have a lot to tell me about." She said. "You'll have a great time." And she hugged me goodbye.

Finally, heartfelt departures completed, I joined Natalie in walking past the barrier, past the event horizon into our lives.

***

Celeste, Chad, and I were seated next to each other on the plane, taking up a centre row, whilst Natalie found herself across the aisle. Natalie, remarkably, found herself a competent plane-sleeper, much to everybody's surprise. Her lights were out the second of take-off, sending her into dreams which contorted her hands into Suneva poses. Chad and I watched on, giggling.

Eventually, Chad asked Celeste how she felt to be returning to her mother after such a long time, and Celeste admitted her worries to him. As always, he listened with an appropriate and keen smile, and responded with wisdom.

"Better to confront and know, than run and never find out." He said. "A mother's love supposedly transcends time, actions, and space. Take James' mother for example. She broke his back letting him go today."

"But my mother was never so affectionate." Celeste hummed.

"But was she loving?" Chad asked.

"Yes."

"Then I'm sure that whatever rage she has for you is stemmed from that. Loss creates anger, but it's the kind of anger you'd feel destroyed if you didn't see." He chimed, his face turning to a frown.

"Did I upset you?" Celeste sensed his shift, although Chad was quick to recover.

"No." He smiled. "My mom was awful, is all." He chuffed, oddly cheery to be saying such a thing. "I don't feel bad about leaving, even if she wasn't the one to make me do it. My dad, though? I'd go back for him." He nodded, then looked aside. "I might watch a movie if that's alright with you guys." Chad avoided further questions, and went to turn on his monitor.

It wouldn't turn on.

"I guess I'll have to watch on with somebody else, then." He smirked, craning his head up to analyse the movies playing by the row in front. Celeste pulled him down.

"I'll switch with you." She said, turning her TV on. "Mine works."

"Thanks!" Chad smiled, climbing over the girl and away from me. "I owe you a pizza, or something."

Celeste squeezed under him to sit next to me. With a forceful push, she shoved my elbow off the armrest, and tilted it back into the chair. She pressed up beside me, resting her head on my shoulder and chest. I froze up.

"Let's watch something on your TV." She suggested, although the only thing my ears could hear was the beating of my heart. "Something to pass the time."

Episode 2

Adding Greece to the Fire.

Chapter 7
Street Fight

Our feet raced hot fire across the roof of the hotel, a blazen trail left in our wake from the maintenance door. Blistered soles pounded fast in the crisp light of the morning autumn sun. Clouds had parted, and let yellow-blue light shine on the silhouette of the great mountains who guarded the valley-city. Spread before us was sea of white concrete; a vast jungle of semi-maintained buildings covering the valley floor like a carpet, hugging the line of the Saronic Bay. This was the great city of Athens, glistening white. We ran towards the edge of the building, but we didn't know what would happen when we got there.

Kiin can fly, can't they? The voice of Boekidin, *The Shiverman*, echoed inside my head. *Why would you be scared? You'll survive.*

Oh, get out of my head Boekidin, I cursed to him.

Sure, I could *glide*, but it wouldn't make jumping off a twelve-storey building any easier. I skidded to a halt at the edge of the tall hotel and peered over.

Staring down twelve storeys, I felt like vomiting. Heights never *look* so bad until you imagine the fall. That was the strange thing about falling – you just keep going, no matter how short the dive. Your body keeps accelerating, getting faster and faster until…

My head was spinning. I turned around to face the door. Zamelle, Genive and Ferrad were half way to the edge, sprinting behind me.

"Go Maiki!" Zamelle puffed, "Jump!"

Do it. Boekidin's voice bounced around the chamber of my skull.

"He knows where we're going!" I yelled. The three Suneva had reached me. Ferrad peered perilously over the edge.

"It doesn't matter." Zamelle insisted.

"It's a trap!"

"He's lying, Maiki. I can feel his quatra. He's coming up those stairs for us right now. Let's go!" Zamelle instructed. She climbed up onto the ledge of the building. Below us, between the cracked concrete façades of the hotel and its adjacent neighbour was a small alley – a consistently double parked, foot wide excuse for a two lane road through a shifty part of town. Zamelle didn't look down

57

as she readied herself, but instead peered across to the next building. She jumped heroically.

"Oh gee." I squeaked.

Genive and Ferrad both followed, showing their bravery gracefully in the face of surrounding adversity. Genive could slow her descent with propulsive flames and huge, bug-like wings; Ferrad could bend the road to soften his landing, but what would Zamelle do? I had the clearest plan to get down safely, why was I worried as I watched them jump?

The maintenance door slammed open. I shouldn't have looked, I was going to jump, but it took me by surprise. I turned to see Boekidin running towards me at full pelt. Flames of hot, wet fire, dripped and slopped from the end of his tripod staff. His predatory bird-face locked on to me, flying atop blazing talons. I couldn't shake the Shiverman.

I turned to the edge, and threw myself off.

It was a straight nose dive – the wind wrapped hard around my head fin. I could see my friends below, Genive jetting hot flames beneath her bug wings, Ferrad riding down the concrete of the building, and Zamelle summoning a wave of dirty water to sweep her up into a safe landing. I fell faster, and my stomach dropped as I heard Boekidin make his leap.

I swivelled myself around mid-air to watch him. Boekidin launched gracefully, feet down, arms to the side, like a black cross falling from the sky. His wings ejected – thick metal sheets fanning behind him to cover the sky. His silhouette was an eagle pouncing for its prey, a dark angel falling from the heavens.

Boekidin's weapon arced with power, energy gathering between its tips. I flipped back to the ground and kicked myself into an aerial spin, jetting away from him. A hot, pink blast of quatra from his staff skimmed my cheek, and I saw it splash and dissolve onto the grimy surface of the road below. I whirled again, blasting faster towards the asphalt. My brain spun – as if falling wasn't fast enough. I forced the rushing air over my back, swooping at the building. I skimmed down the side of it, just inches from the plaster, barrel rolling to dodge air filter units, heating pipes and hanging lights. Blasts of quatra came careening by my side as the white, sandy wall rushed by.

My friends had safely landed now. I had caught up to them and was only two storeys off the ground. Boekidin had not kept up with my descent – how could he? I was a *Kiin*.

I prepared for the landing with all of my might. Then, only a foot from the road, I ground the air stream over my body to a full halt, pulling up hard. Barrelling towards the adjacent building, I banked right, swinging hard down the hill of the road. The street was ten feet wide, to either side were weathered, high white buildings with dingy windows and graffiti scrawled on support columns. I swung myself around hard, arresting my glide and coming to a stop just downhill of my friends. I sprinted back towards them.

I saw Boekidin plummeting towards me. His wings were back, his talons were out. I ran towards him, staff out, firing bolts of quatra, which he absorbed through his feet and redirected with ease. As he swooped for the strike, I leaped between his claws and the ground, slipping out from under his grip and sprinting up the road.

I wouldn't run that way, his Kiwi voice teased between my ears.

"Oh, shut up!" I called out. Swivelling around on one foot mid sprint, I kicked an air blast back his way. His extended wings, with their impressive area, caught the whole gust and drug him tumbling down the hill. I continued to run.

A hot yellow flame engulfed my back. I felt the heat all the way to my bones, cooking my nerves into shock. I jumped into the air by instinct and twirled a nasty eddy around me to fend the flames away. Touching back down to ground, I gripped in and flung the eddy back at the *Shiverman* who had flamed me. His fire parted with the wind, stripping back to his staff.

Boekidin pulled back, preparing another strike. Before he got any ideas, I quick-blasted him with a bolt of quatra and pre-emptively rolled to my left. Just as I summoned the bolt – when its hot, sticky, mass came to fruition at the base of my neck – I heard a bolt being fired from down the street, around the corner shop. Surely enough, as my bolt prepared to leave my palm, I saw *it*, a bright violet blast, coming towards me. I was already shifting my momentum into a roll, in those split nanoseconds I thought I might have been moving right into its path, but there was nothing I could do. My green bolt left my hand, I started to dive, and my quatra got only a foot from my arm before the purple blast collided directly with it. The sound which followed was like a shotgun in a bathroom. The two bolts absorbed each other in a supernova spectacle and imploded into nothing.

I leapt out of my summersault, peering to the cornershop ahead. There was no Suneva there; where had the bolt come from? I turned back to the Shiverman and felt his snide grin. I retaliated with a bolt, and his smirk grew as another purple bolt came flying through the air just at my *thought* of blasting him. My quatra again just left my staff before being loudly obliterated.

Have fun firing bolts, Boekidin whispered into my head. He opened his wings wide to their impressive, imposing span, and leaped high, perching himself onto the ledge of the corner shop. I flung hot and desperate green quatra at his stupid bird face as he flew to his perch, but every single bolt was met by a flying purple assassin. Five little explosions rumbled down the alleyway.

Now, Maiki. Let me find what you're planning.

I was mad now – who could have an aim that good? I glared at the corner, and a Suneva appeared from the shadows. Their strange eyes glowed against the dark, one slanted and purple, the other mechanical and teal. They were expressionless. Strangely, their form was curved, unlike most Suneva who were sharp and pointed. Their joints were even *more* impossibly thin than most, as was most of their strange *alis*.

Grinning, the strange Suneva arched their back unnaturally, snapping their head to the sky and screaming a Suneva ghost howl. The howl was beyond any Suneva screech I'd heard before. It was truly demonic, the sound of death and decay, the shriek of the departed. My stomach twisted in nausea, my eyes wriggled in my skull. This Suneva's armour shifted shades, bleaching from burgundy and silver to grey and blistering white. I was frozen in shock.

I heard Zamelle shout my name from over my shoulder, her footsteps raced towards me. The howling Suneva creaked back upright, their colour leaking back. They drew a staff – a long golden pole with a jewel-encrusted butt. They pointed its end at me, and I felt their energy building.

If *I* could feel the energy building, then there was going to be *a lot* of energy.

I readied my staff, but hadn't expected their next move. Like a machine gun, purple bolts of quatra rapid-fired from the end of their golden rod with deadly precision. Panicking, I spun my staff before me to deflect the attack, but it was too much to handle. The sheer weight of the energy crashing onto my blade had me stumbling back. My heart raced – any misstep, and I'd have ten bolts to the chest. I'd be dead.

Zamelle sprinted past my left, the corks flying off the camel-bags she had strapped to her back. From them she commanded a venomous snake of liquid. She whipped it at the strange Suneva slashing them across their shooting arm. They shrieked another departed cry, their mechanical eye buzzing between every colour of quatra. Where the liquid landed, the armour bubbled and slopped. This was a new trick for Zamelle – acid.

Although, a second later when the acid had dried, their armour was already healed.

Whilst this strange Suneva was distracted by Zamelle, I turned to neutralise Boekidin. As I aimed my staff, an amazing flush of insane heat roared over me, and I was dazed by a blinding, blue glow. A mighty crack screamed by my head, warping air and space. I ducked away from a horizontal strike of pure lightning, which roared in front of me and collided with a lamppost. The bulb exploded, and the pole melted, bursting into flames. Petrified, I creaked my head around to find the lightning's source.

A Suneva stood up the road, their stance firmly planted and straight backed. Their armour was dark and thick. Their helmet was like a bucket with a single, blue slit and copper recesses. *The Space Cowboy* is what I decided to call him in that instant. From his weapons – two thin blades extending form his forearms – plasma dripped.

The earth beneath The Space Cowboy cracked, then lurched. They were toppled from their feet as the road flipped under them. They regained their footing with ease, only to have a boulder of road hafted their way from Ferrad to the right. Undeterred, The Space Cowboy levelled his sword at the flying rock and let rip a blinding flash. His bolt of lightning tore through the air faster than sound, sublimating the rock in its path, setting Ferrad and Genive in a shroud of rock dust.

A bright blue flame erupted from the cloud of stone. The Cowboy stepped from its path and levelled his swords again. He ripped lightning blindly into the dust – the super-powerful arc of electricity creaming the concrete past Genive and Ferrad, blowing more debris onto the scene.

61

With their movement dissipating, the Space Cowboy turned his attention to me. My stomach dropped at eye contact, but I still spread my feet, ready to stand some ground. I'd dealt well with Liktas before, I had a plan, but this would involve lots of carbon and *lots* of time.

As I pondered, they aimed their weapon at my head. *No time.*

I threw the prongs of my *shath* – my Suneva weapon – into the asphalt by my feet. Barely with time to hide behind my weapon, lightning erupted from the Space Cowboy's sword with a mighty *boom*. It raced towards me, but arced into my staff. The ground between the prongs exploded into magma, the staff sent leaping through the sky. I ran, and jumped to catch it, then sprinted for the cover of dust.

The cloud settled just as I reached it. Ferrad launched a rock at The Cowboy, followed by a lick of the hottest Suneva flame from Genive. I found myself scattered again as movement up the hill caught my eye. Something was running on us, fast. It pounded the tarmac on all fours, with the form of a large, metal cat. A silver and red puma.

I didn't have time to comprehend what I was seeing – I couldn't tell Ferrad to clear the path before it pounced on him. It bowled the Bronze Suneva over his right shoulder, slamming him into the ground before me. I thought at first that there was a wild, big cat in the streets of Athens – but no – this was a Suneva. In its tail, which ended in a hand, it held a small dagger – its *shath* – which it was set at Ferrad's neck.

I raised my weapon and shot bolt of quatra, running towards it. It sensed my attack and swatted the bolts off with the dagger in its tail. It turned to me and let out a Suneva cry – much more like a snarling hiss than a ghost shriek. It leaped from Ferrad bounded instead towards me. I screeched to a halt, not sure what to do.

I shot another bolt nervously, but the cat simply evaded to the right and dug its claws into a telephone pole. I shot another blast at the pole, but before the bolt left my staff The Cat had already jumped onto the adjacent building.

I could see its next move in my head, they were getting ready to pounce right onto me. No *quatra* stops this. I gripped onto the surrounding air, and blasted a vertex straight into its path.

This cat had foresight where I didn't. It had waited for my attack, and fleetingly dodged the gust with its airborne agility. The Cat landed on the ground halfway between the post and me; ass up, head down – ready to pounce. This time I would wait for their move.

From behind the feline Suneva came a heavy iron chain soaring through the air. Ferrad's whip, guided by his soul connections, soared for The Cat's ankle. Its eyes lit up – they'd sensed the metal despite its total silence. They pounced to the left and swivelled around before it even hit the ground and landed straight up on two feet, hands already gripping at their element and contorting. They clenched their fingers tightly, twisted their palms, and shifted their momentum onto their front foot. The chain slowed violently and stopped to a hover just above the ground.

Ferrad looked confused. He strengthened his grip and tried to force his will into its movement, but the chain did not obey him. Instead, it whipped back the way it had come. The motion was as if the chain was falling sideways. Ferrad struggled to assert his power, but it was too late, and he was too stubborn. From behind him I noticed another projectile – a manhole cover which had lifted itself up and was falling sideways towards the chain. Ferrad was going to be sandwiched if he didn't move.

I didn't have time to call out. I hurriedly gripped onto the carbon in the tarmac next to Ferrad and pulled it hard towards me. I only just caused his stumble, letting him lose his footing and fall out of the deadly path. The chain whipped around the manhole right where his head should have been, then dropped to the ground with a mighty clang.

Whilst The Cat was distracted using her abilities, I swung my staff and sent two green quatra bolts her way. The Suneva skilfully evaded the blasts, prancing on their feet. They stared me down, ready to strike.

It's magnetism, by the way. Boekidin advised between my ears.

What?

Magnetism. She controls magnetism.

That certainly explained a chain flying towards a manhole. The information wouldn't provide much help, though, as I had even less of a clue what to expect from a magnetic Suneva. But if there was one thing I did know, it was that I could get a cat stuck up a tree.

With a sly smile to combat my nerves, I looked up at the building to my right – about eleven stories tall. This road was only about five metres across from one building's wall to the next. The gap was too wide to leap up continually. I wasn't sure I had another plan to draw the cat up to the top, but she was ready to pounce now, and I had to act.

I threw myself onto the closest building, and launched myself immediately across the gap to the opposite. I watched my opponent, who ripped metal out of the ground and coated it to her claws. I leapt again and again, kicking off the walls like a swimmer, launching myself higher up the structures, leaving the action behind.

Below me, to my horror, The Cat clawed herself up the wall. I was a fast climber, but nothing to match them. They strode up the wall as if the building were turned flat. Long, powerful strides.

They must have been using the metal coating on their claws to hold themselves to the building. Either way, I had no time. I vaulted as fast as I could between the building facades, and finally blasted off the hotel, landing in a backflip onto the adjacent building.

I waited pensively, hearing the roar of The Cat's claws. Suddenly they appeared, flying high into the air off the gutter of the building, claws engaged. Now I had my chance to strike. Lining up my staff, I blasted bolts of quatra into The Cat's falling path. Each bolt was successfully absorbed into one hand and redirected out the other, pocking the building in burn marks and green quatra rings.

They landed on two feet at the lip of the building, one hand extended downwards. I gathered a wind in my grip, a rushed decision, and blasted a column of air into their gut. They bent over backwards in the heavy breeze, but even hanging on the very edge by no more than their weight, they did not fall off. They grinned, and into their outstretched hand, at incredible speeds, flew the manhole from the ground. It should have sent the Suneva flying, but it seemed that they'd magnetically anchored themselves to the floor.

My stomach dropped. There was no way I could combat this cat and her *manhole*. My armour had collected enough dints already. I sprinted towards The Cat, blasting off the floor and vaulting myself over their head. I dove back to ground.

I could only hope that The Cat would be stuck up in that tree, but something told me that she could get down from heights *just fine*.

I spun myself mid-dive to face up towards them. I quickly aimed and fired a bolt of quatra, hoping to disable them on the roof, but I predictably missed. Rolling back to ground, I spotted Boekidin on the balcony. Whilst I had time, I fired a bolt at him too, but a purple one came from out of nowhere and met mine just before his helmet. I cursed, and spotted the Suneva of the shadows standing on the far side of Boekidin's ledge. She switched her focus to me and ejected a flurry of purple quatra bolts.

Storeys from the ground, I fell head first, following a path into a field of flying, purple bolts. I could see my armour smashing off like glass, and my head exploding on the road, my wallet falling comically from my pocket.

My quatra-blood rushing, I grappled at the air over my left side, ripping through the air-field around my body and flinging me to the left.

The manoeuvre channelled me into a hard pull up. Once vertical, I saw Genive throwing blue quatra bolts at the strange Suneva, charting my safe path. I blasted off the closest wall, springing myself towards Boekidin's ledge.

I swooped towards it, towards the now distracted strange Suneva. There was no way I'd be able to disable her thread with a well-aimed shot, regardless of how distracted she seemed. There would only be one way to throw her off, and land a hit on Boekidin.

And that was by literally throwing her off.

Diving towards her, a short blast of air kicked my body into a spin to face feet first. Then, ripping at the flows over my body, I set my position, and piled foot-first into her side.

I blasted air from the soles of my foot on collision, slowing my fall and sending the strange Suneva flying. They thumped up against the back wall, and rolled off the corner of the awning, just as I'd gained my footing. I swung myself around, drawing my staff and setting it to Boekidin's still, meditating head.

I'd leave my mind if I was you. I snarled, before firing.

A shadow fell over Boekidin. The green rings of my quatra were absorbed into it, and the energy pulsed along the black mass under my feet and behind me. I flipped around to follow the trail of energy, as it zipped along the blackness towards the awnings edge. The feet of the shadow crested the gutter, but they were met by nothing to block the light and cast it. At the shadow's end was *nothing*.

My green energy reached its toe and the shadow *peeled* itself up, facing towards me and firing a purple-green toxicated bolt to my face. I let my legs fall under me, crashing to my ass atop Boekidin and then leaping to my feet. The blackness slipped off the edge of the building, and as the last lick of it disappeared, the strange Suneva's hand clawed at the gutter.

I ran away, as was the only sensible option.

In fact, it seemed that fighting was totally useless, we had to run if we were to make it out of here in any state of consciousness at all.

I sprinted for the edge, towards where I could see Zamelle and Ferrad up the road engaged with the Space Cowboy. Genive was just below the awning.

"Run!" I yelled to her. "We have to run!" I leaped off the overhang, clanging to the ground.

As my feet it the floor, so did The Cat's, thudding into the asphalt atop their manhole cover with a mighty crack. They ignored Genive and I, instead pouncing towards the Space Cowboy.

"Oh no…" I knew this could only be bad. "Run!" I yelled again, hoping that Zamelle and Ferrad would hear me.

The Space Cowboy stabbed his weapon into the sky, and The Cat stopped dead behind him, gripping her element with her claws. He struck an awesome bolt of lightning into the sky, and with The Cat shifting her weight, it split into four bolts, each falling to earth and aimed at my friends and I.

I leaped from my position, falling away just as the deadly electrical strike crashed into the ground, melting the rock and ripping the road apart. Zamelle, Ferrad, Genive and I found ourselves in one pile, struggling to get up in the face of our foes. The Cowboy, The Cat, and The Strange Suneva all eyed us, hungry.

Then The Strange Suneva shrieked. Their mechanical eye flickered between colours before setting on pure, starlight, white. Their armour steamed, turning dark. Both eyes were now white, and their weapon aimed, then charged. The Cat and The Space Cowboy threw themselves aside. That was curious.

"By Amsos, we need to run!" Zamelle shrieked, jumping from the pile and sprinting away. I was too transfixed to move, but was tugged up by Genive.

A bolt exploded from the golden staff's end. Twice as big as a regular bolt, and twice as fast, it was the white of pure light itself. It screamed up the road, careening straight for us.

A wall of rock raised to protect us, just as Genive grabbed me and tackled me aside. The white bolt ripped through the wall, sublimating it into gas and lava before slamming into the road's centre. The ground exploded too, sending shards of molten rock flying in each direction. A pool of magma now crested the street surface.

"She's got white quatra…" Zamelle panted.

"White quatra?" I asked.

"No time now." Zamelle stumbled to her feet. "Let's run."

I nodded, and sprung to my feet.

The Strange Suneva's staff finished charging once more, and released another bolt. I could feel its hot energy in my hands, which meant that it was *powerful*. The thing tore up the centre of the street, sending Zamelle, Genive, Ferrad and I into the wall to avoid it. We ran still, as the bolt flew between the next set of buildings and continued off, rising into the sky. I'd hate to see where it finally landed, if it didn't make it to space. With an impressive bang, a lightning bolt tickled the soles of my feet, crumbling the ground under me. I stumbled, but didn't dare look back.

We skidded around the corner of the street, coming onto the bustling main road. We dropped our armour collectively, letting it settle into our souls.

"Time to blend in" Celeste said.

I heard a bolt of quatra before I felt it. The intruding energy ran heavy and hot through my veins. I felt it get sucked into my thread, and instantly my connection to the world around me vanished. I gasped for breath as all sensations left me. Natalie yelped, and fell onto me for support. I turned to Celeste, to see her and Chad fire a bolt simultaneously into each other's chests.

"What was that!" Natalie asked, infuriated.

"Can't let them track us," Celeste said. "These are street tricks. Couldn't warn you, or you'd never let me do it."

"You're right about that." Natalie grumbled.

"Well what about Boekidin?" I insisted, "He's probably still in my head!"

Chapter 8
White Concrete Jungle

We had just screeched around the corner of our hotel, having obliterated each other's threads after fighting for our lives. Celeste led us away from the scene calmly now, fixing her hair to blend into the Athenian crowd. Boekidin's agents were surely stalking us up the alleyway right now. I wanted to run, and I cracked in my urgency.

"What about Boekidin?" I insisted. "He's probably still in my head! Close enough to still *see* my memories. Who knows what he's pulling out?" My ears felt thick, but I couldn't know whether my pressure had adjusted from the plane ride yet. I had no idea if he was still present.

"He couldn't be." Celeste said calmly as she walked. Being a bunch of young kids, we didn't really fit into the morning commute, and it spiked my anxiety. The Shiverman was playing with my head, alright. "We left him so far down that alley. Kidin can't travel in minds unless they let their soul wander, so he'd had to have moved and lay down somewhere else. If we keep moving, he can't keep in your head long enough to know anything lest he become *Natasvoul*."

"But what if he is still in there?" I stressed. "He knows where we're going."

"Then stop thinking about it." Celeste suggested. "Calm down, and let's keep walking."

"Just think *really* unsexy thoughts." Chad said. "That'll make him move on."

I could picture Boekidin's reply to such a quip, but it didn't come. I skipped a breath, finally calming down. Calm gave way to a flood of images from the battle. I was reminded of the Suneva who fired huge, fast, white bolts of quatra, could aim quatra at other bolts before they'd even been fired, and who had disconnected their shadow.

"What the hell was with that strange shadow-Suneva?" I asked the group as my mind wandered. "She had white quatra, does that make her *The White Witch*?"

"She's a powerful witch, absolutely." Natalie said, coming forward to lead the group in our random wander. "She had an amazing connection to herself. If she *is* The White Witch, then that gives Hesslik The White Witch *and* the Shiverman. But I don't think she is."

"What makes you certain of that?" Chad chuckled. "Looked pretty *White Witch* to me."

"She had an amazing connection to herself and her soul – enough to detach it from her body – but something about her was too *strange*." Natalie hummed. "That shriek was too departed. My Yamitse warned me about this, it was like she was possessed. I think she's a *Quatra Daemon*."

"Demons are a part of all of this?" I quizzed.

"Not a demon, a *Quatra Daemon*." Natalie corrected. "It's a Suneva illness, or so my Yamitse said. When you let a black hole power your soul without restraint, it can come to control you as you feed off its energy. It happens when Suneva become dependant on quatra, and it very easy to succumb to if you don't have the right restraint."

My face dropped, stunned.

"Don't worry, James." Natalie said. "You're not a powerful enough witch to succumb to a black hole like that. You need to be better with quatra to fall."

"Oh, thanks…" I took the backhanded compliment.

"My Yamitse warned that she felt a more connected soul than hers recently." Natalie hummed. "She gave up the title of White Witch a while ago, and I hope this isn't her heir."

"Your Yamitse was *The White Witch?*" Celeste burst. "Why haven't you mentioned that?"

"She told me after I learned about the concept, but she denounced the title at least fifteen years ago." Natalie said. "She always maintained there was a better witch out there. It's just that recently she felt an *even* stronger presence than the one she already knew."

"Ridiculous." Chad shook his head. "You can't just *denounce* a position like that. Being The White Witch is one of those things that's just true regardless of what you think about it."

"Maybe." Natalie nodded. "But I think if anybody would know a more powerful soul, it's her. We can just hope that this new witch isn't the one she's been afraid of."

"Not ominous at all." I bit my lip.

"And if this witch *is* the new White Witch, we'll need to get moving to find those Legendaries before she and Boekidin do." Celeste said.

"Then we keep following the plan." Natalie said, walking us across a busy street. Despite the total gridlock, she still had us wait at the light until the green man commanded us to cross. "We'll find a car, and make our way to Sparta to see my family. We'll build our connections and find Argol whilst following the code. We're onto something good."

"And before we find a car, could we find some food?" Chad asked, holding his stomach. "I don't know about you guys, but fighting at dawn always makes me hungry."

"I think that's the lack of breakfast, Chad." Celeste chimed.

"Probably both."

"I'll ask a local what's good." Natalie said, and strayed from our path, walking over to an old woman smoking outside a shop. Natalie could speak Greek, so I learned in this moment, and the little old woman waved her cigarette wand through the air, giving some directions. Natalie nodded, and bowed to the woman.

"Alright, we should go down that street…" Natalie pointed across the deadlocked road to a small, spindly side street. In its thoroughfare was barely enough room for a scooter to move. "As long as I don't tell *you* the directions, James, we should be safe. We should come to some square with a few good cafes."

"Oh, good." Chad rubbed his hands together. I nodded to Natalie, and Celeste barged her way across the jammed road. Chad and I followed, dodging scooters.

"Oh Amasos, guys, there was a crossing light *just* over there." Natalie moaned, finally running between cars to catch us.

The thin, winding street quickly devolved from the tourist-washed boulevards nearing the Pantheon. Gone was the glistening white concrete, replaced with chipped plaster, graffiti, and barred windows, as we shifted into the guts of the local's city. Far enough from the main road that its sounds were simply the echoes off hundreds of dun, cracked walls, hot gas flooded my veins. My connections flooded back, the weight of the air pressing on my hands. I heard Natalie yelp sharply, and I assumed her thread had reopened too. Immediately, I felt for the pressure in my head. Sure enough, my discomfort, the feeling that Boekidin *might* have been following, was just air pressure in my ears. I didn't dispel it, for fear of pulling my brain out of my ear.

"Let's not use our connections." Natalie urged as she led us on. "Wouldn't want to be picked up again."

We delved deeper into the backstreet. One building occupying a bend in the road was no more than a façade. Inside, I saw a thick and healthy tree growing on a mound of rubbish and dirt, whose branches curled out of the open windows.

"I don't know where that woman directed you to, Natalie." Celeste hummed, frowning at the tree. "But I don't think it was to any town square."

"I'm sure it'll be this way." Natalie said. "Let's keep moving."

The tree basked in the strong light of the early morning. Its leaves glowed a vibrant, shining green in the rays that penetrated the patched roof. I slowly peeled off the magical sight to follow. Not one block later, the vines coated in purple flowers emerged, lining the walls to glue the houses and shop faces together. They drew us towards an oasis, a clearing amid the concrete jungle, presenting a tree at the centre of a square, coated in flowers and vines. On each of the clearing's five faces sat a café, each dozing under the shade of the central olive tree.

"Told you." Natalie smiled, hands to hips. "Choice is yours, Chad."

The American boy's face lit up, he pointed across the way, to the furthest of the restaurants. "That one looks the nicest," he said. "Come on, let's eat."

He skipped across the square in the centre of the strange city, taking a table to himself under the olive tree's shade and begging for us to join. Just as we sat ourselves down, a waitress came to meet us.

"Hello." She said in her local accent as she handed us each a menu. I supposed that it must have been easy to spot tourists, even in a hidden square like this. As she passed me my menu, the sleeve of her jumper retreated up her arm, revealing a tattoo scribed up her inside wrist.

It was the Suneva *Mark of the Black Sun*.

"*Na Kafma nas Sun…*" I uttered its *liktan* name as the mark caught my eye. The waitress eyed me with sharp surprise. "*Silo di Liktan?*" I asked if she spoke the Suneva language. The waitress had a curious expression. She stiffened.

"*Nayah.*" She responded with a *yes*, then, "*San sur Suneva?*", she asked if we were Suneva.

"*Nayah.*" I smiled, proud at my ability to start a conversation. Suddenly, however, the chat was swept from under my feet, as Celeste and Natalie barged to talk over me. Chad, however, sat analysing the menu with a scientific eye.

71

"How is it for Suneva in this city?" Celeste asked the girl in Liktan. "We shouldn't be *open*, should we?"

"Not particularly." The girl said. "Not at the moment."

"Why not?" Natalie asked.

"It's never been truly safe for us, you know." The girl said. "But Hesslik just warned that a group of terrorist Suneva have arrived in the city – a group of four macro-elementals. I wouldn't say it's safe to use your connections."

"I see." Natalie frowned. I coughed at the implication, turning red.

"What brings you to Athens?" She asked.

"We're on a pilgrimage." Celeste said, smartly crafting an answer. "We're following Vinavek's Code of Connections."

"That's why I got my tattoo." The girl said, rolling up her sleeve to display it on full. "I got it when I committed myself to realisation as a *Liktas*. I still haven't followed the journey of Vinavek, though."

"We'll be going to Sparta, soon," Natalie said. "I've got family there who plan to help us."

"That's a good idea," the girl said.

"But we're not sure how we're getting there, yet." I added. "We'll need a car. Do you have any recommendations?"

"Ha!" The girl snorted, and craned around to look at the shopfront.

"What is it?" Natalie asked. The girl swung back around.

"I didn't mean to laugh, but it's just such a coincidence." The girl hummed, and stepped away from the table. "Wait, and I'll show you what I mean."

"Destiny, huh?" Chad smiled. "If you're going that way, could we get a plate of dips and pita to the table, please?"

The waitress skipped off, and we couldn't be sure if she'd heard Chad's order as she dashed behind a rear door of the restaurant, into the kitchen. She emerged only moments later, with a tray of dips and hot bread in one hand, and a piece of paper in the other. She laid both on the table, and Chad's ready hands rocketed towards the delicacies.

Celeste and Natalie, on the other hand, were drawn to the paper. The girl picked it up and handed it to me. It was a sign, written in Greek, which immediately had no use to me, but the message was tailed with a phone number and an address.

"They're selling their car," the waitress explained. "They gave us the notice two weeks ago, but they haven't sold it yet, they were in just this morning. They're desperate to get rid of it."

I handed the paper to Natalie, who read it intently.

"Buying a car?" I hummed to the group. "That seems a little gnarly. Wouldn't we want to rent?"

"Do you picture us driving back here?" Celeste asked. "I think buying is the better freedom."

"Do we have the money for that?"

"Only one way to find out." Natalie said. "Here's an address and no buying price. If they're desperate enough…"

"Didn't know you'd drive a hard bargain, Natalie." Chad said between ravenous scoffing.

"I think we'll have to." I said, "Thank you." I nodded to the waitress.

"That's alright." She smiled. "Now, what can I get you all?"

***

The address on the sheet of paper was across the city, so with full bellies, we walked through the rambles of Athens' back alleys, coming to a main road to catch a cab. One was easy to come by, and we piled in, handing the driver the address. He was an old man, skin wrinkled from years of sun, face set permanently to a scowl under his platinum head. In his eyes I met a shimmer, something of a vast expanse behind them. So, I asked if he spoke *Liktan*, and the man did.

"Two coincidences. How fitting." Chad noted.

Although I almost wished that I hadn't asked, because the man's eyes lit with scorn, and from his mouth spewed a rant loud enough to be totally unavoidable.

"That bloody Hesslik," was how he started his rant. "You have him too back where you're from?" He growled, and we all nodded dumbly. "Stupid to think he can combine the Suneva, eh? Those bloody *Kidin* – you know the ones – I don't like them. How can we trust people who can just run through your head? Do you think they care about ethics?"

"I suppose not." I squirmed.

73

"And who does Hesslik think he is anyway, telling us all how to behave, like we don't know that we're dangerous – eh? Suneva have more than shit for brains – and if we didn't we couldn't use quatran – so we don't need him treating us like idiots. Not that I agree with Argol either."

"Oh, of course not." I absently sympathised. I turned to the side window, wishing I hadn't chosen the front seat. The driver slammed a hand to the horn, drifting the struggling sedan around a bend.

"Argol's ego is as big as his flame. He goes around forcing Suneva to bow to him, goes imposing himself on people. What a *vassa*, eh! But we don't need *Hesslik* to tell us when a bloody *vassa* is a bloody *vassa*, do we? Hesslik's too young, he hasn't seen everything. And Argol is too jaded. I don't want to be put in their boxes for how I should live."

"Who would want to be?" I nodded along. "It's hard to agree with either of them…"

"Argol wants rights for his people, not dominance." Celeste put in, "You should see how vocal the protesters are in France. He built the Suneva name in the big cities there."

"Do you know the guy?" The cab driver shot Celeste a scornful glance, tearing his eyes from the road. I gripped the armrests in panic.

"No." Replied Celeste, "but…"

"So, what's it matter to you? He's a terrible guy."

"Sure…" Celeste frowned, and glued herself instead to the window. By this time we were at our destination, and thankful to be there. We handed over the fare but I kept the tip; I didn't really enjoy that ride.

The address led us to a double-storey, gleaming building of glass and polished steel, flanked by sky-reaching towers, whose shadows encompassed all. It was a strange site in a city of white and dust. In the owner's private carpark, red tiles leading straight to the front door, was a gloss-blue sports car sitting idle. The whole car sat lower than my hip, built around a gnarly mid-engine with a mean exhaust. Chad beamed with delight.

"Surely this isn't the car for sale." Chad laughed. "I wouldn't believe it."

"I wouldn't believe we could *afford* it." Natalie said. "How about we knock before somebody tells us off for staring at it."

Natalie stepped past the machine, following the red tiled way to the door. She glanced a double-take of the address stamped above the doorbell before pressing it. We all gathered in behind, eager to let her handle this negotiation. Steps called through the building, and a shadow appeared to strut towards the door. A figure opened it.

A woman stood, even taller than Chad in her impressive heels. She looked down on us through a fringe of grey and chestnut mixed hair. Her hand was placed boldly on a curved hip, pressed against her power-suit. She eyed us, then the paper, and gestured Natalie to hand it over. Natalie had no power against the woman's demands.

"Here for the car?" They asked in *Liktan*.

"How did you know we speak..." Natalie went to ask, but the woman interrupted her with her smooth, aged voice.

"A witch like yourself doesn't leave much to be questioned. I felt your quatra before you even reached my door." The woman said, regarding Natalie, who shied away.

"Yes, we're here for the car." Chad said, smiling and coming forward. "It's not *that one* though, is it?" He joked, pointing to the blue beast.

"No, of course not." The woman chuffed. Chad, although surely expecting that answer, deflated anyway. "I just bought that. No, it's the one to the right..." She raised a finger, her black-painted nail pointing beyond our heads. I craned around, to see a car which we'd just walked past on the street – an older station wagon which would have been unassuming, except that it was bright pink.

"I didn't think so." Chad mumbled. "You got a good upgrade, though..."

"I did." The woman agreed.

"How much for the wagon?" Celeste asked, hands to hips to match the woman.

"Well, that depends on what you can offer me." The woman leaned into her door frame. Chad coughed his surprise, clearly taking the wrong meaning from her gesture. "Where were you planning to drive it?"

"Kalamata. We're following Vinavek's pilgrimage in the hopes of Realisation." Celeste told her lie without any readable hint of dishonesty. The woman smiled.

"So you'll be heading through Nafplio, then?" They asked. We each frowned, and turned to Natalie, who did no more than shrug.

"If it's on the way." Natalie said. "I hadn't planned a route yet."

"And if it gets us the car, too…" Chad added in.

"Good." The woman smirked. "Stay here, I'll be just a moment." She turned, leaving the door open as she walked herself back down her long hallway, one elegant hand tracing the wall to mark her gait.

"So many Suneva in this city." Natalie noted. "The server, the driver, and now this woman?"

"Melbourne is just empty of practicing Suneva." Celeste said. "People are more open over here, especially in southern Greece."

"Clearly." Natalie hummed. I could see her face grow pale.

The woman returned, marked by the clack of her long heels. She carried two items – a small candle in a shot glass, and a potted flower. The flower resembled a poppy, but was bright violet instead of blood red, and with lustrous petals which glimmered in the light. She handed both to Natalie.

"You're an Argol." Celeste noted, examining the candle in Natalie's hand. She grabbed it herself, looking for details that I couldn't perceive.

"I understand the candle, we've been given one before." Natalie said. "But what's special about this flower?"

"You've already received a candle?" The woman chuffed, dropping her authoritative aura. "Then I should trust you for this job. Who gave it to you?"

"Alexis LeGrand, Capo of Melbourne." I said, then remembered another bargaining chip: "He knew my father, *John Grey*." I smiled, awaiting her response, but the woman had none for my father's name.

"Honoured by Alexis?" She pondered. "That's noteworthy."

"And the job?" Celeste asked. "Who is this all going to?"

"Yes, the job." The woman regained her propriety. "I need this flower and candle delivered to a powerful Witch in Nafplio. For the service, the car is free."

"Free?" Chad asked, "How bad *is* that car?" He spun to examine it, frown building.

"The car is fine." The lady sneered, "But I warn you. If you lose or damage *any* part of this flower – even so much as a lost petal, you will owe me and the

Argol family more money than even my car is worth. And I *will* follow you up on that. Is that understood?"

"You can trust us." I squeaked.

"If you don't mind me asking." Natalie said, "Why is the plant so valuable? What will you use it for?"

The woman crossed her arms, grumbling.

"It doesn't have value to anybody else, if that's what you're asking. There's no sale price on it." She danced around the question. "The old *Kiin* people, before Olomb took them over, used to make medicine out of its leaves. We're trying to figure out what properties it has."

"*Studying medicine* wasn't the answer I was expecting..." Natalie hummed.

"There's a lot of cash in medicine, honey." She said. "We're all trying to do our bit for the world, making cures and whatnot. Remember, not a *single* petal of this flower goes missing."

"Or else we end up dead." I finished the sentence.

The woman smiled at me.

"Exactly." She nodded. "Now, do you want the car? Will you do this for me?"

We each peered to the flower, then out to each other. There was a resounding indifference to the task round the circle. Well, except for Chad, who was apparently eager to get driving.

"We'll do it." He said.

"Great." The woman nodded. "Then here are the keys." She tossed them to Chad, who caught them without effort. She then pulled a note from her left ass pocket and handed it to Natalie

"It takes regular unleaded petrol." She said. "There's an address on the note, and two phone numbers. One is of the Witch, the other is mine, in case anything goes wrong."

"Got it." Natalie said. "Thanks."

"No, thank you." The woman said genuinely. "It really feels like the black holes shine down on us, sometimes, when fates line up like this —the only takers on my offer were four Suneva."

"This might seem rude to ask." I said, "But you seem fairly reasonable and connected. Why do you choose to be with the Argols? Don't you think they're a little extreme?"

The woman chuckled, shaking her head.

"I think it's misguided to draw a line between Suneva. We're all brothers and sisters – children of the black suns. We do what we must to get on in this world of humans which, ultimately, doesn't want us around. There are many different views other than Hesslik's and Argol's, but we're together in one thing: we wish to unify, not divide. One day there will be a unified Suneva – although I don't believe anybody can say for what cause, or when."

"For the cause of freedom, clearly." Celeste suggested. "Veritas knows it's coming soon."

"And peace." Chad said.

"And safety." Natalie added in, drawing stares. "Hesslik is right about one thing, we *are* dangerous, to others and ourselves."

The woman looked at Natalie quizzically. She then sighed, rested her hand on Natalie's shoulder. "You, young Witch, are the power to do good on this Earth. Do not convince yourself otherwise."

Chapter 9
In the Valley Castle

Boekidin shifted through the castle's hallways. Cold stones, laid in ancient times with ancient hands, lined the skirting of the wide hall.

This section of the castle was mostly new – an old structure adapted for the times, just like Hesslik's new Empire.

Boekidin was on his way to meet with Hesslik, in a meeting called by the *Fara*. He strutted through the east wing of the ancient castle, coming from his own office towards the central dome. The meeting room would be just beyond that – one of the highest rooms in the structure.

As he strode, his wings, which he had tucked away, would rattle and clank behind his back. Where the raven-like Suneva walked, others would step out of his way. They were repelled, sticking to walls as he passed, snickering whispers to one another. Their making room for him wasn't a sign of respect of his rank – such things didn't happen. They were disgusted by him.

Their whispered distrust would rattle in his brain as he subconsciously pulled their thoughts into his – hundreds of voices which faded in and out of his consciousness, hundreds of emotions he could automatically feel as if his own. His patience for this wore thin.

He had joined Hesslik's cause to create common ground for Suneva and humans in society. He could envision a world where Suneva walked the streets in armour, and it would be *normal*. A world where he could be himself, and not fear being marginalised. But he was coming to realise this might not happen quickly, nor easily. Kidin were widely distrusted. In the ancient *Liktas* lore, there were painted and connivers, and cheats. There would be even less trust for he, *The Shiverman*.

It makes sense. He sighed to himself, passing a group of huddled clerks. They slunk around him, as if their careful movements would hide them from sight in clear daylight. *You can hear their thoughts, you can access their memories, and speak into their heads. That breeds distrust.*

Although, it wasn't as simple as most Suneva thought. *Finding* memories was hard. It was an involved process. You had to sit down, find time, concentrate, and be close enough. Still, it was incredibly invasive, and he could do it to *anybody* near him, at *any time*. This was clearly unsettling. However, he had great restraint – he knew this as he walked with his head high. He spotted two of his agents up ahead, they smiled at him, and did not deviate from their paths.

Boekidin had restraint, in that he barely used his abilities. If he did, it would only be because the Empire required it, or the person was causing detriment to others with their secrets, and *deserved* it.

Maiki deserves it, he thought of me, as he heard a disapproving woman he passed in his head.

Maiki is a rat, and I am right to invade his head. Boekidin convinced himself, striding towards his colleagues. The rift between himself and everybody else was accentuated now, as just two Suneva stood before him, not shifting with the parting streams. His internal monologue yelled a little louder.

Maiki corrupted a trusted, morally strong agent of Hesslik, and conspired with the Argol daughter. He was carelessly reckless, sending years' worth of scientific discoveries into ashes,

79

and almost burning the whole Melbourne facility and its library to the ground. He is truly selfish — the most dangerous Suneva threat.

Yet Hesslik still has hope for him…

That thought gnawed at Boekidin. Hesslik had made it clear in their last meeting. *It would be a shame to remove my thread.* It made the *Kidin*'s blood boil. *I was a traitor to the people, yet I deserved regard?*

Boekidin had tried to lead me to my capture before, in Melbourne. He had first gained my trust by leading me to *Salak Nolver's* book, then planned to trap both Celeste and I by using my misguided anger and confidence against me. All he saw was a boy with a weak mind, easy to manipulate.

And in Athens, when he had gotten close enough to *see* into my head — not just talk to it, which could be done at a considerable distance — he had found more damning truths about my nature. In the short time he had in my head — and thank *Veritas* his agents could keep us distracted and in range so long — he found memories, fogged over like frosted glass. *Quatra visions — so many quatra visions.* Either that, or memories corrupted by Omercronius. *He is either clinically insane,* Boekidin reasoned, *or the pawn of a black hole. Neither is good.*

Boekidin couldn't see into quatra visions. Like trying to spy through a bathroom window — the details became obscured. The emotions usually accessed when feeling a memory were twisted, vastly misrepresenting what little of the situation he could see. In Athens, he'd needed every minute that his agents could give him to find a useful memory. If Zamelle hadn't sensed him close by, squatting in the broom closet, it wouldn't have turned into a fight for information.

I'll have to watch out for that witch, more than I thought.

There was something in those glossed memories which makes Maiki a dangerous Suneva. That was the nature of being a kidin, it seemed to him. Those details which mattered the most were always unobtainable. But those which he could see surprised him more.

Legendaries? It shocked Boekidin again as he thought of it. *He's trying to find Legendaries.* Boekidin hadn't expected such ambition from us — although maybe he should have. *Maiki's interest in Vinavek's texts and the original founding were an early clue.*

Boekidin reached his two agents in the hallway — The Space Cowboy and The Cat. The Space Cowboy nodded, and they turned to stride with him, towards Hesslik.

"Boss." The Space Cowboy greeted, glaring at those who stuck themselves to walls.

"Talik." Boekidin greeted flatly.

We shouldn't be here. The thought came to him, rocking him with its apparent urgency. *We need to be out there, on Maiki's tail. That group has charisma, and Argol connections. They are dangerous.*

And they'll find a legendary soon. Boekidin could feel it, despite how mythological the task was. Veritas screamed it at him down the pipeline. Another voice to fill his head and bounce there – but not a voice, rather a deep-rooted *feeling*. Destiny – it was real, and powerful. Boekidin feared for my destiny, because if my friends and I were destined for greatness, and Boekidin was against us – what did that mean for him?

"Is there something wrong, Boe?" The Cat asked.

"We shouldn't be here, Vasloka," he said bluntly. "We can't stall."

"Fisira is still with her family, remember?" She said to *The Shiverman*.

That's right. Toxication to that. Boekidin huffed. The girl did need her time, but the success of their mission would decide the fate of the empire. He couldn't afford to be lenient on such time off.

"Why didn't you start your hunt earlier, if you're so concerned about timing?" Talik asked. "I don't think there's a rush. I doubt they'll *ever* find a Legendary."

"I know you should be right…" Boekidin agreed, "But my soul is telling me to rush."

In truth, it would have been risky to have started earlier. Boekidin did not underestimate the power and knowledge of *Lion's Foot*, nor did he underestimate our witch, *Zamelle*, or the supposed *Iva Argol*. We were such a perfectly formed team, that he had to take time to study us – our thoughts, our problem solving, our powers. Without a team initially, and without proper support from Vestas' library base, it would have been too risky to get close enough to any of us and figure out what we were planning. Reading minds involved a certain proximity, and left him easily detectable, and entirely helpless.

He soon discerned that I had the most penetrable mind, but still had to act from afar – only close enough to talk into my head, not read memories. Still, the rogue conversations which he glimpsed in the limited time he had in

81

Melbourne, as if by destiny, had given Boekidin enough to know what we were planning, and where we were planning to go. To get closer, and get better information, he had to form his own perfect team, who could protect him as he did the risky work. He had found them, and they had fought us.

And they still got away. They shouldn't have, we had them easily beat.

"Why not attack earlier, Boekidin?" Talik repeated. Boekidin snapped from his thoughts.

"Too risky without a perfect team," he replied. They were almost at the door now. It lay just beyond the foyer they entered. Beautiful light streamed in through a stained-glass dome, fractal colours painted the floor vibrantly.

"Perfect?" Talik asked, and grinned deeply.

"Don't get ahead of yourself," Boekidin instructed. "If we can get to a Legendary before them – if we hurry – we'll have these traitors more easily than we already should."

Yes, Legendaries were out there. He could feel his soul being pulled, Veritas tugging his mind to agree with the statement. If a Legendary existed, *somebody* would have to know them. And it didn't matter if people wanted to openly share their answers or not, when you could hear their subconscious surface thoughts and scan their memories. Answers lay in a field of Suneva, ready to be discovered.

Boekidin would find the Legendaries.

Then I can save the dream. He smiled. *The dream to be myself.*

Chapter 10
Special Delivery

The city of Athens ended abruptly, the white towers meeting a stark edge at the rim of the basin. The station wagon we drove, although nothing special, attracted many sidelong glances with its colour scheme, and we were glad to be out on the open road once clearing the city's gates.

Chad drove, being the only one of us with significant driving experience. Natalie and I *had* our licenses by now, but neither of us wanted to take responsibility. Natalie was quite happy, really, to take the shotgun seat, her head buried in a map, handing out the directions. Celeste and I sat in the back, Celeste being trusted with the all precious plant, and I with the candle. When I bought up the fact that she could easily burn the whole flower in blue flames, everybody agreed that it was better than the inevitability of me dropping it out the window.

Before we left, we snuck back into the hotel to pay the bill and get our bags. With the trip ahead, and escaping Boekidin on our minds, we'd almost forgotten to do it until I mentioned it. I was upgraded from holding nothing, to holding the candle, for my demonstration of intelligence.

After half an hour of driving through the sparsely-inhabited countryside, we had to make our first turn, just as we passed over the canal at Korinthos. The exit threw us only a tiny, one-lane road cutting a path of dense forest. Natalie demanded that we pull over to check that she read the map right.

"I think you got it." Chad said to her, laughing. "I drove roads like this for Hesslik all the time. These roads were built for donkeys, not cars like Australian cities. Don't expect them to look the same."

"Yes, Chad, I get that." Natalie rolled her eyes. "But look at this road. You can't even see the sun!" She pointed a palm to the sky. "We're in a forest, but we couldn't be off directions yet. Look, there's the canal, there's the exit..."

"Well, I'm going to keep driving, and you look out for the side roads. I bet that you were right." Chad smiled.

And Chad was right. Soon the forest opened into vast plains at the foot of distant mountains, road signs gesturing towards towns on the map. The autumn sun shone strong in the sky, the scents of imminent winter swirling through the windows.

The mountains which loomed continued to sit on the horizons all around, even as we came into the town of Nafplio. They parted to make way for the small city – a collection of tall, white low-rises living in the shadow of a castle on a sea-facing cliff. As we continued through the town, the drab white buildings were set aside, the town taken by streets of quaint pastel shops and houses. The town became the smattering of a colour wheel, walls to building faces set right up to the cobbles of the road. We navigated the busy stretch right through the town to its far edge, coming to a door set into a street-long wall of houses sharing the same façade, looking over the still bay. We had arrived at the address. Chad parked the car on the packed street as best as possible, and we all climbed out.

I stared across the bay. The water was an endless expanse, capped only at the very horizon by mountains, seated at the edge of the earth. The sun had begun to set behind them, letting the shadows of giants loom across the sea.

"This is the place," Natalie declared, stealing my attention. "I think Celeste and I should handle this. Chad, would you mind getting some groceries? We should probably stay the night."

"Yes ma'am." Chad nodded.

"And James, would you get some coffees?"

"And not find out about the flower?" I protested. "I think we're forgetting who has the candle here…" I held the artefact out, only for Celeste to sneak it off my hand.

"They're going to be tight lipped, James." Celeste said. "And I'd really love a coffee." Her hand trailed down my arm as she drew the candle in. I followed her arm to her smile. Suddenly, getting coffees didn't sound like a terrible idea.

"Okay, but don't leave off any details on the recap." I said, and turned to leave.

I walked through the pretty, pastel streets. This town was just divine, I had decided, prettier than the postcards hanging in the tourist shops.

I could see the main square of old Nafplio down the alley I was walking. I could also see a coffee shop ahead, just before the street's end. The intersection I walked into had a coffee shop on each corner. I considered my options – not a connoisseur of coffee myself, I couldn't smell the differences between the brews. I hummed, looking to the only person sitting at any of the cafes. It was a figure in a broad brimmed hat, reading a local newspaper, face hidden. They had *two* cups of coffee on their table. It must have been good then.

And yet, I was rocked by a compulsion – there was a strange vibe about this figure. I didn't want to approach them.

I followed the feeling, turning to the opposite shop. I walked across the intersection when a voice called, and forced me to freeze.

"Maiki!" It said, strong and rich, coming from behind me.

I knew this voice. But it couldn't be, could it? I checked around me, and with a clear coast, let my armour consume my body. I felt the air swirling on my cold metal skin.

"Maiki, over here." It said again, and I turned sharply to it.

The newspaper and hat were now set aside of the figure, revealing the voice's owner with their two coffees. *Fara Hesslik* sat with their drinks, a grin behind their helmet.

I summoned my staff, there was nothing else to do, and I aimed it straight at his face.

"Woah, easy." Hesslik grinned, throwing hands to the air. I fired my bolt. It steamed hot and green across the way, aimed poorly. Hesslik threw a limb into its path, catching it and redirecting it through the ground. "Wouldn't want to hurt somebody with that, Maiki." He soothed. "You know that people can't see our bolts, right?"

"I've got to go…" I said, panicking. If I ran, he could follow. I'd lead him to Natalie and Chad and Celeste. *Oh dear lord, what would Celeste think?* Her trust had been stretched many times. I couldn't have her thinking that I was always luring her into a trap. She'd pin it on Chad too. And *Chad* would hate me, bringing the guy who wanted to remove his thread. I was stuck, frozen. Was this a battle that I had to face alone? Why *me*?

"Go so soon? But I bought you a coffee?" He pushed the second cup across the table, letting it rest near me. I could feel the hot air rising off it through my palms. "Boekidin knows your coffee order. It's just as you like it."

But did the bird-Suneva know my *Greek* coffee order? Well, I didn't know it either, so it was bound to be a good coffee anyway. I hummed. I was no match for Hesslik as a Suneva, so was adhering to his demands the only way to get out of this situation? Surely it was a trap.

Well, I guess I was trapped, then.

I advanced cautiously. Close enough to grab the mug, I snatched it, and took another step back to sit on a far table. Hesslik nodded at my reservedness.

"Yes, wise." He said.

"What are you doing here?" I asked, stalling for time and thoughts.

"Here? In the Suneva *homelands*?" Hesslik chuffed. "I'm ruling from the Old Electric Throne in Mount Olympus. Greece has been the home of every Electric Nation, and it is mine."

A man of tradition, then. I mused, although it meant that we'd inadvertently come stumbling into Hesslik's backyard, and he'd followed us from Mount Olympus to here.

"This is a trap, right?"

"Depends on what you think I'm after." Hesslik sat back in his chair. "Traps aren't always for things which are physical. Use your senses, did you feel a trap coming?"

"I'm feeling it now."

"And did you see a trap in a vision?" Hesslik asked.

"No, but…" I paused, how did Hesslik know about my visions? I hadn't mentioned that. "Did Boekidin tell you about my visions?" *What has he seen?*

"No, Boekidin didn't." Hesslik smiled. "But you did, just now."

Ah, damn. I frowned, sitting back in the chair. "Good job…"

"I'm not the Fara for being an idiot, Maiki." Hesslik said, and let his words ring.

I didn't want to say anything more on the subject, lest I incriminate myself. Surely, though, he hadn't trapped me in a conversation to hear about my visions. Boekidin could have told him about them, really.

"What is this about?" I asked. "Why aren't you just attacking me and my friends right now? You know where we are, you have us trapped, and you've apparently convinced the wider Suneva community that we're terrorists. Play your cards, man."

"A smart game isn't won by playing every hand at once," Hesslik countered, leaning towards me, into the table. "And I have no interest in apprehending you today. What would give me the right, anyway? You've not done anything illegal, and I have no authority."

"Don't play good-guy." I rolled my eyes. "I know you're planning to remove the threads. You can't hold a moral high ground."

"Strange visions you're having, Maiki," Hesslik said. "I wouldn't trust everything you see. Vestas informed me of that raving."

"Sure, whatever." I rolled my eyes. "Can I go? Have you got what you need?"

"No." He asserted, cyan eyes beaming hot. I simmered down in my seat. "When I first met you, I said that I would monitor your progress closely, and that's what I'm here to do. I wasn't kidding when I thought you could one day fill the void that Muhrakiin left."

"That's flattering." I grumbled. "But I haven't trekked across the globe to spin on a dime and join you. I'm stopping your movement."

"And you think that the Legendaries will help you do that?" He prodded.

"No." I said. I didn't want to give too much away, but Hesslik leaned in expectantly. I needed to be more like Celeste – she could deliver a perfect diversion straight from her head. A good white-truth told without a hint of guilt. "We're only here to achieve realisation. We're following Vinavek's path."

"Ah, the path to *Sunasera*." Hesslik nodded. "Noble. You'll become a great Suneva out of that."

"I hope so."

"It's nice to see that you're taking serious steps to be the Suneva that I know you can be. Lots of travellers come here, to the Liktas Nation homelands, to achieve realisation. If I may suggest that you might have more luck finding the answers you seek in southern Macedonia, the home of the *Vochduh* – the ancient *Kiin*."

"The ancient *Kiin* home?" I quizzed. The place had come up in Olomb's diaries, but he'd never given an indication of where it was. Either Hesslik was misdirecting me into a trap, or he'd just given me good, valuable information for me to waste my time finding. "I will consider that." I said.

"And, just a tip…" he continued, leaning closer. "From what Boekidin has been able to gather, you're looking to solve the code by expanding your social web. It's a nice idea, but the code is less about how many people you know, but rather how well you know yourself and love those closest to you."

"Why do you need to ask me anything at all when Boekidin sees into my head?" I asked. "I'd rather him than having to deal with… this…"

"Finding information as a kidin isn't easy work. He doesn't see everything, but he did see that," Hesslik said. "You don't like our chat?"

"I'm fearing for my continued existence right now." I gulped, peering around. "You're much more skilled than me."

"Ah, but don't doubt yourself Maiki, you're an intelligent young Suneva." He said. "I'm sure you'd be able to solve any situation that came your way."

"That's flattering…" I noted. "But perhaps you're overestimating my ability."

Hesslik hummed, frowning. Finally, he stood. "In that case, I think it's time that I made my leave. I wouldn't want to make you uncomfortable."

"I'm sorry, what?" I laughed. "*You're* leaving? You're *actually* not taking me with you? Or following me to my friends?"

"No, or course not." Hesslik shook his head, dusting his armour off. "You've got to trust me more, Maiki."

"Hard to do when you're the enemy." I chuckled.

"We may be enemies now, Maiki," Hesslik said. "But I'm sure not *forever*." He put the broad brimmed hat atop his head, tipping it to me as he turned to leave. His metals heels clanked away across the cobbles, until finally he was out of sight. As if by instinct, my armour retracted and my body fell into every nook of the chair all at once, a wave of relief so powerful that it melted my bones, forcing me to sit in strange satisfaction.

With my only sliver of energy and stiffness, I managed to flag down a waitress, and ask her for three more coffees to take away.

"Good day?" She asked, reading my odd elation.

"Not *good*." I reminisced, "Just...*strange*."

How much does Boekidin know about me? I wondered. *How much does Hesslik know?*

***

I returned to the car with four takeaway coffees in hand. It was afternoon now, with the sun beating down on the strangely warm autumn's day. When I got there, I saw Chad, Celeste and Natalie waiting for me.

"Is everything okay, James?" Natalie asked. "I sensed a bolt of quatra being fired. I couldn't say anything, because we were with the old lady..."

Could Natalie really sense a bolt from halfway across a town? Her senses were frightening.

"It wasn't me." I said, playing dumb. "And I couldn't sense anything."

"No, I wouldn't picture that you could." Natalie hummed. "Oh, well, I'm glad that you're safe."

"So am I." Chad smiled, grabbing a cup from my tray. "Boy, have I needed this."

88

"Did you find anything out about the flower?" I asked.

"They were tight-lipped, just as I thought." Celeste said. "Argols won't share their secrets."

"And did you ask if they knew where Argol was?" I asked, and the thought came to me that we *really* could have asked the woman who'd given us the car, too.

"Once again, no answer on that." Celeste said. "They're not inclined to give that information away. I knew he was going to be hard to find."

"No information, even for the flower?" I asked.

"The flower got us a car, James. I think that's all we could hope for." Natalie said. "Hopefully my family in Sparta will know more. They'll want to help us, in any case."

"But the old lady you gave the flower to didn't know that we'd been paid." I suggested. "Could have wrought an answer out of her."

Everybody gave me a sharp look. "Now you're thinking like an agent, James." Chad said. "Wasn't expecting that."

"And we did get a payment from her." Celeste smiled. "She got us a room in a local accommodation, so you can thank me for that."

"She did?" Natalie asked. "I didn't hear that."

"You walked out first." Celeste said. "I've had years of on-off street-living. I know how to get a bed from a favour in minimal time."

A *local* accommodation? I tried to hide my face as I wrestled with the fear that Hesslik was still in this town, somewhere. I stifled the feeling. Luckily, I wasn't the centre of attention.

"Good work team." Chad said, hands to hips. "Let's get some rest, then. Tomorrow, we'll hit the road and get to Sparta."

Chapter 11
My Big, Fat, Greek Family

The man who housed us, Spiros, suggested a way to get to Sparta as he fed us breakfast. "If you follow the mountains…" He instructed Chad, his finger tracing the outline of the bay, "You will come to a beach. I know that it's

89

December, but today will be warm enough – it would be a shame to miss the only good day to see it whilst you're here. It's a bit out of the way, but worth it."

"Well, the code is all about the journey instead of the timely destination, right?" Chad said. "Spending a day at the beach when on a holiday can't stop us from finding Argol or the Legendaries. Might set us back a single day…"

"It'll probably throw Boekidin off, too." I said, keen to get out of Nafplio. I hadn't seen Hesslik since our encounter, and nobody had mentioned sensing him, but I was still nervous. "I'd be keen to get moving. We've got a lot to get through."

We truly did. Hesslik and Boekidin knew our plans, and they were tracking them. I didn't know *how much* they knew, and that was the danger. We had a lot of ground to cover to build our connections to the Legendaries.

"It's a nice idea." Natalie agreed. "A little off our ideal path, but my Great-auntie isn't expecting us until afternoon, anyway. We could use some fun."

"I'd like some fun." Celeste agreed. "This has been too stressful already – and you should never ignore local advice."

"Except maybe for…" *following your responsibilities*. I was going to say, but was drowned out by Chad's deep voice.

"Great, beach it is." He smiled. "It'll be fun." He slapped me across the back, forcing me to cough up my breath.

And so the route was planned. Natalie manned the map again as we set the car off around the great bay, towards the southwest. We soon came to the foot of the once-distant mountains and tracked around its base. The road hung off the cliffside, dangling precariously where land met the gentle, expansive sea. The land on the mountain face was untouched, raw as the day it was created.

The road snaked under a cliff face, away from the sea and into a valley, where we crossed over an old, unkempt stone bridge. It then continued over the valley to the next mountain and back out to sea. The view was incredible, looking out onto the endless blue abyss from an insane height on top of a sheer drop. The water, stretching out to the horizon, was the deepest, purest blue imaginable – more blue than the sky itself.

On the map, the beach didn't look like it was too far away, but we found out that the road wound very far from straight. It hugged the face of the mountains and valleys, twisting down the coast. The length of the drive sparked my anxiety. I sat analysing my wrist watch, mainly to keep myself from looking at the winding, deadly road, but also in fear of Boekidin. I would force myself to have fun if I had to, but it had to be quick. I couldn't tell anybody why we had to rush – I couldn't tell them that I'd talked to Hesslik and *not* stopped him.

It took us an hour of scenic driving, evading death and managing the narrow roads, but we made it to where we thought the beach was. The turn off wasn't on the map, but the directions Spiros gave, which Natalie had written down, were good. We followed the beach bar signs to the correct turn off, then navigated the squealing car down a nearly-vertical switchback to a dirt patch under an olive tree, known as the car park.

We sat in the narrow cove between two mountains, where the beach bar – a three story building with a small inn, owner's quarters, and a bar - was built into the side of the north cliff. On the pebbles in front of the bar's chairs and tables were beach lounges with umbrellas and drink benches. Natalie picked the closest lounge to lob her stuff onto, stripped down to her bathers, and started fiddling with her watch.

I stiffly settled into the next lounge, my muscles creaking in their attempt to relax. It was all well and good for Natalie – the one who could sense other Suneva – to be comfortable, but *I* couldn't feel the danger, and I *knew* it was there.

"Alright…" Natalie flicked her hair aside. "It's two hours from here to Sparta, and my *Yamitsira* isn't expecting us until about three o'clock, so we've got two hours on the alarm, *now*." She pressed a button on the watch, threw it into her towel, and sprinted for the water.

Two hours, I could deal with that, maybe.

I cracked into position, attempting to sink into the lounge. Footsteps came by me, and a hand wrapped itself on my shoulder. I panicked, sensing the power held in that palm. I seldom cottoned on to the feeling of quatra energy outside of my body. My staff beckoned me to draw it, but then the person spoke.

"You've got to relax, James." Celeste said. I turned to the hand, to see that it was, indeed, Celeste's. It migrated down my arm, to rest atop my own hand. "You were about to crush your watch in the car ride here. It's fine, we've got time."

"I don't think we do." I said, my anxieties flooding in. "We're on Hesslik's doorstep and Boekidin is after us, yet we're at the beach? *I* can't sense the danger, I know you all can, but…"

"We're on Hesslik's doorstep?" She asked.

91

"Yes! He's ruling from the Electric Throne in Mount Olympus." I blurted, then gasped. I'd found that out from Hesslik himself. Did Celeste know that?

"He's taken Olomb's old throne?" Celeste asked, eyes wide. "Where did you read that?"

"I…" *Oh god*, my mind buzzed. I had to make a lie, fast. "Boekidin. Boekidin told me. He assumed that we knew."

"And you didn't tell us?"

"I assumed he was right." He coughed. "I didn't want to appear stupid."

"Right." Celeste frowned, removing her hand from mine. "Well if you'd told us that…" She hummed, staring out to the beach. "Look, we'll be fine." She finished. "Two hours spent here is no different than two hours spent in Sparta if Hesslik is only a few cities away. Natalie and I will keep sensing in the field. You keep an ear out for Boekidin."

"Well, I can *definitely* do that." I grumbled. Celeste sighed at my attitude.

"Enjoy a holiday whilst you have one, James." She said. "We are here for one too, as well as whatever mission we've dragged ourselves into. It will all work out. It always does, somehow."

"Somehow…" I nodded to Celeste's sentiment. My compulsions of destiny had only led me into continued existence so far. I had to assume that they'd keep sustaining me for at least two hours longer whilst we sat on the beach.

Trust your friends, and trust your senses. I told myself, and I finally settled into the chair. I felt a drowsiness overcome me, as if weight had just fallen off my brain. I reached for my earphones, dangling from the Walkman I'd brought along with me, and plugged them into my ears. With my favourite band playing against the sloshing of the gentle sea, I quickly nodded off, lingering on my connections to the eddies around me. Meditating.

***

A girl floated before me in the sea of blackness, hung by her chest in the forever abyss. Her limbs and black hair floated up, drifting in the current of the world, except for an ankle, which was tethered down into blackness below. Her aura was white, like a halo that surrounded her body, a corona imprinted on the universe.

Her eyes, radiating her living soul, were a drab grey.

"I fear for the fallen." A voice echoed from the deeper sea. "For they aren't aware that they've lost control."

And the girl's head snapped to face me.

***

"Boo!" Natalie's voice shook me awake. I spluttered, snapping upright in the chair, to be met with her face and it's deep, blue eyes. "We've only got fifty-one and a half minutes left here, and if you don't get in that water with us James, I'm bringing the water to you," she said. I noticed her hands swirling, controlling. I could almost sense their power. Her eyes pointed up, and I followed their gaze.

An orb of water swam above my head.

"Ah!" I shrieked, lobbing my discman aside to the sand. "Cheese, Natalie..." I caught my breath, my face becoming hot as I remembered again where we were, and who's backyard we'd come into. "Natalie, you can't use your abilities here!" I urged.

"Look how much the locals care." She said, gesturing towards a gaggle of disinterested kids a few chairs over. "We can use our abilities. Suneva are common here."

"That's not the issue." I grumbled, holding my tongue as the orb of water followed my head. "The issue is that we're in Hesslik's cheese-damned backyard. Didn't Celeste tell you what I told her?"

"She did." Natalie smiled. "But I agree with her that we're either here or in Sparta, and we'll definitely be using our threads around my Suneva family. I can't believe I'm the one to tell you this, but lighten up, James. Use your abilities as yourself in the real world. It feels magical." She twisted and snaked the water which held me ransom. I stood up cautiously onto the sand, and she raised it to match my new height.

"Lighten up and use abilities?" I growled. "Natalie, we've gotten nowhere in the time we've been here, and we're being followed, and those following us can see into our heads! We're nowhere near knowing who the Legendaries are or finding Argol, or even following the code of connections. This is all just too *real* for me... I can't believe we're here..."

"Gotten nowhere?" Natalie huffed, dropping her orb of water to the side. It caused a wave of sand to wash across the beach. "I suppose gaining the trust of random Argols, talking in Liktan, and standing our own against Boekidin's team is us getting *nowhere*, is it?"

"No... but..."

"And we didn't expect to find any answers before we saw my family, but we've already built connections to the Suneva in this country and learned from them. We're better off that you think, you know."

"Are we?" I urged. In my mind, we *still* didn't know how the code led to the Legendaries. We'd been acting off my assumption that expanding our connections to others would help us find them, and I had no idea why anybody played along with an idea of *mine*.

"Yes, we are doing well." Chad added, bearing over me from behind my chair. He cast a shadow over my head. "Plus, Boekidin is smart, but he's got more jobs than just following us, trust me. Hesslik might have made us a public enemy, but that's just so he doesn't have to deal with us, and he can deflect blame for our actions. I doubt we're as important to him as you think we are."

If only you knew... I gulped, thinking to the fact that Hesslik had personally sought me out. "Okay, if you're sure." I nodded along, then frowned. "How didn't you know that this was Hesslik's stomping ground?" I asked Chad, craning up to his head. "You were his personal agent."

"When I was working for him, I was operating out of remote bases across the world." Chad reminisced, frowning. "He never mentioned a central location, although the castle at Olympus did come up as a base. I never thought he *lived* in any one place."

"Strange." I hummed. "It's almost as if he knew you'd defect from the start."

"Maybe he did." Chad shrugged. "Good thing Boekidin let the base's location slip."

I nodded, letting Chad believe the lie.

"If you're that uncomfortable sitting around, though, maybe we should leave." Chad hummed, looking at Natalie. "It couldn't hurt to get ahead."

"And ruin a fun part of the holiday?" Natalie's face dropped to offence. "No way. We've still got forty-seven minutes of allocated fun left, and Amasos-damn-you, James, you will unwind a bit."

Natalie reached for my hand and tugged it up, yanking me from the chair. Still firmly grasping it, she sprinted for the shore, dragging me in her wake. I struggled to match her pace, stumbling on the beach's pebbles. When we reached the lapping, calm ocean, she ditched my hand and leaped into the water, forcing the sea to meet her half way and take her body. She surfaced next to Celeste who was already in the water, rubbed her eyes, and beckoned me in.

"You don't know what you're missing out on. Forty minutes of fun, it can't hurt."

"Forty-seven, don't you mean?"

"Forty-*six*, by now." She snorted. "Now leap, *Maiki*." She called to my soul, and I felt that spark, that call of the void, and it soothed my anxiety. Everything would be okay, I knew it.

Gripping at my soul connections, I blasted at the ground, high into the sky off a jet of air. A crater of sand was hollowed by my feet, my leap sending me over Natalie and Celeste's heads, far into the sea.

And once I was in, I wished I'd taken to the water all of seventy-four minutes ago.

***

The drive to Sparta was treacherous. The mountains here were even more frightening and magnificent than their coastal counterparts. The peaks extended taller, with higher cliffs and sheerer faces. Instead of tracking the valley, the road twisted its way up, and then down, each impressive mountain. The constantly winding track turned the peaceful outing into a rally.

"Alright, one-hundred metres, double sharp one-eighty bends, then straight." Natalie would instruct to Chad.

"Got it." He would say, and apply his concentration into the art of turning. These drifting roads were still only one-and-a-half cars wide. Nearing the top of each mountain, there was an unprotected tumble awaiting a bad mistake or a collision. I held on to the back seat for dear life and Natalie rambled on. Celeste looked at the scenery, at the sky, at me, at anything but the road. She grabbed my hand on particularly dangerous corners, and I grabbed it back. There was a lot of comfort in that.

One mountain cleared unexpectedly at its peak, bringing us to a plateau. Here the forest disappeared, to be replaced by endless fields of olive trees on dusty red soil. For another half hour, I didn't see a single other plant.

Only a little while longer and we pulled into the city of Sparta. It didn't appear much different from the other cities we'd seen – squat, off white apartments of flaking plaster extending to the bowl of the surrounding mountains, clothes hanging from balconies, and roads of double-parked cars.

"Okay, so the most important person we'll meet here is my *Yamitsira*, my *Yamitse's* sister." Natalie said as we neared the address. "Her name is Eleni Floros, or *Surawelle*. My Yamitse told me that she is a Witch with particular talent for reading souls through the eyes. According to *Yamitse*, she's the best in the world."

"Best in the world?" Celeste asked. "That's a bold claim."

"Well she's certainly better than any other Suneva we'll meet." Natalie said. "I've asked her if she can do a reading for us. I think it will help our journey."

"I'm sure it will." I said, feeling a little silly that I'd been so worried two hours ago. I still had questions, but I was sure that witches of acclaim could answer them. Why didn't Natalie ever mention that her family was so prolific? How had Natalie's Sunevahood been kept such a tight secret all this time in the presence of great witches?

"Eleni Floros." Chad repeated. "Good. Anybody else important?"

"Well, there's a lot of family." Natalie hummed. "I've got it all written down somewhere." She reached for her bag, but Chad laughed and stopped her.

"You've never met them before, right?" He chuffed. "Maybe it's more natural that you *don't* know their life stories."

"Right…" Natale sighed, putting the bag back down. "But my Yamitse said that she's not the first *Ocras Quatrona* to come from the *Menas* family. If she's right about there being a new White Witch, they could be in the very house we're going to. I suspect there will be many important Suneva here."

"All better for the connections to make, then." Chad smiled.

We soon parked before an apartment building identical to each around it, rising tall and white. Stepping out of the car, I could hear a tremendous amount of noise raining out from the open windows a few floors up.

"Sounds like them," Natalie said. "They all speak Liktan, so we should be fine to hold our own."

"Good." I said. Even though I had no eerie feelings about the situation, staring up to the apartment, I had the realisation again that we were on Hesslik's watch list. "How loyal to the Empire are these people?" I asked, although when I looked for my friends they had all started walking. Natalie turned around.

"What, James?" She asked.

"Because we're on Hesslik's watch lists, and we're going to introduce ourselves. Should we use fake names, or something?"

"Give a fake name to a soul reader?" Natalie chuffed. "James, this is my *family*. I think you'll find that family is more important than politics."

In Natalie's word, I could only hope. I followed them up the set of external stairs, passing between balconies to come before the door from where the noise was flowing. This balcony was alive with potted herbs and vines, the door sitting amongst a wall of green. Natalie checked the card she'd written with the address, and scrutinised the door.

Finally, she nodded, and reached for the handle.

"If my family at home is anything to go by," Natalie warned, "be prepared for hugs and food."

"That's nothing I can't handle." Chad smiled.

"You say that now…" Natalie smirked, and pulled at the door handle. The door swung outwards.

"*Yamitsira?*" She called into the house. Immediately past the door was a dark living room lined with wood panels and floored with faded carpet. There was a wall of voices emanating from the back room, all with typical Greek sounds and accents. Once Natalie's voice had rung into the unfashionable abyss, a silence fell, followed by a unanimous and uproarious "Eh!"

A stocky old woman with dark curly hair and thick glasses appeared in the hallway, waddling towards us. She marched towards Natalie with determination to spite her little, worn limbs, and threw herself around Natalie. The young woman gasped as the hug wrenched the air from her lungs.

"Yamitsira!" Natalie finally leant into the hug. "You're strong…" She pulled back, kissing the woman's cheeks. I finally deduced the meaning of this name. '*Mit*' referred to mother, '*sira*' meaning 'sister of' and '*ya*', in title context, meaning 'one generation above'. This woman was her grandmother's sister, or her Great auntie.

"The photos I see of you, in them you are so young. Here is a *woman*. Just look at your eyes, young lady. You are like my sister." She said in *Liktan*, closely inspecting Natalie's irises.

"And these are your friends?" She asked and turned to us. I could feel the industrial grip of her strong arms before she'd even grabbed me. Her hand crushed mine in her attempt to grapple me in and kiss my cheek.

"Yes," Natalie replied. I wanted to demonstrate my prowess of basic *Liktan* sentences, so I made my own introduction.

"Mi nasos James Grey." I spoke proudly. The old woman had just finished strangling my hand, and stood before me.

"Ah, I did know your face." She pondered, smiling. "You are John Grey's son, no?"

"I…" I furrowed my brow. How did so many people know my father? Was I always going to exist in the shadow he left behind? "Yes…" I agreed. "How do you know him?"

"Oh, he stopped by here once. Very kind man." She nodded. "*A chi alisdi nasi?*" She asked the name of my *alis* – my Suneva form.

"Maiki." I said flatly.

"Ah, Maiki." She nodded. "Very tall and strong young man, Natalie." She spoke to her great niece, "Very interesting eyes you have." She commented cryptically, staring into me, into my *soul*. I could feel her reaching through my eyes, her grip extending into my being. This woman was a powerful Suneva. "I am Eleni, or *Surawelle*, Natalie's great auntie." She nodded before moving on to Celeste.

"I think you're right about her being a good reader." I whispered to Natalie.

"I trust my Yamiste." Natalie said. "Hopefully a reading will help us out a bit, even if we don't find Argol from anybody we meet here."

"I'm sure," I said, "And sorry to get so upset at the beach. If I knew we were walking into the house of such skilled Suneva, I…"

"Everything works out, James." She said, "It's all okay."

"Ah, a very beautiful young *Ivaer*! I see the passion in your heart" The strong, old lady said as she stood before Celeste. "And the mark of powerful family, too." She caressed Celeste's earrings. The French girl blushed.

"Thank you." Celeste said with a smile, and leaned down to give the lady a closer look. "They're sapphires from Egypt. A gift from my mother." Natalie's Great-auntie felt them in her finger tips.

"A chi *di* nasi?" Eleni asked.

"Celeste, se alismi nasos Genive." Celeste smiled.

"Beautiful names," Said the old woman, and kissed Celeste on the cheeks.

"And the last *Raduk* travels with my *Nesiratas*?" She said, astounded as she turned to Chad. "How strong you are, boy – of heart and muscle, just like the earth."

"You read my *quatran* from my eyes?" Chad blushed. "I'm Chad – my Suneva name is Ferrad." He kissed her cheeks.

Tables and chairs shifted and scraped on tiles around the corner. Suddenly there was a whole stampede of family rushing from between the cracks in the room, all coming out with huge smiles and open arms. I got rid of pleasantries and just said "James, Maiki." to each of them as I shook hands and kissed cheeks. There were uncles, aunties, Great-uncles and aunties, Natalie's cousins, her mum's cousins, their second cousins, Nick from apartment sixteen – and his cousin, John who met up with one of the family members earlier today and came back for coffee. The whole city seemed to converge in this single apartment.

The crowd rustled us back to where they had come from. We walked left, around the dividing wall at the back of the lounge area, and came to the dining room. The table, at this point, was simply a pile of food suspended from the floor. Not a square inch of space was spared as even more food found its way from the kitchen to the mass of delicacies. There was goat, pork, chicken, potatoes cooked three ways, ten different salads, at least five tubs of feta spread over the accumulated dishes. Through the back window, I could see three men surrounding a spit, which had another whole animal – probably a goat – rotating and cooking.

Suffice to say, the feast was one of the best I'd had. Just like Orthodox Easter back home with Dad's side of the family, the sheer volume of food required strategy to taste the whole table. I took small amounts of everything, then waited half an hour to chat and let it set before I went back to take more. Chad was simply overwhelmed. His uncultured eyes had never seen such a mountain of food so fresh, so healthy, and so lovingly cooked with local ingredients. He topped his plate way past its filling point and plunged his face deep into the mound of flavour. The silly man, he conked out way too quickly – before he even got to the good salads – and fell back in his chair with a full belly, trying to fight the induced sleep.

Natalie, like me, knew what was going on. She also knew that there would be even more dessert, and that discretion should be taken not to fill up now.

"Hey, James." Celeste called to me from behind as I eagerly tip-toed to the table full of said desserts. I put my plate down, disappointed to be delayed in my feast of sweets, and turned around.

"Hey," I said back. "How good is all of this food?"

"Oui, it's very good," she said, putting her plate down. "Look, I was just wondering if you are doing alright." She smiled at me caringly and grabbed my hand. I was taken aback.

"Yeah, I'm great. What makes you ask?"

"You were stressed before at the beach, and you were basically crushing my hand in that car ride. Are you a little less tense?"

"Oh, sorry." I coughed. "I didn't realise…"

"It's fine, I was crushing yours too." She smiled. "It's just that you always make sure I'm okay, and I really like that. I just wanted to make sure you're alright. Natalie dismissed your concerns."

The way she smiled at me, and caressed my palm with her fingers, it made me forget that the world was happening around me. I hated that she could so easily sway me like this, when she kept giving me such conflicting messages. I thought that Celeste just wanted to be friends, that her affection meant nothing, but I was beginning, and hoping, to doubt it.

"I was concerned." I said, "And I don't know why Natalie didn't tell us how important her family was *before* this. I'd have been much more relaxed if I knew who we'd be meeting here. It seems that everything might be working out."

"It is strange." She frowned, "But I agree, we're in good hands. Glad that you're feeling better."

"Are you doing okay?" I asked in return, our hands still held.

"Yes, James. I'm having a nice day." She said. "Anyway, if you ever need to talk, I'm here. I owe you that much."

"Same to you, Celeste." I returned her sweet smile.

"Oh, *madame*." A member of Natalie's family touched Celeste on the shoulder. We broke our gaze on each other. "I'm sorry to interrupt your moment, but I had to talk to a French *Ivaer*."

"Of course." Celeste smiled. "We'll talk later, James." She said to me and let go of my hand. I lingered on the feeling of her palm in mine, staring off into space as she was whisked away over to a group of Natalie's supposed relatives.

I finally took my plate to the table, eying up the dessert sitting tantalisingly atop it, when I felt *watched*. There were eyes and hands on my skin, crawling under my shirt up my back. I turned to the sensation, feeling the power of the seer who watched.

My gaze met them. Tall, emaciated, platinum hair, pale skin, and a clouded-over left eye. She stood tall and straight, smiling at me through a placid, yet gaunt, face. The lines of her skull were prominent. I gasped, and turned bright red from my own rudeness. The girl, however, didn't seem to notice.

"Yosas." I coughed, introducing myself in Liktan. This person made me severely uneasy. I could feel my being crawling, writhing. "Silo di Liktan?" I asked, and they nodded, indicating that they could say Liktan.

But they said no words of their own.

I turned to the dessert table, to find Natalie right in my face.

"Ah!" I gasped.

"Ah!" Natalie yelped at my surprise.

"Who's dead-eye over there?" I gestured behind us. Natalie caught a glimpse, and her expression dropped.

"Okay, my Yamitse told me about them." Natalie whispered, "That's my cousin, Christina."

"Your cousin?"

"Somebody's cousin. They're my age at least." Natalie clarified. "They're quatra-sick, that's what matters."

"Quatra sick?" I hummed, turning to the girl. Her gaze was still wriggling on my skin. "What does that mean?"

"Look back here, for Amasos' sake." Natalie spun me around. "It means that she had poor thread control. She used the black hole energy to power her soul and never its connections, and she let the energy pool. Using quatra that way can make you heal, increase your mood, make you more lively, it takes away pain. But,

101

if you never control the flow, the black hole can start to control you. It's called a possession."

"Like Boekidin's *Quatra Deamon*?" I asked.

"Yes, similar." Natalie said. "Although that Suneva looked functioning, at least. From what my Yamitse told me, Christina first forgot how to speak anything other than Liktan, then she forgot that too, then forgot how to write, and she's now losing the ability to eat. She used to be a normal kid – never even fired a bolt of quatra. But now nobody knows if *she* is still in there. It's frightening."

"How the hell does that happen?" I asked.

"Weak mind." Natalie said. "Too strong of a connection to the black hole. Not enough determination to hold onto yourself. Apparently, there's a few avenues to become sick as a Suneva, but they're all slippery slopes."

"Cheese…" My hairs stood up. I wasn't in-tune with any of this *deeper* connection stuff. "Can we get sick like this?"

"Everybody can." Natalie said. "But you've just got to stay mentally strong when you become powerfully connected. It's the risk of using these abilities we have, apparently. Right now, I don't feel you're at risk of *falling*."

Falling… my memory triggered, my vision at the beach. I spun back to the possessed, pale girl. Her dead, grey eye still stared at me, gnawing to see my soul. Then, her head cocked up, her eye meeting mine.

Grey like the girl in the endless water. I fell into it.

I was floating in a grey mist at the centre of a blank nothingness. The blinding colour of the purest white reflected and bounced around the space. It pierced the fog around me and shone through to my bones.

I found that I could move in the sea of nothing. I could swim through the clouded grey fog, which seemed as endless as the white around it.

"Maiki." A nightmarish howl came from all directions. It rang as a man's grimy, deep voice imposed upon the cry of a small girl.

"Ah!" I let out a shriek as the sound of my name rocked my spine. I flipped around in all directions, frantically trying to catch the face of the monster. Where my limbs flailed, they left streaks of black smoke in the grey mist, until suddenly all that was around me was pitch darkness.

Then I saw a distant blue light glowing. A blue halo around a deeply black centre, flames radially spitting from the light disc. A mark of the black suns.

102

From its centre emanated the purest dread I'd ever felt.

"Maiki." The voice painfully repeated, and it came from the dark centre. "You don't understand what you're seeing. You don't understand your direction. Nobody is as they seem. Nothing is as it seems."

I floated in the abyss of dread, staring at the face of fear itself, unable to look away. Then there was a tap on my shoulder. I turned around.

I was standing by the dessert table, infatuated by an emaciated girl's clouded eye.

"I sure hope she puts up a fight soon, or it could be too late." Natalie said, but I couldn't concentrate on her word.

"Let's have some dessert." I diverted. "I'm ready for the sweets."

I turned from the possessed girl, but I knew that she still watched me.

Chapter 12
The Reading

Eleni, Natalie's Great Auntie, led me into her meditation room. The journey there led us through her bedroom, a dark and homely room with off-white curtains blocking the sun, and a bed laden with a fluffy floral bedspread. Past the varnished wood vanity dresser was a door, which Eleni opened and gestured me inside. I found myself in a broom closet of sorts – a small, empty room with two cushions on the carpeted floor.

"Please, sit." She instructed, and I did so on the furthest cushion. Eleni closed the door behind her, casting the room into pitch black darkness.

"Darkness is good for Suneva." She explained, taking her own seat. "As people, we depend too much on our eyes. Limiting this biological sense forces us to open our minds the world visible only through quatra."

My thread hummed at the base of my neck, and the darkness made me aware of it. Without sight, my brain seemed to make its own swirls of colour before me, patterns which disappeared when I looked directly at them. Without distraction, I found myself able to sense the buzz of the old woman's energy. It was the smallest pinprick on my fingers, the weakest connection, but there still. The silence between us reigned.

"I don't know what to expect out of this." I said, filling the void. Then, two hands grabbed mine, and an *energy* of being watched creeped through my eyes. It was the sensation of being seen, being deeply *exposed*. I stiffened.

"Your soul is tangled about questions." She spoke softly. "You have worries, and they respond to me. What do you need to ask?"

"I…" I wasn't expecting to be challenged so soon. Wasn't she meant to be telling me things about myself? What was I drawn to ask her? As we sat silent, I could *feel* my concerns pooling. They voiced themselves.

"I know nothing about the Code of Connections, really," I said, and a floodgate opened. "And I'm the guy who thought of our plan to find the Legendaries using it. I suggested that we should follow the connection to others to find Argol, then use his social web to find the Legendary Suneva, but is that missing the point? What is realisation, and why is it important in finding the Legendaries?"

In asking the question, a weight was lifted from me. I relaxed into the cushion, my back falling against the closet wall. Eleni sighed, and I could feel her bearing closer.

"I like your plan, actually." She said. I wasn't expecting that answer, which plastered a smile across my face. "The Legendaries are mythical at this point. I don't think a strict following of the Code of Connections would help anybody locate them. I think your idea makes good headway into becoming connected to them."

"So why is realisation important then?" I asked. "What does it mean? Do we even need it?"

"So many questions, I can see why you're so tangled." She chuckled. "Realisation is what will untangle your soul and allow you to be the most connected, best Suneva that you can be, but it's also unobtainable."

"What?"

"It cannot be obtained." She repeated. "Realisation, or *Sunasera*, is the total alleviation of conflict from the soul. To solve conflict, one must understand their place in the universe, their place amongst others, and must understand themselves, and accept these facets. You must understand your suffering, and the suffering you cause, and in doing so, create *peace*. One can never solve *all* of the conflicts and suffering, nor understand and accept all of that which you cannot resolve. New conflicts are always born, hence, *Sunesera* doesn't exist.

"Following the code, however, *will* make you a better Suneva. In attaining greater peace, you will untangle your soul, and strengthen all of your soul connections, and even might discover more. Is that clear?"

"Yes." I said, remembering what Hesslik had told me. Upon my lie of realisation hunting, he congratulated me on taking steps towards becoming the Suneva I always could be. "And how does that relate to Legendaries?"

"The world is always trying to pull you, James." She said. "If you understand your place in it, and if you are receptive to all of the connections you have to it, you will be able to better navigate these pulls towards your goals. You may even stumble upon the more subtle of callings – those that you might have otherwise missed. *Sunasera* isn't necessary to finding the Legendaries, but it will absolutely help, and it should be a personal goal, anyway."

"Right." I let the information settle. "So, by studying my connections to myself and my surroundings, I can understand my conflicts, and solve them to create peace. Doing so would give strengthened soul connections, which could help us find the Legendaries more easily?"

"That's a remarkably astute summary..." Eleni quizzed. "But yes. You understand the process."

"Can you see any of my conflicts?" I asked.

"A reading will tell me some general idea of what troubles you," she said. "What I read in your soul should spark truths for you. Anything I hint to will be something that you *already* know to be wrong, but may not know is hindering you. Listen carefully to what I find, and reflect on it."

Then there was silence again, as the woman's fingers drifted across my palms. In the darkness, I could feel my connections flourish. I knew Eleni's movements by the air which she displaced. I knew the size of this room. And I knew where her eyes were when they locked onto mine, penetrating my soul.

"There is a stale conflict resting in your soul, so old that it must be from your thread's creation." She hummed. "The deepest level of your soul expects that you hate yourself, or what you know you will become."

"That personality doesn't sound like mine..." I cringed.

"And the rest of your soul, everything built atop of it, is a personality of optimism, jealousy, self-doubt, and impatience."

"That's more like it."

"Is this thread yours?" She asked, and my stomach dropped.

"I'm sorry?" I stammered.

"This thread expected to be aligned with a different personality. I've never seen this before. I think this is something that you must search yourself to find an answer for."

Never seen it before? I coughed. The implications were astonishing, that my soul was so incompatible with being a good Suneva that the world's greatest reader had never seen such a case. "Could it be The Shiverman?" I suggested, trying to find justification in the face of my born ineptitude. "He's been playing in my mind recently. I don't know what he changed."

"No, but that's a good guess." She encouraged. "Using *kidin* abilities is more akin to reading a book. They can open up your thoughts and read them, but they are not the authors. They cannot rewrite what is there. Some event has happened to you some years ago. You'd do well to resolve it."

"Okay." I hummed. I didn't know what to make of that fact. I didn't think there was a point when I was self-loathing or scared, not even when mourning for my father. "What else is in there?"

"Well, your soul wants to be one with the sky, that is clear." She said. "Although flying is a way off without some steps towards realisation. And beyond this, you're the harshest critic of your own ability. You're jealous of your friends."

"Yes," I responded. I knew this truth well. Natalie's face came straight to mind, and Eleni shook her head.

"I can feel your reflections." She said. "I don't think you should let your judgement be clouded by jealousy. Certainly, your friends are advanced, but they have a different relationship to quatra. Yours is succinctly different to anything I've seen before."

"So, what good is in my soul?" I asked.

"There's a lot of positive in here," She said. "You're kind, you always mean well. You have a solid intuition and instinct. I believe you should always follow your gut."

"Noted."

"But you do harbour some concerning character traits. Among jealousy I see a lack of confidence and belief. You have a lot of potential, Maiki. The black hole Omercronius choosing you is not random. It is fated, and has a reason.

106

There's a lot of power in your soul. The ability to form deeper soul connections is in there. Nearing realisation is attainable, but it will require your focus."

Deeper soul connections, I pondered. As a Suneva who couldn't read the quatra field, even after many months of trying, I was doubting my ability to form these deep connections. It was relieving to hear a strong Witch tell me that it was within my scope.

"And your impatience won't serve you well." Eleni noted, as if scouring my thoughts. "Self-discovery is a long process. Do not expect everything to come quickly."

"Of course," I frowned. "What about my destiny, then? I was told by a reader, before I knew of my powers, that I was destined for leadership. Is that still there?"

"Yes," the Witch replied. "But you will have to learn to be a leader before you will take your role." She then sat back, collecting her thoughts. "My advice to you, Maiki, is that you must focus on strengthening your closest connections instead of broadening weak ones. I sense that there are many people with whom you are close, but distancing yourself from."

I gulped at the suggestion, thinking clearly of Simone and Tom, who I'd avoided notifying of my abilities. "Be free to find yourself in new places, but remember to learn about yourself by strengthening aspects of your being with which you're already familiar. Expand your web to chase your goals, but do not neglect to understand deeply those closest to you. Don't look too far for the connection between you and Omercronius, look to the thread you share."

"Thank you." I smiled, "How did you learn so much about spirituality, and purpose?"

"These are the birth lands of the Code. In fact, this family is descendant from its writer, Masalik Vinavek. We've had secrets of the code and her ancient belief system passed to us," she recollected. "But It's not about the interpretation I know, it's about how you discover yourself."

"I see," I smiled. "I'm just glad that you gave me some straight answers. It's taken a while to hear anybody explain the code."

This made the witch huff. "Those who do not explain the Code to others do not understand it themselves," she snarked. "The journey is not ruined by having the purpose explained. I believe that if you follow the code as I have told you, towards peace and away from conflict, you will solve the issues with your thread. I believe you can overcome this Maiki, and be the powerful *Kiin* I see hidden in your eyes."

I did not say anything immediately. I just smiled and sat there holding onto the bliss that it might all get better.

"I appreciate your words," I finally said. "And this opportunity."

"I appreciate the opportunity to see a soul and connection as rare as yours." She conceded. "But I have one favour for you."

"What is that?" I asked.

"Watch out for your friends," she implored. "Especially Natalie. You'll all need to support each other through your personal journeys. You've each got a way to go. Some will need more encouragement than others."

"I will do that for you." I smiled, and felt it was time to leave. I stood up and walked past Eleni. As I came out into her room, Chad was at the door waiting to come in.

***

It was the day of readings for us. Surawelle was a famed reader of souls and foreteller of destinies. She did not reveal to me how that kind of Witchcraft worked, but said that it relied on *auras* and the colours of the soul. As a Suneva, you either saw them, or you didn't. Even those with Suneva biology – those born with quatra veins and the cones to see quatra energy, but no threads or powers – could see soul colours sometimes, although it was rare.

Natalie and Celeste were still waiting to be read as I exited my session. They waited on the couch in the entrance room, eating the leftovers of yesterday's feast. In and out of the house bustled members of the family and guests of yesterday's gathering. They said hello to us as we waited.

"How was it?" Natalie asked.

"That's a loaded question," I frowned. "I learned what we should be doing to follow the code…"

"That's good," Celeste said.

"But I also got to hear *'I've never seen that before'* from one of the world's best readers."

"That's...good?" Celeste strained.

"No, it was bad."

"Oh..." She ruffled her hair and looked away.

"But it wasn't all bad. I've got potential, apparently. And I know where to put my efforts." I thought immediately to Simone, and Tom, and then Mum, even. Eleni said that I had to resolve conflict and strengthen those connections that I already had. I wasn't going to tell Simone or Tom that I was a Suneva yet – especially not my sister – but thinking of them reminded me to keep the contact I had promised. I'd also do well not to lie to my own mother. That could be source of future hardships. Right now, I had to be a good friend, brother, and son. I had to take steps to be honest and open.

"I'm going to go down to a souvenir store." I said. "I need to write Tom and my family a post card. Do either of you want one to send home?"

"No, I'm okay," Natalie said. "But thanks, James."

"No thanks, James," Celeste said.

"Alright then, I'll be back," I said, making my way out the door.

Like yesterday, the sun shone down through the pale blue, near-winter sky. A gentle breeze made its way through the city – I could feel its flow in the back of my mind. I tried to focus on this connection to the wind. This was a connection that I could strengthen by better understanding what I was in relation to it, which involved having peace in my soul. The reasoning was solid to me now. Understand your place, purpose, and relationships to resolve conflicts. In doing so, attain peace and strengthen your connections because of it. Find peace and become a better Suneva.

I continued down the crumbly, concrete steps and out into the street. I had no concept of what day it was, as happens on holidays, but the streets were bustling. The sounds of nature echoed all around – the sound of car horns, people yelling at each other, revving engines, distant telephones and shuffling feet. All disturbing the breeze which ran along the street.

Natalie's relatives lived near the city centre. I did not know where a souvenir shop would be, but I figured one couldn't be hard to find.

Then, I felt a great disturbance to the breeze, like a white void disturbing its tide. This was a Suneva presence, it tickled my fingertips with its discomforting energy. I froze, suspecting any number of powerful, enemy Suneva. I readied my wrist and my armour, clutching at the air around me, and craned my body to the source.

Behind me was a short, skinny girl, with platinum hair and a grey, glassy eye.

"Oh, hi Christina." I said, both relieved and frightened as her grey eye observed me. I refused to look at it. She raised her hand and waved. "What are you doing?" I asked, even though I was aware that she couldn't talk back. Instead, she raised her eyebrows and glanced to the side, down another street.

"You know where I can find a postcard?" I asked, and the girl nodded. I wasn't sure that I wanted to follow her, but she didn't give me the option. She stalked to my side, grabbed my arm, and pulled me along. Her hand was bony on my flesh, digging like a claw. I tried not to show my discomfort. She pulled me along for a few blocks, before we came to a squat little shop with various wares and curiosities spilling out. There were lots of wooden phalluses, much to my surprise, as well as models of monuments and evil eyes. We walked inside.

The cashier at the souvenir store lit up when we stepped in. I assumed it must have been for the quiet day he was experiencing, so I browsed postcards with a smile to make the store look busy. The shop was warm and inviting, with crème, beachy paint lining the walls inside. The vibrant sun crashed in through its open face, casting a warm glow on the wire racks of useless crap and gifts. The cashier made his way over and knelt next to Christina, uninterested in his potential customer.

"Bringing boys into my shop, Christina? I didn't know you could chat up boys without a voice." He winked at the girl. She blushed, albeit robotically, if that was even possible. He spoke Liktan to her, instead of Greek, which I found interesting.

"*Sa tan Suneva?*" He asked her if I was a Suneva. She rolled her head around to me. The eye caught me off guard, and I tried to look over her instead to face the man.

"I don't suppose everybody in this town speaks *Liktan*, right?" I asked.

"Just about," he laughed. "I've never seen you around though. What's your accent?"

"I'm Australian," I said. "Although my dad is Macedonian."

The man gave me a suspicious look, expecting more.

110

"Greek-Macedonian." I clarified.

"Good man," he smiled. "What are you doing in Sparta?"

"On a journey of pilgrimage." I told our standard lie. I supposed, despite the conflict that lies might have created, this lie deserved to be told. "Following the Code of Connections. I'm staying with Surawelle, because I'm travelling with her Grand-Niece."

"Ah," he smiled. "Well, keep this one out of trouble." He nudged Christina. She smiled. He leaned in to my ear and whispered. "And you're a good boy for taking her out like this. She doesn't need pity, but she's very ill and I bet she really appreciates this kindness."

"Thank you," I said, for lack of knowing what else to say. This man attributed to me too much kindness.

"She likes the ice-cream down the street," he continued into my ear. He picked a postcard off the display and handed it to me. "That one's on me if you take her. She'd appreciate that even more."

"Thank you," I said again, and picked another off the display. I handed him   the   amount   on   the   card.

"Thank *you*," he said to me, and waved me off.

I took Christina, against my intense discomfort in being around her, to get some ice cream from down the street. She held my hand the whole time too, despite my willing that she wouldn't. In it, just as I could do with Surawelle, I could feel the intense radiation of her Suneva power. I noticed her energy brighten as she had the cold treat in hand, and suddenly, the uncomfortableness I felt evaporated.

I took the smiling, ill Suneva back home and wrote the postcards I needed to. It was hard to write a postcard about our activities that excluded any Suneva details. It took me longer to think of anything non-supernatural on the trip than it would have taken me to write the whole thing out. Eventually I had something I could work with, and I posted it that afternoon.

As I waited for my friends on the couch, talking with Natalie's relatives and whomever else happened to be around, I found that Natalie, Celeste and Chad's reviews of being read by Surawelle were about as uplifting as mine.

Celeste came out with a wet face, perhaps from some very confronting truths. She said that she was destined to be as powerful as her mother as an *Ivaer*, maybe even more powerful. However, she had a lot of personal issues to sort out before she could get there.

Chad came to the realisation that he would have to go home to face his parents, and the kids who almost tried to kill him. "I ran away," he put it, "and if I ever want to progress, I'll have to go back and help them understand why. Their closure is mine, apparently."

Natalie was much more solemn on her return. Her face was blank, and she chose to stay silent. "It's a lot to take in," she said to the group, "but I learned a new trick, which is nice. James, get out your armour," she instructed. I did as I was told, and let the *alis* Maiki consume me.

"You've still got those dints from when we met Chad, haven't you?" She asked, searching my armoured body.

"Yeah, and many more." I added.

"Great, well you'll have them no longer…" She hovered her hands over the scar running down my back, holding the peace-sign pose. I felt the crack as my armour popped back into place. A twang of pain shot up my back, but was quenched by immediate ecstasy. She had healed a soul's injury. She did the same process on my arm, which had amassed a large dint.

"Wow, that's incredible," I said. "How did you do that?"

"Armour is weird. It's pure mass, like quatra, but it's not made of quatra. Still, if you have the proper connection, you can heal it using quatra. It's not easy though."

I patted my scars in disbelief. "Well you sure are amazing." I said.

The old witch Surawelle emerged from her room after this, and pulled up a dining chair to face the couches. We all took a seat to form a circle around her.

"I hope that you've all got a better idea of your future in your head," she said. "You're a strong group of Suneva, but you're not without your own personal struggles. Whilst I might not be able to help you further on your own personal journeys, I do have something to aid your mission…"

She dove her hand into her pocket and pulled out a card which she shuffled over to hand to me. It was a business card, much like the one LeGrand had given my father. One side was white, painted with the Mark of the Black Suns. The other had a blue border, and personal details printed on it. The card was from *The Green Dragon*: Naxear Argol – Adam Leroux, and gave an address.

112

"You have Argol's address?" I awed. How had my plan worked? It seemed stupid that it did – I wasn't this smart.

"It is where you can find him, yes," Surawelle said. "I believe it will lead you to a candle shop, although I cannot remember what to do once you're there. I know you'll figure it out."

"How did you get this?" Natalie asked. I passed the card to her and she inspected it, brow furrowed. "Mr. Argol has always shown an interest in this family due to our White Witches – both present and past. He could never get into contact with Tess, who wouldn't work with him. He did hand me a card though, just in case either of us changed our minds. All things are handed and kept with accordance to destiny. I could see this card having connections to the future when I was given it, and now those connections are realised."

"Interesting…" Natalie pondered. "So you've met Argol?"

"I have talked to him twice. He's kept my name in his files," she said. "If he asks where you got the card, mention my name. I'd like to hear what he has to say."

"Certainly, Yamitsira." Natalie said with a smile and handed the card to Celeste. Celeste sighed deeply as she held it in her hands. She frowned, inspecting the address. Finally, she passed it to Chad.

***

We stayed in Sparta for a week before we moved on. There were lots of sights to see around the area, like the Byzantine settlement in Mystras and the ancient Spartan ruins. I spent time in the dark room trying to unwind and meditate, sometimes under the guidance of Surawelle. The first step to realisation, I figured, was getting rid of the stress I held on to. Surawelle agreed, and coached me through relaxation.

Now that we had a way to Argol, we planned the next stage of our trip. We would drive back to Athens and give the car back to the Argol lady – as we only saw to be fair. We would make a road trip of it on our way. Despite the decided urgency in our current events, neither Hesslik nor Boekidin had impinged on our week of sitting still, and we still wanted to see a few sights whilst we'd payed the money to come to Europe.

Then we would catch a plane to Paris, where the business card's address led us. If Eleni's card and LeGrand's candle didn't let us in, I joked that we could pretend we were bounty hunters here to sell back his daughter, given that Celeste was already branded with that mistaken identity. She slapped me for the suggestion.

Episode 3

A Story About Getting Lost to Find Yourself.

Chapter 13
Art of the Deal

We left Sparta the next day and started our winding road-trip back to Athens. We made sure to thank Natalie's Yamitsira one-thousand times for the help she gave us. We each had our own personal advice to think about, and a clue to our next destination of business.

Where I had earlier been worried about Boekidin and his potential White Witch, it had become apparent that despite their power, they were still on *our* tail and no closer to the Legendaries. As we holidayed, I was occasionally graced with his presence – that feeling of water stuck in my ear. When I felt him I would put a blindfold over my eyes, and all knew to stay silent. We knew when he was close, and I knew when he was listening.

Natalie could feel his team silently following our journey. I could sense her powers growing here. The trip to the homelands and a reconnection to her family really let the quatra flow through her. After a week of studying under Surawelle, her *Yamitsira*, she was so much more attentive and in touch with the world around her. She constantly walked around with her hands in the peace-sign pose.

We each had our input into the destinations we visited, but Chad, the driver, and Natalie, the navigator, did most of the choosing. We cruised around the Peloponnesian coastline for a week and a bit, stopping off at cheap hostels, apartments and hotels along the way to absorb the wonderful sights. It was, however, well into December, and without high temperatures there wasn't much enjoyment to coastal towns. Once we'd seen enough culture and walked through enough castles, we packed it up and headed back to Athens to keep moving. We had to get to Paris to find Argol.

There was the question of what to do with the bright pink station wagon we'd acquired. Its internals were fine, although in need of a service, and it had taken a few dings and sideswipes on the crazy, narrow and unpoliced highway mountain roads. We weren't sure that the lady would take it back, given that its worth had decreased from when she'd handed it to us.

"I mean, what are we going to do with it?" I expressed to the group as we looked over its declining state, the now winter Sun rising behind it. "We can't sell it as is, and I doubt she'd take it back like this."

We took a moment each to consider. Chad's eyes sparked up, and his mouth   quivered   with   excitement.

"Oh, do I have an idea for you, Jimmy-boy." Were the words which graced his glorious brain fart. It was an idea so glorious, so astoundingly perfect, that I got my hands out and started work immediately. I used them to tear carbon from the Earth. I trenched it from deep in the ground and heaved it up. Chad started fishing iron from the crust as well. We amassed our piles and started work.

I made a pencil with graphite and we drew out concept sketches as Chad described them, and when we had a design we were happy with, we got to work.

We pressed carbon and iron together to make steel. I flattened carbon into rigid plates of weaved armour. We rebuilt the entire body of the car. Of course, we had to keep the headlights, internals, seats, controls and everything mechanical, but we made a hot rod out of what we had. It was an aerodynamic beast, streamlined to be fast with those eighties style pop-up headlights. It had a custom undertray to direct airflow, and a comical spoiler to give traction on the winding mountain roads, a profile designed by my *kiin* senses to generate downforce. The finishing touch was a set of tail light fins, like the old Cadillacs.

We bought some paint and primer and had a fun time using me as an air gun to apply it. We painted it bright pink again, with two thick, white racing stripes down the centre. We used steel to cap the tail wings and to line the body with shiny details. When it was done, it was an unholy, cool and dramatic beast. A real dream machine.

The drive to Athens was, of course, eventful. According to Chad, it was the best handling he'd ever felt. It hugged the road, stuck into the corners, and screamed on the bends. I'd never before felt safer when on the verge of shitting my pants.

We made it back to the big city and took the car to a dealer. He looked at it, inspected it, told us that it was an unorthodox machine and that he wouldn't accept it. Having put in our 'best' efforts to sell it, and more or less being too lazy to drive around town to any more dealers, Chad and I made the executive decision to just hand the car back to the lady.

"I didn't expect to see you so soon." She said as she opened the door. She flicked her long, grey hair aside to talk. In her glass heels, she loomed over Chad and I. "Is there something wrong with the car?" She asked, "I did give it to you for free…"

"No, we improved it." Chad said, and gestured to the monster parked outside her house. "Its value is through the roof. *Unorthodox*ly cool, said one dealer."

"What under the Black Suns…" She pushed her glasses down her nose to gape at the machine.

"It's had a full aerodynamic package upgrade." Chad said proudly.

"I can see that." The woman gawked in disapproval.

"We came to hand it back to you," Chad said, and threw the keys her way. She floundered to catch them. "You could sell this thing for a real profit."

At that moment, a very run-down, rusty hatchback pulled up behind our dream machine. A fat, balding man in a dirty, pinstriped suit bustled out of its door. He performed a waddling-jog all the way to the door step, where he just about fainted from exertion.

"Jesus, that's a powerful Witch." He stumbled away from Natalie as he came to his senses. "Sorry, don't mean to be rude darling. You're leaking quatra, is all."

"I know." Natalie glared at him. He gulped, causing a ripple to traverse his wobbly, fat head. He snapped his pudgy face to the beautiful, older woman.

"You weren't just about to sell the car to these kids, were you?" He asked. "I've been meaning to come here for weeks, and I've only remembered now."

"Two-hundred thousand, they offered me." She said plainly, but gave us a cunning look. We stayed quiet, except for Chad.

"No less!" He said dramatically. "I mean, just look at those curves," he gestured to the car with his whole body, "and those aerodynamic shapes."

The portly man twisted his blubbery body to witness the sight. "Yes, it's quite a marvel of engineering," he agreed. "Two-hundred and fifty thousand," he declared.

"Two hundred and sixty-thousand!" Chad shouted over him.

"Three-hundred thousand," the man said, a grin forming across his face.

"Oh, well you can have it then," Chad said. "I know when I've lost."

The man smiled widely, then noticed Chad and the woman grinning in unison and didn't know what to think. His eyes rushed between the two parties, but by the time he'd figured out what had happened, he'd already shaken the lady's hand.

"Done," she said with a grin. "Come inside and I'll get the paperwork." She looked at our group. "You all wait here for a minute. I'll be back." She winked at Chad as she bustled the stout gentleman inside. I could see Chad's heart melt and come out his ass. He gasped for air, as if her wink had winded him.

She came back only a few minutes later with a check. It was for seventy-five thousand drachma.

"A quarter cut seems fair," she said. "You did the car up and played along. I owned it for ten years."

"Seems fair to me," Chad said. Celeste tried to push her way to the front, but Chad held her back with only a finger. "Good doing business with you." He smiled, and turned us away.

"This is enough for tickets to Paris," Chad said, directing us back to the street where our suitcases were.

"And it could have been more," Celeste interjected. "You let yourself get walked over in the deal. We added the value to the car, and there's *four* of us. We could have taken a much larger cut!"

"Ah, but the art of greed is not the art of the deal," Chad smiled, and wagged his finger at the *Ivaer*. "We have exactly as much as we need. That's what I call fair," he said, and would take no more input. Natalie directed us to a main street where we quickly hailed a cab and were on our way to the airport.

***

"The first *Ivaer* was a man from modern day France, Monsieur André Basille. Before the Suneva were known in the region, and when people were only starting to work out what it meant to be a Suneva, nobody knew what to do with quatra." Celeste told a story. It was going to be a three-hour flight to Paris, and it seemed that my question of 'Why are the Argols and the *Ivaer* French?' sparked a tale of lore. We all listened closely to Celeste as she explained.

119

"The first to contact destiny were the *Kiin*. They lived in the windy plateaus on the ranges of Macedonia and Albania, and felt connected to the movement of air. Eventually they learned that they could influence the flows of the sky and clouds. Soon after the *Kiin* naturally came the *Raduk* in Spain, and the *Welle* in Greece. Each group understood some ability to alter the natural world around them. From the waves which crashed on the shores to the mountains and valleys of the landscape.

"After the macro-elements came the *Liktas*. They were led by Zeus, Greek god of Thunder, and chased storms to bend their arcs of lightning. They did not understand that electricity was the movement of charge, they only understood it as beams of light from the angry sky which they could twist.

"The *Kidin* of Sicily were the next to find their ability. Naturally, they found that they could awaken in other people's dreams, and were able to refine their abilities from there. They built empires on secrets and broken trust, eventually becoming the Romans and the Carthaginians.

"The last of the ancient powers to be discovered was *ivaer*, discovered in the dark ages. Without an understanding of modern science, it was hard to know what a flame was, and harder to know if you could control it. In addition to that, a Suneva flame isn't like a regular flame – it doesn't burn from fuel and it doesn't consume.

"The first *Ivaer*, André Basille was not a romantic man. He was a man of many women. He would visit cities and take one night to find many lovers, and did not build depth in any relationships. He had little drive except lust and charm.

"One night, in one village across the south coast, he came across a woman so beautiful that he thought she was descended straight from the heavens. He felt compelled by great forces to talk to this woman, and to make her his. But when he did, she rejected him.

"He came back to that village every night for the next few weeks, to the same spot he saw her before, and tried to woo her. Each time he brought a more extravagant gift. She was severely uninterested, but after a few weeks gave in, and agreed to give him her time.

"He felt complete around her. It wasn't her looks which attracted him, it was her soul. He wanted to know this woman, and the way he talked to her made this genuinely clear. She grew to crave his interest and his care. Eventually they got married and he brought the property on the street corner where they met and made it their house."

"Well that's cute." I added in with a smile.

"...And stereotypically French." Natalie chuckled.

"Yes, very cute, and French," Celeste smiled. "They lived in the house for fifty years. He became the village baker, she became a renowned seamstress – until the plague swept through town. She became dreadfully ill and was on her death bed when the dark Suneva *Artkis* came to end her misery, like he did for so many other people. The moment that Artkis' scythe came upon her, the man realised what he had lost – the soul he would never get to spend another moment with. She was gone.

"In that moment, he was overcome by wild passion. The passion and magnitude of his love rippled through his bones. He felt her soul being ripped from him and in his last act of love he let his passion for her consume him. It is said that in the moment a ten-foot flame erupted from both of his palms and scorched the cobbled stones of the street.

"The next morning he was gone from the town – his house lay as a pile of ashes. He went searching for her soul in the world, and found many others that reminded him of hers. From young boys to old women, they reflected some of her qualities. He taught them all of the power of love, and the flames born of passion, and spread the knowledge of *ivaer* abilities all over France.

"So that, James, is why the *Ivaer* are from France, because only they could understand the flames – as the embodiment of passion and love." She smiled at me and lit a tiny little blue fire in her hand – presumably so small to stop a stewardess seeing. "Here is my passion. When I show you my flame, I show you my soul."

***

Celeste grumbled, sipping her coffee on the Champs-Élysées, looking out over the crowd flowing past on the busy street. All kinds were visible here, from humble and obvious tourists, to the impatient locals. I sat next to her, my own coffee in hand, waiting for Chad and Natalie to get back to us. Chad had insisted on taking a photo in front of the Arc de Triumph, to which Celeste had sighed and refused. I chose, despite my keenness to see the sight up close, to stay with Celeste at the café.

"I hate this city," she mumbled between sips, and said no more. Instead, her head fell to rest on my shoulder. She sighed.

"Why?" I asked. "It's been nice so far. Nothing like people say it's meant to be…" I admired the architecture opposite. Wealth emanated from this street and many like it. The buildings here, unlike those in the cities and villages of Greece, held modern history of aristocracy. Everything on our walk today, from our hostel all the way across the city, was beautiful, even the people.

"It's fake," Celeste grumbled. "I idolised it so much as a kid. I thought everybody who said that it would be dirty and rude were wrong, but no, they were right."

"I don't know," I hummed. "People have been good so far."

"I guess you never held it with childhood admiration," she sighed. "This was the place I'd always imagined was the *future*, you know? This was the place I first came to when I ran away. There would be so much here for me, fashion, people, opportunity. Surely, you know how it feels to have your childhood expectations crushed?"

My mind raced to hugging the Easter bunny at a shopping centre, only to have the mascot's head roll off. What was left was human-sushi – a greasy man wrapped tightly in a costume, face of shock. I had cried for an hour.

"Yes." I replied.

"Then you know what it's like to have your dreams ruined," she spat with disgust. From my brief encounter with the city, I could only disagree. We had only arrived last night, getting enough time to sleep before waking to tour the sites, and I'd already been entrenched in this place of high fashion, class, food, and people. We had gone already to Notre Dame and the Eiffel Tower. Chad, much to the shock and disgrace of Celeste, had accosted random locals with his low, booming voice to take pictures of us with our disposable camera. The loud American was her bane in this city, and she chose to slink behind me where we went. I had expected to find the French girl in her element here, but it felt almost as if she was an ashamed cat dragging half-dead mice into her home.

"Chad's enjoying himself at least," I said. "He's taking in the culture."

"Oh, please, you could feed the boy a snail filled croissant and he'd think it was the genuine French experience," she huffed, then reconsidered. "Although his cultural naivety is endearing. He really *did* get excited about that crepe..."

In that moment, Chad and Natalie appeared in sight. Chad wore a massive grin, waving with one hand and holding a monstrous crepe in the other.

"And he found another. Amazing," Celeste chuckled.

"It's a traffic-circle," he laughed as he came by. "I don't know why, but I thought it would be something grander than a traffic-circle."

"And you found another crepe?" I pointed.

"These things are everywhere. I tell you." He grinned.

"Weren't you an agent for Hesslik?" I asked. "Surely the novelties of the world can't surprise you this much."

"Didn't get to do much exploring as an agent," he shrugged. "Hell, I'd probably have lived here if I knew the food was *this* good and everywhere." He took a hulking bite out of the pancake, chocolate oozing from it. Natalie swung herself around to take the seat in front of Celeste and I, turning herself into our view.

"So, it's eleven-thirty now," she said, looking at her watch. "I reckon we walk to the Louvre – should take about thirty minutes – eat, then see some art."

"Eat near there?" Celeste raised an eyebrow. "No way. That's how you get caught in tourist traps."

"Is this a tourist trap?" Chad asked, scoffing his desert.

"Everything you are attracted to is a tourist trap, yes." Celeste nodded, and Chad deflated. "Let me lead this one Natalie. I promise we'll get to the Louvre by at least one o'clock."

Natalie analysed her watch, considering, then looked up to the sky above our heads. "It sounds like a good idea to trust the French person here," She admitted. "Lead the way."

***

The Louvre was expansive. Each corridor and room of the palace was filled with the most expensive finery known to a man who valued oil and water spread upon a canvas. Such *classic* pieces, hundreds depicting political scenes and figures I wasn't educated enough to know, and of course, the Mona Lisa.

123

We had passed the crowds surrounding the painting, restraining Chad from taking a prohibited photo, to find ourselves lost in the rest of the museum. Each piece was met with quiet contemplation. For some artworks, the world built by the artist was obvious and intentional – a scene of individual characters, smattered across a canvas to write a story standing still in time. Other works, however, were impossible to see with any critical depth. I had seen my first depiction of a cherub urinating on a naked breast when I decided it was time for a break.

"I'm going to find a toilet," I declared to my friends. "I'll catch up."

"We shouldn't be too far," Celeste said. "We're going clockwise."

"Just use some quatra if you get lost. I'll find you." Natalie said before they continued to the next room. I turned back, powerwalking my way through the lumbering, dumb crowds to a bathroom I'd spotted earlier.

I slipped down a corridor, toilets in sight, and marched towards the signs. A maintenance door ahead of me opened, right into my path, forcing me to stumble. From the opening emerged a gunmetal, armoured hand. It grabbed my arm and pulled me in.

The door closed, and there was nothing but darkness – well, until my eyes adjusted, to reveal a cyan glow to everything.

"Hello Maiki," Hesslik's voice said to me, and I rushed to summon my *alis*, the form of Maiki rocking my body. I turned to the glow, to see his iconic eyes and face partition. His helmet was illuminated in my green glow.

"Hesslik, cheesus!" I gasped. "God damnit, we're never safe, are we?"

"Oh, you're safe," he smiled beneath the helmet. "Safe with me. Nobody knows I'm meeting with you. Boekidin is still trying to track you down."

"And you found us first?"

"It seems so," Hesslik shrugged.

"Look, I don't like this," I said, backing into a set of racks. I panicked as the stack shook – any storage in this place could have held priceless works. "Why do you want to talk to me again?" Once more, any wrong steps and we'd be in Hesslik's clutches. I still couldn't outmatch the Suneva. I had to play his game, and I shook in my metal boots.

"Checking progress," he smiled.

"After a week?" I stammered. "Not much has happened."

"You stayed a week in the house of a powerful witch," Hesslik cooed. "I doubt that *'nothing'* happened in the *Menas* household."

"You knew where we were and just let us stay unimpeded?" I huffed, brow furrowed.

"Well I'd only assumed that was your location. I didn't *know*, though," he grinned. "What did you learn?"

"Damnit," I cringed, and rubbed my glass eyes with my sharp fingers.

"You're bad at the information game, aren't you Maiki?"

"Don't condescend me," I growled. "Just get on with whatever you want and let me be."

"Well, I'd *really* like to know what you learned from your soul-searching eye-reading," Hesslik smiled. "I imagine you progressed spiritually in your time with the great reader Surawelle Menas."

"We all did," I nodded, staying tight lipped. Hesslik huffed and shook his head.

"What a spiritual journey it must have been," he said, "because you stopped your journey of pilgrimage to Kalamata to come here to Paris. Achieve Sunasera, did you?"

"Nowhere near it, Hesslik," I said, my brain buzzing to think of a good reason to be here. It couldn't be for the Legendaries or Argol, and any answer of pure tourism would have to have been a clear lie. I sweated.

"Some of our answers lie in this city," I said, finally. "Especially for Genive."

"Oh, I'm sure." He smirked, "She would have a *lot* to rediscover about herself in this city, what, with her father in the catacombs."

"Argol buried her dad in the catacombs?" I coughed.

"No, Argol lives in the catacombs," Hesslik clarified. "You still don't believe that Genive *isn't* Iva Argol, right?"

"Do you still think I'd protect her if I didn't think that?" I crossed my arms.

"Probably," Hesslik shrugged. "You do think that she's hot, after all…"

"Hey!"

"Lust is the one killer of logic," Hesslik said. "I think that there's obvious signs of her deception, anyway."

"Like what?" I quizzed, bearing into him.

"Did you know that there are many ways to read a soul beyond the eyes and their colours?" He asked. Hesslik was avoiding his own accusation, it made me grin in victory.

"Like what?" I pressed, smug.

"Ancient Witches devised charts of how to read the shape of weapons and armour. Apparently, there are personality traits attributable from everything to the distribution of colours to the angle of a weapon's hilt."

"What do these scriptures say about a lightning-shaped sword?" I quipped, but Hesslik passed them comment off.

"I don't know," he said lamely. "But they don't shine favourably on those who alter their armour, and your *Genive* is one of those Suneva. Her sword has obviously been worked on. There's alterations over the whole blade."

"Probably because she cracked it against a door hinge in Vestas' lab," I rebutted. "You can't attribute everything to maliciousness." I had never noticed anything strange about her weapon, and I'd had a good eternity when first meeting her to stare down its flaming barrel. Nothing came to me as *odd* about it at all. Not even now.

"I admire your naivety," Hesslik chuckled. "But stay careful. You'll appreciate my foresight."

"I'm sure," I grumbled. "Now if you've manipulated me enough, I'd like to leave."

"You don't like our chats?" Hesslik frowned.

"Omercronius, no," I grumbled. "If Zamelle caught me with you, she'd have my head cut off. I'm considering doing it to myself anyway."

"Ah, *Zamelle*," Hesslik smiled. "If only you'd not been so dismissive of your friendship with her and brought her to me on our first encounter. Then maybe I'd have been a friendly face to her too, and could track her progress. She's quite the witch, you know."

"You could easily follow her progress instead of mine," I teased, working my way towards the door. "But it's much easier to trap me – a Suneva you know to be unskilled. I bet that if you trapped her alone in a room with you, you'd walk out without armour."

Hesslik, the coward, shook his head. His calm, glassy eyes gazing into mine, a blue glow sparked in his fingers. Then the sparks joined, roared, and screamed with red light. I slammed myself into the door, fumbling for the knob. A red whip of plasma, so hot that it melted my metal skin, sagged limply from his hand, charring and bubbling the floor below. The tiles spit and hissed.

"Oh Maiki," Hesslik sighed. "Following you is due purely to my interest in your progress." He advanced on me, drawing a black line in the ground, marking the palace. My senses locked on to every atom of carbon and every tether of air around me. It would all be useless to that snake of death. "If this was about prowess, Maiki, you'd already be missing a limb."

His free hand lunged for my body. I shrieked, and leaped out of the way, crashing into the wall in a powerful blast. Hesslik's hand landed upon the door's knob, his plasma extinguishing. He pushed the door open as I recovered.

"Remember, Maiki. You're safe because I order it. As long as I'm interested in you, and you entertain our chats, no serious harm will come to you or your friends. Trust my word."

I couldn't do that. No part of me could trust Hesslik, but he had me cornered. I nodded.

"Good." Hesslik hummed, and gestured me to the opening. I slipped through it, removing my armour and stumbling out of sight.

Chapter 14
Sunesca in the Streets

The winter sun teased us the next day, throwing the city in the shade of a glowing blue sky, but allowing none of its warmth to seep through. We traversed the calm riverside, working our way towards the candle shop marked on the business card Eleni Floros had given us. Natalie navigated, once again asserting her prowess with a map. Chad followed keenly, his baseball cap worn backwards, doing nothing to deflect the morning sun. Celeste trailed silently, eyes glazing over the river and its rowing boats.

I wonder what it would be like to row on that river... I found my inner rower intruding. I would have asked her what was wrong, but her debacle was plainly obvious – if today went as expected, she would come face-to-face with the man

127

who murdered her father. The man who set her life's trajectory spiralling, until she wound back here. I frowned as I watched her. I couldn't be so brave.

"This is what I need," she told me this morning when I found her awake before light. "If I'm to follow the Code of Connections as outlined by Surawelle, and resolve the conflicts I have, then I must to talk to Argol. I can't back out of this. I can't be afraid."

But she was afraid, and that much was obvious.

We turned a corner, and in the near distance, the shopfront we sought was obvious. *'Bougies de la Riviére'* it read in cursive white letting upon a simple, black, hanging sign. I heard Celeste's sigh as it came into view.

"And there it is," Natalie smiled, as if to spite the French girl. "I can't believe your plan worked, James. We *actually* found Argol."

"Well, don't praise me yet," I warned. "I trust your Yamitsira, but I don't trust myself to have it right just yet."

"Oh, you've done fine." Chad smiled, patting my shoulder. "I don't like to attribute too much to destiny, but your urges lead to some good ideas. Now, Celeste, did you remember the candle?"

"Candle?" She asked, face turning pale. Natalie ground to a halt, spinning on her foot. Her eyes leaped from her head. Celeste grinned. "I've got both. One from LeGrand and the one from James' dad. You should see your face." She laughed, and strutted past the stunned witch. Natalie brushed herself from her shock, and jogged to catch up.

"By Amasos, you gave me a scare Celeste. Jesus."

"I'm surprised you didn't trust me to remember them," Celeste tutted, her joviality only thinly masking her nerves. "You should trust me, you know."

"I know," Natalie sighed, and relaxed, following in step behind. Then, she perked up, her hand darting to peace-sign poses. "There's a Suneva trail here," she said. "Somebody is using quatra."

"That's promising," Chad nodded. "Hopefully it's not bad for us."

"*Hopefully.*" Celeste coughed. "That could be useful, though."

"Not many Suneva in this city, I've noticed. Not compared to Greece," Natalie mentioned, eyes closed as she engaged with the field.

"Not really," Celeste hummed. "It's a little more taboo. It would be worse, even, if Argol hadn't carved a path for us. Not to praise him..." She trailed off, coming to the door of the candle shop. With a shaky hand, she pulled at the handle, and gestured us inside. I ducked in, and Natalie followed, only to be held up by Celeste.

"I think it's best if you waited outside," she said to Natalie, whose face fell to objection. "They'll think we're a threat if we march in with a Witch like yourself. Plus, if this turns out to be a trap, then at least you don't get caught and you can save us."

Natalie was charmed by the slew of confidence, and instead of arguing simply nodded. She moved aside to let Chad in, and then held the door for Celeste, closing it behind us.

"You think Natalie's a threat?" I asked Celeste as she grappled Chad for his backpack, reaching in and producing our two candles – our tickets of entry to see Argol.

"She leaks more quatra than she uses," Celeste said. "It's unusual. They'll think she's up to something. Better to play it safe." She turned, and waltzed towards the far end of the shop.

Only natural light, and that of hundreds of flames, lit the space before us. Rows and rows of coloured wax sat on shelves, some in jars, some standing naked, to be sniffed and admired. There were a few other patrons in the shop fondling the products. Celeste moved towards the back of the shop, to the antiquated wooden counter there and the young woman behind it. Chad and I moved our separate ways, trying to appear indiscrete as we browsed the products. I dipped my nose into a coconut scented candle, keeping Celeste in my line of sight.

She approached the counter casually, surprising the dozing cashier by placing the candles atop their benchtop. The young woman was shaken awake, before hearing Celeste's request. I could hear them exchanging in French, locking me out of the conversation. The exchange was enthusiastic, however, complete with hand waving, pointing, nods, and close inspections of the candles.

Soon, Celeste picked the candles from the bench and strolled over to Chad and I. She yanked at Chad's bag with an unfitting smile, placing the candles in, and dragged him towards me and the exit.

"Wrong shop," she said.

"What?" I asked. "How long ago did Surawelle get that card?"

"I don't know," Celeste shrugged. "The girl suggested another shop to try. Come on."

"That's disappointing. We were so close," I frowned, following Celeste to the door. She ushered me quickly out, and closed the door firmly.

"Where to, then?" Chad asked.

"This isn't the place?" Natalie butted in, but Celeste kept walking away from the shop face, back towards the river, leaving us to catch up. She stopped two stores down.

"They were leading us to a trap," she said. "The girl didn't believe our candles, although she acted as if she did. She told me to go to another shop further away from the river, which is the decoy. We haven't been let in, so we'll need to find another way."

"How do you know that?" Natalie asked, putting herself in Celeste's path. "That's a big assumption."

"I can tell that she was lying," Celeste asserted. "I can see enough of auras to sense her dishonesty."

"And what if we set off this trap?" Natalie asked. "Wouldn't that lead us to Argol anyway?"

"From my experience with traps, no…" Chad butted in, coming between the girls. "When you get caught by an enemy, usually any claim you had to see their leader is immediately thrown out. Then they decide what to do with you. With thread removal technology on the rise, I don't want to see what Argol's henchmen have access to."

"Exactly," Celeste smiled, leaning what she could of her arm on Chad's high shoulder.

"Okay, good point," Natalie nodded. "Then where do we go?"

"That depends, can you still sense that quatra trail?"

"Yes, it's still around," Natalie hummed, gripping into the quatra field. "Actually, I think it originated in the candle shop."

"Perfect," Celeste grinned. "And where does it go?"

"Towards the river."

"Good. Then we'll follow it," Celeste said. "Lead the way quickly. If the trap shop was in the other direction, then this has got to be the correct way to Argol."

"You're making lotsa number of assumptions there." Natalie hummed.

"I'm not sure we have much else to go off," Chad said. "We should trust our guts. Let's get moving."

Without having any sense for the danger, or the wavering paths that cut through the quatra field, I had no sensation of which route was correct, so I shrugged. Natalie keyed into my indifference.

"Okay," she said, "follow me." And she walked at a power pace, first towards the river, then cut a quick right-hand corner to lead us into an alley.

The alley looked to be a disused service way, marked by the large iron loading doors pressed into the building's walls and the platforms before them. The alley ended in a stone hut before the abutting building, whose wooden door was marked with a 'no entry' sign.

"That's where the trail leads, right?" Chad pointed to the door, chuckling. "Predictable. The old 'keep out' sign to conceal a lair. I've seen these before." He waltzed through the alley to the hut.

"That looks like a catacomb entrance," I pointed out, remembering the brochure for underground tours I'd read at the hostel. The pamphlet had made sure to mention in bold lettering that entering those tunnels without an experienced guide would mean death. I squirmed, hoping that Natalie wouldn't follow Chad, but she did.

"It is a catacomb entrance," Celeste confirmed, sighing.

"Talk about *underground* crime, right?" Chad huffed, and nobody laughed along. He deflated.

"This could be dangerous," I ummed, stopping near the alley mouth.

And, without warning, without even a sound, a green plume of flames roared past my cheek, just missing my face. I screamed, grappling with my connection to air and blasting off to the left. Once in the air, my body slowed, pulled back by some tether, I drifted helplessly on my arc.

"Sunesca!" Celeste yelled. Another flame roared past me, this time aimed at Natalie. Natalie was quick to evade, although just out of the flame's path her motion slowed to a freeze.

Sunesca, I pondered, levitating in my jump path. They were the *energy transformers* that Kuvalik had spoken about, the beings who defied their destiny to receive a thread, and stole real energy to power their soul connections. *Oh cheese.*

"Don't move. Don't give him power…" Celeste said, and would have said more, but her voice was drowned to nothing. Suddenly I gained speed back tumbling through the air and thudding against the stone floor. I flipped up to my feet and turned to the alley entrance, to be faced with a young boy whose hands dripped with flames. I had no idea what to do.

"What do we do?" I yelled.

"Armour!" Celeste screamed. "Then I don't know…"

Don't know? I squeaked to myself. Not knowing was *my* job, not Celeste's – the Suneva with the most experience in these things. I sweated. Movement wasn't allowed or else the Sunesca would use it for his flames, and striking at the boy felt *wrong*. It went against what Kuvalik told me, didn't it? That moral code he told me about – 'don't hurt regular people' was a part of that, right? Did a Sunesca count as regular? I didn't think he could redirect or take a quatra hit, but I had no idea.

An orange bolt flew towards the boy. His flames, idly brewing at his fingers, extinguished as he threw his arm into the path of Zamelle's quatra. He caught it in one hand, redirecting it, and throwing it back towards Genive. I didn't dare move to see the outcome, instead just staying still. If I didn't give the boy power, I couldn't lose us the battle…presumably.

On the street, a car was silently ground to a crawling pace, it's motor whirring and smoking, trying desperately to drive. The boy's palm erupted in a flame that ran from red to green, and he threw it towards us. I grappled into the air, and blasted a jet stream into the centre of the flame, diverting the licks of fire around my body.

Then they stopped, a brick of stone flying past the boy as he ducked from its path.

"Interesting," I heard Ferrad note. As the boy stood, the ground at his feet rumbled and shook. Then it flipped under him, throwing him onto his face before my feet. A brick of the earth landed on his calf, pinning the leg.

"Maiki, trap him!" Ferrad yelled.

"Trap him?" I squeaked. The boy was wriggling, writhing to stand.

"Quick, man!" Ferrad urged. I hesitated, watching the poor boy struggle. I bounced on my feet, then almost against my own will I threw myself on top of him. He yelped as my weight constricted him, fire dancing off his palms. My instinct was to grab and hold them, stopping him from using the flames. I didn't know how these powers worked, but holding him down ought to stop them, right?

"Good work," Ferrad said, jogging over. He pulled iron from the massive loading doors, and melding it in his hands, formed shackles. He drove them into the ground over the boy's wrists as I held them, and piled another pair over the boy's ankles. The boy yelled at us in French, and I pounced off his body, my heart sending me into panic

"Leave him like this?" I gawked.

"It looks bad, and it is, but he'll capture us," Genive said, coming over. "We've got to leave him to get away."

"Somebody will help him," Ferrad said, dropping the armour to become Chad. "Quick, before anybody sees." And he ran for the forbidden door. Conflicted, I backed away from the boy, dropping my armour, to see Celeste also running for the catacomb entrance. Natalie grabbed my arm from the other side.

"It feels bad, but we have to go," she urged, and she tugged me along. I ran with her, through the door held by Chad and into the catacombs.

Chad raised the earth behind us, sealing the entrance.

Chapter 15
Maze of Darkness

The entrance to the underground catacombs was thrown into pitch darkness. Somebody fumbled with the zipper of Chad's bag, and a light turned on. Celeste held a torch in her hand.

"Did you know that would work?" Natalie asked Chad.

"No idea," he admitted. "I've never had to face a Sunesca. I'm not sure why he didn't steal my attack's energy."

"Argols haven't used Sunesca on you before?" I asked Chad, but he shook his head.

"I'm surprised that they would use one. From what I know, Argol has particularly conservative views on being a Suneva. He'd think Sunesca are thieves and manipulators…"

"So, was that an Argol attack then?" I asked.

"Oh, definitely," Celeste said. "We chose the right path, and they tried to stop us by sending an attacker we couldn't sense. It's smart."

"Well, whatever it was, Chad saved the day," Natalie smiled. Chad blushed red, and laid a hand on her shoulder.

"Now it's time to do your thing. Let's follow that trail."

Natalie nodded, and held her hands to her side, sensing the quatra's direction.

The corridor we were in was thin and low – barely the height of Chad standing. The sandy-coloured stone walls were cemented together by cobwebs, creepiness, and a loving coat of spray-paint. The darkness was thick – the torch barely cut through mystery of the tunnel.

"Well, there's only one way." I pointed out, as Natalie seemed to have trouble regaining her steps. "Let's walk a bit and see if you find it down there."

"Hold on James, I'll get it," She protested, thrusting her posed hands in the field. "It's just hazy in here. Maybe it's the pressure? I'd want to find the trail before just walking so we know we're in the right place," she grumbled, then opened her eyes. "But you're right, there's only one way to go. Maybe the field is easier to read further on."

"Let's hope," Chad nodded. Natalie sighed, and walked ahead, into the dark corridor. Walking a few steps behind them, a weight of dread build upon me. There was pressure growing – Natalie was right to suggest it before – and it wasn't from the air. I knew that. I suddenly felt as if we were going to become hopelessly lost.

"Wait," I called, and everybody stopped. "We should leave markers, so we don't get lost." I tore carbon from the air around, causing the corridor to alight with millions of micro-flashes. I formed it into a crude, unshaped stone of diamond. I threw the first to the floor.

"Diamonds?" Celeste asked.

"Shine a light on it," I suggested, and Celeste threw the torch's light upon the stone. The gem burned with a brilliant fire against the dull sandstone.

"Oh…" Celeste hummed. "That's why people like diamonds, hey?"

"Yes," I explained. "They've got a property called brilliance. I'll leave a trail of them."

"Better hope nobody comes to vandalise the place whilst we're down here," Chad said, pointing to the rampant graffiti. "That's a good prize for a vandal."

"Then I make the stones, and you imbed them in the floor," I suggested to Chad, and he shrugged.

"I like that idea," he said, and I handed him a stack of diamonds. He let one drop to the floor, and stomped it into the earth, where it stuck. Celeste shone the torch on it to produce the fire effect.

"Okay, good," Natalie hummed. "Now, let's keep moving."

Natalie reassumed the lead, driving us further into the pressurised darkness. This corridor was long and narrow, the stones underfoot wobbling and creaking with dust. Soon the corridor dipped into a steep, broken staircase, littered on each side in vandal's scrawl. The footing was loose, and I could see a slip in this space being dangerous. Finally, the path came to a T intersection. Natalie, grappling with the trail of quatra, led us quickly left and then right. We followed on her heel.

Natalie gasped, spreading her arms to the walls. We piled into her, rocking her dangling toes over the edge of a vast shaft. Chad grappled Celeste and I around the waist, pulling us back and off the frightened Natalie. She regained her breath on the edge of abyss.

Before Natalie, the floor had fallen away, an endless column looming to darkness with a ladder on its opposite side.

"The trail goes down here," she puffed, then turned to Chad. "Can you sense how far down this goes?"

"Probably," Chad shrugged, coming to the opening. He grappled his meaty palms around i's ring. "A long, long way," he noted. "Hopefully we don't have to climb the whole thing."

Natalie hummed, stepping across the gap and grabbing onto the ladder. She began to descend. Chad followed once her hands were clear, and Celeste moved to go next.

As she put her weight on the ladder's first rung, it snapped, and she screamed, falling. Adrenaline kicked my body, my limbs searching for quatra, my thread was snapped into action. I launched myself at her, grappling her waist with one hand, and kicking into the void with a gust of wind. The blast flung us both backwards, and she landed on top of me in a heap of dust.

She coughed, her palms spitting flame, and rolled off me.

"All good?" I spluttered.

"Yes," she said, stepping back over to the hole. I grumbled as I stood. *A 'thank you' would have been nice...*

"I'm sorry," she apologised, gently testing the second rung. "This city has been hard for me. I don't mean to be rude."

And only Celeste could manage to make me feel guilty after I had saved her life. I sighed, following her through the gap, descending the long drop.

Natalie exited before the bottom of the endless shaft, bringing us into a semi-circular room some tens of floors below the surface. The air here was thick, I felt on my palms, but the atmosphere was thicker. Natalie's voice died at her throat, the light of our torches rang black. There were three exits here, all black and ominous.

"*Amasos*, the trail is hard to follow here," Natalie grumbled. "Something is muting the quatra field."

"Which way does it go?" I asked.

"Just...*quiet* a second. I'm trying to find it again," she hushed me, searching with her hands. "I swear it shouldn't be this hard..."

Chad dropped to the earth, pressing his hands to the stone. His fingers felt about. "There should be footprints, if there are Suneva..." He hummed to us, more to explain his strange actions than anything.

"That way!" Natalie exclaimed before he could find an answer, pointing to the rightmost exit. "Finally." And she led the way.

The tunnels here were darker than those above, and devoid of graffiti and unsettled dust. These halls had not been touched since their creation, walls cemented from brick and bones. Skulls periodically jutted from them, their shadows dancing across the torchlight. Although, *all* shadows seemed to dance against the spotlight's grain. I turned, frazzled, numerous times to see the silhouette of a man dart across the current hall's end. We were being watched, and the feeling only intensified.

Eyes, watching not our skin but our *souls*. We remained silent as we followed Natalie's path, bunched close against the unsettling darkness. I'd lost memory of our path now, with its many turns. It felt as if we hiked in circles, but

136

no new direction we traversed had the diamond studs which would indicate our travels.

Weight in the atmosphere built, pressing on our beings, and we turned a final corner to discover the source.

The small room we entered was a sea of hanging lights. Orbs, spread like stars across the Milky Way, smeared their luminescence across the drab sandstone of the catacomb walls. Like a pack of jellyfish in the deep sea, they hung and bobbed, thin streamers of light dancing from their bodies in the current.

It was the current of the quatra field.

Strangely, every ounce of dread and pressure lifted from my body at once. I could feel myself floating into the deep-sea abyss, swimming amongst the lights. There was peace here, lined with the radial despair.

"Orbs…" I uttered, unsure of what my sentence would be. "Are they…?"

"Souls," Natalie gulped. "Now wonder the field was so hard to read. These catacombs hold a sea of souls."

With each mention of the word *soul*, the sea vibrated – a wave of pulsing and dancing orbs which radiating through the room. The dead eyes and ears were centred on us, hanging on our actions. Their judgement was palpable.

"Not surprising, with all of the dead in the walls," Chad said, stepping past Natalie and I, into the room's perimeter. I walked with him, extending my hand out to a nearby orb. It glowed and danced under my touch, its tentacles wrapping to the next orb, passing the light along the daisychain of the dead. Stepping into the space, I could see a door on the other side. A way through.

"I think it's safe," I said to the others, as I embarked another step in.

"This is it for the trail," Natalie warned. "I can't sense anything through *this*."

"It's fine," I said, not looking back. "There's a door, all we have to do is…"

"*MAIKI*," a breathy voice caught my attention. I turned left to face it, to see the outline of an exit I hadn't yet noticed. I edged towards it, pushing aside the orbs and ducking between their streamers of light, to peek around the portal's corner. I saw now a short hallway, whose bricks dissolved into the vast expanse of space. In the vacuum, appearing both infinitely far away and just at arm's reach, was a halo of light – the eclipse of two moons.

137

"Uh, guys," I called out, and realised that everything had become quiet. I turned around to see that there was nobody else left in the room, it was just me and the blue orbs. "*Guys?!*" I called more desperately.

"*Maiki?*" The voice summoned me again. I turned back to face the mirage. Clearly, I was in a vision, but everything felt so much more *real*, and that voice was so familiar.

"Omercronius?" I called to the anomaly, but it remained mute as I creeped towards it. "Omercronius?" I asked again and stood on the horizon of stone and space. Beyond my toes lay the vast, empty void of the universe. The eclipse before me, now clearly a living corona rather than two separate bodies, looked as if I could reach out and touch it. It was in the room with me.

"Change is coming, Maiki," the halo whispered to me.

"I know," I replied, "that's what you mean."

A piece of stone cracked under me. I lost my footing on the edge of the world, and scrambled for earth, but fell into the starry abyss. The catacombs behind me crumbled and collapsed – the corridor cracking, shrieking and finally compressing into a singularity, disappearing. All that was here now were the two moons, myself, and the millions of stellar onlookers.

"Who are you?" The halo asked me.

"Who am I?" I hummed, confused. "You just called me Maiki. You know who I am." And then it sat silent, it's ring of light buzzing, shifting.

"I know Maiki, but who are *you?*" It asked.

"*I* am Maiki," I repeated. "Maiki is my soul...I think."

"Maiki is a name given to you. You are not who I expected to hold it."

"You...what?" I frowned. I was swept by a strange isolation. This halo, the two moons I'd seen, had been a symbol I'd associated with my Suneva journey, the hint to my life as more than what I'd assumed it could ever be. It had been my calling, the symbol for *me*. It had called *me* from the void. But it didn't know me? Its presence in my life was accidental?

"Who are you?" It asked again, and I huffed. I had only one answer for it.

"I am James Grey," I said, and the being considered my answer. Space hung dense between us.

"It was not John Grey's son who I chose," the halo said. "Who could oppose destiny?"

138

And then I was falling. My stomach hit my ribs, my arms flew upwards, my body fell. I flailed, the corona whispering into the night sky, distant. Specs of stars plastered over the dome of the world. I landed on my back, splashing into a cool, black sea in the dead of night. I sank under the churning, spitting water, rolled by the coursing waves. I regained myself and forced my mouth to the surface, breathing in the wake of a large, crashing wave. I propelled myself to its peak, riding over the top of it to see a dark beach. On it stood my father.

"Dad!" I called, and he turned to me, his jaw dropping.

"James?" He bleated. "How did you...?" And he paused, saying no more. I hit something solid in the water, and I grappled it, holding as the waves tried to pull me off.

"Dad, am I strong like you?" I shouted. It was the first question that I had, even if I never knew it. "How can I live up to your name?"

"James, that's..." he went to answer, but the earth rumbled. The man's body had turned to a brick, floating above the sand.

"What...?" I stammered. All around, it began to rain rocks. Bricks fell from the sky, crashing into the water, hitting the surface and smashing to dust in a roar of shrapnel. Hundreds of impacts rang around, dust flying into my face, forcing me to squint my eyes. As I did, the world was sucked from its hold on reality, like paint bleeding into a drain. The whole scene peeled off the plane of existence, oozing into a singularity behind my head, revealing a dry, rotten skull jutting from a wall which was my handhold.

I shrieked, pushing myself off the skull. It rolled from the neck, falling past my feet. *Way* past. I watched it fall, to see it smash on the floor far below, making one ting abundantly clear.

I was levitating.

The realisation seemed to make the situation impossible, and I fell quickly. I drew my staff, blasting air below my feet to catch my fall. The ground was a mess of cracked bricks, dust, and the broken skull. My mind jumped to a strange, but obvious conclusion.

"Chad must be in trouble."

I sprinted from the chamber, following my intuitions to where he must have been.

***

"I think it's safe," I called back softly.

Natalie felt ill at the sight. Before her sat a sea of vast colours, each orb radiating with tendrils of quatra energy. The atmosphere was thick, weighting on her palms with the collective power of hundreds of late personalities. The field was a wave which crashed gently against her hand, but with ill intentions.

The trail was gone, too. She had been able before to feel the snake of force between her index and middle fingers, but in this vast sea of unsettling energies, the single trail was lost – drowned by one thousand scents and sorrows.

"This is it for the trail," Natalie said. "I can't sense anything through *this*."

The colours were responsive, they could feel Natalie's power and ability. The orbs drifted towards her, tugging on her senses. She fell into a tunnel vision as the room's worth of energy began to converge on her palms. Her sight and hearing faded, replaced by the waning drone of intensity, an imposing rainbow smeared over her eyes and ears. Her heart now beat with the field. It owned her.

"*Help. Please help!*" Voices called to her from all around. They pressed on her soul, individual cries lost to the fast-growing crowd.

"What do you want?" Natalie squirmed, "I can't help you."

"*Please help!*" the ghoulish voices pleaded. "*Please help young witch…witch…witch…*" their voices all blended into a grey, growling moan.

"I can't help you! I don't want this…" she yelled back and stumbled in her blindness. The single word echoed in the chamber: "*witch, witch, witch…*"

She held her hands out to feel a wall, or even the field beyond this mess. Her foot caught something instead, and she tripped, falling to the floor.

The world turned black as she crashed into the soft ground. Warmth encapsulated her, and the depressing groans of late souls were drowned in the white noise of a rainy night under a tin roof. Natalie snuggled at the blankets around her. Peace had settled. She sighed in relief, relaxing.

A deep, grumbling snore pierced the quiet. Natalie opened her eyes. She was curled up in a bed, lit by the blue haze of midnight which crawled through a small window. She knew this bed – it was her mother's. Natalie flung the covers aside, jumping to her feet. Wasn't she just in the catacombs of France? What happened?

140

"Mum?" Her voice echoed against the peaceful room. To her left, down the hall, the snorer rumbled. *"Mum?"* Natalie furrowed her brow. Her mother didn't snore – not that she slept at her mother's house very often to know the fact. Natalie toed out of the bedroom door, sneaking into the hallway.

Another rumbling breath moaned towards her, and Natalie caught a static in her palms, a sensation that repelled her hair to stand on its end. The breath whined on the exhale, then broke into a high-pitched shriek which rattled Natalie's bones. The static roared in her palms, the Suneva cry billowing in the hallway.

"*Yamitse?*" Natalie gasped, and ran to the room. Natalie had spent her childhood mistaking the woman's sleep apnoea for possums fighting outside, but now knew the true source of their struggle – quatra nightmares. She burst through the closed door, letting it slam against the wall. In the bed, a body slept with covers pulled all the way over the head. It thrashed violently beneath the covers, growling between rushed breaths. The atmosphere in the room was prohibitively thick, stained with radiating quatra. Above the pillow swam an orb of water, sloshing steadily.

Another Suneva howl roared through the air – so powerful that it paralysed Natalie, forcing her to wait. Finally, she pounced, throwing the covers off the bed to shake the sleeper awake.

Orange light burst onto the ceiling, painting it in a brilliant fire glow. Lying in the bed, eyes open and throwing out orange energy, was the body of Natalie Athanas. It was she who commanded the water, who howled like the departed. Her limbs twitched and rocked.

Natalie shrieked, throwing her back up against the wall. She stared at her own hands – those on the body she was in. How was she both standing and in the bed? Maybe it didn't matter, she realised as she watched herself convulse, suffering a powerful quatra nightmare. Natalie didn't want to know what would happen if she didn't wake from it. She lunged to her sleeping body, slapping it across the face.

"Wake up!" She urged. Natalie grabbed the body by the shoulders, throttling wildly. "Come on, you're too young for this. Wake up!" She shook and slapped her sleeping body, but it growled its demon shriek in return. Natalie teared up as her attempts failed.

"Help! Help!" She cried into the night. She looked to the door, but was caught by her reflection in the mirror instead. Natalie Athanas was in bed having a fit, the woman staring back from the mirror was her mother, her face red and wet, but most of all *tired*.

There was a crash of metal striking earth. Dust came down in front of Natalie's eyes. She followed it to the ground where it landed, to find that the floor was made of stone. She peered back to her mother's reflection to see that she was in the catacombs, in a room with a full length, scrawled on mirror. Behind the markings, she saw her own wet face obscured by her dark, curly hair. She patted her cheeks to make sure that she was real, and then laughed nervously between deep, panicked breaths.

Her hysteria was interrupted by another crash of rocks. The mirror was kicked forward by the force of the vibrating catacombs, and fell. It shattered across the floor with a crash. Natalie jumped out of the way of the cascading glass.

"Chad must be in trouble," she thought to herself. She tried to calm down and analyse the energy around her. Natalie held her palms out and let the streamlines of quatra in the field go through the centres of her hands. Quatra moved with the blood around her body. It was complimentary to the circulation of life. She felt the energy pump through her. The field was still thick, but amazingly she could see through the madness to Chad. She followed his trail.

***

Celeste turned the gooseneck of the catacombs, coming into the hall of orbs behind Natalie. She awed at the sight, hundreds of souls hanging still like starlight across the glowing room. Celeste had met many ghosts before, but never in this *volume*. The field was thick with colour, bursting in its intensity.

She had never been formally taught to read the colours of auras, despite seeing them and feeling them with her palms. Yet, she knew intuitively what many colours meant by the way they *felt*. Her quatra, which circulated with the heat of her body, connected her soul to this field as it imposed itself upon her. Through the colours which streaked her palms she could feel despair, regret, anger, but above all, *evil*.

She shuddered, and I stepped past her and Natalie, wading into the tendrils of quatra which danced between the orbs. "I think it's safe," I said, but Celeste had to disagree.

She stepped in, chasing to grab my arm and pull me out, when the weight of sorrow and anger in the field pressed on her, crushing her. The tendrils of the dead were knocking at her skull, trying to scream into her thoughts. She fell to her knees, grappling her ears.

Celeste grappled at the quatra in her body, and used it to power her connection to her own soul. Just as a *quatran* was a connection to the surrounding world, a Suneva could have a strong connection to themselves, which they could fuel. Celeste, unlike most other Suneva, viewed the mind and soul as a single entity, occupying the same plane. Using her connection to herself, she strengthened her mental barriers, and the world began to drown out. Sensations were lost, first sound, then sight, then touch, until she was no longer sure where she lay.

Now she would be safe.

"Belle Dame?" A gravelly voice broke her *nothingness*. Her vision returned, as if the blackness of nothing was only the lid of her eye, to reveal a black fireplace set on a white wall, burning with purple flames.

Her mother's flames.

Celeste shot to her feet, swinging herself around. This was her childhood house. She stood on the white, fluffy rug at the centre of it all – a calculated array of black and white surfaces with hard edges – the amazing heat of her mother's flame warming her skin.

"Mama?" She called out, but the walls stole her voice, smouldering it out. "Mama!" She yelled, but her cries fell again to her feet, dead.

"Belle Dame," the unfamiliar voice spoke again, "you're back." And from the black wooden floor the cloud of dust rose. It spun about itself, black ribbons dancing in its belly, with eyes of fire and embers.

"Who are you?" Celeste stepped away, knocking into the family couch. She summoned her weapon, and ignited its flames. They sputtered into existence, red instead of blue.

"I should be familiar to you," the beast spoke, and with a twitch of its gut-ribbon, the cold flames were sucked from Celeste's sword and into its gut, its eyes glowing bright with sparks. Celeste's flame was extinguished.

"You're a demon!" She gasped. A demon – a dead Sunesca, a soul which could only live by gorging on the energy around it.

"We've all got demons, don't we?" It cooed.

"Where's my mother?" Celeste spat.

"Mother? Why, you *ran* from her, didn't you?" The demon accused. It paced about the room now, circling Celeste. Its black soot body settled on anything it touched, slowly staining the room black. "I suppose she probably died of grief."

"That's not true," Celeste growled. The beast only delighted in her anger, its ribbons dancing faster.

"You had better hope not. Because you avoided seeing her to come to Paris first. Where is your love?"

"It exists," Celeste insisted. "I know that I have to face up to her."

"And yet you've come to seek answers from your father first?" The Demon hummed. Celeste turned to face it.

"I need to know what happened to him," she said. "What happened to the man who loved me."

"*YOU KNOW WHAT HAPPENED, CELESTE*," the beast roared, its voice splitting into three discordant, dead singers. The house shook, crumbling. Brick dust fell from the ceiling, covering the white rug in sandstone soot. "You have taken a life! You have seen that aftermath twice! You know what happened to him."

"And I understand just how terrible it is, now," she nodded, "I am ready to forgive. I'm ready to be myself, *finally*."

"And this is your first step? Forgiveness instead of *revenge*?" The demon banged on the floor, its ember eyes roaring with flames. Celeste was shaken from her feet, and fell. She grappled at the rug as she crawled away from the monster.

"If you will not act, *I* will kill that evil man," the beast yelled, and its form erupted – dust and soot expelling radially in a puff of smoke. The beast left only its ribbons and red ember eyes, which caught a gust of wind and soared into Celeste's heart. They painted her black, smacking her into the floor and crashing through her body and soul.

"No!" Celeste yelled, and her voice finally reigned. She launched to her feet, and sprinted for her parents' room. By the doorway, a glowing gem called her – a firestone. Just like a lit *Ivaer* candle, a firestone contained the essence of a Suneva

144

and their will. It could radiate instructions. She palmed the stone, connecting to its message.

In here. Was all it said, and it was enough. Celeste kicked the door in before even bothering with the handle. The ground trembled with an almighty roar, and Celeste fell into her parent's bedroom. Dust rained from the roof, a brick soared past her face. Celeste backed herself against the nearest wall, to feel it was made of stone. Suddenly, she was back in the catacombs, and she had never been in her childhood house.

There was a deafening crack from above, forcing Celeste to stare above her head as the roof of this cavern shifted and split. Celeste screamed, and kicked a flame to life in her palm. The light showed her an exit, and she launched herself through it just as the pivotal brick broke. The cavern collapsed behind her, ejecting her from its portal in a cloud of dust and stone. She rolled across the rocks, flopping onto her back in a dark, clouded room. She coughed for breath.

"Oh my lord, I didn't mean to do that," she heard Chad gasp. His footsteps ran towards her.

***

Chad was indifferent to spirits. In his months of travelling the American wilderness with the old man Vasilli, he had encountered them in the thousands.

Many Native American doctors and healers were Suneva. They had an understanding of the energy of the body, and the energy of plants. Suneva like myself, Chad, Natalie, Celeste, and mostly all Suneva we'd met so far, had come from the Mediterranean. These Native American Suneva, in their isolation, had developed and embraced a different culture of Suneva understanding, so separate that their abilities cannot be defined by any European *quatran*. In fact, the idea of *quatran* is based in the Mediterranean experience of quatra, and only limits the possibilities of the energy's use.

From these tribal elders, who spoke a language not dissimilar from *Liktan*, he was able to garner a new respect for the afterlife soul. A dead man wasn't dead, but simply living on another plane of existence. The same plane where his armour and weapon lived – up there, somewhere in the *void*.

Chad walked into the Milky Way chamber after Natalie and I. He saw me venture off down a hallway, he saw Natalie stand still and wave her hands about, he saw Celeste fall to the floor. He sighed – the ghosts were projecting a strange atmosphere, but it could not affect him. Chad was too *grounded* for the ghosts to touch – too detached from their realm. They could not control him.

"I should find a safe space to move everybody, before they hurt themselves," he hummed to himself, brushing past the long tendrils of the field. Even accounting for the ghosts, this field was unnaturally thick. Chad could barely see the darkness past the little glowing lights, so he turned to his sense of earth, to find openings in the rock.

Chad focussed, closing his eyes. He had been taught to feel his soul through his connection to the earth, rather than feeling the connection to the earth through his soul's extension. The rock here contained some of the *fullness* of iron, but mainly his palms gave him a visualisation of all rock around him. Chad quickly located an adjacent opening, and strolled towards it.

There was something strange about this new room, he noted as he stepped into it. There were no walls – it was *infinite*. The entrance through which he had arrived no longer existed.

He opened his eyes, finally. There was no stardust smeared in this space. Rather, there was an unending expanse of blackness, broken by a hooded figure standing beneath a spotlight.

"Nerios damn it…" Chad growled. Everybody was relying on him to not fall to this madness. He was too far from the higher plane to have visions, wasn't he? He was too far to feel all but the biggest pulls of destiny, even.

Chad summoned his axe. The weapon, instead of materialising in his palm, flew from a location in front of him – darting at light speed across the abyssal room to land in his grasp. He truly was in another plane.

"You can't do this, field! I can't see fantasies…" Chad wound his axe and threw its blade into the earth. It cracked like regular stone. It *felt* like regular stone to his soul. He hadn't imagined the higher planes to feel so real.

"Hello Lion's Foot." The cowled figure said, removing their hood to reveal their distinctive yellow, pointed helmet with cyan eyes.

"Hesslik?" Chad quizzed. "How did you get here?"

"I'm here, am I?" Hesslik scrunched their face behind their sleek mask.

"Games…" Chad grumbled. It would be like a quatra field to play games. "What is this about?" He asked, before craning his head to the unending, black sky. "What am I supposed to learn from this? Give me the lesson, let me out."

"So cynical," Hesslik tutted, stepping towards him. Where Hesslik walked, the spotlight followed.

"I don't suppose I get a light, do I?" Chad asked the sky. He was momentarily blinded, as a beam of divine light extended from the heavens into his face. He too, now, was illuminated. "Thanks," he chuffed.

"I've got a mission for you, Lion's Foot," Hesslik sauntered closer. "It's dangerous, though."

"You've got a mission for me?" Chad huffed. He couldn't help but smirk as he shook his head. "You try to kill me, you abandon me, you order my thread removed, and now you come crawling back for a mission? Who do you think you are?"

"And that's precisely why you need to take my mission," Hesslik smirked, leaning closer. The light glinted on his yellow helmet. "I need you to ask yourself *why* I did what I did."

Chad paused, furrowing his brow. What kind of an assignment was that? Chad *knew* why Hesslik had abandoned him, didn't he? Hesslik knew that Chad had learned too much about his plans and secret operations, he was dangerous to the Empire as a possible defector. But then, Chad had only *assumed* that, really. Hesslik had left him with a mission even when abandoning him, one which he had convinced his new friends to join, even. *Find the Legendaries.* Hesslik shook his head at Chad's consideration.

"Even when you gave me all of your loyalty and heart – and when it seemed I'd done similar for you, I left you for dead, multiple times. Why did I do it?"

"Because I was dangerous, I knew too much," Chad defied the apparition. Through his feet, distantly, he could feel the *real* earth, not this strange crust. He'd descend from this fantasy, he just had to root his soul in the *real*. "I know why you disposed of me."

"You're assuming that," Hesslik contorted, and finally stepped back to let a breath's space hang between them. "You never asked, you just accepted."

147

"Healthier, I think," Chad gruffed. "Why linger on people doing bad things to you? Just be happy and live on…"

"Even when it happens multiple times?" Hesslik hummed.

"What are you on about?" Chad asked. Hesslik reached for their own helmet, and hands wrapped about it, pulled it from their neck. From underneath, long, blonde hair fell. The woman revealed was Chad's childhood crush and tormentor, Stacy.

"If this is real…" Chad choked to himself.

"What about when you devoted your loyalty to me, and I turned into your bully?" She asked.

"You turned into a nasty teenager. You got obsessed with yourself. It happens."

"You're assuming!" Stacy yelled.

"I'm allowed to," Chad defied. Stacy then reached for her chin, nails grappling under the skin. She pulled it back, tearing her face off like a wet wrap. Chad recoiled, "sweet *Jesus*." He gagged, too entranced to look away as his own mother's face grew from under the mask of Stacy.

"And what do you say to me, the woman who should have loved you? You loved me."

"You were an actual narcissist," Chad rolled his eyes. The figure reached for their chin again, and Chad did the honours by lunging in and pulling up the mask for them. Now the old man Vasilli sat in Hesslik's cowled armour.

"Vasilli?" Chad quizzed. "You didn't abandon me."

"I handed you over to Hesslik when I knew he was evil."

"No…no you didn't," Chad hummed. "You were showing me a community with a leader you trusted. Not even Hesslik knew he was evil at that point."

"Why do you keep assuming?" Vasilli insisted. "When will you turn to *ask?*"

"Alright…" Chad threw his hands in the air, and he turned to the sky once more. "I thought visions were meant to be insightful. Why show me *this* show reel."

When he looked back, there was a new face in Hesslik's armour. It was his own, from several years ago. His chubby cheeks were red with shyness. His eyes

148

were wet under long, black hair. "If you don't ask, you'll never know why everybody left you behind." The boy sobbed. Chad could only shake his head to the pathetic sight.

"That's it," Chad said, digging his axe into the earth. He could feel it down there – his soul, the *earth*. "I'm out."

"If you never ask you'll never grow!" The boy insisted. Chad felt the ground at his fingers now, too. He urged it towards him.

"I grew plenty-fine, thanks for asking."

"You'll keep giving your love to people who'll leave you behind?" The boy whined.

"Yes, because the world needs more love and kindness. I'm being the change I want to see."

"Then you'll never learn why you drive people away!"

"I don't," Chad insisted. He was grappling the ground now. It was *right there*. He was on it. How did he return to it? "People use me because I'm open and trusting. That openness naturally attracts malicious people."

"How can you be so wise yet so *stubborn?*" The boy growled, "why did I become an asshole?"

Chad laughed. "Kid, everybody else is an asshole. You're a little self-absorbed, but you're a good one."

Finally, Chad had it. This vision was a painting over the real chamber, and he knew it. This world was no longer infinite, and he just needed to crack this illusion – show it that it was fake. There was a wall by his younger self's head. Chad raised his axe.

"See-ya later, kid." He smiled, and wound his swing. It landed through young-Chad's face, colliding with a real wall and spitting rock and dust across the illusion. The colour bled from the area, but the world did not budge.

"You can't do this!" The kid urged. "You need to ask…"

"Come on…" Chad ignored the false apparition. He swung harder this time, ramming the axe edge right into the stone. It crunched into the wall, and the crack it made exploded across the whole room's length. Suddenly, the whole vision was sucked into the rift, screaming out of existence. The catacomb was revealed.

And it was rumbling. In Chad's soul, he felt that the next room's ceiling was collapsing.

149

"*Oh no…*" He cringed, and ran towards the portal to the adjacent room. He could save it. As he neared, a rain of bricks hailed down with a final rumble and a cloud of dust burst through the doorway. With it came Celeste, who bounced across the ground.

"Oh my lord, I did *not* mean to do that." Chad apologised, running to her side.

Chapter 16
Secrets Underground

I ran into the room, skidding to a stop over the dust and rocks. Celeste and Natalie had beaten me to Chad's location, but it was Celeste who was being helped up. This room had four entryways, one to each wall, and the one near Celeste was blocked with debris.

"Hey, what happened in here?" I asked. "The place has been falling apart."

"I got caught in a vision," Chad said. "That doesn't usually happen. I took a dramatic solution…"

"Right," Natalie frowned, "well at least everybody is okay. Celeste, are you fine?"

"Oui, I escaped," she said, dusting herself off. Her arm was grazed. "That room almost fell on me."

"Here, let me get that," Natalie said, slinging around her bottle of water. She charmed its water over to Celeste's arm and held it there to wash the wound. "This dust looks nasty…"

"So, what now?" I asked the group. "You don't have that trail, do you Natalie?"

"Not anymore," she admitted. "Field is too dense here. I might be able to find it somewhere else, but we have to pick the right direction from here first."

"That seems hard," Chad admitted. He got down to a knee, rubbing his palm on the stones. "I can feel most of the passages from here, but none look more complete than the others. This place is a labyrinth."

Natalie finished up on Celeste's arm, and we hummed in unison. I didn't feel very useful here, although I did my best to connect to the air around and sense the fullness of carbon. I couldn't draw a conclusion even as large as Chad's. I just wasn't powerful enough to sense the air beyond the next room over.

"There is a strange signal in this room, thoughm" Natalie said, eyes closed. "It's coming from there." She pointed to a far wall. Celeste shined her light, and something in the rocks glinted back.

"One of my diamonds?" I asked, but I had felt no such rock.

"No, but it's what *I* was hoping for," Celeste shook herself off, strolling towards the anomaly. "In that quatra-trip, I found a heat-stone in a wall. I was hoping there would be real ones around."

"Heat stone?" Natalie quizzed.

"Ivaer use a more…*country* style of witchcraft," Celeste said, pushing her palm to the gem. "You can infuse a heat-stone with a message. It's kind of like leaving a signature in a candle and burning it to extract it, except you don't need to burn the rock. You just need to read its heat."

"That's what the candles are for?" Natalie quizzed.

"Yes, I mentioned that, didn't I?" Celeste hummed, growing quiet. "Candles will tell the doorman who sent us — they're infused with the sender's quatra scent…" She closed her eyes as she massaged the rock. We stood by awkwardly, Natalie frowning.

"Argol left this one," Celeste said. "It tells the direction. We should take that door, back into the spirit-room, then right. From there, there'll be another stone."

"If it's written by Argol, it could be a trap," Natalie warned. "How do you know it's not dangerous?"

"This isn't a trap," Celeste said, "with a stone this hard to read, he'd only be trapping his own men."

"Are you certain?" Natalie insisted.

"Natalie, you're going to have to trust me," Celeste said. "I know the way."

"Okay," Natalie nodded, smiling, "then lead."

Celeste drove us towards the room of lights, the eminence of the field hitting us again. A hand grabbed mine, and I turned to see that it was Natalie. She gestured me towards the hand of Celeste, and I grabbed it to form a line. Chad holding Natalie's other hand, we walked together through the oppressive field, saving each other from its insanity.

151

Once past the sea of souls, Celeste read the next stone, and lead us further into the maze of darkness.

Behind us, shadows continued to dance, well beyond the field. There were souls about each passed corner glaring, shifting, *waiting*. Nobody else seemed to turn to them, or notice them. I had to assume that my friends were braver than me, and just weren't paying the spirits any attention.

Soon, Natalie found multiple quatra sources in her palms, and we followed her and Celeste's joint direction down another set of long hallways. Midway down a narrow pass, we came to a haunting sight. A skeleton, clothes still attached, a man lying where he died.

"Far out," I cringed, "that's terrible."

"Did well to get all the way down here," Chad noted, "not that I think he was trying to…"

A shriek echoed down the hallway. Its cry resonated with the structure, bending the walls and floor. The skeleton rattled. Our heads craned around to face the source.

Behind us, the end of the hallway was cast in a dark shadow, one inilluminable by our torch. It was in the silhouette of a massive, robed figure. It shrieked its harrowing moan again, and its eyes squinted, focussing in on us. Chad transcended his shock to raise his hands in surrender. He backed towards us.

"If we lose our threads down here, we'll be dead," Celeste whispered to the group. "We might be too deep underground to reconnect. No quatra means no pathways."

The spirit growled, and I gulped. We still had my diamonds, and the firestones in the wall, but they'd be much harder to find without *quatran*.

"Woah, we mean no trouble," Chad called to the ghost. Between he and I was the skeleton, and he obliviously stepped towards it.

"Dude!" I floundered.

"Don't worry, I got…"

There was a crunch under his foot. "Oh.." He deflated, the blood draining from his face. He lifted his foot to eye the crushed skull under it, then turned back to the apparition with a guilty laugh.

"Oh, was that yours…was it?" He asked.

The ghost shrieked an unholy cry. It charged – its form clinging to the walls, roof, and floor, running like a dark halo. It shrieked, we shrieked, and we tried to run. I fell over on a loose stone, Celeste fell over me, and Chad fell onto us. The thing raced on, and we were helpless.

The hall was illuminated by orange light. A singular bolt of quatra, sent from one of Natalie's twin swords, soared down the catacomb way. It collided with the beast right between its eyes, just as its tendrils of darkness wrapped at our feet. The ghost barely cried out, as the bolt's rings bulged on its apparition and converged on themselves. The soul of the thing was sucked into the singularity, which twinkled from existence with a pang. The shadow was left as black dust, which settled down onto us from the ceiling.

I melted into the ground, laughing in my nervous relief. Chad wrenched his jelly body from the ground, and pulled Celeste off me from behind him. He clasped at the wall to keep himself up. Peering back to Natalie, I could see he drawn face. Her sword tips drooped to the ground.

"Good aim, Natalie," he said. "You hit it right in the thread. You saved us."

"I'm sure I did," she sighed, nodding, "although it wasn't what I was aiming to do." She turned, dragging the blade tips across the stones. "Come on, let's keep moving."

"Hold on," Chad hummed, stepping towards her. Natalie dissolved her swords, walking off. "What's wrong?"

"I wasn't trying to *terminate* a soul," Natalie grumbled. "I don't have the *right* to decide who lives and dies…" She mumbled, then stared off down the corridor with blank eyes. "I have a feeling this will hit me harder when the adrenaline wears off. Let's keep moving." And she strode off. Chad lunged after her, grabbing her shoulders and swinging her about. Her face was blank.

"You know, Natalie, ghosts don't pass until they've fulfilled their last destiny. That's the reason they're trapped as ghosts in the first place."

"Is that so?" She asked, almost dismissive.

"They don't *get* to die until they fulfil their role."

"*Get* to die?" She quizzed.

"It can be *very* difficult for a dead soul, drifting between here and the void, the figure out what do to."

153

"I imagine it would be."

"Especially *down here*. We're probably the first light this ghost has seen."

"I imagine so."

"You *saved* this ghost," Chad urged, "he'd be doing this forever if you didn't free him from the torture of an eternal task."

"I did?" Her face turned, suddenly. Chad's words caught her subconscious off guard. The blue returned to her eyes.

"I hunted spirits for Indigenous tribes back in Ohio for months. Always got thanks for the job. Spirits need release."

"Okay," Natalie nodded, then turned her chin up to Chad. The two of them were intimately close, now, "thanks."

"Now let's keep moving," he mimicked her tone, and gestured her ahead.

***

It was not long until we came up to the Argol stronghold. Natalie and Celeste's careful reading of stones and quatra pathlines led us to a solid mahogany door with a giant brass knocker, set into the stones of the catacombs.

"Well, here we are," Chad remarked. "Nice work everybody."

I turned to Celeste, whose face had flushed white at the sight of the door. I could see her hands shaking in her pockets. "You know," I said to her, "you don't have to go inside. It might even be stupid for you to see Argol..."

"No, James, it's fine," she interrupted, "these are my demons to face. Plus, I'm the only one who can use the candles to get us in." She smiled, and grappled with Chad to get into the group's backpack. She produced from it two candles — one given to us from LeGrand, and the one which my dad had been given.

"Bang on the door," Celeste instructed me, and I obliged. The knocker was thick and heavy, and its ring echoed in the chamber. By the third strike, the door was being pulled open from under me, and I stumbled to stay on my feet.

A bulky, mechanical Suneva held the door. They stood taller than the doorway, with an untelling expression worn below their helmet's single-slit visor. In their free hand they held a mace — their Suneva *shath*.

"And who are you?" The doorman grumbled in Liktan. Celeste pushed a candle into my hand, and lit both it and her own with her blue flame. She then held them both to the guard for him to inspect.

"We were sent by LeGrand of Melbourne, and told this address by Surawelle, the Great Reader." Celeste said. The guard hummed, grabbing both candles from her. With a posed palm he analysed the flame, and with careful eyes he scrutinised the glasswork.

"One of these isn't for you," he said. "And the other…well…if the first one isn't yours, I doubt the second is. You know, you could have just made an appointment to see Argol. This isn't some secret society."

"It's not?" I quizzed. This whole operation could have been so much easier! My annoyance was written on my face, and the guard chuckled.

"Who did you have to coerce to get these, anyway?" The guard returned to a scowl, handing Celeste back one of the candles. "Who are you?"

"My name…" She carefully lit the flame with a click of her finger. "…is Celeste Leroux. I believe I have an eternal appointment."

Leroux? I quizzed. That sounded familiar, but Celeste's last name was *Bouvé,* wasn't it?

"You expect me to believe that?" The guard asked.

Celeste smirked, "hold this." She instructed, pushing the candle back on the man. He frowned at being bossed about, but hadn't time to respond before there was another candle in his hand.

Celeste held cupped her hands in front of her, and took a deep breath.

A red flame sparked into life in her palm. Just like she'd done for LeGrand's guard, she transitioned the flame all the way from red through to blue. She held it with a smug grin, but the guard rolled his eyes. "You're not fooling me. Sanavaer gets a purple flame."

Celeste narrowed her eyes, and took a breath so deep that I felt the wind of it in my palms. On her exhale her body slumped, the flame spittled, growing, *growling* with blue might. The hallway around Celeste grew hot, and I was sweating under my shirt. Water dripped from her brow, her face flushed red, and her breathing grew militaristic. I could see the guard losing patience, and Celeste looked like she was on the edge of blowing up. Cautiously, I extended a hand out to her shoulder to turn her around. We could try another way in. We could try a different guard, even.

My hand burned as it touched her shirt. "Ah!" I yelped, pulling it back from her burning skin. Celeste stiffened to my surprise, thrown off her cool. The boiling flame crashed down to a red crackle in her palm.

My face fell. I'd just ruined everything. I peered to the guard with puppy dog eyes, whose mace swung in his hand. "Oh no," I laughed. The guard however had stiffened in his own shock. He stared at me with the same awe.

"She was *that* hot?" He stuttered.

Our shared gaze was suddenly broken by a roaring light. Celeste grinned quietly as a red flame spewed from her palm all the way to the ceiling. The stones charred black as the hot beast spat from red through to green, white, blue, and finally to violet. The amazing heat of the plume threw everybody up against the nearest wall, grappling to the cold.

"By *Veritas*," the guard mumbled, "I don't believe it. I…I'm sorry."

The flame retracted as the guard stumbled back into the hall. Celeste dusted her hands.

"Our appointment?" She demanded.

"Foretold in the candles. Of course it is." The guard nodded, catching himself on the walls. "Follow me."

Celeste led us behind, into a hallway depraved of modesty. Dark, oiled wood and white marble layered the surfaces, walls lined with old photos and prizes. I paused to examine a family photo. Both daughters were present, which made the photo at least seven years old. Argol and his wife were some symbol of beauty, though. I was allowed to see no more as Natalie pulled me away.

The guard palmed a buzzer at the halls end, and spoke reverently into it in a French tongue. A deep, full voice was quick to respond to him. The guard nodded to Celeste and spoke a sentence of French to her, too; handing back the two candles. Celeste straightened, her face painted with determination. Behind her eyes she was calculating, I could sense it. Many words would have to be said to the man who ruined your life. The gravity of this meeting now dawned on me, too, and I felt my stomach slip out of my body. The guard opened the door.

The revealed room was a high ceilinged, white marble masterpiece. The floors were thick, dark oak, and there was a stage at the back of the room, where a large desk sat. To the left and right of the room were tall white vases which housed bonsais and an array of candles. The back wall was a closed off, glass fireplace which held a wall of bright green flames. Hanging on a copper chain from the ceiling was a sleek, glass chandelier.

Argol stood from behind his desk as we walked in. He wasn't a man of stature, but had a strong jaw and a solid build; just like Dad – the last of the *old bulls*. His face was stoic, although the façade cracked upon seeing us. A tear came to his eye, which he tried subtly to wipe.

"Did we come at a bad time?" Natalie whispered to the guard.

"No, you've just made the man's life," the guard replied to her, and stepped aside.

I looked to Celeste. Her confident, battle-ready expression had melted to match Argol's. A pause ensued – Argol and Celeste eying each other with reverence and glassy eyes. Natalie, Chad and I stood confused.

Then Celeste and Argol both spoke at the same time, and paused. Their faces were twitching – writhing – with emotion. Celeste gestured to the man, and he spoke first.

"Celeste...?" Argol simply uttered her name. Her face was pained, trying desperately to hold all emotion in. Against strained lips, she nodded.

"*Papa...*" She gagged in her meagre, French voice.

"Oh...no..." Natalie caught on – dots immediately connecting in her mind. Her face flushed red, rage boiling like a sonic kettle. "I...I can't...*I can't!*" She growled, and threw the guard aside, swinging the door open.

I was mortified, unable to act.

"You *are* Iva Argol?" Chad asked – although he got little more than a nod in response as her father, Adam Leroux – Mr Argol himself, vaulted his desk to embrace his daughter.

"*Fuck.*" I uttered. Natalie's awesome footfalls rocked the hallway and the catacombs beyond. I was beyond understanding what to do, or how to feel in the moment. Natalie seemed set to explode, so I rushed foolishly after her.

"Wait, Nat!" I called. She came to the grand entrance, and with the force of her rage, tore the knob from the handle. I winced, the guard poked his head around behind me.

"Hey!" He shouted.

157

"Go *fuck* yourself!" Natalie yelled at him, her face red and her eyes alight with powerful scorn. She screamed into the catacombs. I raced outside to join her, Chad bustling with me.

I swung through the entrance, and grabbed Natalie by the shoulder. She dug at my hand with her claws and flung it aside.

"Get away!" She hissed. "*God.*"

"Hey, it'll be alright…" I tried to soothe her – although, I was unsure what a change like this would mean for our mission.

"Alright? *ALRIGHT?!*"She seethed, spit bubbling between her teeth. "I…I *can't…*" She bumbled, not even coming to terms with her emotions. "I can't believe she would do this do us!" She roared. Quatra poured from her thread – a vibrant orange so strong that even I could sense it.

"Is it that bad?" I asked. This was not the correct question to ask.

"James, did you pull your brain out?" She hissed. "I get it, you think she's hot…"

"*Hey!*"

"But my god, we all just got deceived! She's lied to us this whole god-damned time!" Natalie clenched her fists, a force so powerful that she threatened to break her own fingers. "I won't stand to be fooled like this, James! She goes on about how hard is was to trust us or anybody, back when she abandoned you to Vestas, and then pulls shit like *this?*"

"That was so long ago."

"Why are you defending her?" Natalie shrieked. "You just had your life uprooted. If it wasn't for her, you wouldn't have been flung on some far-off, fantasy fucking *goose chase* right into the face of danger! What of all the months of life-threatening worry about being captured by some goddamn lunatic with magical electric powers? What about being branded a *terrorist* in an international community? All for *this?*" She pleaded with my reasoning. "No, *fuck* this, and *fuck* her."

I was blown away by the magnitude and emotion of her argument. I backed away with hands in the air. Honestly, I couldn't tell her why I was defending Celeste – I guess I defaulted to standing up for the little guy. Even then, I hadn't had a moment to compute how this situation made me feel. Natalie must have been anticipating this exact turn of events for a long time.

Natalie summoned her blades and stabbed them far into the wall, cutting the stone and blasting it full of quatra. Chad pushed me aside, and grabbed the girl by the shoulders in his grasp. She was seething, her breath of hot fire burning his chest. Chad's face was calm, and his voice was calmer.

"We've all been burned, Natalie," he said, soothingly, "this is hard for us all, but we'll all work past it."

"Is it?" She tilted her head. "Last I checked, James is having a great time! And *you*? You didn't give up *shit* to be here."

I could see Chad stiffen in offence, but he didn't let it show to Natalie. "I gave up my reputation and life till that point to save you guys. I gave up a lot in trusting Celeste, too," he said, "I think we need to hear her out before we draw any conclusions."

"Hear her out?" Natalie scorned. Her eyes were crazier than a madman. "I can't believe you're both against me on this. Am I the only rational one here?"

"We're not against you," he said, and promptly stepped on my toe, forcing me to give a thumbs up. Natalie disregarded my gesture. "I just think you're letting yourself be consumed by emotions. Peace and calm is the only way to reach resolution."

"Oh, *buddy*," she mocked his accent. "I don't want peace and calm."

"What *do* you want?" He asked her.

"I want my god-damned life back!" She barked without hesitation. "I want to go to the moment where I met her, and hit her across the face for lying to me so *mercilessly*."

Chad sighed deeply. Natalie's hysteria raged on, like an endless blowtorch of hate.

"Do you?" I asked, drawing her gaze. "You say this has been awful – and *sure*, it's been tense – but look where you are."

"In a filthy plague cemetery," she quipped.

"No…well, yes… but halfway across the world. Without her, we'd probably have joined Hesslik. And *hello*, we were independently on Vestas' kill list; she *saved* us. Without her, we wouldn't even know about the impending end of the Suneva people – nobody would unless she led us to capture. Without her, you wouldn't have had to become who you are. Everything happens for a reason."

159

Everything happens for a reason. The saying I would have rejected just a year ago as an unwise man's nod to fatalism, a misread few instances of coincidence. This was, however, the catchphrase of destiny – a deep web of experience which guided us to this very moment. A set of compulsions which we held dearly.

"*Destiny,*" Chad said, catching my drift. "It all happens for a reason. We're a part of something great, here. With *her*. We know it's going to be hard, but we're all going to have to *trust* one another, here."

"Pah, *trust*," Natalie dismissed, her hysteria crumbling as emotions ran dry.

"Now, I'm going to ask you again – and answer honestly this time – what do you want from this?" Chad asked. Natalie silenced briefly, bar her strong, heavy breaths. She spent a while considering – calming herself.

"I want to know *why*. Why did she think *this* series of events was her *only* option?" She said, finally. "And I want a *damn* good apology for being deceived."

"Then I'm sure you'll have it," Chad said, patting her shoulder.

Argol emerged from around the doorway. He nudged me on the arm.

"Is everything alright out here, Maiki?" He asked me. I was astonished – he knew my name.

"Just a bit of shock, is all." I said to the man. My level of composition surprised even myself – I was talking to a man whom I believed to be powerfully evil, yet I did not falter. "Celeste told us she was *definitely* not your daughter for a long time, you see."

He nodded, clearly having been briefed by his crying girl.

"I think we should all come into my sitting room, and chat."

"I think that's wise," I spoke for the group. I followed him into the hallway. Chad led Natalie behind me.

***

"Why?" Natalie asked. It was the first thing she'd said to Celeste. The French girl had tried to cry on her shoulder – the force of her emotions, years of familial exile, bubbling through her eyes, but Natalie rightfully rejected her.

We sat in Argol's sitting room. Like Surawelle's, it was little more than a closet with cushions spread on the floor. We formed a circle in the small room, around a set of three golden candles – one of which we had given Argol just now, from Alexis LeGrand. The wicks of the two unfamiliar candles spluttered with Argol's green flames, painting the room a vibrant, flickering green. Our candle had been lit by Celeste. Her blue flames were hotter, but not nearly as bright and *warm* as her father's.

The room was soothing beyond all measure. There was a deep atmosphere of peace and belonging which purveyed all things within its walls. One would have to *try* to hold onto anger in here. I could see why Argol chose this spot to talk.

Celeste held my hand for comfort, and it made me feel giddy.

"Why did I run, or why did I lie?" Celeste asked. She sat opposite to Natalie in the circle. Her cheeks were still wet, and her eyes tired.

"Both," Natalie clarified. Her hysteric rage had long subsided – and in this room, was impossible to keep – but a cutting attitude had risen in its wake.

"I ran because my sister and I witnessed my father kill a man," she said, and the room immediately fell into unease – Argol's face guilty. "We were hiding under a table when he had an important guest over. He blasted a bolt of quatra straight through the man's heart."

"*Far out,*" I exclaimed.

"I didn't know what to do, or think. Amalie, my sister, said that we couldn't live with Dad anymore, and I agreed that we couldn't trust him. But then she wanted to tell the police, and I didn't. So, we separated too. It seems silly now, but we were only kids when it happened..."

"Okay," Natalie seemed to accept this. She turned to Adam Leroux. "Why did you kill the man? Is this something you do often?"

Adam stiffened against Natalie's tone – he was not used to being so bluntly addressed. He steeled himself, and gave an answer.

"The man killed Celeste's cousin, Thomas, whilst we were out getting ice cream, minding our own business."

"So, you invite him over and kill him," Natalie surmised, "and you've accepted this, Celeste? Hence you've come back." Her tone bit, but the words were neutral – *logical.*

"No, I hadn't accepted it until Dad explained it before," she said. She and her father been talking together in the time that Natalie was shrieking an unholy argument. "I get it now...but it's still traumatic. It's still *hard* to think about." Her eyes welled again. Natalie did her the grace of connecting to her tears to wash them away.

"The man was a policeman," Argol explained. "They don't care about Suneva here – nobody does. We're the enemy in their eyes, cultural invaders and heretics. The church looks to ostracise us, the government looks to stop our progress. It's why the Argols formed in the first place.

"Killing the man was brash, and I accept that now, but at the time I felt it was what I needed to do to protect the Suneva who sought my aid. It was a message to send to other corrupt bigots in the system."

"Why not take Hesslik's approach?" I asked. "I know you don't like the man – we don't either – but I like his message. *Treat others how you want to be treated. Act with ethics and morality.* Why didn't you make these the key points of your campaign?"

Argol scoffed – not condescendingly, simply a laugh from a man who'd seen too much. "It doesn't work, James," he told me. "It's idealistic to think that not posing a threat will earn you respect. Humans like to hate. Our brains are still tribal – focussed on in-groups and out-groups, family and the *enemy*. If the out-group is too weak, they get bullied. *We* are the out-group, and we need to appear strong. It's the only way we'll garner any respect in the world.

"And it's working. The fact that you made it halfway across the world without getting pulled up is a testament to what we've done here for years. We've been keeping Suneva safe from harassment.

"That said," he continued. "I don't condone the efforts of my father, Seros Argol, or his father before him. They took the job much more like a Sicilian mobster. For them, it was about money and blood. That never helps the people – and its hard to turn around years of bad public image."

"And for you it became about blood?" Chad asked, "I mean, if you had to kill to get the message across?"

"No, it was a brash mistake," Argol defended. "My father had just died, and I'd only just assumed leadership. It's hard to think you can fill those big footprints which you step into. You make stupid decisions."

Celeste nodded along, in agreement, a smile finally across her face. She squeezed my hand.

"That's all well and good," I said, "but the Argols I've witnessed *have* been violent and unruly. The first Suneva I ever saw were Argol men threatening to kill one of their own."

There were nods of ascent in the room. Natalie hummed, sharing my memory.

"Melbourne is notably corrupt, as far as Argol controlled cities go," Adam defended. "It's why I installed LeGrand to oversee it. We're having many issues with rogue Suneva adopting our name to get away with what they want, too. He will bring an end to it."

"Fair," I nodded. "You know, you're much fairer and friendlier than rumour would paint you."

"I'm trying hard to prove people wrong every day," he said solemnly. Behind his pained face were years of accusations.

"So, why didn't you come back?" Natalie asked Celeste, swinging the conversation back. "Why did you have to lie?"

Eyes shifted onto Celeste. She didn't hide from the stares. Rather she met them, gathering her composure.

"Once I realised I could come back, it was already too late," she said. "When I was young, it was my father who I feared. If he could kill a man, what did I *really* know about him? I feared what he might do if I came back. And if I came back, I'd have to grow up with my name. I'd have to take his role. I didn't want to be a murderer, if that's what it meant."

Celeste sniffled in the face of the memory, but steeled herself. "By the time I realised that he wouldn't harm me, I was already far from home, and without my sister. There was a bounty on my head too – and even though it was done from love and longing, it made my life frightening. I couldn't trust anybody. I kept hearing rumours, too, about my father's vengeful tenacity. Suddenly home was the worst place to go.

"Then, when trying to escape one attack, I killed with quatra. In that moment, I understood how devastating it felt. I thought then that I could never forgive a person for doing that willingly. For *planning* to do it. I could never come home and face a father who was that monster. I had to move on." Celeste sniffed, her face cold and wet. She squeezed my hand, and I squeezed back.

"So, I had to lie, Natalie. I didn't think I could come back here. I wasn't ready to face it, and I certainly didn't want to take this throne. Years on, and every day the guilt of leaving my mother in the cold ate at me, but I wasn't brave enough to accept who I was. I'm sorry you got dragged into this…" Celeste said, then stumbled. Locking eyes with the cold Natalie, her emotions bubbled all at once. "I tried so hard to make you hate me, to think joining me was a stupid idea, but you did it anyway! You and James are so loyal and trustworthy, it broke my heart every day to lie to such caring people, but I had to. I mean, I *felt* that I had to. I'm so sorry, please see that!"

The small room was once again consumed by a tense silence. The green flickering of the candles caused our shadows to dance up the high walls, to the ceiling. The little flames held so much comforting warmth.

We all waited on Natalie, eyes intent, ears listening. Her head was bowed, her eyes closed in contemplation.

"Okay," she said, finally.

"Okay?" Celeste asked, sniffling.

"Okay," Natalie said. "It's okay, I guess." She held her hand out, and Celeste took it, abandoning mine. "You've been through a lot. I hate that you lied, but maybe it's okay."

"Do you forgive me?" Celeste asked, sobbing.

"I don't know right now," Natalie hummed, "but I will. I'm sure."

Celeste's face gagged a tear, stretching into a smile. She squeezed Natalie's hand tightly.

"But," Natalie continued, "don't any of you *ever* pull shit like this again."

We all nodded, even Argol, who sat in silent reverence.

Suddenly Celeste dropped Natalie's hand, throwing her own posed palms into the air. Her eyes shot wide, her breaths rising in excitement. She chuffed a laugh of disbelief, chuckling giddy, "Oh my god…" She awed, her eyes buzzing about the room, following invisible spectres.

"Hey, are you okay?" Natalie asked, her hands also adopting the sign. Celeste did not respond. "*Celeste?*" She asked again. "The field is so thick around her…what's are you sensing?"

Adam rushed up to be beside his daughter, and at his touch she came to herself.

"Amalie is here," she coughed. "I know where my sister is!"

Chapter 17
Gravity of the Situation

"Your sister?" Chad quizzed. "But the second Argol daughter isn't Suneva…" He peered to Argol himself, who could hardly notice Chad past his own surprise and elation.

"Amalie is here?" He whispered. "What kind of a day is this?"

"What just happened to you, Celeste?" Natalie cut off all other questions, grabbing the girl's arm. "The field around you just condensed like nothing else. Did you achieve realisation?"

"Realisation?" Celeste laughed, her head bobbling on light shoulders. "No, not at all. But I feel so *connected*. Your Yamitsira was right, all I had to do was solve conflicts. That's where peace and connection lie…"

"Her Yamitsira?" Argol asked. "Surawelle sent you? She still has my card?"

"She gave it to us. She's not inclined to follow your offer," I said to the man, who had his first disappointment for the day, finally breaking a frown.

In the centre of the circle, the candles' flames burst into violet light. A purple flame jetted from each of Celeste's fingers, and with its light she sprung to her feet. "Forget having conversations, I've got to follow this compulsion before it goes away," she urged, kicking towards the door. "Who's coming?"

"Hold up!" I called, forcing myself up. "You can't leave without us." I offered a hand to Argol, but he declined.

"Then hurry up," Celeste sang, and threw herself out of the closet, into the grand lobby. Chad rushed to follow, dragging Natalie up behind him.

"You're not coming?" I asked Argol.

"I'll follow," he said. "Celeste is radiant – I'll be able to follow her trail. I think I need to call my wife first. This is getting a bit much to bear in one day."

"Then I'll make sure we bring Amalie back to you, if we find her."

Argol smiled, but shook his head. "I'll make it there with you, kid. Just watch," he smirked. "Now, go and catch them before they get away."

"Right." I nodded, and jetted out of the room.

I shot myself through the lobby, soaring past the guard and blazing down the hallway into the catacombs. I skidded to a halt in the dark hall, throwing my head each way to see a light. I spotted it to the left.

"Hey, wait up!" I called, and tore after my friends. They were jogging into the dark halls, following on Celeste's heel. I rounded a bend, and a second, finally finding them in the dusty blackness.

"You didn't want to wait for your dad?" I asked.

"He'll catch up," she said. "He's got four trails to follow. Let's move before I lose my sister."

Celeste jogged us through the labyrinth on an unending path. This far down, walls were made entirely of the dead, barricades of skulls and skeletons crushed under the weight of the earth.

We passed through an atrium, then turned a corner into a long hallway. Celeste's bright purple fire lit it up to the end, to reveal a cloak shaped, in-illuminable shadow. We paused in place, frozen, but Natalie stepped forward of the group. The tunnel's thick atmosphere seemed to part around her. Feet planted, she spoke.

"You want to talk to me?" Natalie asked the ghost. I hummed, hearing nothing of the request. I'd rather just avoid the dead after this insane day.

"And you need to talk to me," its golden voice echoed in the long hallway.

"Yes, I do," she said, "I need to ask you a question: Do you like your existence?"

"I'm not sure we have time for this…" Celeste whispered, but went ignored.

The ghost didn't take long to consider the question. It was clear that he had already thought about this before.

"There was first grief in death, and then pain, and then nothing. I had to run through the endless void to make it back here, only to find that everybody I loved is now dead. The Mother doesn't tell you what happens when your time is over – when it's all been said and done. I know I still had more to do with my life, but I can't see light anymore and I just can't influence the world in this state."

"You don't like being alive?"

166

"I'm only sad, lonely and frustrated. It's not worth the pain," it said. "but you're the first person to ask me about myself since death. I've been waiting for this moment, and I don't know why. Thank you, young witch. You've made me feel happy. That's something I haven't felt in a long time."

"Thank you," Natalie blushed. "You've made me happy too. I needed your words. I hope the Mother takes you on."

"She will." The ghost smiled, "I'm sure she will."

The black shadow's large smile lit up in yellow quatra. The light of the mass energy radiated from his mouth, consuming his body until he was a golden, glowing shadow. A bright, white light appeared from his orb – the kind of light people talk about in movies when they're dying; the divine light which harks the end. His yellow spirit was sucked into the orb like water into a drain. The bright light of the orb winked as the ghost fully disappeared into it, and then closed. His thread had disappeared. He had passed on.

"Now," Natalie grinned, spinning to us, "*that's* how you deal with a ghost."

"Damn, Natalie," Chad awed, "you just helped it find peace. That's incredible."

"It's what I should have done before," she said. "Now, Celeste, aren't we in a hurry."

"Yes...of course." The French girl was shaken from her amazement and fright, she dragged herself to the front of the pack. "Let's keep moving...come on." And she walked herself back into a jog.

From here, the catacombs quickly advanced into twisted, broken ruins. Cave-ins blocked our path, and those paths which Chad helped to clear were no longer flat to the ground. Floors became walls, which became rooves, as the tunnels began to twist and bend on themselves. We crawled through impossible spaces, leaping over chasms in the floor and hallways which now extended down into the earth. Coming to the end of a long climb, we found ourselves spat onto the roof of a large atrium. This chamber had turned completely upside down.

"Insane," Chad hollered at the sight, lit with Celeste's violet light. "How the hell did your sister get down here?"

"I don't know," Celeste hummed, "but she's close. I can feel her."

"I can too," Natalie nodded along. "There's a Suneva presence near here. A *strong* one."

As usual, I couldn't sense the presence, only the dust floating here. Mind wandering, I threw my hand into my pocket for a muesli bar I had there – you know, hard work is hungry work - and peeled the wrapper. I fumbled with it so catastrophically that the bar flew from its packaging. I flailed to catch the treat as it fell upwards, past my eyes.

Hold on a moment.

I watched it whiz towards the sky, before it bounced onto the ceiling, disturbing a great bed of dust held there.

The dust also fell back to the roof.

"Uh…guys…" I uttered, pointing to the magical act. Natalie hummed in her curiosity, following my finger's direction.

"What is it…*oh.*" Natalie gawked too, now. Soon all eyes had been diverted to the muesli bar on the dusty ceiling.

"Why is the roof so dusty?" Natalie asked, "How does a roof get dusty?"

"I think you're missing the key point here," I said, deadpan.

"Yeah, who's the Suneva of Muesli?" Chad joked, arms on his hips. Then his smile faded, and he fell serious, dropping to the floor.

"Did you hear that?" He asked us as he mushed his palms to the rocks.

"Hear what?" Celeste asked.

"Footsteps. Movement." His eyes darted around the room, and he swung to the entrance on our left. "Somebody is here. They're closing in. But *something* is not right about them…"

"Is it the Suneva of Muesli?" I asked. Next to me, Natalie's armour crawled over her body. Her twin swords fell into her hands.

"They've got more power to their trail than a Suneva of muesli," Zamelle hummed, hands gripping her weapons tight. Chad had now become Ferrad, and to my left Celeste adopted her armour also, to finally become the infamous *Iva Argol.* Where her plating had once been highlighted with blue, it now had midnight and purple marbling. The reds were bolder, and her sword, which roared into life in her grasp, had a hilt of grey and purple with sharper lines.

Hesslik was right about the sword. I hummed, and donned my own *alis*, Maiki. *Celeste did alter it.*

168

As we stood shoulder to shoulder, *shaths* drawn to the doorway, two red eyes appeared to break its blackness. They bounced down the adjacent, pitch dark space, their wearer coming to rest just in the shadows.

"Who are they?" I asked, but nobody could answer me. "Not who we're here for, then."

"I can't tell," Iva said. "I'm not sure."

"Are there any other Suneva?" I asked, and Ferrad spoke.

"I can't feel any other feet."

"Fine, then *we're* the threat here," I surmised, dropping my stance and stepping forward.

"*Maiki*, what are you doing?" Zamelle hissed. I frowned, and turned to her.

"Its four on one, we have the power here if anything goes down," I said, and swivelled back to meet the eyes. I stood between my friends and the dark entranceway, and I smiled beneath my helmet.

"Yassi," I called to the eyes. "Silo di Liktan?" I asked if they spoke the Suneva language. The eyes squinted, and a powerful Suneva hiss roared from the darkness. I heard the flick of a wrist behind the curtain of shadow, and the square edge of a long, *massive* weapon broke into the chamber, tip held high to the cieling. "Okay…" I squeaked.

"You might be wrong, Maiki," Zamelle urged. "Get back here."

I nodded, heart racing, and paced backwards towards the group. For each step of retreat, the eyes advanced, the long shaft of their pick-hammer weapon riding into the chamber's light. Finally, they stood on the precipice of light and dark.

They were standing on the ceiling.

"What?" I squeaked.

The Suneva was a woman of powerful form. Their armour gleamed bronze, silver and red in the faint torchlight. More noticeable was the zebra-stripe plating, which marked their chest and thighs.

They raised their axe to the sky – or our ground – and slammed it into their floor. They fell to a knee, dragging the hammer tip along the cold stones.

Natalie, not perplexed, and sensing the danger, lined up her twin swords and fired a bolt of quatra. The orange bullet whizzed towards its target.

169

Suddenly, I felt weightless. Nothing holding me to the floor, I started to drift up. The bolt of quatra, lined perfectly on target, fell away. It arced through the air, as if by magic, and curved off into a far wall.

"What?" It was Natalie's turn to utter, and she flailed to understand her bearings. Nobody had much time to comprehend what had happened though. The zebra-striped Suneva clawed at the floor with her free hand, and the room span. The ground was above me, not below me. Or, rather, I was upside down, hanging above the floor.

Then I was hanging no longer.

Thinking quick as we began to fall, I flicked my staff to life and threw all of the air in the room beneath us to soften the fall. I flipped in the air, landing on my bulky feet. Iva's flame extinguished, and the room was cast into the dim glow of Suneva eyes. I saw my friends fumble on my cloud of air, landing on arms and asses.

I adopted a stance, the only man left on their feet, and went to fire a bolt of quatra. The zebra-striped girl would not have that. She dug her fingertips across the old stonework, then rammed the hammer towards me. The sound of her nails alone was enough to make me collapse, but I also found that my legs were no longer strong enough to hold my weight anyway, and I barrelled into the ground. I was flattened there against the stone, as was everybody else. I tried to pry myself up, but I was held solidly to the floor with no room to move. It wasn't the feeling of something crushing you, rather, being *pulled* into the earth. I couldn't fight it.

Was this another Suneva of Magnetism?

Their hammer still yanking at the elastics of their soul connection, they raised a posed palm to Zamelle. Zamelle squirmed.

"Please don't!" I urged. "If we lose our threads down here, we're dead."

"Didn't stop her from firing at me," the zebra-striped Suneva spat. They spoke Liktan in a mutt accent. I couldn't pin it to any place. "Why are you following me?"

"We weren't." I said, and the force on my body doubled. I gasped under the crush. "We were trying to find her sister…" I gestured my head's fin to Celeste, by my side.

The Suneva's face scrunched beneath their helmet. They pointed to Iva. "Who are you?" They asked. "Too few Ivaer have the purple flame for you to be unknown. I can't afford to be followed by high-profile Suneva."

"Who am I?" Iva huffed. A purple light flickered into the room, a flame lit in her fist. "I am *Iva Argol*."

Iva's words held power – likely the first time she'd spoken of her identity so boldly. I could feel the heat of her flame across my whole body. It radiated with her new truth.

The Suneva before us dropped their armour, eyes wide and mouth agape. They were slender and tall, with a great discolouration, like a burn, running over their neck and up their face. They stood, and suddenly all was returned to normal. I gasped as the weight was released from my body. I wrenched to my knees, panting.

"Celeste!?" The girl before us spoke.

"Amalie?" Iva coughed. She retracted her armour and shot to her feet.

"Really?" Zamelle quizzed. "Your sister is the Legendary of Gravity?"

"*Gravity?*" I shrieked. Our mission had worked? My stupid plan – find Argol, and use him to find Legendaries – had worked? A smile rang so full across my face that it threatened to break through my helmet. I laughed and fell back to the ground. What would we do now? What was the next step? I hadn't got this far in my thought process.

Celeste leaped onto her sister, who took the hug as stiffly as a handshake. Their face was unique, I noticed as they freed themselves from Celeste's grasp. It was *almost* perfect, but not quite. A strange beauty.

"You're not meant to be a Suneva…" Celeste awed as she retracted herself. "How…what?"

"It's a long story," Amalie said, "but I am *Vectra*, it seems. Suneva of *Vectis*."

Vectis – Gravity, it was confirmed. I squealed.

"Long story?" Ferrad hummed. "You went from nothing to the Legendary of Gravity? That sounds like an epic."

"How long have you been back with Dad?" Amalie asked, ignoring Ferrad's amazement.

"I just came to him now. That was the first time I've called myself *Iva Argol* since I last saw you." Celeste sighed, face red. "Why are you here?"

"I came back for him too," she said, "only I got lost misreading firestones. Then I felt you here…"

"This is crazy," I said finally, rising to meet Amalie, "I never thought my stupid idea would work, but we found a Legendary, and it's *your sister*." I pointed to the girl, as if Celeste wouldn't believe the fact until I pointed it out. "And you're Argol's daughter too. I mean, what else will today bring?" I turned to Zamelle, trying to extract *anybody* else's amazement to this situation. She looked solemn, viewing the world through posed palms. "Next thing you're the White Witch, Chad's long lost cousin controls time, and another of us can teleport! It's just madness!"

Zamelle didn't share my elation, although Ferrad had joined my celebration.

"It's crazy," he noted, "we might be getting somewhere."

"Not for long," Zamelle said, finally. "Boekidin's witch is here. I couldn't sense her through this mess of mazes, but she's close. *Really* close. They're all here."

"What?" I hummed, my stomach turning to dread. At the word, Celeste and Amalie reassumed their armoured forms. Together, the two had similar shapes. Genetic inheritance of *alis*, perhaps?

"How much time have we got?" Iva asked.

"Almost none," Zamelle warned.

Chapter 18
Escape

"We should have expected this," Ferrad said. "Of course Boekidin would ambush us when we found a Legendary. This is what he was waiting for."

"I wouldn't have expected it," Zamelle noted. "I couldn't follow a single trail all the way down here. Their witch must be even *more* powerful than she appeared."

"I think that's impossible," I squirmed. The air around was pressing on me, boiling thick. I couldn't sense the danger coming like everybody else seemed to, but the tension was riding me. I summoned my staff, and I held it for dear life.

"How good are you in combat?" Ferrad asked Vectra. She flicked her wrist to form her massive, sprung-head hammer. The bronze anomaly glinted in the dim glow of quatra eyes.

"I can stand my ground well," she said. "I've avoided it by staying relatively hidden. I've always tried to avoid Suneva searching for Legendaries..." She snarked her tone, and the room fell mute to her words.

"Being an Argol, I don't think staying under the radar was ever a permanent option," Ferrad said finally. "Good to know that you can hold your own."

"Should we run?" Iva asked.

Yes. My mind screamed, only, it wasn't in my voice. "Oh *no*, he's close!" I warned, only now feeling the water as it dribbled out of my ear. When did Boekidin get in there? How much did he just find out? "Can't run."

"Definitely don't run," Chad said, "we've got a defensive position here."

"Who are we even facing off against?" Vectra asked. Her concern – moreso her realisation of the inevitable – cracked into her voice.

As she asked, the glowing of eyes separated the blackness of the doorway. Boekidin burst into the room, his wings filling the portal and spilling a black silhouette over the entire wall. From under his impressive rustling feathers prowled the cat-Suneva, followed by the Space Cowboy and the powerful White Witch.

Zamelle, without hesitation, fired a bolt of quatra. Boekidin's team didn't move a muscle, bar the Witch, who perfectly countered the shot with a bolt of her own. Their collision mid-air blasted a shockwave with the force to rock skulls.

"Well," Boekidin smirked, recovering. "I can see that..."

Vectra slammed her hammer to the rocks, and Boekidin and his team dropped to the floor. Their bodies fell faster than they could comprehend, and clanged into the stones. The Space Cowboy wretched to get himself up, but Boekidin scolded the Suneva. "Stay down," he said, "we're on a diplomatic mission. No need to appear violent."

"Diplomatic mission?" Zamelle mocked. She blasted another bolt of quatra at the held Raven-man, as did Celeste.

The Witch roared. Her body, crushed into the ground, spasmed and deflated with a crack and a hiss. From it darted a shadow with deep violet eyes. It

173

lay itself across Boekidin's body, absorbing the two bolts of quatra. The bolts reappeared out of the Witch's physical feet, slamming into the wall behind.

The shadow peeled itself back from Boekidin, rising up the wall, its eyes watching.

"Yes, a *diplomatic* mission," he continued. My frustration was sparked, my mouth ran hot.

"You play around in my head, throw us off a roof in Athens, follow us across Europe and into the catacombs, and you claim that you're on a diplomatic mission?" I hissed. "Get lost."

"It's not for *you*, or your terrorist friends, who I'm showing my diplomacy, Maiki," he sneered, "although you'll have my protection for the time being if you hand over your hostage."

"Hostage?" I quizzed, peering over to Vectra, Suneva of Gravity.

"I am no hostage," Vectra asserted, "I *belong* to nobody except myself. Who are you to suggest what happens to me? I am the Legendary of Gravity, I define my own path." She raked the back tip of her hammer across the stones, and the Suneva at her fingers' grasp groaned and gagged. Boekidin, however, could never be silenced. Face to the dirt, he spoke.

"Destiny controls us all, *Vectis*. It drives us to be better, and it prints our paths, so we know where we should walk. Don't risk taking an unbeaten trail before you."

Vectra let a silence linger – a silence punctuated by cracks of stone as weighted Suneva squirmed to avoid their crush.

"Let's go, quickly," Iva suggested.

"They'll just follow us," I warned. "Boekidin can get any information he wants. Vectra, can you hold them here for long enough?"

"We can't neutralise them to stop them, either," Zamelle added, "not with their witch."

"You *must* make a decision, don't let it be made for you," Boekidin broke our discussion, talking only to Vectra. "You're no longer unknown, in hiding. You are one of the single most influential Suneva alive. Who do you align with? What changes will you help implement?"

Vectra huffed, and frowned. She raised her hammer.

Boekidin smirked, and he planted his hands down to rise. All of his team did.

"Uh, what are you doing?" I uttered to Vectra as she let them stand. I backed myself away, nearly to the back wall as they ascended with hungry eyes.

"What do *you* want?" Vectra asked Boekidin's group. "Who *are* you?"

"Amalie…what are you doing?" Celeste appealed to her sister, but the girl did not budge. All Suneva hands in the room were hot with quatra. Energy was present in everything, bulging to break free.

"We can all exist here with no hostilities," Boekidin said, trying to dissipate the room's fermenting anticipation. "This is a stalemate, after all. If anybody moves, this room explodes." He assured, then stood tall from his stoop. His wings rustled in his regality. "I am Boekidin, the *Shiverman* for the people. This," he pointed to the shadow hanging on the wall, "is *Fisira*, a most powerful young witch. This is *Talik*, a *Liktas* proficient in high-power strikes. And with the tail and on all fours, she is *Vasloka*, Suneva of *Vastas*, magnetism.

"Together we are Hesslik's lead intelligence team, searching for gifted Suneva to make the dream of a united, integrated, Suneva-human world a reality. Don't you want to be a part of the community that changes cultures?"

"No," Vectra delivered her answer. I sighed my relief, and she snapped to me. "I'm not joining *you*, either," She quipped to my remark. Boekidin grinned, Iva gasped.

"What?" Iva demanded. "You're going to leave me again?"

"I'm coming with you," Vectra emphasised, "but I'm not joining your cause."

"Why not?" Iva asked.

"Its Suneva like you, Boekidin, and like everybody else in this room who have stopped me from being able to join this *community*. Constantly hunting for Suneva like me, chasing me with ancient codes. It's madness! There will never be a community for me when I'm forced to hide my own identity within it. Call me selfish, but I don't care much for a world where Suneva are in the limelight. It doesn't suit me, and I won't join you."

"I have to implore then that you don't associate yourself with these terrorists," Boekidin urged, drawing his tripod, golden staff. Each of his cronies, *Talik*, *Fisira*, and *Vasloka* in turn drew their own weapons. My heart skipped a beat of anxiety straight into fury. "They too want to use you, but their plans will devastate us all. Make this decision for those of us who *want* to be in society. Don't ruin our dreams for us by taking the wrong side. Please."

"Where do you invent these terms?" I roared at the bird. He stumbled in my explosion. "How are we *terrorists*? Why did you brand us like this when *you're* the ones working for a guy who wants to destroy the threads?"

"Let's see," Boekidin hummed, "you destroyed an entire warehouse of scientific research, terrorised its workers, and have seemingly vowed yourselves to disrupt everything happening in the Suneva community. I'm out here fighting for peace and acceptance, Maiki. I want to be a part of society exactly as I am. Peace is the aim of all Suneva after all – the ultimate path to enlightenment. You want the Empire and its teachings to fail, and so you want Suneva to suffer. That is why you are a terrorist to peace."

"We want Hesslik to fail, not the Suneva," I yelled. "What about the threads?"

"Thread removal is a policing method to ensure a certain quality of moral fortitude amongst Suneva. It will generate our acceptance."

"You know that he wants to remove *all* of the threads, right?" I remarked.

"Excuse me?" Boekidin tilted his head at me. He didn't get to finish his thought though. A great, green light spewed into the room from behind us, casting Boekidin and his team in our shadows. I turned about as strong footsteps, glowing in the welcoming warmth of a green flame, stepped into the atrium.

A tall Suneva of dark-grey and crimson armour stood in the room. Its helmet was like a dragon-wolf, cupped from behind by a thin-webbed, royal collar which spewed bright green flames onto the ceiling above his head. He carried with him a longsword with an elegant handguard and helix of green flame. This was *The Green Dragon* himself, *Naxaer Argol*.

"Dad?" Vectra exclaimed.

"Dad?" Boekidin spat. "That's interesting."

"Boekidin," Argol nodded, "wasn't expecting you down here."

"And a powerful family grows stronger…" Boekidin chuckled, shaking his head. "Your reign is ending, Argol. Ending your stranglehold over oppressed and confused Suneva will be a gratifying day indeed."

"Let's go," Argol directed us, and we all nodded. There was no way to refuse the hulking, inferno of a man.

"I'm not going to let you do that, Naxaer. We're in the middle of negotiations. Your daughter is needed for the good of the Suneva people, you see."

Argol eyed his eldest daughter, who spoke to defy.

"I'm needed where I feel I should be. And that's not with you," Vectra gave her final word. "I'm going to leave." And she turned her heel to step towards her father. As she faced me, I could see her expression fall to paranoid fear behind the helmet. Her free hand immediately assumed a peace sign pose.

A tension snapped.

"Oh, so that's how we have to play it..." Boekidin whispered.

Fisira, the shadow of a soul, fired a bolt from their intangible hand right at Naxaer Argol. He snatched it in his longsword, redirecting it at Boekidin. The Raven-man flung his golden staff to the bolt, and chaos fell.

Vectra commanded her hammer, grappling with her soul connection to slam it into the ground. Fisira fired hot, purple bolts upon her, and threw her concentration off. Zamelle fell in to cover the Legendary, and was fired upon by Vasloka now too.

I knew I could handle the agile Cat-woman only marginally better than anybody else. I flung myself in her direction, blasting off the floor and firing a bolt of quatra. They leaped away, and I gave chase about the room, darting between bolts that flew and whips of elemental power.

This, however, wasn't the answer. If we all became locked with opponents, we'd go nowhere. Boekidin's witch, Fisira, was his main power. If we could shut her down, we could win.

A plan hatched.

I gave up my chase of Vasloka and gathered all of the carbon that sat around me.

"Watch it!" Ferrad shouted, and I felt the insanely hot *ionisation* of air. I flopped to the floor, an arc of lightning flying overhead, crashing into the wall and blowing the bricks into oblivion.

I sprung back up, vaulting away with my carbon. I formed it into a disc, and leaped my way around the room, over heads, Vasloka still running from my chase.

With Fisira's body in sight and her shadow distracted with Iva, I bounded off the floor, flipped, kicked off the roof, and dove onto her body. Without a quatra attack, her senses weren't alerted. She only noticed me much too late. A bolt of quatra launched from her dead body towards me, but I threw the disc into its path and landed with my hand wrapped around her ragdoll neck. I blasted.

The shot was redirected – absolute insanity. A shot to the neck *couldn't* be redirected. Nobody had *that* much control over their quatra pathways. The attention in the room was captured by my blunder, and the break in concentration gave Vectra just enough time. She swung her hammer at the ground.

Talik, from the other side of the room, raised a blade to Vectra, which glowed hot. Zamelle, seeing the attack, ripped water from the bottles in the room and whipped the snake of liquid at the Suneva's firing arm. Talik's arm was smashed upwards, where his strike of lightning collided with the ceiling, causing the cavern to rain with debris.

Vectra's hammer slammed into the earth.

Boekidin's agents once again dropped to the floor, glued down. All except the shadow, which hung smug on the wall.

"Damn you!" Vectra yelled, and tugged with her hands and hammer. Suddenly the group of agents soared through the room, flung onto the rear wall with a crash.

The spirit of Fisira shrieked, filling the destroyed atrium with her harrowing, soul-stopping wail. My legs shook numb under me, I struggled to stand.

And the shadow raised it arms to fire.

"Block them off!" Vectra screamed at Ferrad, but he was already ahead of her. His hands clung to the stones, and when he heaved them up, the rock and brick of the floor ran to the wall, raised into barrier. Fisira's shrieks cried through the cracks.

"Can you hold them there?" I yelled to Vectra. She nodded.

"Not when we're too far."

"Then let's bloody run!"

"Follow me," Argol said, "I know an exit." He ran to the nearest portal, and we blindly sprinted in his footsteps.

He led us swiftly around corners, up stairs and across corridors. We came to another orb-field, where Argol drove the pack to a halt and instructed us to run with hands held. I grabbed Ferrad's assuming to grab Iva's, and sprinted into the Milky Way. On the other side, and all together in one piece, we made the final sprint, launching ourselves around a bend and coming to a unique opening.

This atrium was paved in blue stones, unlike the dusty and decrepit sandy colour we'd come to see here. Opposite us in this room sat a dark shaft, built into the wall.

"I use this chute to get bulky goods down to my office," Naxaer said. "But if we shift gravity the other way, I assume we can use it to get things up, too. Everybody out of your *alis*, this thing opens to street level."

"Great idea," Zamelle hummed, her armour washing away. "How would you usually get out though?"

"There's a ladder in my office," he said, then frowned, "I didn't really want to lead Boekidin to my office."

"Understandable," Natalie nodded.

"One issue, I'm not reversing gravity," Amalie said, stepping up to the chute and peering into its blackness. "I can't let people *fall* all the way up this thing. But I can do something else…" She gripped into her element, grabbing with her hands and shifting her stance, *pulling* at the threads of the world. "Step in." She ordered her father.

Adam Leroux stepped past his eldest daughter, up to the boundary of the infinite column. He stared into the blackness.

"Go on," his daughter urged. He puffed his chest, and stepped into the void. And he floated.

A huge grin ran across the stoic man's face. His arms flailed, and his body tumbled in the shaft. "Ha!" Adam laughed, green flames tickling from his fingertips. "I've always wanted to try this…" He faced his palms to the ground and unleashed two roaring green plumes. He flew up the shaft on a dazzling emerald trail.

"Looks fun," I commented.

"Okay, everybody else, jump in," Amalie said, gesturing us with her head. "Get in."

I went to move, but nobody else came with me. I ground to a halt, staring back.

"You're not coming up, are you?" Celeste asked her sister. "You're sending us all up…"

"Of course I'm coming up," Amalie said. "It takes a *lot* of concentration to hold a field like this. I can't jump in and climb up. You all need to go first."

Natalie found this appropriate, and stepped forward to join me, but Celeste didn't budge.

"I can't lose you again," she said, voice wavering. "I won't let you leave."

"You don't trust me?"

"You just said that you wouldn't join us!"

"But I said that I'd leave this place with you," Amalie huffed, still straining at the field. Then she sighed. "Fine, you come with me. But you'll have to carry me up and blast fire from your feet, or something. It's up to you."

"Fine," Celeste nodded, smiling. She strode to her sister's side, leaving Chad, Natalie, and I to peer into the shaft.

I stared down into a great nothingness. A fantastic blackness, robbing me of my senses. No green eyes to light the way, just void. My feet tingled on the edge.

I stepped in.

The feeling was insane. I was falling, crashing down at stupid speeds, so fast that the earth was falling with me. Both of us together, suspended. I hadn't moved, but my stomach was lurching out of my throat, going at a million miles an hour.

"*Omercronius*," I gawked. I looked to the top, to see light pouring in, illuminating the roof of a shack all the way up, past the mouth of the shaft.

I grappled at the air around me, and blasted it down into the column. Finally, I could truly fly.

***

We emerged on a night time street, the sky paved with Christmas lights which hung across the road. As soon as Amalie and I emerged from the service hut, Natalie threw her demands.

"Alright, threads off," she said. "We can't get chased." And she extended her hand to Celeste, then Adam, blasting them with quatra consecutively. Adam gasped, but praised the effort.

180

"Yes, good idea," he hummed, annoyed.

When it was my turn to take Natalie's thread, both of our hands lined up for simultaneous shots, and she winced. Her eyes rolled back when my quatra met her thread, and she awoke from the daze gasping and clenching in pain. I had no such feeling as my sensations washed away.

"What now?" I broke the silence.

"We should walk away from here, probably," Chad said, stepping over to help Natalie upright. "Not a safe place to be."

"Sure, man," I sighed. "Then what? You're not going to join us, will you Amalie?"

"Well, I'm coming with you now," she said. "I came here to spend time with my family." Adam smiled to the note. "But I won't *join* you. It would make me a target. I'm not ready for that yet. I don't know what I want to support, either. I know that my decision has weight for..."

"Ha! *Weight!*" Chad burst, then shut himself up. "Sorry, continue." But Amalie said no more.

"Let's start moving," Adam Leroux suggested. "We can talk as we move. I've got a safehouse on the other side of the city that we can use tonight. I've got guards to keep us safe."

"That sounds like a good idea," Natalie nodded, and urged the man along. We strolled in his tail.

"This is what I'm getting at, then," I continued, "we found a Legendary, and I have no idea how, but they won't join us. So, what do we do?"

"Find the others," Chad said. "The fact that Amalie won't join *either* cause still works for us. All we have to do is convince the other Legendaries not to join Hesslik. They don't really *have* to join us, although it would be nice."

"Right..." I considered. Chad had a good point. It didn't matter that we had no Legendaries. If we could stop them joining Hesslik, it did the same thing to foil the Empire's ambitions. "But how did we find *one* in the first place? We weren't even trying just now."

"I just followed Eleni's advice," Celeste said. "I faced my conflicts so that I could find some peace, and in that peace, I realised just how strong my connections could be. I connected again to my sister."

"Following the code of connections, in other words," Chad smirked.

181

"But you didn't know your sister was a Legendary," I hummed.

"No, but did it matter?" She asked. "I still haven't faced *all* of my issues either, but I found enough peace to feel an important connection. Regardless of whether finding peace leads to Legendaries, I think you should all do it. I feel great."

"So, in essence, the plan doesn't change, then," I surmised, "we're still following the code, we're just not doing it through Argol…"

"What about me?" Adam piped up from the head of the line.

"Oh…nothing," I hummed, having almost forgotten we'd found and befriended the man, something that seemed so far away only a few weeks ago. "So, has anybody else got any life-altering problems they've been running away from? Now seems like a better time than ever to just jump right -on into those." I tried to think of one my own, but nothing sprung to mind. Where did my conflicts lie? I certainly didn't have anything as stand-out as running away from home and lying to all of my friends.

"I've got an easy one," Chad nudged me, "I also ran away from home. Haven't seen my family in about three years – not that I'd care to see them again. But, you know, I did leave a whole life behind…"

"Before we get to that–" Celeste interrupted, "I would like to spend some time with my family. Maybe just a week to sit around and get everything out."

"I'd be disappointed if you left sooner than that," Amalie nodded. "We've got things to work out."

"It's just over a week until Christmas," Adam said. "I think it would be the story of the decade to have the whole family together at *Imaeres Avoul*. Have you kids had a Suneva *Day of the Soul* before?" He addressed the question to Natalie, Chad and I. We each shrugged. "Then it's settled. Come celebrate it with my family. It'll be the best you'll ever have."

I turned to Natalie, who had been strangely silent, eyes lost to the cosmos hanging in the sky.

"What do you think?" I asked Natalie. "Do we go with Argol, or do we leave Celeste for a while and keep moving?"

It took Natalie a good moment to be shaken from her gaze, but when she snapped to, she was staring at me with tired eyes.

"I could use a week's break," she said, weary. "A lot has happened in half a day. We could all use some time to think."

Chapter 19
A Tale of Two Sisters

On an afternoon seven years ago, an hour after dusk, the cocky policeman adjusted his hat as he entered the front door of the Leroux home. His gait was authoritative, his grin was toxic. One hand locked onto the handle of his pistol, tempting him to draw. He observed the artwork upon the walls with contempt. He had no guilt. Suneva were elitist, self-segregating cheaters. They had earned their reputations.

Adam Leroux had sent his daughters off to their rooms in apprehension of his guest, but Celeste and Amalie had more curiosity than they knew what to do with, and had never seen their father so anxious. Police hated Suneva, and Celeste knew this. What trouble was Dad getting in now? With light feet, they snuck back into the dining room, hiding under the central table and its long cover. Their game was to be quiet – undetectable, and the sisters played it well.

Adam greeted the officer and led him past the main entrance way and into the hallway. The policeman was much taller than the barrel-chested, stocky Leroux, and with his combat boots and hat, he was forced to duck under the divider into the dining room. The feet of the two men scuffled close to the edge of the table's fabric. The two sisters held their mouths closed, not daring to breathe. But the adrenaline was kicking in, and it was hard to keep from panting in anticipation. The men were talking but the girls were too anxious to listen, they could only hear their hearts in their ears. The boots stomped next to a chair, right in front of Celeste's face. She gagged, holding her chest. The chair shifted, but the boots pulled away, leading towards the door.

The girls dropped to the floor, eyes under the cloth, capturing both men in their line of sight. They saw their father raise his finger to the officer, close enough to jab at their chest, scolding them with stern instruction. The officer smirked, and chuckled as they turned from the accusation. Adam grappled the man's shoulder and swung him back around, yelling now. The officer's hand tightened on his pistol. He drew it.

The girls gasped, breaking their disguise. Adam jumped, finger turning to palm to shove the man away.

And that's when it happened.

Quatra is silent, mainly. Unlike a gun, a bullet of the energy makes almost no discernible sound as it escapes its barrel. And unlike a bullet, it doesn't leave any clear, traceable evidence behind – at least not to a human.

The teal light of Leroux's bolt appeared holy and pure between his palm and the officer's chest. The silence of the pure moment was shattered by the destruction of the man's chest, as his ribcage exploded into chunks flesh and cooked blood. The table cloth splattered red.

The girls fell flat, silenced in their shock. The destroyed body slapped onto the floor after them, unrecognisable.

"Oh *Veritas*," Adam Leroux sighed.

"Come on," Amalie whispered to Celeste, pulling her up. Celeste's body was heavy, her mind running empty, vision taken by the bloody mess before her. A man slaughtered by her father.

"*Come on*," Amalie urged, somehow pulling the younger girl up and dragging them away, up to their shared room.

The girls slumped into their bedroom, Celeste falling across her bed, Amalie racing for her bag and assorted supplies.

"What are you doing?" Celeste asked. She wasn't sure that she was in a mind to understand the answer, let alone do anything. She just wanted to lay. She wanted to get the image out of her mind. It was burned there. Who was her father? Who was a man who could do such a thing?

"We've got to go," Amalie said. "Get a bag. Pack it full."

"Where will we go?" Celeste rolled onto her back. Light shone into her eyes. "Why?"

"Why?" Amalie hissed. "Celeste, Dad just *killed* somebody. He killed a *policeman*, of all people!"

"I…"

"Do you think we're safe?" Amalie huffed, rushing to pack Celeste a bag.

"I don't know," Celeste said. "Dad isn't a bad person."

"Well he is, and he probably has been this whole time," Amalie remarked, throwing a backpack at Celeste. "Look, maybe you can't see it because you're too ittle to understand…" Her sister, at the grand seniority of eleven mocked, "and you're a Suneva so he loves you more, but what he did isn't worth staying here for. Let's go."

Celeste was hurt by the comments – or maybe it was just the insanity of the whole situation. Her dad had killed a man, and maybe that meant that Celeste knew nothing about him. But that was just it, there would *have* to be a reason he did it.

Before she could ponder, Amalie was dragging her to the window in their room, and pushing her out onto the abutting tree. They ran from home. They ran towards the centre of town. Celeste didn't know where her sister was leading her until they ended up at the doors of the police station. When Celeste spotted the building's sign, and noticed Amalie's determination, she snatched her sister aside, pulling her against a wall.

"No!" Celeste protested. "You can't tell the Police. Dad will go to jail!"

"No?" Amalie huffed, pushing her sister off. "What about the officer's family? Dad gets what he deserves."

"But I'm sure he had a reason," Celeste rebuffed. "We didn't even ask!"

"A reason?" Amalie halted, her face a mess. "A *reason?* Something that makes it okay to kill?"

"Maybe…"

"No, you don't get it," Amalie shook her head. "You Suneva don't get it," and she stepped away, back to the street.

"But Dad will go to jail, we'll never see him again!" Celeste leaped after her sister. She grabbed Amalie by the wrist, but her sister swung her weight around with the tug, spinning Celeste onto the cobbled ground. She lay there dazed.

"Why even come with me if you're going to be an idiot?"

"Because you made me!"

"Then go home to the killer," she spat. "Maybe the police will give you a lift," and she turned to walk.

"No!" Celeste yelled, again. Her sister could not be stopped, and Celeste's anger at her own *powerlessness* boiled in her blood. Her hot rage beckoned her to use its might, use that so-great *equalising* force that roared with the heat in her bones. Celeste could stop her sister.

185

She flung her hand before her, willpower connecting to heat, an extension of her *soul*, bursting into a yellow flame at her palm's edge. The blaze thundered through the air, engulfing her sister's turning head, setting it in a lick of flame.

Amalie's face bubbled and spat. Skin like liquid, it oozed and peeled. Bursting in a blister, all in an instant.

Celeste's eyes fell through her skull. She vomited on the spot, slumping back to the ground. She heard only her sister's frantic stomps as she ran off, sprinting far away, screaming.

Celeste was done-for now. Her life was over. The only thing left to do was run *far* away.

***

Celeste ran quickly. She found herself on the central city outskirts, not having found a place to fall asleep. It would be late soon, and she was scared of the police finding her, her father finding her, and her sister finding her. She was drawn by a beating rhythm to an old sandstone inn covered in vines. The top floor was peaceful, whilst yellow light threw itself out of the lower windows, riding with the beat. Celeste figured that she could sneak into a room on the top floor if she was quiet enough, and then she'd be safe.

Under the waist height of most patrons, she entered undetected. Louder than the music, on the darkening afternoon, was the chatter of one thousand tipsy conversations. Celeste sleuthed under their blanket, her footsteps masked, as she moved past men in well-done suits and ladies in magnificent dresses, looking for an entrance to the upstairs. Past the farthest of the two bars, she spotted a stairway. She slipped towards it.

Celeste's father had spent a lifetime teaching her ways to fit in as an outcast, and here, ascending the first step of an unfamiliar staircase, Celeste took his most prominent bit of advice – act like you belong, and nobody will question you. Instead of sneaking onto the step, she stormed up it, feet falling with disregard. She didn't look back to the crowd, but she was certain that not a head turned in shock to see her rise to the first floor.

The flight turned a corner out of sight of the crowd, and Celeste rounded it to be met with a face staring at her from the head of the stairs. She gasped, a spittle of flame dancing from her fingertips before she could control it.

It was the face of a young boy, younger than Celeste even. She steeled herself, but the possibility of being caught out was real, and frightening. Celeste sweated.

"Are you staying here?" The boy asked.

"Yes," she said, forcing her eyes to smile sweetly.

"With what family? In what room?" He asked, flat faced. Celeste just smiled dumbly, brain spinning for an answer. Any answer would do… "My parents own this hotel," the boy continued, and Celeste was outsmarted. She sighed, giving up.

"I don't have a room," she let the guise drop. "I just need a place to stay."

"Would you like one?" The little boy asked, still without a smile.

"I don't have any money."

He shrugged, producing a single key from his pocket. He slotted it into the first door of the squat hallway and opened it with ease. His actions were robotic, as if he was forced against his will to open the door – compelled by a higher power.

"Thank you," Celeste was dumbfounded. Still, she put on her pretty smile, and kissed the boy on the cheek. He broke his demeanour and blushed immediately and Celeste, covering her adrenaline and anxiety, bounced into the room.

"I know who you are," he said with a warmer tone, "it is the least thanks my family can give yours." Before Celeste could question him, he closed the door behind her. Celeste immediately went to open it, but the boy had disappeared in a second.

Celeste walked back into the room and slumped herself on the bed. Her father helped Suneva families – he had a real impact, and that was all she needed to hear. Celeste hadn't told on him, and it was the right decision.

Although Amalie *had*, and Amalie might have said bad things about Celeste, too. The consequences were enough to keep Celeste from *thinking* about going home. She was safe here, though, and she needed to set aside her anxiety if she could rest. She got up to have a shower, to wash reality away.

Amalie ran along the street, her face throbbing. Her instinct was to hold it, to press against the skin and scream, but her mother had always taught her better. The woman who toyed with a purple flame, she knew a thing or two about fire safety. Never touch the wound. Wash it, and get antiseptic.

Surely a police station will have that. Amalie reasoned, coming to the door. She threw the door aside, stepping fully into the lobby before an officer behind their desk. The officer, with their cheery smile, turned to Amalie before their face paled, and their grin fell to the floor.

It was then, that the weight of Amalie's own situation hit her.

Where will I go once I tell them what Dad did? She thought. The officer almost vaulted their desk, jogging over. *I don't have money. I have nobody to turn to who wouldn't send me home. If I get Celeste in trouble, she'll go to jail. If I get Dad in trouble, Mum would never have me back at home. She'd probably get investigated too...*

"Oh my *god*, what happened to you?" The officer crouched down to Amalie. They had to restrain their own hands from leaping to the wound. "Get a medical kit, quick. Get an ambulance sent out..."

"No!" Amalie interrupted. Going to the hospital would mean taking details, would mean getting her parents involved. She couldn't have that.

The officer seemed shocked at the outburst. "You're burnt. You must be in shock..."

Amalie had to think of a lie, *anything*, but her brain wasn't good at thinking of falsehoods. *Why can't I think more like Celeste. She tells such good lies. Never ends up in trouble...* "It was a cooking accident." Amalie supposed, thinking aloud. "I pulled down a pot and it was full and hot."

"Where are your parents?" The officer asked. Amalie could sense their suspicion. Of course this situation was fishy – it was a terrible lie!

"No," she shrilled defensively, realising the officer's direction. "I'm...I'm a gypsy, I don't have parents." *Yes, brilliant!* "I was trying to steal food. I tripped the chef." Amalie was impressed with herself.

The officer hummed. Amalie now had to hope that they hated gypsies enough to ignore her.

"Come with me," the policeman said. "You'll have to get under a cold shower, then I'll take you to the hospital myself."

Amalie would have to find an escape before the 'hospital' part of this man's plan. Still, she went around the back to the shower. That *was* something she needed. The running cold water stung horribly as it washed over her. Another nugget of her mother's advice was to use soap. It would hurt, but it had to be done. Tentatively, Amalie raised the soap to her face.

It was the worst thing she'd ever felt. But she had to endure it.

When it was over, she patted herself dry, leaving the water running. She snatched her clothes from outside the stall, getting dressed and peering into the hallway. There was a clear line to the exit. She turned the other way, to see a policeman coming for the front of the building. She closed the door, waiting for them to go by. She could feel their presence leave, that familiar sensation of sharing the room with a Suneva. It was only to be expected when they possessed so much energy.

Peering again, Amalie could see two clear directions, and her exit straight down the hall. Adrenaline kicking, and with no plan in sight past that door, she bolted.

She burst past the desk.

"Hey, wait!" The officer called, but Amalie would not wait. She slammed herself through the entrance, falling into the street beyond. She caught herself, but did not stop. She had no answers except to run. Run to a place where nobody knew who she was.

Amalie was drawn by the sound of music in the dusk of the city outskirts. It was a club of sorts, or maybe a bar. A tall, two storey building made of sandstone with vines hanging over its walls. A second storey window was wide open, with vines leading right to it. Above the window was a perfectly framed sign reading 'Inn.' *Perfect.*

Amalie, without second thought, clambered up the vines. She was strong, something her father had taught her from a young age. Her mother was a very intelligent woman, very fashionable, and very sociable. Amalie didn't take much after her mother's lessons on image. Celeste was the pretty one. Rather, Amalie had taken her mother's logic but her father's grit. Somehow, Celeste had inherited all attributes to become a princess and a fighter, even at nine years old. But Celeste was a Suneva. That made it easy.

Amalie hurled herself into the window and tumbled over the bed. She didn't notice the bag, much like hers, which sat on the foot of it. The shower caught her attention. She'd stumbled into an active room, just at the perfect time. Amalie toed her way to the room's entrance, setting the door ajar and peeking into the hall beyond.

There were five other doors to the left, and a stairwell to the right. She quietly creeped out into the hallway, creeping towards the other doors. Amalie peeked through the peep-hole of the first room – it was full, so she moved to the next door. The stairs creaked behind her, somebody was coming – heavy boots trudged the steps. Amalie's heart skipped. Even though this person probably had no idea that she didn't belong, they *might*. Who knew? She pushed off the second door, throwing herself to the far end of the hall. The boots reigned louder, a silhouette painted onto the corner wall.

Amalie jiggled the handle but it didn't budge. Desperately, she mashed her palm against the keyhole and yanked at the handle. Curiously, the little clacks of the tumblers rang through the door, and it came free. She flung herself inside the room and rammed the door shut.

The footsteps kept coming, heavy on the carpeted hallway. *They might be coming for this room.* Amalie gasped, and looked around frantically, not seeing any evidence of belongings. Still, she found the closet and locked herself into it.

The boots stopped, and they were close. She heard a key enter the lock as it reverberated into the wall, and she heard the tumblers snap into position. The key turned, the handle clicked, and the door creaked open.

But it was not the door to her room. Amalie stepped out of the closet, sucking in the biggest breath of her life. She flopped onto the bed and lay there, adrenaline pumping.

She slept under the bed that night, just in case anybody else decided to come in and scare her.

Chapter 20
The Tale Continues

When Celeste awoke the next morning, she'd almost forgotten her paranoia. But when the sun hit her face she remembered that her sister had told the police about her and her father's actions, and she'd never be safe at home again.

She could never go home again.

Celeste knew there was only one place to go: Paris. A city of dreams, of late-night lights and fame. Monuments and tourists and women of acclaim. Paris was where fashion was born, where ideas bred and people gained wealth of all kinds. The streets would be clean and her life would be complete. It's where she had always seen herself anyway, as a grown Suneva.

Oh, how the real city disappointed her.

She'd snuck onto a train. A small girl, cute as a button and with a smile to melt all suspicion, she'd snuck under the waists of conductors and gates, fitting into families as a mystery extra child. Celeste drew no suspicion, she was perfect at hiding in plain sight.

And she'd rather had not been hiding in Paris. Clean streets were trodden by tourists who spoke loudly and blundered without personal regard. The locals were jaded, storming streets with sneers and letting their dogs shit where they pleased. Heels clacked, and the women who wore them had fashion to the highest degree, but Celeste had no money to participate. Celeste had *nothing*.

Every time her stomach growled, she remembered a friend of her dad whom she could go to. Each city had an Argol network. Any Suneva would house a young, lost Ivaer, but she was too known, too public. Her first night she spent ignored on the street, her bag wet as she was left ignored in an alley. Nobody would look at her past the inflection of their noses.

The bells of a church pierced the morning, stirring her awake. Celeste cursed groggily at them, retching from her unfulfilling, cold sleep. The ringing reminded her of an adage from her mother. Juliet Leroux, whilst never encouraging religion, and being no spiritual magnate herself, had always noted churches as a safe place for Suneva – as long as you never made your abilities clear.

Of course, one could never be open with Suneva abilities in a church. The reason for Suneva isolation in this country, after all, was their denial and ideological contradiction to the teachings of the catholic faith. Despite this, Juliet Leroux claimed that Veritas could hear you more clearly within a cathedral's walls, and that Suneva congregated to churches as a place to attain peace and introspection.

Celeste forced herself towards the knelling. Stumbling in the cold morning, she felt drawn to their buzz, her soul warming her as she grew closer. She was being guided, and she leaned into the sensation.

The church she found wasn't large, nor ornate, but it radiated an aura that Celeste could only know as *holy*. Its thick, wooden doors gleamed in the orange sunrise, set in the ancient stonework. They were open, but the inside was too dark to see in. Celeste cautiously entered, not sure if she was allowed to in the first place.

Rows of pews lined the stage before an altar, which sparkled in the rising sun's glare. Just to the left of the door, however, flickering lights and lingering smoke caught Celeste's attention. She turned to see the silhouette of a hunched man before a raised sandpit of candles. The man was mumbling something under his breath.

Celeste inched closer, drawn towards the flames. Her soul wanted to wrap around their warmth. As she neared the man, she could hear that he didn't chant in French, but rather in Liktan. Celeste froze – anybody speaking Liktan could be a man of her father's influence, although her father didn't conspire with men this old, did he? Before she could make a decision about him, he turned and greeted her.

"Bonjour," he smiled and nodded to her. His face was old to match his arched posture. Wrinkles danced in the candlelight.

"Yassi, Tano," Celeste responded in Liktan, and the man sighed relief, letting down what guard he held.

"You have come here to connect too?" He asked her in *Liktan*, "All by yourself?"

"I ran away from home."

The man didn't know how to respond to this. He looked back to the flame of his candle. "Do you usually come here when you run away?"

"I've come a long way from home," she said. "I can't go back because I did something bad…but after a bad night, I felt like I needed to be *here*."

"The Black holes watch us, you know," he said slowly, conjuring wisdom to give. "They lead us in the right direction, because they know where our destiny lies." He reached for an unlit candle and handed it to Celeste. "Light a candle and place it in the sand, young Miss. Perhaps you will find out why they bought you here."

Celeste took the candle. It felt drab compared to the ones her father lit at home.

"Celeste Leroux," she said to the old man, "that's my name."

"Kyros Olomb," he smiled at her, reaching for his lighter, "although I've gone by many names…" Before he could flip open its top Celeste had flicked her fingers and cracked a vibrant yellow flame between her finger and thumb. She lit the candle.

"You're *the* Olomb?" She asked.

"That's a bold move in a church," Olomb eyed her fire, ignoring the question as he pocketed his device. "Although, an impressive flame."

Celeste placed the candle into the sand, and a deep sensation rushed her body and mind, crashing through her like water from a dam. Celeste could trust this man with her soul. It was why Veritas brought her here. There was a path for her in this world.

"Thank you," she whispered.

***

Amalie found herself in the streets of Paris. Why? Because that's where she knew her sister would be. She had caught the train, early in the morning, when nobody was around. She snuck her way in, moving quickly between walls and laying low. As the non-Suneva of the family, she had to learn to be defensive without abilities. Adam Leroux was prudent to teach her proper defence against Suneva, as his position brought danger to those around him. Amalie learned to dodge, roll, duck and hide, embrace the darkness, redirect quatra, and move herself swiftly.

She smiled down the streets of Paris – there were lots of people and many places to hide. She was never the centre of attention, and she never enjoyed attention. When surrounded by fire-breathers, mind runners, spark spitters and water flingers, it was beneficial to stay under the radar. Especially with a mind-runner in the room, a *Kidin*. Nobody knew how *kidin* abilities worked, except for

Kidin, who could not be convinced to tell. Nobody knew just how much they could see, just how much they had access to, or just how much they could manipulate. That's what made them an asset, and a dangerous enemy. Amalie did not like *Kidin*.

She found herself – after being surrounded by so many Suneva for most of her life – to have this uncanny ability to spot them in a crowd. In the streets she roamed, she could tell the Suneva from the regular men and women. They had an air around them, they had the way they walked, the way they conducted themselves. They stood more upright as if they were above others, they walked with perfect grace, and they were always so in tune to what was happening around them. A soul connection – it was a useful thing to have but ultimately what gave them away. They blended into nature but not into crowds.

And yet, without their movements separating them, Amalie could tell a *Liktas* from an *Ivaer* from a *Kidin* from a *Welle* from a simple witch. As weird as it sounded to admit to herself, they each had their own unique *aura*, and through these sensations she could see the people behind the powers – their most basic definition of character. For this reason, Amalie's father had her on the front-lines of the household. She would be the guest-investigator, telling her father if those with whom he entered into agreements with were good and honest people – if they had a good aura.

Her father had a very good aura. The policeman did not have an aura.

That always seemed weird to her – she thought as she walked past a church, bells sounding in the sunrise – that only Suneva were touched by this weird divinity. Everywhere she went, she saw people who were connected to gods – the real gods who demonstrably gave divine power. She could sense the power, but was shunned by it. She would never go to heaven as many might think, she would never have an afterlife, she would never connect to Gods, for these were only privileges granted to her entire family and not her.

And they all believed in this idea of destiny too, this idea that the universe called them to certain places and that their lives had a purpose and a meaning. It was all bullshit, of course, because a black hole wasn't conscious – it couldn't think or control anything. A black hole was just a super condensed ball of pure mass. They weren't even real Gods. They were liars.

A day of searching and being lost in her thoughts, and her sister was nowhere to be found. Amalie was getting hungry, and the sun was setting. She needed something to eat and somewhere to sleep. She wasn't like her sister, who was cute enough and charming enough to get handouts. She could not beg for food – she would have to bin dive for it.

***

Olomb had offered to take Celeste under his wing. He, of course, knew exactly who she was, and understood that she could use protection if fleeing was her wish. At least, that's what Celeste believed. She didn't have the ability to tell people's intentions like her sister did, despite seeing the auras – and her sister was always right. Celeste chose to always trust, because people were much more open if you gave them trust. People could be swayed if treated well.

So, she followed Veritas' wishes, and she went with the kind old man. He was staying in a house in the city's east, and had a very nice lunch cooking in the oven awaiting his return. A roast lamb, inexplicably for two, as if he expected a guest to arrive.

Over the hot lamb lunch Olomb explained his situation. He was in Paris for a meeting between the remaining powers of the electric nation to discuss important issues of the future of the Suneva people. Olomb would be in Paris for a week, but then needed to return to Melbourne, where he lived the normal life of an old man with God-given electric powers.

He handed Celeste an ultimatum, she could come with him to Melbourne, and he would help to enrol her in a boarding school for Suneva children which he had himself established, or she could live in the city of Paris with his contacts, being given a list of people she could rely on to care for her properly.

Celeste immediately accepted the first offer. Paris was too close to danger, and she already hated the place. Her best plan would be to go far away, so far that nothing of this life mattered. Not the police after her for burning Amalie's face, nor the disruption of her home life. Celeste was going to move to Melbourne.

"Right," the old man accepted her decision. "You might think it strange that I help you in running way – which I feel is not the right decision for a girl your age – however, I feel that this is right, weirdly. I'm old enough to know that a Suneva's instincts are always right." He grinned kindly, and took another bite of his lamb.

195

"You are the same Olomb from the diary, aren't you?" Celeste asked, and the man could not ignore the question.

"Yes, of course."

"Then you must be one million years old!" Celeste exaggerated. "That book was written so long ago."

"Five hundred years old, actually. Five hundred and thirty-two years to be exact." He grinned beneath a moustache.

Celeste dropped her fork on the plate.

"You can't be that old! You'd have to be dead. People can't live that long."

"Ah, it's an old secret," he winked. "Only a few Suneva have ever done it. Nobody has done it as long as me."

Celeste examined the old man's contempt face. His skin sagged no lower than any other old man, he was more mobile than any gentleman Celeste had seen. Not even her grandfather, Seros Argol, had been so spritely, and he'd died before reaching sixty years of age. This old man was magical beyond any Suneva she'd ever known.

***

Amalie had spent a few days on the streets. She sleuthed around Paris like a stray cat, lurching in and out of small alleys, stripping bins of fruit and bread, laying low and observing the people.

Paris was populated by many *Ivaer* and *Kidin*. Not too many *Liktas* this far north, but she'd seen a few. *Funny*, she figured, that the two least understood Suneva abilities should congregate so heavily in one city.

Where *kidin* might have been understood, but kept a secret, it was no secret that nobody understood *Ivaer*. It was called a macro-element, like *kiin*, *welle* and *raduk*, but the soul connection to *Ivaer* was not the same. With the other macro-elements, the soul connection was one to the most abundant substance of a physical state. The *Kiin* had control over the gaseous state, realised through their soul connection to breathable air which surrounded them. *Welle* had control over liquid, realised through their soul connection to the vast oceans, deep lakes and flowing rivers which covered the world. *Raduk* could control solids, which was

196

realised through their connection to the silicon rich crust of the earth – the dirt, stone, and the flesh of the planet which lay at their feet.

Ivaer was not like the others. A fire is just hot gas realising light due to a reaction – and the Suneva flame didn't even need the reaction. It was not a state of matter, rather it was the realisation of something else, something misunderstood. *Ivaer* claimed that it was the realisation of their passion, but you couldn't have a soul connection to passion – passion is an *element* of the soul connection.

Liktas used to be much the same. The first *Liktas* sought their connection to lightning. They later discovered that this was a connection to electricity, which they then realised could be expressed as the connection to the flow of charged particles, which then became an expression of a manipulation of the electromagnetic fields. Although, even now there is still another level of understanding to go, because why else would some Suneva feel a disposition to electricity, while others, the *Vastas*, felt a disposition to magnetism?

Amalie often pondered this world she'd never know. She'd studied the Suneva history books, the only things that her mother could convince her to read when she was younger. As she roamed pondering, she began to sense what felt like her own soul connection. It came to her over her week in isolation, reading auras of those who passed by. She felt a connection to that which brought strangers together, and that which pushed them away – their interactions. The social glue seemed a weird thing to feel this connection to, and she was almost certain that it was not a Suneva ability, but rather the gift of Suneva biology. Her mind had time to think, and she wondered why she had the sense to see whether people would attract or repel.

Amalie's week led her to a marketplace in the north of the city. She'd heard word of a famous fortune teller coming to the Sunday market. Amalie wished she could be a better sceptic towards such a profession, but her life so far hadn't set her up to reject the amazing. Plus, with so much she was unsure of in herself, now that her life had totally flipped around, what light could a fortune teller shed?

The marketplace was a thick swarm of colourful tents and tables arranged in haphazard rows over a sea of cobbles. People bustled in and out and between each other, trying with intense concentration to find a nice knack or ware to add to their antique home décor. The fortune teller's tent would be somewhere in the centre, as she'd seen on a map.

She pushed past the bustle in the marketplace. In every stall hung an extensive range of jewellery and handmade clothes, being whipped between hands and exchanged with a strange leisurely haste. People shuffled between each other nervously, trying not to smack into one another as they fought for bargains. Amalie could see the bare looking tent of the fortune teller – she recognised the logo from what a poor hungry man had told her. *Na Kafma nas Sun* – the Mark of the Black Sun – a calling card to Suneva in the crowd.

The stall was free, and there-in sat a kind old lady. She had kind eyes, nested in an un-telling, wrinkled face, bordered in jet-black hair. She saw Amalie coming, and sat tall in anticipation, clearing the desk and pulling out a pack of cards. *A good fortune teller*, thought Amalie, *is one who knows when a customer is coming* before *they ask for a service.*

Amalie smiled and livened her pace, rolling through the crowd to take a hastened seat at the black-clothed table. The opaque orb between the two women was pushed aside as the Fortune Teller leaned closer in. She peered into Amalie's eyes, then *past* them, into the space of Amalie's soul.

"What answers have you come here seeking?" The fortune teller asked, breaking her gaze upon Amalie's soul.

"I…I don't know," Amalie blanked out.

"Your confusion is certain. I see it in your eyes. What is causing your soul's turmoil?"

"I feel stupid," Amalie laughed at herself. "Because I don't know what you can tell me. I'm not looking for my future, I'm looking for *me*."

The lady leaned in knowingly.

"I think I'm going crazy, or I've been crazy my whole life. I'm the only normal child in a family of Suneva, but I keep seeing auras of Suneva around me. I can see the colours of their personality and thoughts. I can judge characters…"

The old lady grinned.

"But I'm not a Suneva. I know I'm not. I've got the biology…"

"Nobody with a Suneva biology can do what you do without *the blessing*, young witch," rhe lady smiled.

"*Witch?*" Amalie protested. "No, you must be wrong. I'm not a witch."

198

"I've been spotting Suneva for over fifty years, young lady," the woman said. "You're a very intuitive witch, but very hard to spot. I've never looked into eyes which locked away so much information, but it's in there. You're a witch."

"And nothing else?" Amalie asked, examining her hands, finally aware of an energy's pulse at her neck.

"I think not," said the witch, shuffling her cards. "Now young *quatrona*, allow me to read to you your future. This is a fortune teller's tent after all."

The old witch, Surawelle, drew cards and placed them on the table in a Christian cross about the crystal ball. She flipped the intricately patterned cards from the bottom of the cross up, revealing a block of colour on the front face and a colour name.

Kera-li – Pink – the colour of instability, in the space of the immediate past. Predicting emotional and decisional uncertainty.

Mesa-ka – Cool Orange – the colour of self-introspection, in the space of the immediate future. Predicting a period of personal reflection and change.

Kera – Red – the colour of charisma, in the space of the journey. Predicting that the journey to self-discovery will be aided by a friend.

Assa – Blue – the colour of strong emotion in the space of future thoughts. Predicting an emotional shift, and perhaps hardships.

And finally *Ocra-Lik – the White Light* – The symbol of the black hole's power in the space of the outcome. Predicting an important and powerful destiny.

***

Celeste boarded a plane to Melbourne. Not her first time on a plane, but certainly the longest trip, and done without family. Olomb did not come with her that day, as he still had business in Paris to complete. Celeste, however, needed to be in Melbourne sooner to meet the school's headmaster. Olomb had set up a travel sitter to go with her, an older gentleman, probably her father's age, whom was on Olomb's apparently unending list of contacts.

Upon landing in Melbourne, the sitter escorted Celeste to Olomb's house – a nice weatherboard cottage in the inner south east, sat on a T-intersection by a train line. The freeway ride from the airport took Celeste on the scenic route – cruising over the Bolte bridge and capturing the view of the whole city. Celeste was

199

amazed. The city wasn't all that big, but the buildings were tall, and the dense urban landscape was so spread. Beyond that, in amongst the concrete and hills were trees and plants – trees lining every single street. The duality of green and grey was something she didn't often see at home, but here it was, even in the most dense, urban areas the trees grew regularly and green.

The travel sitter, a man named John Grey, walked her to the door of the weatherboard bungalow. He was somewhat of an unreadable man – uneasily stern but also unfathomably kind. He was apparently a police officer, so naturally always held a straight, intimidating face, but he talked to her like a father would to a child. There was care in his tone. He told her about his son and daughter, James and Simone, near Celeste's age. Celeste was always welcome to come over if she wanted somewhere to go or a place to feel at home.

John Grey led Celeste over the brick path, up onto the porch, to the front door. He knocked on it lightly and, to Celeste's surprise, footsteps sounded from the house. The door opened to reveal Olomb in his finest old-man clothes with a cup of tea in hand. Celeste didn't believe what she was seeing.

"Surprised, are you Celeste?" He said with a grin. "You'll get used to it. John." He turned to the man and shook his hand. "Thanks for that. I trust the flight was good."

"Long," John sighed, "but fine. I'm glad to be safely home. Travelling with you can be a chore, Vasilli. I just hope it's not all going downhill like you think it will. I have hope, but the Argols here aren't making it easy."

"Do what you can, John. This can't happen in a night."

"Of course," he said and looked around to his car. "I should probably head home anyway, I'm expected soon." He looked down to Celeste and produced a card from his pocket. "Have a great year at a Suneva school. I know somebody as strong as you will fit in. Here's a number anyway, if the old man doesn't get back to you." He winked at Olomb and handed Celeste a business card.

"Goodbye Mr. Grey," Celeste said sweetly and hugged the man's leg bye. She and Olomb waved him off.

"Now," said Olomb, "let's get you inside. I've got headmistress Tona Narelle in the living room, and she's looking forward to meeting you, Celeste Bouvé." He winked. Celeste had to remember that she was going by fake name now. A weak disguise, but of course necessary for her foreseeable life on the run.

200

Amalie travelled with Surawelle. The older witch saw a lot of potential in the young girl. Surawelle's connection to quatra was to reading, rather than to tracking, smelling or seeing. Quatra manifested its connection through many senses, which meant that no two experiences of the energy were the same – as is the nature of the personal connection. Surawelle saw the potential in Amalie – who had now called herself *Vanna* – to perform great feats of reading and have an unspeakable connection to the energy which surrounds all.

Surawelle agreed to take Amalie with her to Sparta, where *Liktan* was spoken freely in the streets, and to send her to a local *Liktan* school for Suneva. She taught Amalie most of what she knew about reading, and every school holiday they would go on a trip to set up their gypsy-esque fortune telling tent and earn good money whilst practicing the art of quatra.

For the most part, Amalie was conflicted by how her life seemed to be turning out around her. As she solidified her connection to the black hole, and learned to manipulate its power in the ways she was taught, she felt incomplete. Yes, she loved to use her ability to hide, and feel a part of the shadows, to sleuth and to have this extraordinary sense of awareness, but it wasn't completely *her*. There was something missing. Surawelle's teaching focussed mainly on emotions themselves, but not how this formed the interactions *between* people. This was what interested her the most. Plus, whenever a non-Suneva came to the tent, Surawelle just shuffled the colour-cards and gave them a false future. That seemed wrong to Amalie, even if she personally didn't believe in destiny or the control of the black holes.

And she also felt a different pull – this deep connection to the earth, Not to the rock itself, or the elements in the rocks, but the actual Earth. Just like she did with people, she had an indescribable interaction with it. In some way, the giant inanimate rock talked to her. She didn't understand this connection.

Amalie didn't tell Surawelle about these urges either, instead letting them brew inside her between trips to school and the daily run from bounty hunters. Her connection clearly wasn't just to people, or the rock at her feet. In the world around her she saw the forces of nature. Objects were attracted and repelled, objects could move together, deform each other, orbit each other. Just as people did between themselves, in a sense. People attracted and repelled, they orbited through obsessions, they violently collided in arguments. Interactions were the forces, fuelled by emotional energy, and people were the objects. There was this base connection between everything in the universe. Everything went by these same rules – everything was strung together by the same glue.

She found some answers in her weapon – the giant spring loaded hammer which lay at her command. It was truly the ultimate symbol of force and power. Surely that's why the black hole gave it to her. Surely, she was missing something.

Then one day it clicked. She sat in school, eating lunch by herself under the shade of a giant, ancient olive tree. She thought about the connections, or more the irony that she felt this connection to human interaction yet kept minimal friends. She pondered how she felt about the Earth. Her connection to it, just like to everything else around her, felt like a tether between her and it. There was a force behind this interaction, just like every other interaction, she just had to *focus*…

Her face was forced into the red clay earth – surprisingly as if she was pulled towards it, rather than pushed from the back. The impact shattered her focus, but suddenly it seemed clear. *Gravity – that which binds objects in the universe.*

***

Celeste spent her years at the school, under the fake name Olomb had given her. A funny fact, she often thought, was that Olomb admitted his disguise to her too. Olomb was not his name, as no old Greek man would actually be called Kyros Orion Olomb. The last name was preposterous. He had given himself the name to create a political character as he rose in Suneva Politics. His real name, as it turned out, was Vasilli Dimos.

Na Taneste Suneva Mathenesia – the uncreatively named '*School for Young Suneva*' was situated in a collection of old bluestone buildings deep in the Victorian countryside. It sat on the centre of a large property, far from the view of any roads, and in an incredibly remote part of the state. Those who lived in the closest town knew of it, but didn't bother with it. From all else, it seemed to be a secret.

Celeste quickly rose to popularity in the school. She was intelligent, somewhat reserved, incredibly powerful, and certainly pretty. The boys who fawned over her would do her bidding, and she was not shy to their affection. She certainly didn't give them any hope though – if you crossed the young *Ivaer* of the blue flame, you got burned. Even being an *Ivaer* was especially out of the ordinary at this school. About three-quarters of the kids had a *quatran*, and of those only a fifth had an ability other than a single periodic element. *Liktas* and *welle* were common amongst special *quatran*, but *ivaer* was unheard of.

She, despite Olomb's warnings, still wore her earrings. They were given to her by her mother, they were a symbol of what she would become, but now represented who she was. The earrings were an *Ivaer* thing, family traditions that marked your ancestry. Of course, like most traditions in Suneva, they were passed down from the mother. How many Australians would know Juliette Leroux's ankh? Not even Naxaer wore them.

During the summers she went to live with Olomb in his meek suburban house near the city. She loved every moment near the bustling heart of Melbourne. To Celeste, it was what Paris was meant to me. Taste, class, food, and fashion, just with better people.

But then when summer ended she found herself back with the cows and kangaroos, trudging a mud pit in the middle of a nothing grassland in the most isolated old bluestone building in all of Victoria. It wasn't a prison per-se, but after four years of longing for the city life, complacent in her safety, it had her feeling a bit beside herself.

Her notoriety as an *Ivaer* had earned her animosity from some of her peers. With blue eyes, blonde hair, chubby build and unimpressive height, Taylah Seeker came to be the classic nemesis and exact opposite of Celeste by her ninth-grade class at the school. A *Welle* by training, and an absolute teacher's pet. Despite Celeste's clear ambivalence for the girl, Taylah went out of her way to annoy and disrupt Celeste. She wanted to see the French girl fall. Celeste could see it from her pedestal – and perhaps her nonchalance about her popularity is what set poor Taylah off.

So, the day when a trio of Argol firebearers burst into the school, Celeste had a pretty good idea of who ratted her out.

The fight was intense. Celeste was fourteen, barely able to produce her iconic blue flame. Its very licks of heat stunned the trio who had come to take her.

The Argols here were corrupt, she had learned from days spent with John Grey. They were driven heavily by money.

Teachers came out to see what the commotion was about, but were immediately disabled by the Argol trio. It seemed that teachers had never seen a moment of combat in their careers. Celeste was a good fighter. Olomb had trained her, and her father taught her well. Nobody had taught these men well. They used the fire like a weapon. Rather than being a soul expression, the flame was a tool. For Celeste, the flame was the pedal which drove her spirit, the pinnacle for her passions. Its tendrils whipped hot fury where she commanded, and they enacted her very will beyond her body's limits. This was what being a Suneva was about.

She ducked, rolled, dodged, and fired blasts of hot quatra. With the whole school watching from behind windows, the situation was ground to a hot stalemate. With no way out, and her body growing tired, Celeste did what she had to – she ran. She sprinted for the gate, storming the dirt track for the exit with bolts of quatra and licks of flame marking her tail. Celeste knew that she couldn't outrun the three men forever, but she had no other option.

Just about touching the gate, on the edge of escape, Celeste was thrown aside by a powerful force. A wave of mud had surged from the ground and beaten her down, followed by a bath of water. Her flames were gone and she was soaking wet. In her panic her soul constricted, dampened, and her passions refused to form flames. She rose quickly, not bothering to scrape herself dry before charging the gate.

But standing in the exit was the large body of Tona Narelle, with whom Olomb had entrusted Celeste's safety.

"Didn't think you'd get a free ride here, did you?" the *Welle* headmaster grinned. "Not for what I owe Vasilli, and not with that bounty on your head. You're about to make me rich…"

Her words spluttered from her fat lips with ambition and pride, but the headmistress hadn't won anything yet. With her physique, she hadn't won a battle in years…

Celeste didn't have time to think of concentrate. She could feel the Argol trio radiating as they closed in. With no flame, she had only one option, quatra. Celeste launched off the ground, leaping onto the Headmistress, who's impressive girth miraculously stopped her from being bowled over.

"What are you doing?" Narelle shrieked, grasping for water. Celeste's hand grappled the woman's neck, quatra amassing from her thread, surging to fire.

Celeste couldn't have seen the bolt flying towards her. Through her adrenaline, she had no sense for it. It zipped past her hip just as Narelle shifted, just as Celeste fired.

It hit the Headmistress in the chest, just as Celeste's left her hand for the woman's neck.

The first bolt disrupted Narelle's connection. Celeste's bolt tore through the woman's neck, spraying her with burning flesh and blood.

***

Amalie left Surawelle's home. She did not tell Surawelle why she was leaving, she did not even see the woman as she left. She knew enough about the Legendaries to recognise the target above her head. Amalie's Sunevahood might have saved her form her father's men, but it now bought with it its own consequences. She would always be on the run. Nobody could know what she was.

Amalie had time now to figure out how this power of hers worked. The first thing she'd discovered was altering her own attraction and repulsion to the earth. It let her fly. She leapt out of Sparta by muting her interactions with the earth and launching off a wall. She sailed of her bounce, soaring across mountain faces.

Next came strengthening and weakening her bond to all other objects around her. Gravity was a force that acted between all masses. It cannot be perceived regularly, as your shoes do not attract you as strongly as the earth, but the tethers still exist, and can be altered. Amalie learned to strengthen these connections to draw herself towards objects. Occasionally objects would fly towards her, as she was more massive than they were – so she learned to only pull on objects which were especially heavy, like trees, or mountains, or boulders, or buildings.

Amalie bounded over Europe, pushing herself away from the Earth and pulling herself towards the landmarks she could see. In the cities, she hid in the shadows, attracting food and money to her hand out of unsuspecting mitts. Little by little she made a sustainable life of supernatural theft.

Her power turned to incredible liberation, despite the isolation. As a controller of gravity she got to choose how tethered she got to her surroundings. If she didn't like a place, she simply moved and grounded somewhere else. What had seemed a curse was truly a blessing. She had freedom.

Still, she couldn't be too obtuse about her power. She learned that lesson quickly after being ogled by tourists on a northern Greek mountain road. She kept her movements to the night, when she could be out of sight in black clothing amongst the stars. She'd become nocturnal by this point. It was freedom at the price of friendship and sanity. But it worked.

***

Tona Narelle's body, or what was left of it, fell in all directions. Behind it, a figure was revealed standing in the gate, with gleaming gold, black and purple armour. It had its hooked sawblade drawn by its side, a thunderous crack of electricity arced to the ground beneath it.

Olomb marched onto the ground with confidence and height which defied his old age. The three attackers pushed on, but were wiped out in a second when Olomb raised his weapon and sent a split arc of hellish lightning to each of their chests. All at once they convulsed and dropped to the ground. He scooped up the shaken Celeste, put her in a car, and drove off away from the school.

He settled her back down at his house and went to prepare the guest room for her. Celeste was shaking as she washed the dried blood off her hands, face, neck, *everywhere.* The shower ran dirty brown beneath her soiled soul. Through her eyes, she could see her hands grow bigger, bulker, hairier. She saw the golden ring of her father's hand splattered in crimson, sewn to her arms. Celeste had run away from Adam Leroux, but in doing so she'd never been closer to him. She would never escape.

Olomb drew her from her obsessions, giving Celeste a hot tea and a hand-crafted blanket to wear upon his old-man couch. Olomb had led great battles before, and he told Celeste that the brutality of death by quatra had never faded. The experience of killing with quatra was life altering. Celeste would have to grow with the guilt, but understand that it wasn't her fault.

Celeste didn't feel that his words were comforting, and the old man trailed off, muttering that he knew a psychologist. He would get her somebody to talk to, and then get her back in the world with a new name, and a new contact. She would be safe again, and he promised it as he trudged into his office.

There was a knock on the front door. Celeste peeked from her place on the couch down the hallway. She could see an inhuman figure through the obscuring glass window. She tossed the blanket off, standing to peer through the door, but before she could get halfway down the hall, the window erupted into a massive flash of light. She drew her flaming sword and pulled her armour from her soul. It encapsulated her as the door crashed open, the sheared door-jam sweeping across the hard-wood floor.

The yellow, purple and titanium armoured figure stepped in. Only just taller than Iva, but with a dominant demeanour. Their helmet was sleek and thin, with two protrusions around the chin like mandibles, and a face separated up the middle by a strip of glowing cyan which split into eyebrows above the cyan eyes. Two thick fins ran from the mandibles to stick up the sides of its head, with little lightning bolt horns adorning their tops.

"You're not who I was expecting," the Suneva said bluntly. "Olomb you coward, where are you hiding? Come out and face the day."

Iva hissed a Suneva screech. It was powerfully haunting; the most chilling ghost scream she'd ever produced. She flared the blue flames on her sword crouched low, ready to strike.

The yellow Suneva called Iva's bluff. They advanced on her and raised the tip of their jagged, titanium sword to her neck. It buzzed with electricity. Iva froze, and the Suneva pushed her aside. Olomb appeared from the doorway in his gleaming golden armour. Iva noted the similarities between Olomb and this new Suneva, their helmets were almost identical, and their colours were starkly similar.

"Hesslik," Olomb greeted, "why would you make such an entrance? Have you no manners?"

"No manners for you, Olomb, and no time for you either," Hesslik hissed.

"That's not the way one should speak to the Suneva who taught them their quatran…"

"Olomb, the time for niceties is over!" Hesslik doubled his volume, raising the sword to Olomb. "I'm not your student any more. I would never admit to being taught by such a coward."

"You know that what I did…"

"You failed the Suneva Olomb. You abandoned the Electric Nation when the people needed it most. What of the people now?"

"The *people* abandoned us, Hesslik," Olomb retorted, calmly. "They went to live normal lives. They decided long ago that they didn't need the nation."

"And what of the Argols? You're soft, Olomb, you let him get away with it."

"His actions were brash but he's better than his tyrant father. Why shouldn't we let the Suneva seek his protection?"

"Because he kills innocent people with quatra. That's extortion. You should have toxicated the man till his thread came loose! Your council of old people - that White Witch, her gypsy sister Surawelle, and Muhrakiin – have failed everybody."

At that moment a tall, black Suneva came through the door. Dark as the night with a pointed bird-like face and beady pink eyes. His cape – what looked like a collection of metal strips, rustled behind him. Boekidin.

"Now Hesslik, there's no need to be brash," Olomb said, still standing tall.

"There is, old man," Hesslik snapped, "I won't see the Suneva let down by you. You claimed to be the saviour of our people! You were meant to bring us united into the modern world. But I can't wait for you to act." Hesslik raised his weapon, Olomb backed up.

"Social change doesn't happen overnight, child," Olomb scorned, "I've had my plan underway for centuries. This is my doing and if you interfere with my plans now you could ruin everything I've spent four lifetimes setting up. Your anger at my recent actions isn't worth this. You *will* destroy it for us all."

"Four centuries is enough time," Hesslik said calmly, "I think it's time somebody stopped talking about change and started to implement it."

Arcs of energy sparked from Hesslik's jagged blade tip. The erratic blue tendrils violently burst, and then converged into a single tentacle of energy. The plasma turned red as Hesslik concentrated, its energy becoming almost uncontrollable. The room glowed with its ominous red buzz. He cracked the red snake like a whip, burning a line in the roof.

"Go!" Olomb shouted to Iva. He dropped a piece of paper by his side and discreetly gestured to it. He held his weapon strong in his left hand, and with nothing more than a flick, a thick, red rope of plasma erupted from his blade's tip.

"Don't try to beat your master at his own trick," Olomb scowled. Hesslik swung his red whip. Olomb dodged, rolled, and spun. Another cut tore through the roof and floor. As Olomb spun he flared his power. The rope of plasma stretched out and almost cut Hesslik's sword straight out of his hand. Boekidin and Iva jumped back in alarm.

Hesslik sparked his plasma and swung again. More marks in the roof, with Olomb evading once more. Olomb's only retaliation was to dodge each blow. He wasn't going to kill Hesslik, but Hesslik had no second thoughts about killing his old master.

Olomb retracted his plasma, instead switching to a quatra attack. Hesslik kept swinging, using the red line of superhot material to dissipate the blasts. The room was quickly becoming scarred. Another whip of plasma and a section of ceiling fell between Olomb and Hesslik. They both leaped clear as it crashed down, but Olomb wasn't so lucky. A beam came down atop of him, pinning him to the floor. The paper note was flung towards Iva by the resulting wind. She lunged forward to catch it and help Olomb, but the piece of paper shifted course and slotted itself through a plasma-burned line in the floor.

Hesslik raced to his feet, plasma arc burning. Olomb struggled with the beam. Iva was almost there. She dove forward, grabbing the old Suneva's arm. She went to tug him away but was blinded – a red snake of energy coming down right next to her. It burned through the beam, through the chest of Kyros Orion Olomb, and straight through the floor. His arm went limp in hers.

Iva thought she'd scream, or run, or fall further into her shell – but the death didn't scare her away. Rather, her blood burned hot, her passions seething, calling the might of her soul. This rising wasn't rage, it wasn't vengeance, it wasn't hatred. This was some feeling she'd never known before. It was pure defiance, and absolute strength.

Iva screamed, throwing herself at Hesslik. Her arm collided with his shoulder as he knelt, and he was sent flying backwards onto his arse. His head slammed against the wall and his plasma dissipated. Iva scrunched her claw-like toes and kicked him in the face, then grabbed him with her powerful, long fingers and threw him as hard as she could. Hesslik crashed through the coffee table in a daze, and started to struggle himself up, his armour scratched and dented. Those marks would *hurt*.

Iva wasn't done. She picked up her sword, flared its power, and sent a torrent of blue flames to the downed Liktas. A pink bolt of quatra skimmed her face – thrown from behind her. Boekidin fired another round from his golden staff, which Iva deflected and sent right back.

She was hit by intense pain in her right side, sending her into convulsions. Hesslik now stood, and between Iva and Hesslik was an arc of blue power. Iva fell from the shock's path, miraculously rolling under the shot fired by Boekidin and landing back up to her feet, standing in the door to Olomb's secondary hallway. Two bolts came at her at once. She fired back on one and deflected the other, but realised she was outnumbered and outmatched.

She sprinted into the hallway, slamming its door shut behind her. Without a second consideration, she charged through the bathroom and launched herself out of its obscured glass window, rolling to a stand in the house's side alley. She vaulted the fence before her and let her armour fall away. Celeste saw a thick bush behind a shed in this yard, and she sprinted for it, hiding amongst the leaves.

She heard Hesslik and Boekidin rush the broken window and come to a stop. Their voices carried across the yard.

"Do you think it's her?" Hesslik asked Boekidin. There was no concern to his tone about the murder which he had committed.

"It's definitely her," Boekidin said. "No *Ivaer* outside of the Argol family is that powerful. She even has his sword."

"This could play well. If we return her, we'll get the sympathy of Argol's men."

"I think that'll be harder to earn back, considering our large efforts against them here. The Melbourne section of the gang would never side with us."

"Maybe…" Hesslik trailed off. His foot turned on broken glass, and he stepped back into the destroyed house.

Celeste waited quietly, absorbing her shock. Her heart raced, and her mind didn't believe her own circumstances. The only person she could trust was dead.

It was then that she heard Hesslik and Boekidin leave the house, slamming the front door without abandon. She jumped up from her spot, vaulting the fence to sneak into the back yard of Olomb. She needed that piece of paper he'd written her.

She summoned her sword and sliced through the back door. Olomb's body was gone from the floor, with no signs of being dragged anywhere. The ceiling and floor were a mess, and dust hung in the darkness between. She saw the hole where she thought the note for her had gone, and drove her sword into it. The charred wood cracked away easily, and she could see the paper resting on the earth below the floor boards. She reached for it and turned it over.

Names. The first was John Grey. The rest she did not recognise. At the bottom, hurriedly written, was a sentence telling her that these were safe places to stay – a final list of contacts for her to use.

She gave her sword back to her soul and its higher plane of existence, and shut off her quatra once more.

There was a noise, a rustling from the small hallway. Iva paused, her first instinct was to rip her sword out again, but she thought against it, least she alert Hesslik's senses. She *really* shouldn't have gotten it out in the first place, but her mind wasn't working right. Instead, Celeste snuck behind the couch, peering to the hallway entrance.

Slow, heavy footsteps rang from the hall, echoing intensely into the living room. Celeste shivered, frozen, as the creaks moaned loader. Finally, their owner came to the door, and halted.

But there was nobody to make the sound.

Instead, an ominous purple light hovered at neck-height in the doorway – small branches of light arcing from it. A shadow growing to fill the space.

A single word, maybe a name, consumed Celeste's thoughts – *Kuvalik*.

Celeste held her scream at the sight of the ghost, but she couldn't stop her legs from running. They carried her through the broken back door, and she kept running despite the possibility of drawing a scene, all the way to John Grey's house.

Little did she know that John Grey had passed away that morning.

Episode 4

New Year – New Me: If I survive It.

Chapter 21
The Reunion

On the long train trip from Paris to Marseille we had become engrossed in Amalie and Celeste's stories of the past seven years. It was an odd conversation, to be a passenger in a family reunion, to know the depth of the deception we'd been fed. Certainly Natalie was keen to hear the details, and fished them out herself when needed.

We received strange, sidelong glances from the servers aboard the train as they entered to offer snacks. A man had been sitting in our compartment when we came to occupy it, and he was quite happy to stay until we all started speaking Liktan. He moved quickly after that, making no excuse.

"Most people still don't trust a darker man speaking Liktan," Argol explained when the man had left. "They think we're gypsies...and, well, my mother *is* a gypsy, so I suppose I am. One day, speaking Liktan won't earn you such stares."

I waited until the end of Celeste and Amalie's stories to start asking questions, although my mind was bursting at the seams, the pressure of curiosity driving me insane.

"So, that house you're describing, *Olomb's* house, is the one where we've been living with the Ghost Kuvalik?" I asked Celeste.

"Oui," she nodded, "I'm certain that Kuvalik *is* his ghost. Although the ghost hasn't admitted it. The ghost has the same voice, just...different. Cheerier, I guess."

"And Olomb is also *Vasilli Dimos*, the old man who led Chad across America?" I asked.

"Oui," Celeste said. Chad chuckled, shaking his head.

"So, *my* old man, is *your* old man, is James' ghost?" Chad asked. "*And* he's *Kyros Orion Olomb*, the historical leader of the Electric Nation? The man who's been avoiding his responsibilities for hundreds of years?"

"I think he was doing an awful lot, Chad," Celeste defended. "Like he said, big plans take a long time."

"However long he took, it makes *more* sense that the man was three people at once," Argol reminisced. "I thought I had rich connections, but Olomb had an astronomical number, all varied. He quite literally got me off murder charges."

"He did?" I sputtered.

"Yes," Argol frowned. "And I have no idea why."

"I think it's clear that he had some grand plan," Natalie said, finally adding her contribution. She'd stayed strangely quiet since the catacombs. "He wanted to bring us all together for some reason. The four marco elementals, as he put it himself."

"I wonder what the plan was, then," Chad hummed. "Surely we aren't his *grand plan*, the five-hundred years in the making *grand plan*. That's just unbelievable."

"Maybe we're the backup plan," Natalie suggested, "I doubt he *intended* for Hesslik to kill him."

"But he met Chad and I before Hesslik killed him," Celeste said, "and he had connections to John Grey and Lilawelle since long before that. We have to be a part of what he was planning."

"And what was he trying to achieve with us, then?" Natalie asked. "I wonder what his final vision for the Suneva was…"

"I guess we can just ask him," I said. "He's the ghost we've been living with. He's not *dead* dead yet. Maybe this is our purpose."

"Our *destiny*," Celeste corrected, and we all nodded along, except Natalie, who hummed.

"So, you think you're a part of his plan for the Suneva revival, and you want to take down Hesslik," Argol quizzed. "Seems to me like were fighting the same battle. Only, I've been in the game for many more years. There's just one thing I'm worried about that might underpin your plans."

"What's that?" Natalie asked, waiting smugly on criticism.

"You dislike Hesslik mainly because what you think he'll do to the threads. But who first learned of his 'plan?'" Argol eyed us each in the cabin. I raised my hand. "And how sure are you that you're right?"

"I saw the sequence through Vestas' eyes. I saw the inception of the thread removal device…" I glanced about the compartment for support, but I was met with only cynical, quizzing eyes. "The vision showed Hesslik ordering Vestas to make a device to send the signal across the globe, before he wiped the scientists mind." Still, frowns looked on. "You don't all believe me?"

"I'm doubting it all after yesterday's encounter," Natalie said. "You confronted Boekidin on his beliefs, and he was fighting for the Suneva wholeheartedly, chasing peace. Boekidin couldn't be dumb, and he seems incredibly passionate. He thinks we, rather than Hesslik, are the threat to his freedom."

"Yes, because Hesslik erased the memories from Vestas!" I pleaded.

"Would he erase the plan from his own mind, though?" Natalie asked. "Boekidin feels like the kind of Suneva to scan the minds of everybody he talks to. The kind of guy to not take any risks. You believe he would trust Hesslik without running through his brain?"

I had no answer to this. Boekidin was the Shiverman, he was connected to a web of minds, a plethora of perspectives. He was also an asshole, and I believed that the bird-man would have to have ventured into his boss' brain.

"I…uh…" I stammered. "You're putting a lot of trust in Boekidin," I said. "We know that he's manipulative."

"He wasn't lying yesterday," Amalie interjected. "Not a bit. His aura was full of passion and honesty. It's why I heard him out."

"I see…" I hummed.

"And if Hesslik *is* planning to build this huge transmission device, Suneva would have to know about it, or else there'd be nobody building or researching it," Natalie continued. "Boekidin would have to come across the idea at some point."

"Vestas is building it, though. He says it's a 'free-energy' device," I defended.

"And maybe it truly is, then," Natalie crossed her arms, "I don't think we've got enough evidence to say otherwise."

"Doesn't mean that it *couldn't* be used like James thinks it will," Celeste noted. "Surely somebody has opposed Hesslik to suggest that the thread-cutting signal could be put through it."

"Maybe they have," Natalie agreed, "we just can't prove those intentions yet. We haven't come across these concerns, and we've been meeting a lot of Suneva."

"None from Hesslik's castle, though," Chad added. "None of the people who count. If only there was an easy way to get into Hesslik's castle to find what we need. Knowing Hesslik, though, everything will be guarded. It would be too risky."

"Then I think, amazingly, I have your solution," Adam Leroux smirked, reaching into his travel bag. "I received these in the mail, but I don't think it's wise for me to attend." He handed Natalie three slips of pink paper, marked with an illustration and date.

"New-year's Ball at the Electric Throne…" Natalie read from the slip's header. "*A masquerade party to bring in the year 1999, with a special announcement.*" She turned to Argol, "Hesslik gave these to you? Surely it's an ambush."

"So I thought, but I chased it up and it seems that many of his respected friends received the exact same slips. An invitation to a first-of-its-kind, no-armour-allowed masquerade ball to gather Suneva and supporters of the Empire. Of course, I'm sure if *I* turn up, it will be an ambush. But three young Suneva in masquerade without their identifying *alis*…" He grinned, sitting back into his chair, "I think you'll make good use of it."

"It's a good opportunity to investigate, if not a little dangerous," Natalie hummed, passing the tickets around. I grabbed one, feeling the high quality of the material. "I know I've seemed cynical, James," she said to me, and I turned my head up to her. "I just want to make sure we're fighting for the right thing."

"I think a reality check is always good," Chad answered for me, speaking as I was about to. "And this seems like an opportunity we can't miss, if we're looking for evidence. The circumstances are almost perfect."

Natalie snorted, "It's unbelievable that some Suneva don't believe in the power of destiny, when these insane contrivances keep happening." She shook her head, "what evidence will we hope to find, though?"

All eyes turned to me. Under the stage fright, I fell inside myself, mind running blank. I knew that both thread removal technology and this device existed, and I had to make the link between them. The only real link so far was my vision, so how could I affirm it?

"If I can find the lab where the vision occurred, then we know that the vision was of something real," I said, reciting my plan as it came to me. "I couldn't have imagined a real place that I'd never seen before. I guess you'll just have to believe me when I recognise them."

"And what says that the labs are in Hesslik's Castle?" Natalie asked.

"Nothing," I admitted.

"If they're not, we've still got access to Hesslik's most powerful adversaries, and hopefully some of his files," Chad said. "I should be able to find information, even just from conversations heard through the floor. It's what Hesslik trained me to do."

"Okay, it sounds good then," Natalie hummed, relaxing into her seat.

"So, who stays behind?" I asked. "There's only three tickets, and four of us."

"I'll stay behind," Celeste interjected before anybody could claim the absence, "it'll be good to have more time with my family. I want to spend the new year with them."

"Can't argue that," I shrugged. "I guess it's settled then. Another insane plan."

***

The Argol household was a modest, a terraced house which slotted directly between the other identical, three storey facades of the street. Sandwiched between the abutting houses, there was barely five metres of off-white stone to its girth. Stepping up from the outside, it was just a standard looking terraced house. Up its face, flower pots hung from balconies, vines growing down from the roof.

Argol set his key in the heavy, dark wood door, and opened it to reveal a stark interior. Cream walls, dark floors, monochrome outfittings. He called into cold house as he opened the door, something in French which I believed to be to the effect of 'darling' or 'honey I'm home'.

From the staircase descended a woman of commanding posture, embroidered coat hanging off her body, fanning her stride. One hand draped over the railing, her every step was marked with poise, her nose held high, her heels clicking with precision. Her head of half-greys sat as if undisturbed by her calculated step.

She greeted her husband back in French – something along the lines of 'oh love, thank god your home' – but then her eyes drifted over to her daughters.

The woman fainted.

No signals, no heavy breath, simply the loss of her legs as they collapsed under her, sending her sprawling backwards across the stairs.

***

Their mother – Juliette Leroux – *Sanavaer* – had been revived, and filled in on her daughters' past seven years over a fast-moving glass of wine. We sat around the kitchen's bar, a spread of cheeses neatly displayed on the table, raided by Chad and I. It was only morning, but that didn't stop Madame Leroux from her frequent sips of red wine between her huge, bug-eyed black glasses. She kept her lips pursed tightly between words and held her nose high. On her ears, like Celeste and Amalie, hung a pair of ankh earrings. Juliette's, however, were silver in colour.

"Well I couldn't have imagined Olomb and Surawelle to raise such accomplished Suneva." She remarked, dabbing her cigarette against the ash-tray. The fire at its tip was bright purple. "Neither could barely guide a nation."

"Olomb is behind something bigger than you believe, Mum - Even in his death." Celeste suggested kindly – without a hint of snark.

"And the two of you are greater than you believe," she said to her daughters. The memo was nice, but the words were still cold as they creeped out of her stark, red lips. "You avoided all of the forces of this world for seven years. One of you controls an indigo fire, the other is a Legendary. What would you need to come back for? You've already succeeded in life."

"To see you and Dad again, of course. To apologise for leaving. To make some amends. To come home and smell your cooking again," Celeste said.

"It's a compliment, but you were doing well, darling."

"Aren't you excited that we're home?" Amalie was shocked.

"I thought you were dead," their mother remarked, taking her large, black sunglasses off her head. "I grieved for a long time, but I accepted it. I learned to love what I had. It's hard to think that all of the years spent depressed were for nothing." She looked back to her cigarette and took a long drag. The smoke fell dully from her pointed nose. Her face seemed paler. She turned to her daughters.

"I…I'm sorry, Mum," Celeste said, her voice unstable, "really, I…"

"You were always my fire," she addressed them both. "You did what you did. Things will never be the same, but different isn't always bad. I'm glad you're home, but don't apologise. You both turned out to be good kids and that's all I could have hoped for. Anything that happened is better than dead kids."

Celeste started to cry. Amalie started to cry. Chad started to cry. Their mother Juliette did not cry, she'd already cried these tears, she just wanted to be happy again. She squeezed her daughters' hands from across the bar. The emotions in the room were exploding – spilling out in all directions. The one thing I noted most of all was the thickness of quatra around me. The energy pooled with the spirits of its users, and was dense with the energy of the soul. I could see Natalie meditating on the power around her. I always wondered what the energy did to her. What was she feeling in this room?

Chapter 22
Imeres Avoul

I woke on Christmas day in the guest room of the Argol household. I was on the third storey of the thin, modest abode. I tossed aside the thick, comfy doona onto Chad as I got out of bed. He groaned, his unconscious body grappling the thrown covers and drawing them in. I pulled myself up, peering at the white morning-light shining into the bedroom.

Outside it was snowing. I'd never seen snow.

My eyes blared wide. I toed out of the room, then threw myself down the central column of the stairs, jumping straight down to the ground.

"Amasos, *James*," I heard Natalie gasp as I landed on a cushion of blasted air. The house was still dark here, no souls yet stirring. Natalie raced to the foot of the stair set.

"Christ, James, I forget you can do that..." Natalie caught her breath, whispering. "I thought your legs would break."

"Would have been more than that," I chuckled, and she eyed me sternly.

"What's the rush to get down here?" She asked.

"There's snow!" I grinned, pointing to the front door. "The street is covered. I saw it from the window."

"Snow?" Natalie's face turned, concern rising to a smile. "I've never seen snow. I was wondering when we would."

"Neither," I said, "come on, let's check it out." And I slid towards the door, turning the handle to let the white light of day spew in.

The ground was white, and the day cold and biting. A gust caught my bones through the doorway. I should have trusted a family of flamethrowers to keep a warm abode.

Natalie stepped out before me, hands in her peace-sign pose. Water slicked up from under the white cover, charmed in her grasp.

"It's…" she stumbled for words. I joined her out on the front path, past the short gate and onto the street. The snow was but a layer of slosh. Only half frozen, only a millimetre high. It felt more like somebody had tipped a frozen soda machine over the earth.

"It's disappointing," I hummed, finishing Natalie's sentence.

"Yes," she frowned, "I mean, it's fun for a *Welle*. But I expected it to be more *structural*, you know?" She reached down, abandoning her amassed water to pick up a wad of snow. It slipped in between her fingers.

"You guys want *snow*?" A deep voice rang from behind. We turned to see Chad. "You'll have to come home to central Oregon. Up in the hills we've got real snow. This stuff is just cold water."

"I'm sure," Natalie hummed, and stepped back towards the entrance. I frowned, kicking a lump of slush. "And I'm glad you're up. We've got some work to do getting this place ready for today."

Ah, today, *Imeres Avoul* – The Day of the Soul. It was the twenty-fifth of December, the day commonly associated with Christmas, which the Suneva had hijacked for their own holiday largely built on the same principals of family and food. There was a lot to do to get the Argol house ready, as there would be more than one hundred guests coming to the esteemed event, and we'd all agreed to help with the chore list. Natalie and I had never seen an Imeres Avoul, and had no idea what to expect of the day. Chad had celebrated one or two with Hesslik, but Celeste and Amalie were the two among us who were hungrily awaiting today. Strangely, they weren't awake at the break of dawn.

I followed Natalie inside, where the house had stirred awake in a matter of minutes, and chores were distributed by Madame Leroux. Celeste, stumbling groggily down the stairs, was to help her mother cook the feast. Chad was on lifting and rearranging duty with Adam, clearing space in the ground floor for visitors. Natalie was on cleaning floors and counters, and I was assigned to clean the walls, ceiling, corners that nobody could reach, and anything else just out of an arm's distance because 'you can fly, can't you?'.

Being emasculated for my inability as a *Kiin* wasn't exactly how I wanted to spend my morning, and I made the best effort to make clean those tricky places as demonstration of my skill. A traditional lunch of roast goat with mountain herbs was being prepared by Celeste and her mother, the smells of which wafted into the highest corners of the house and set me salivating for the whole morning. I was told that all the guests would bring their own food, but it was up to the hosts to cook the traditional goat.

At midday the house was clean, and purple flame burned in the fireplace, giving a soulful warmth to the living room. The firsts guests arrived just as the last chore was done. They came in droves, first the older, geriatric relatives, with souls hanging by their last threads of quatra, afraid to be late lest they not make it till the lunch. Then came the more vibrant family and friends, and finally orbital friends, Argol gang members, Vince from down the road. I struggled to hold onto all the names and faces I'd been introduced to. They swum loosely in my mind as I wafted from guest to guest. To my name, most Suneva mentioned John Grey, the human who was doing his gallant effort to further the Suneva community. Across the party spread whispers that Maiki was John Grey's son. I huffed, keen to be known as *James*, to not live in a shadow.

The names *Maiki, Zamelle,* and *Ferrad* were well known now, too, even in the Argol sphere. Somehow, the name John Grey was bigger. Just who was my dad?

Celeste took the time to introduce me to a young man – one of the only other young Suneva our age.

"Yvon," he introduced himself.

"James," I greeted back, shaking his hand.

The boy was some image of style, dressed much better for the occasion than I could have packed for. Shoulder to knee waistcoat offset with a tartan scarf, posture held high as if his neck was wired to the gods. From his perch a good inch above me, I felt his reigning charm.

"Yvon was one of my childhood friends," Celeste explained. "He's a *kidin*, we used to go to school together, until I ran off."

"And I think we've got a lot of catching up to do," he said with a sly smile in a strange, mutt accent of French and Liktan.

"I would think so," I said. "It's not often that you miss out on *seven years* of somebody's life."

Yvon nodded his acknowledgement, then turned his shoulder to me, speaking directly to Celeste in French. I frowned, and would have moved away if Celeste hadn't grasped my shoulder for dear might as she doubled over laughing at the man's incomprehensible joking. She cried from the exertion. I felt a pang on my soul, and my eye twitched, but I was pulled aside by the call of my name.

"James," the voice said, and I found myself facing Alexis LeGrand, Capo of Melbourne.

"Mister LeGrand, I didn't expect to see you here," I put out my hand for him to shake. Celeste's hand dropped from my shoulder, but her sweet, thunderous laugh still pounded the back of my skull, forcing my grimace.

"All of the Dons and Capos come to this party," LeGrand explained. "If you wanted more connections, this is the right place." He gestured to the mass of people congregating around the food, "but I just wanted to congratulate you on finding a Legendary, and Mr. Argol."

"Oh, thank you, sir," I said.

"Didn't want to bring a Legendary along to the party?"

"They didn't want to be identified," I said, "and I think it's better that way."

"Very well then," he smirked. "I'll take your word, but I'm still sceptical. I'm not convinced they exist yet." He winked and patted me on the shoulder. "But nobody was convinced that Amalie was still alive, and you and your friends really showed us all. Finding a regular person is more impressive, in my opinion, than finding a super powerful, ancient Suneva."

I laughed at the dramatic irony. "Don't look at me – it was Celeste who found her. We just followed the Code of Connections."

"In all my years, kid, I've never heard of anybody doing *anything* that fantastic with the code. We follow it, but nobody finds lost loved ones, Legendaries, or Argol lairs," he said, gracefully grabbing cheese and a biscuit from a passing platter. "As a team you're all very, very impressive."

222

"That means a lot, sir, coming from a Suneva so revered by Argol himself," I smiled. LeGrand took the compliment in his stride, smirk glowing.

"So, what's the plan now?" He asked. "Coming back home?"

"That'll be soon, I think," I said. "Following the code will lead us there, and plenty more places."

"I see…" LeGrand nodded, eyebrow raised. "Well, when you do come back, make sure to drop by my office. I could give you some guidance, but I'd like to hear whatever stories you have to tell."

"Of…of course, Capo LeGrand," I smiled, "I'll make sure to swing by."

"Please," Alexis nodded, and turned to leave, but paused. "The witch, the girl you all follow, what's her name?"

"Natalie," I said.

"That's it, isn't it? Thanks." He smiled, and followed a tray of food away.

***

The afternoon banquet of food covered all counters in the kitchen. The display of flavours was vast and varied – moreso than the Christmases at home, even more than the feast at Surawelle's. Chad learned from his experience there, and followed my lead in taking small portions of everything. It was all delicious, and the desserts afterwards delivered the final blow to my stomach's walls. I made sure to thank Juliette and Celeste Leroux for their hard work putting together the centrepiece of the feast, and promptly sat down to stew in my gluttony amongst the other casualties.

To disturb the peace of my stomach was the sudden eruption of folk music. Trumpet and accordion bounced over bass and drums. The oldies in the room hoisted themselves up, everybody flocking to the cleared living room.

"What's the next event?" I asked Celeste as she came from the kitchen. She grabbed my hand, pulling me up off my stool and twirling me into life.

"This, James, is Suneva dancing."

"Suneva have dances?" I mused. "But Suneva are so varied…"

"Traditions are strong. I'm French, but I'm a Suneva. Amalie was culturally Suneva before she even had abilities."

"Right," I hummed, "so, can somebody teach me the dances before I make an idiot of myself?"

"I'm going to, silly," She smiled. "Come on. I'll show you." And she skipped away, releasing my hand to float towards the staircase. I followed her trail, up the set of stairs and into her room. Once inside, she closed the door and dove her hand into a chest of tapes. The party outside was drowned in this tall, narrow room. There was nothing in here but the air between us.

Celeste palmed a tape into the player atop her dresser, and the silence was replaced by a beat. She spun to me, her hazel hair shining in the white daylight. Her eyes locked to mine as she grabbed my right palm. My blood stopped.

This girl was beautiful, and despite the lies, she always had some genuine care for me. The last time I asked her how she felt was standing outside Vestas' Melbourne labs, Kuvalik's book in hand. That was an eternity ago, how had I let so much time pass and never asked again? Hell, she'd been reaching for my hand on every bend on every road in Greece, on the floor in her father's office, when she shed tears. I shouldn't have been confused at all, yet here I was.

But I knew I'd screw things up by talking. Being a Suneva was all about following the soul, following the pull of the world. Maybe I had to trust that.

"This is the *Zola*," Celeste said, drawing me back to the music, "if you need to know only one dance, it's this one." She stood to my side, putting one foot before the other. I clumsily emulated.

"You hold hands in a circle and dance with your feet. You dance next to your friends, or, if you like the look of somebody else, you dance next to them and it's a traditional way of showing interest."

"So, flirting?" I wheezed, my cheeks flushing red as her lips.

"Exactly," She smiled, "now, look at our hands." She squeezed mine, taking my full attention. I was sure she could sense my heartbeat. "See this? The man's hand is always on top. Now, first we take three steps to the right..." She pulled me off to the right, off my balance. "Then back on the left, forward on the left, back on the right, together, then it starts again." I didn't struggle to follow along. That much was easy, and she led me for laps around her cramped room.

As I picked up my confidence, Celeste threw more skilled moves in. Her heels clacked and span as her legs moved to a blur, kicking and rising between the basic steps. "If you've been doing it for years, you add in your own variations," she said, noticing my amazement.

"How do you know what to put in?" I asked, trying my own kick and losing my rhythm.

"It's the day of the soul – you do whatever you feel. There's no *correct*, but it can certainly look wrong," she teased, and ground herself to a stop.

I fell into her, too tied up on my left feet, and she caught both of my hands, spinning me around to pull me up. We were close now. Standing toe to toe, her nose at my throat. Her eyes slowly raised to meet mine.

There was no air between us now. Save our breath.

"You know, James," she almost whispered, the tone of which sent my legs giddy, begging them to topple, "I really do appreciate how kind you've always been to me."

"You…do?" I stumbled on my words.

"You didn't have to take all of *this* so well. My past, my story, my admission. Even if you haven't been taking it well, and you don't want to admit that you're mad, I really appreciate that you've been supportive."

"I have?"

"Although I'd hope that you'd tell me if you feel wronged. I don't want you to hide that," she turned stern, and my brain was too hopelessly lost swimming in a pool of lust and confusion to comprehend the change in tone.

"I'd tell you if I had mixed feelings," I said. "I get your situation. Lies intended to protect you snowballed. You couldn't have known that we'd all end up friends."

She raised an eyebrow to my statement. I literally had no idea what she was getting at. My mind froze.

"Although, I mean, you should take some of the blame," *No, that's stupid!* "Like, learn from it, is all. Learn something…" Goodness, I couldn't have screwed up more badly. I knew I shouldn't have talked. Just smile and nod, that's all it takes.

She smirked, shaking her head in a chuff. "Sure, James," she said. "But thank you for being somebody I can trust. I'm sorry that I betrayed that, but I hope we can build it again."

"Of course," I smiled dumbly, still transfixed in her gaze. Her hands moved from mine, finding instead my waist. Her fingers gripped in, she raised onto her toes. I lost my breath as she came up to meet me. Hot breath on my lips.

And then she stepped back, turning to walk away. "We shouldn't miss the dancing," she said, and I fumbled into the bed, holding myself tall against its frame.

"No, we shouldn't," I gasped, and stumbled to follow her out the door.

Downstairs, four giant circles of the *Zola* tracked, two groups to the living room, two to the hallway and the kitchen. Natalie spotted me searching in the crowd, and called me over, making space for me next to her in one circle.

I grabbed her hand, watching Celeste brush past the group. Craning my head as we stepped around the room, I gestured for her to join me with a roll of the eyes, but she wasn't looking. Instead she waltzed purposely over to the spry, young circle, her hand locking with a familiar face.

Yvon.

The way he smiled at her, the way she smiled back, the way their hands squeezed at just the right pressure. It pinned down my chest, forcing me to growl in my jealously.

Celeste was playing games with me. She'd been doing it this whole time.

Chapter 23
The Grand Ball

Truly, the hardest part about buying plane tickets was always trying to sell diamonds. It wasn't finding the right flight, or getting there on time without forgetting something, or even fitting your legs between your ass and the seat in front of you – no it was *definitely* the diamonds.

It was how we got around anyway. *James*, Natalie would instruct me, *just go find some diamonds and sell them somewhere. That should cover the tickets, right?* So, I'd go out in the city and I'd find some carbon just floating in the air, supercondense it, and we'd have diamonds ahoy. But again, that's the easy part.

Argol *had* offered to pay for our flights and tickets to Hesslik's grand ball, in fact, he offered to fund the rest of our trip, but Natalie had refused the money – I'd hope out of principals rather than pride. So here I was, running around as the scam boy for our extra cash. I was happy to get out of the house and be useful. I didn't want to be around Celeste, rather, I wanted to stew on our past interactions alone, until I, by the power of self-deprecating thought, had construed her intentions well beyond the facts. Surely it was the only healthy reaction, to *assume* that she was playing with my heart, and create convoluted reasons as to why.

The *hard* part about selling diamonds, anyway, was finding a jeweller who would take them, and at the right price. The first jeweller never bought – otherwise it would be easy. They would be shackled up in a fancy shop, mirrors on every surface trapping all light that entered, prohibiting society's most vein from leaving. Surrounded by the glimmer of gold and silver, transparent rocks watching on like thousands of encrusted eyes, jewellers would scrutinise my diamonds. Truly the purest diamonds the jeweller had ever seen, yet they would refuse to buy them. Surely something so perfect was so obviously fake, overdesigned to imitate the real thing. I couldn't tell them that I could fart out one of these rocks or they'd pay nothing for them, so I would have to swallow my boiling irritation and move on. The first *never* bought.

Today's hunt for a jeweller gave me a playground upon which to practice my skills. I stepped out of the first shop and into the colder street – a stiff winter breeze blew past me in the centre of the city. I felt the power in the wind, the energy of the air's motion was the energy in my soul. Feeling that power allowed me to reflect.

Celeste told me that her and Yvon were just friends. I thought to myself. *She was excited to see him was all. But that's bullshit, right? Why would she lean in for the kiss with me then pull away like that and go straight to him? She's clearly into him and dragging me along.*

I peered to the row of buildings across the road, eying the squat, stone façade directly adjacent. When the traffic lulled, I blasted air at the wall behind, kicking off into a sprint across the road. Slamming my palms down, I generated a gust that threw me into the sky. I blasted downwards again, double-jumping into a spin over the road. So far, I'd mastered a double-jump just fine, as long as I was close enough to the ground to push against it.

I soared towards a lamp post hanging over the opposite side of the street, and *just* reached it with outstretched pinkies. I clasped on, hauling myself up, then leaped off it onto a building's awning. I landed with the thud of metal.

She's never confessed any romantic interest in you, you know. I barked at myself. *Our first kiss was her being 'overcome with emotions'. The only reason she's possibly holding out a hand to you is to keep you interested. Maybe she likes the security of you being there, or maybe she just likes attention. Both could be true.*

There was a distance from the awning up to the roof of the building, and I leaped it easily, rolling onto the roof and springing to a stand. I let my hands drop by my side, feeling the pull and stretch of my soul's connections. The world was rich with carbon, but only in a jeweller's shop would it be dense and *flavourful* like a diamond – the blue hot on a heatmap. I sensed first the haze of pollution in the air, the glow of people and birds in the sky. I honed the feeling, finding a patch of condensed flavour on the map where I had just been. There was another place, though. It was just across a few rows of buildings.

If you're the string-along, then you're also the backup. My mind reminded me. *She knows that you're there, she's just hoping that better will come along. Look at how Yvon made her laugh. You've never done that.*

Fine, then he should have her. I grumbled back to myself. *Why do I need to get so upset about a romance between her and I that's not even happened, not ever will? Why should I hang my worth on this?* And with that, the argument was over. I frowned, feeling no better in my conclusion. Now I just had to sell diamonds.

I kicked off my back foot into a sprint, running across the roof in line with the street below. I used a blast to jump onto the air conditioner unit, then *pushed* off it with a strong burst to bound up a storey to the next building. I landed on the run, letting the armour of Maiki take over me. I turned towards the next street, leaping off the building's front edge before properly gauging the gap. I was falling short, too far from the ground to push away, falling too fast to land the target. Desperate, I reached with my claws and drove them into the adjacent building's brick façade. Safe on the wall, I hauled myself up and flopped over the gutter. I could sense the dense carbon of this new jeweller, only a few streets away now. I kept running.

I leaped over ledges, onto higher buildings and bounded between walls to reach into the sky. I swooped down from tall drops and glided across streets. I jumped with the powerful force of the air around me, performing acrobatics I could never before imagine. It was so natural to me now, but still wrong. As I leaped between buildings with all the freedom in the wind, there was still something I was missing. Flight.

I was just playing with the air as I gave it energy around me. I was *using* it…but there was more to being a *Kiin*, I could feel it. A soul connection wasn't about *using* your element, it was about a deeper connection than that. I was missing something.

The words of Kuvalik, or now Olomb or Dimos, crawled through my head. He told me that it'd been centuries since a *Kiin* flew. It relied on a different level of connection – a very high spiritual awareness. I think he was implying that I wouldn't achieve that awareness, but I could prove him wrong.

I made my final leap, slamming the air with all of my might against the lip of a low set of apartments, and launching myself across a four lane, tree divided street below. I landed and bounded off a tree in the median, giving myself enough height to double-jump to the other side.

The carbon was coming from the abutting building below. I strode across the rooftop, coming to the next road, feeling the carbon at my fingertips. It was diamond alright, sweet and salty and dense, too. Satisfied, I pin-dropped off the edge of the four-storey building. I came to land on a cushion of air on my feet, not even a thud in my wake.

This jewellery shop was different from the ones which preceded it. It wasn't retro with dark wood struts, gold trims and mirrors – instead the shop sported a black and white interior. The floors and table tops were of a prestigious marble, the counters built from white painted wood, the cabinets being in black. The selection of jewellery was limited, which only made the present pieces within more valuable by their curation. I walked through the white door, tripping the bell. The owner was hunched over a workbench at the rear, soldering metal on his mat, goggles perched on his forehead. He turned to me at the bell's chime, standing almost to the roof with his incredible height. His face was wrinkled into valleys, but still gave a smile.

"Yassa, chat mas mi di alfo?" He asked me how he could help in *Liktan*. I almost responded, too, before realising what he'd said.

"How did you…" I stammered in *Liktan*.

"Quatra, boy. And I saw you land on the pavement."

Oh. I squirmed. If I didn't want to be picked out for my abilities, though, I shouldn't have been practicing them so vulgarly.

"Albanian?" The man asked, turning back to his piece.

229

"Macedonian."

"Ah," he said into the ring between his hands, "I didn't know there were any *Kiin* still around."

"We're rare."

"Understandable. I wouldn't be sitting here in this shop if I could *fly*."

He assumed too much, and I didn't want to give anything else away. I coughed without response.

"What can I do for you anyway, Mr *Kiin*?" He asked and put down his work. I produced a diamond from my pocket – a purely clear crystal – and handed it to him. He put the goggles down over his eyes and examined it.

"Beautiful brilliance…" he commented, and puffed a short breath onto it, "yes, that's good…" He put it up to the light and examined the way that the rays shone through. He frowned, "too perfect…"

"It's pure," I assumed him. "The biggest, purest rock you'll ever see in your life."

"I have no doubts about its purity. I know the work of an elemental Suneva," he smirked at me, and I immediately stiffened.

"I work with *Agris* – silver. You, *Kiin*, clearly work with *maikess*."

"It appears so."

"I didn't expect somebody with a name as big as yours to be so bold with their abilities. You never know who could call you out."

"Big name, sir?" I squirmed. There were two, *very* distinct opinions this man could hold for *Maiki* – the terrorist to Hesslik's peace. Recent articles by Hesslik's propaganda site had not painted a pretty light on our 'assault' of Boekidin and a Legendary down in the catacombs. The online Suneva world was buzzing at the implications – a Legendary found, and by the great Boekidin no less.

"Famous in Hesslik's circle, at least," the man articulated, frowning. "That's where I've heard it."

My stomach dropped. I considered just giving him the diamond – leaving the store before he could stop me. I scooted on my foot.

"Now, I'm not going to tell anybody you stepped in here…"

"You're not?" I gasped.

"No. That would be a waste of good hands," he said. "In fact, I'll pay you for these diamonds too, but you've got to do *one* thing for me before you leave…"

The old man invited me around to his bench, pulling out a tray of diamond specs he had there. His task for me would have been simple enough – to shape the rocks as he made pieces for them, and to purify them like the stone I presented him.

Only there was one issue – I couldn't shape diamond. Creating diamonds was easy enough, but holding the tight bonds whilst moving everything around, that was tough. As I tried to smooth the rocks, they would crumble to graphite and dust.

The old Suneva, *Agrinn*, gave me advice as I struggled. He told me not to give the lattice energy, nor to focus on the bonds, or anything quantifiable. Rather, he recited that moulding the elements is much like singing – if you imagine the note, and you can hear it before you speak, you will sing it. Shaping elements depended on imagination and visualisation. You had to believe in where you wanted the pieces to go, and communicate this through your hands and your *soul*. One needs to give their soul to the diamonds.

Lo and behold, my frustration was ended as his method worked. I gave my soul, my imagination, and my intentions to the diamond, and it formed in my hands as I intended it to.

I was then able to help the man. Satisfied with my work at the end of the morning, he paid me and sent me off. The money was sufficient for two tickets, and I didn't trust my luck with any more jewellers. I just had to hope that Chad struck luck selling iron.

***

The week had passed, and it was now New Year's Eve of 1998. Natalie, Chad and I walked down the beaten hillside path on the Liktas homelands – the Mount Olympus national park, having left our car over the knoll and out of sight. We advanced on Hesslik's Castle for tonight's grand ball.

Signs led our way through the dense pine scrub, with occasional fairy lights and lanterns to show the path. Cutting through the dusk, the hanging lights set a magical mood to the woods. Quatra buzzed in the air.

We rehearsed our personas as we trekked through the crisp undergrowth. Tonight, Chad would play the role of Larry Hugh, a more toned-down and sensible

231

version of himself with only the powers of a witch. I would be his cousin, John Hugh, a witch and Argol gangster from New York, blessed by Argol with tickets to such an exquisite Suneva event. Natalie would be, by her own choosing, *Adamantia Papadopoulos*, my Greek-speaking, non-Suneva friend who I had chosen to bestow my third ticket to for her love of Suneva culture.

For the occasion, Chad had renewed his skills in disguise and make-up artistry, learned in his time as Hesslik's agent *Lion's Foot*. Despite the fact that we wore masks to what was a masquerade, he insisted on touching up our prominent features with his fine craft. For his own disguise, he'd chosen a wig. Chad's distress about his own looks was understandable – at over six feet tall and as wide as a small bus, with his distinctive crew-cut blonde hair, Chad would have been a stand-out in the Suneva crowd, especially to Hesslik who had known him for two years. The red-headed mullet of a wig he donned was more than enough to draw attention from his figure.

To complete the disguise, just as we crested the final knoll before Hesslik's castle, I blasted Natalie with a bolt of quatra to neutralise her past the doors. Her thread was our greatest threat to being discovered, after all. She winced and gasped in the momentary agony, but fast steeled herself by clutching her locket. I thought it was a risky idea to wear such an identifier to a ball, but Natalie had almost slapped me at the idea of removing it. It did look nice against her sequined, blue dress. Natalie regained herself, leading the charge to the Castle gates.

The castle stood separate from the mountains, straddling the valley between Olympus and it's surrounding peaks. It's stone walled perimeter housed a city, at the forefront of which was a tall and spread stone building webbing from a central glass dome atop a grand atrium. The wall's gates were wide open, and guests were already streaming through them.

Between the walls and the surrounding forest was a wide, muddy clearing, bisected by a road. Cars strolled past to some distant parking lot, carrying men and women in suits and gowns. Coming into this clearing, the air at my fingertips was an unending expanse. Unlike in the forest, where it gave me awareness of the trees and all around, here in the open, my senses were drowned. The open made me uneasy, and I skulked across the road behind Chad and Natalie.

We passed through the gate, coming to a stone path amidst a grassy knoll before the grand entrance. The two figures at the door were tall men with tan skin and thick features. We strode up to them, hiding our nerves.

The doorman on the left wore a yellow and blue mask with lightning-bolt horns. The much taller, more slender man to the right wore a feathered, black mask. They appeared to be of some Polynesian decent. These men had to have been Hesslik and Boekidin.

Boekidin, the man who runs through my mind. The man who probably knows me more intimately than anybody else. Who could *probably* sense my mind out of a field of souls – I couldn't be sure what a *Kidin* could and couldn't do, but now wasn't the time to be downplaying the man's abilities.

I froze with bulging eyes. My limbs went dumb.

"Yassas, sule Suneva," the supposed Hesslik spoke with a smile. "Mastes der derres prosaki?" He asked if we had our tickets. Natalie pulled the slips from her clutch and handed them over.

Boekidin was staring at me. I made an American accent in my head and thought of nothing but wild, untamed plains.

"Very good," Hesslik said in Liktan. "Welcome to the party. Always good to see young supporters of the Suneva vision. I am *Fara Hesslik*, and this is my right-hand man, the *Faraku Boekidin*."

"Incredible to meet you." Chad outstretched a hand to shake. I could barely move. I didn't even acknowledge a hand as it came to me, and I forced myself to take it.

"Please, go in and find your tables. The festivities will begin shortly." Hesslik gestured us in, and my legs found their life. I zipped ahead of Natalie and Chad, rocketing down the long, stone hallway of the Castle.

"What's wrong?" Natalie asked as she caught up. She grabbed my hand and pulled me back towards her.

"That's *Boekidin*," I whispered, eyes intense. "And I'm *me*. I think I ruined our mission."

"We've got time before he realises," Chad said, butting in.

"He's the Shiverman, though," I shook. "He's the most powerful Kidin, surely he can smell my mind out of a crowd."

233

"He'd have to be looking for it," Chad said. "I don't think we've given him a good reason to search yet."

I nodded my acceptance. If we were to be useful tonight, I'd have to calm down. But I could feel the walls closing in – the ancient stonework riding on its bearings, crushing us before we could even know we were trapped.

To keep my mind from doom, I focussed on the artwork. The old stones of this hall held tapestries of battles, ones which I hadn't read about in Olomb's diaries or in Salak Nolver's book of tales. Soon, the hallway ended, coming to a mezzanine of the ballroom.

I latched to the balustrade, craning my head to admire the impressive room. A massive glass dome, some three storeys above our heads, opened the theatre-like dining room to the shining night's sky. One level below was the ground, a sea of tables covered in black cloth. Opposite us was a grand stage, it's curtains almost rising to the dome. Plastered around the balconies, rising up the walls, were banners of the Mark of the Black Suns – a black mark printed on a white backing. The one screen in the room, sitting at the back of the stage, displayed the symbol in inverted colours.

"Odd obsession with black and white," I noted as Natalie and Chad joined me at the railing.

"Hesslik is all about tradition," Chad hummed. "There's some superstition about the use of black and white. I forget what it is."

I hummed, scanning the black-covered tables. Few people were sitting yet. Most people had gathered by the foot of the stage, socialising over drinks.

"Let's find our table," Natalie said, walking off to the left. I saw her moving towards a set of stairs I hadn't noticed. I peeled from the railing, following her to the ground floor. The stairs landed us in another long hallway, extending well beyond the large vomitorium we took to exit onto the dining room floor. There were two of these entrances, directly opposite each other in the hall. On an easel in the arched doorway were the seating arrangements, and we scanned for our fake names. It seemed that there would be five others joining on our table.

"Let's hope they don't want to dig into our stories too much," I hummed.

"It's a good thing you're the one sleuthing tonight, and not doing the talking, then," Natalie said to my concern. "If we stick to our roles, this will be smooth."

Our roles. I hummed to myself as we traversed the crowd to our table. Natalie, being trilingual, was to be the socialiser. It was her job to find interesting conversation wherever it lay, and draw details out.

"Might be hard to listen in tonight," Chad alluded to his own role. He had elected to listen to conversations through the ground vibrations. He should be able to hear the details that parties didn't want to be heard. "I've never tried to focus past this many people, and this much talking and music. The ground is white noise. I'll need to adapt to it before I'm useful."

"I'm sure you'll do great," Natalie praised him. She pulled up a seat placated with her fake name. Our table was to the stage left of the ground floor, close to the entrance through which we'd come. I stared between the two fake names to her side, forgetting which I had taken. I sat down at the place reserved for Larry, and chad sat next to me, swapping my name plate for *John.*

"Like your dad," he chuckled. "Didn't think you'd forget it."

"Neither did I…" I was becoming flustered. I could feel the walls constricting again. I could sense Boekidin out there, his mind wandering like a lazy fisherman on a vast sea. His line was out to catch, and he didn't know what he was going to pull in just yet.

I shot up.

"I need the bathroom," I said, just to get away from the table. I had to investigate the surroundings if I was to feel safe. I had to know my exits, and where I would run off to find this supposed lab. I passed through the crowd, traversing the ballroom, to come to the opposite vomitorium on the ground floor. A sign for a bathroom hung on its stones, and I followed. The hallway connected to this entrance was identical to the one we'd used to enter, and it continued past the stage, all the way to a corner. I wandered if the other hall was just as long, so I turned around to investigate.

I was pulled in by Chad as I passed our table. He grabbed me out of my path, orbiting me by his arm to throw me down on my chair. There were five new faces at this table, each smiling.

"I asked about the black and white," Chad said to me, as loudly and American as he could. It reminded me to shift into my terrible accent.

"Oh, did you Larry?" I drawled, and I could see the offence of my impression strike across Chad's eyes.

"Yeah," he smiled. "John, this is Ms…"

"You can call me Jean," the older woman said. She was plump and dark, with a broadly smiling face. "I'm Boekidin's mother." She raised an eyebrow on her proud, jaunty face.

I coughed loudly, clasping at the table. "You must be proud," I choked.

"Very," she said. "You can never predict where your kids will take themselves. I'm glad he got involved with his Suneva identity. He hated it for so long."

"And you're a *Kidin* too, then?" I asked the only question which would come to me. My eyes darted, searching for the tall, slender man I'd seen at the door. He could be coming for his darling mother at any moment.

"Oh no, I'm not a Suneva," she smiled, "but he's taught me a lot."

"Tell John here about the colours, Ms Jean," Chad said, pulling me in by the shoulder. I tried to feign a smile, but I knew I had to get far away from his table if I was to keep us safe.

"So, my son says that white light is pure and true because it reveals all that it knows – all wavelengths, all spectrums. White objects are impure, because they reflect all of this truth and purity, taking none of it into themselves. Black light is the manipulator, because it tells us only that which we can't see, but black objects embody the truth, because they absorb all white light and embody it."

"Hence the black tablecloths…" I palmed the covering.

"And the white *Kafma nas Sun* on the TV screen," she pointed towards the screen set on the stage. "The Kafma is white when being lit, but black when a drawn image." Her finger shifted to the banners I'd seen earlier draped over the balcony levels, showing a black Mark of the Black Suns.

"Interesting," I hummed.

"Then black-covered Boekidin must be the most truthful Suneva going around." Chad joked, and Jean chuckled. As much as Chad was joking, it was a strange and interesting set of circumstances, then, that had Boekidin covered in black, to be majestic and truthful to Suneva, yet evil and imposing to all others.

I didn't really want to think of the guy any longer. I had a lab to find.

"I'll be back," I said, standing. "I was still stretching my legs."

"See you later," Natalie called as I left. When I glanced at her, I was expecting a glare of worry for my ineptitude, but I didn't find it. Instead, I found

236

myself falling into her shining, blue eyes, into her *soul*. For a moment, the ballroom melted, pieces of it falling away like wet paper, slipping away to reveal a white void to envelop me. In this white void, I was compelled to feel Natalie's concern. Rather than anxiety about my foolishness, she was worried for my safety. Natalie trusted me to do well. She trusted me that the lab would be here. She knew that I could find it. I was surprised – Natalie hadn't expressed her praise in *anything* for a while now, let alone by abilities. My surprise kicked me from the void between us, shaking me back into the ballroom. I found myself lost in her eyes.

"Thank you," I nodded, solemn, and walked away.

I passed through the closest vomitorium, turning towards the stage, away from the stairs. There was a long, broad hall ahead to track past the back of the ballroom. I walked down it on light feet, trying to appear confident in my stroll. If I gave the air that I knew where I was going, nobody would question it.

There were only two doors before the end of this hallway, and they both appeared to be toilets. I continued past without looking, the labs would be further into the castle, I was sure.

I checked my pocket before I went any further – I had a walkie talkie there, which I could use to ask for help. I also had a disposable camera in the other pocket, and a tape audio recorder. If I forgot those, there would be no way to verify anything I saw.

I turned right at the end of the hallway. It led to another corridor, slightly wider than the last, which joined up to the hallway on the other side of the theatre's floor. There were doors against the stage wall in the centre, likely to access theatre. I didn't try to open them as I moved in towards the middle of the corridor. Adjacent the big, metal double doors, was a shorter, taller passage leading to a flight of stairs.

My footfalls echoed up the marble steps, the clack of dress-shoes on stone. I rose into a marble lobby between towers of the castle. The centre of the foyer rose into a tower itself, and the lower surrounding ceiling was supported by a perimeter of white stone columns. Each wall of the square room had an entrance like the one I'd walked through. In the lobby's centre, under the dome of the tower, stood a grand basalt statue of the black sun mark atop a pedestal.

I did not step into the room's centre – instead I slunk between the marble pillars to reach the closest entrance. The sound of the party dissipated behind me, absorbed into the white stone. I reached the rightmost entrance and peeked into it. It led directly to a stair set. I could hear no sounds coming from the second floor, nor was there any air moving down the passage. I decided to move to the next portal.

Whispers were coming from this entrance. I flattened myself against the adjoining wall and listened, but could hear no more than a mumble. The voices didn't seem to be moving – they weren't getting louder or softer. Through my palms, I sensed no more than an empty hallway, without people to make the sounds. Slowly, I edged my eye around the corner to...

Static roared behind me. I sprung off the corner, throwing myself right in front of the hall, and scrambled to my feet. It crackled again, softer this time, carrying a whisper.

The walkie talkie! I cussed, flinging myself back behind cover. I slung it from my belt and pressed the receiver.

"James?" Chad's voice rang through.

"Yes?" I whispered.

"The food's come, and..."

"Permission to eat it, man," I hushed back. "Can't talk."

"Got it," I could hear the man's smile. I threw the talkie into my back pocket and peered around from cover.

Before me was an empty hall, leading to an ajar double door set behind a row of lab coats. The door was covered in hazard warnings, and had an obscuring window which shone white.

Convenient, I hummed. I stepped into the hallway – now far too deep into the castle to pretend I belonged, but with nowhere to hide, I skimmed against the walls, somehow hoping to camouflage myself. Reaching the lab coats, I pulled one from the rack and lay it over my suit, pulling the mask down.

I set my hands to my side, sensing the air behind the ajar double doors. There were few objects as far into the hall as I could sense, and none of them were moving. Even here, the voices were more muffled than this door could account for. Walking into this next section was a risk, and perhaps not one I could avoid. I steeled myself, and pushed the door aside.

This next hallway was stout, it's left wall constructed of dark glass and a heavy, metal door, its right wall covered in sterile white, over a sterile linoleum floor. At its end was an open door peering into a dimly blue-lit darkness. From it came a voice.

I panicked, throwing myself over to the white wall, on an odd angle to be seen from inside the open room. I kept myself glued there for a moment, listening for more voices which didn't come. Intrigued, I worked my way down the short hallway, hugging the right wall.

The voices started again. At full volume now, they streamed towards me. I toed closer, quickly, activating the tape recorder in my pocket. My heart beat was surely the only sound it heard.

"Alright, pass me the em-three key, Niskidin." A voice called, and I immediately knew it as Vestas. I was pleased, albeit frightened, to hear his slimy tone. It meant that I'd stumbled into the right place.

"Here, boss," Niskidin's gravelly voice creaked. Slowly and cautiously, I peeked my head around the doorframe to glimpse the scene.

In a blue-lit room clad in black mirrors, Vestas hunched over a machine. It was as tall as a man, deep black, and bulbous. It hissed and glowed, spitting colour across the scientists' faces. Its two, sleek antennae climbed to the tall ceiling.

I pulled myself back around to cover. *The signal device.* I thought to myself. I couldn't snap a picture of it, but I could save this memory for later.

"Okay, take note Serallius," Vestas sighed. "I've adjusted the third rheostat, in board N-A-T-two-five-seven-W-one, to have a resistance three kilo-ohms lower. More current here should keep the energy where we want it. *Should...*"

"Noted sir," a smaller, woman's voice said.

"Great, now let's try this again. It should work better this time..." He grumbled. "Preparing the charge up..." There was a click, like a lever being thrown, "...and in three...two...one..."

I covered my ears in anticipation, but no crack or flash came. I wanted to look around the door frame to see what went wrong, but stopped myself.

"Four point five kilo-watts, Vestas," rhe female voice said again.

"Damn," he cursed, "I put *ten* through."

"It is over twenty metres," the gravelly voice of Niskidin echoed.

"Yes, but I've had enough time to perfect this," Vestas said. "I should be able to transfer *at least* eighty percent of the power through such a short distance of air."

"We have time, sir," the female voice said.

"It's less than a year. Less than a year to get ninety percent transference over ten kilometres. There's not enough time in the day."

So far, I'd heard nothing that Boekidin couldn't have confirmed for me – this machine was being built, and it was being used to transfer electricity. If I was to prove anything tonight, I'd need to link this device to the thread removers. I'd need to find some evidence to support my vision. If only I could find the lab I'd seen, then I'd have something…

"I'm going for a tea break. I'll be back," Vestas grumbled. His two-toed feet clanged towards the door.

I froze. If I ran, I'd be seen. If I stayed, I could only hope that Vestas had a renowned lack of spatial awareness and a startling talent for ignoring peripheral sight.

"Before you leave, look at this result," the meek woman spoke, and Vestas paused.

I savoured the moment to act. The stout hall's end was too far to reach, but to my right was a large, metal door. I leaped towards it.

"I'll look when I get back, Serallius," Vestas moaned.

Panic spiking, I jiggled on the handle frantically, but it was locked. I turned to the open lab. Vestas, head drooped to a clipboard, danced through the darkness towards the hall's light.

There was carbon in the door's deadbolt. Finesse lost, I mashed my hand into the door's lock and clumped the carbon out of the steel. The door clunked, falling ajar from the frame. I slipped into it like water down a drain, pulling the door flush behind me.

This room was dimly lit, bathing only in a light machine hum. A glass wall at the rooms rear let in lazy white light from an adjacent room. Under the white spotlight sat a chair covered in bracers, and before it I could see that this room was lined with the silhouettes of rows upon rows of computers on lab benches. Bunches of wires snaked across the tile floor.

This was *the* lab.

I whipped out the camera, snapping a quick few pictures. Still, this evidence wasn't enough. Only *I* had seen the vision, and I didn't know any *Kiin*

240

who could pull the memory from my head to verify that. I hummed, stepping further into the banks of computers.

There had to be something in here that was evidence of what I'd seen. The Suneva in the chair was gone, but what about...

I spotted it as it came to mind – a thread destroying device. I gasped elation and simultaneously shuddered away. So much power was held in that device, power greater than the charge it let off. And still, it wasn't good evidence. It and the power transmitter existed separately, and I hadn't found a link.

I hummed, stepping away, when my foot tripped. I thought I'd snagged a wire, but I'd come across some other irregularity in the tiles.

One of them was melted and charred.

Black as the four gods, raised on its edge, as if the singular stained tile in the sea of white had at one point been liquid. Evidence of the conflict – of Hesslik's great rope of plasma. I snapped my picture.

And before I could look for further evidence of the altercation, the door to the room had torn itself open, slamming into the glass wall.

I stared into the opening, forgetting any self-preservation in the vein of habit. It was Boekidin who stood in that doorway, his wings covering all its light.

"Oh Maiki, you've made a mistake," he smirked.

Chapter 24
Party Fowl

"I shouldn't be surprised to see you here," Boekidin growled, talons caressing his large, golden staff. "What have you come to ruin?"

"I...I...I'm just here to prove a point," I stuttered. There had to be another exit. I snapped myself in all directions, but I could see nothing beyond the darkness.

"Prove what point?" He snarled. "What are you planning to do to the innocents here?"

"I'm not doing anything to the people here," I stumbled on my nervous words. "It's Hesslik who's going to deceive them. I've been trying to tell you."

"You've certainly been trying to convince me Maiki," Boekidin said. "Tell me, what did you discover by breaking into Vestas' lab? What evidence did you plant?"

"Plant?" My brain – now a wet noodle flapping in the wind – strung from flustered to frustrated. "There's a burn mark in the floor right here, from when Hesslik almost killed Vestas. I didn't put this here!"

"Come on Maiki, that's where Vestas' assistant dropped a hot computer."

"That hot?" I yelled, snapping my head down to the scorch mark. It formed a long, jagged trail of bubbled ceramic. A computer couldn't do that, could it?

When I looked back up, a bolt of pink quatra was flying at my face. I screamed, summoning my staff and throwing myself aside. I rolled behind a computer, sticking up against it to take refuge. Boekidin didn't fire again – he was clearly reluctant to destroy the computers in this room.

"You're believing Hesslik blindly, Boekidin," I said. I heard his claws stalking into the lab. If I could draw him away from the exit, I could run. "Hesslik is intending to put the thread removal code into that free-energy machine, Boekidin. That's his plan."

"You're believing your own machinations, Maiki," Boekidin snarled, stalking closer. "Your memories are clouded. You're being seriously deluded by quatra daydreams. Take your own memories with a grain of salt."

I wasn't sure what to make of Boekidin's quips. I had visions, that was my *thing*. Should I not have been trusting these? They'd proven to be useful snippets of destiny. "You should take Hesslik's leadership with a grain of salt, Boe." I taunted, drawing him closer, "and listen to my words. He's going to sabotage his free energy to end the Suneva. You love the Suneva, you have to believe me."

"I'm afraid that I don't, Maiki," Boekidin said, stalking slowly. "You've got nothing to support such a mad theory."

"I've got visions! Visions that happened in this room. Visions that *showed* me Hesslik's plan!"

"You've got madness."

"Visions are *destiny*," I retorted, appealing to his beliefs. The bird-man paused.

242

"Your visions are insanity, Maiki. They're way too clouded to be from the black holes," he dismissed, toeing closer again. "I think you've been choking on quatra in your daydreams…"

Boekidin jumped out at the end of my bank of computers. With his staff levelled at me, he fired a bolt of pink quatra. I leaped from my crouch, blasting off a jet of air to backflip over the buzzing tower. Boekidin's pink blast melted the tile where my feet were, presumably destroying the charred floor. The door was wide open, and unguarded. I sprinted for it.

The air ran hot by my head, a wall of yellow flames roaring towards the door. I skidded in my tracks, remembering my fleshy skin would be melted, and drew forth the armour of Maiki. Boekidin fired a bolt of quatra which I turned to catch in my staff, redirecting it into the glass wall. The pane shattered in the heat, spooking Boekidin enough that he let down his flames. I jetted off a blast of air, launching myself through the doorway. With me, I surged a wind out into the hallway, sucking the door closed behind.

Then I sprinted.

Vestas was dead ahead, right in the double doors.

"Is that Maiki?" He coughed as he peered up from his papers. I didn't have time for shenanigans, I simply bowled past him, pushing him over and sending his papers flying. Behind me, Boekidin's sharp claws raked against the linoleum floor. He kicked into a sprint, and I blew through the doors, racing into the lobby.

There was no stopping Boekidin, there was only running. I launched a hand into my pocket, scrambling for the walkie-talkie, only to realise that my pockets were on *me, James*, not *Maiki*.

Natalie and Chad are not *going to be happy.* I gulped, vaulting off the steps into the marble lobby. Boekidin raged behind me.

With no time to dodge, I barrelled straight through the lobby's middle, sliding under and arm of the giant *Kafma* statue. Boekidin's pink bullets of quatra grazed my helmet, pulling my heart out of my chest. I came to the next set of stairs and threw myself down them, then clawed around the corner, vaulting off all fours. Boekidin glided over the stairset behind me, swooping around the bend on his mighty wings. He was right at me now as I barrelled down the side hall to the theatre. Close enough to grab.

A patron stumbled into the hallway right in front of me, dawdling from the toilet door. I knocked into them, and panicking, threw them backwards into Boekidin and blasted off their body. They were slammed into the bird, who grunted to catch them. Finally, I swooped about the final corner, careening out of the vomitorium. Natalie must have smelled my quatra, because her eyes locked with mine before I had even found her.

Run! I mouthed, just as a set of black, enormous wings sprung into a silhouette behind me. I didn't run towards Natalie or Chad, lest I give them away. Rather, I eyed up the first-floor balcony – the main exit, and leaped for it.

I soared true for the railing. Hands out, desperate to grasp it, but I was stopped by an insane force. It compelled my whole body, tearing me from the sky and tackling me to the cold ground. People stumbled to clear a circle around me, and as I went to stand and flee, I found that I couldn't. I was glued to the earth.

Boekidin pounced on me, pulling my arms behind my back with a strained effort to cuff them together. My head raised, I could see none other than Vectra atop the stage, her Gravity Hammer focussed squarely on me.

Bolt of quatra rained onto Boekidin, orange and red from Zamelle and Ferrad, who had adopted their armour and ran to my aid. Boekidin snarled, flinging his staff and talons at the bolts to deflect them back. The stage then roared with the clang of feet as Hesslik blew through the rear doors, black cape flapping in the wind. He joined in on the fire. The crowd scattered to the hall's peripherals.

I felt Vectra's focus drop, and I blew from my helmet's mouth a blast of air which threw me to my feet. Without my arms, I felt useless, and I writhed to be free of the cuffs. I summoned my staff.

Vectra leaped from the stage. She was launched away from it, before spinning mid-air to fall towards the third-level balcony. Nearing it her body slowed, as if she was *repulsed* by the surface, rather than falling into it. She then grounded herself to the other side of the room, zipping across the roof of the party.

Zamelle and Ferrad were lifted from the ground, yanked in the direction of the Suneva of Gravity. They soared around her flying body in an arc, being pulled high through the air to be slingshotted into the cold ground next to me. Boekidin swooped upon them as they writhed in the dust, tying their hands up. I fiddled with my staff, but felt a jolt of cold *power* hit my neck, I froze. Prongs of a thread remover were nestled into my armour.

"On your knees," Niskidin growled. I did as I was told, kneeling by my friends.

Vectra returned to the stage, her gravity spells lifted. She hovered there next to Hesslik, feet refusing to touch the ground.

"Well, ladies, gentleman and esteemed guests of my house," Hesslik stirred the shocked silence of the hall. "I was going to wait until after dinner, dancing and fireworks to make my New Years' address, but it appears I've been called to stage early. I'm delighted to announce to you all, at a time when you're all gathered here, that my plans to bring Suneva into the modern world have finally gained traction. The year nineteen ninety-nine will be the year of our people."

There was a nervous, soft cheer from some in the crowd. Most of the audience was too shocked to do anything. People shuffled to a seat where they could, to awe at what was to come.

"Yes, for this week several great things have happened which will take us in the right direction. I note that this introduction I am about to make is very significant in the history of our people. This is the first time since Vinavek's founding that anybody will have ever seen such a *quatran* in action. Yes, ladies and gentlemen, I am pleased to introduce you all to Vectra, the Legendary Suneva of Gravity!" He gestured to Vectra, who waved from her invisible podium. Her expression was dead behind the helmet. I was not staring at a woman I'd just spent a week with.

"There's something wrong with her," Ferrad noted it aloud. "If only we could read auras…"

"Vectra has decided to join our cause in the New Year, to bring Suneva into the modern world," Hesslik continued. "Having a *Nafarisos* side with our messages is truly honouring, and marks the righteous path ahead. We're standing on the road of destiny, people.

"Tonight, we also mark the end of an era in our history. It may have only been within the last century – a blip to our collective – but the Argol gangsters forged an alternative path for Suneva which only drove our segregation. I'm glad to say that this faction should be no more. I'm not sure how much the agents of terror before you received for handing over the Argol daughter, but for their sakes, I hope he paid them, because he won't be giving many handouts in the future…"

245

Hesslik reached into his cape and drew an object high before him for all to see. He held the dragonesque helmet of Naxaer Argol, free from its body.

I tried to gasp, but my breath was stricken. My eyes hung out of my head. "You *killed* Argol?" I yelled as I thought it. We'd only left the house for a day, yet Vectra had been captured, Argol had been killed, and "What about Celeste?" I shrieked.

"Naxaer Argol is no longer a threat to the goals of the Suneva," Hesslik smirked. "His daughter won't be any use to you now."

"Outrageous!" Ferrad roared, although the crowd was against him. An applause rose to diminish our protest. The crowd *loved* Hesslik. "How can you decide who lives and dies?" Ferrad growled, and his voice projected louder than I'd ever heard a human shout. It dwarfed the crowd, drowning the hall. "Where was that morality that I supported you for? That I almost *died* for? Killing was never the way, you have words."

"Foolish, Lion's Foot. Argol would never respond to words. I had to play his game, and I won." The crowd cheered to this too, amazingly. I couldn't believe it – although really, I should have. Hesslik had killed Olomb, the most influential Suneva of recent times. Hesslik was not above murder for his gains, yet this still shocked me. Argol was a good man, mostly. I'd only just found that out, and now he was gone.

"Vectra, where is your sister? What did Hesslik do to you?" I called to the stage. Vectra's eyes did not shift. She regarded me, but refused to respond.

"Now, my next announcement tonight will be a live demonstration, if you will," Hesslik continued, rolling over any protest. "I have been working on the technology to prove to the people of this world that we're serious about handling our deviants and miscreants. For our integration, we need accountability if we are to be trusted to use our powers. I have developed the technology to limit the bad apples from spoiling the bunch. This is *thread removal.*"

Hesslik reached for the lectern and held to the crowd a device placed on it. It was a thread remover, just as was jammed into my neck. "Of course, punishment cannot exist without law, without expectations and proper codes of conduct. I assure you that these devices represent only the last resort of law and order. But it is a measure that we ultimately need.

"Now I call upon you an ultimatum, Maiki," Hesslik said, pointing the prongs of the device at me from across the room. "I've given you many chances to join my ranks and make something of yourself, and in our recent meeting you've seemed so promising..."

"Recent meetings?" Zamelle interrupted. She turned to me with eyes of fire.

"He ambushed me in Nafplio!" I retorted.

"Ambush?" Hesslik laughed, "Don't spread hollow lies. We had a meeting..."

"I didn't agree to be met with, nor make any arrangements to do so!"

"But you certainly didn't leave, now did you?" He smirked. "Not when we met in Nafplio, nor Paris, nor Marseille."

"Marseille?" I scoffed, and turned to Zamelle, but I was barred from looking past her eyes. That trusting, encouraging soul I'd fallen into earlier tonight was barricaded off to me. I growled in my frustration.

"As if you believe him, Zamelle?" I coughed. "Hesslik is a manipulator!"

"I don't know what to believe any more, Maiki," she gritted, snarling. "You *have* met with him, and you didn't tell us? That's what's important here."

"I..." underneath my helmet, my face flushed red. I had no good reason for that, other than protecting myself.

"If you've had enough bickering," Hesslik cooed. "I am in the middle of making you an offer – for which the time should have well and truly passed. But, I'm generous enough to give you and your friends one more chance. The choice falls upon your shoulders only, Maiki. Do you join everybody in this room to fight for the rights of our people, or will you act against the needs of the Suneva and cause me to take ultimate action upon your threads?"

"You're a disgrace too, Hesslik – an arrogant monster," Zamelle harked up to the *Fara*. "You can't expect us to join you. Maiki might be naïve, but we know your true intentions, you're..."

"Of course I expect you to join me, *Natalie*," Hesslik waved her off. "Because you know that I'm the only one who can help you. You're the only monster here, just ask your mother. I know what she thinks of this..."

The crowd hushed. I went limp at such an accusation, my head lolling to Zamelle. White rage engulfed the slit of her helmeted face. She was trying

247

desperately to contain herself, but the energy was pooling at her thread, enough that I could feel it *pushing* on my soul. Even the guards holding the thread removers seemed to nudge away.

Then she shrieked — a roar of her incredible power. Devastating, aggressive, *dead*, her Suneva shriek resonated through the souls of even the ancient bricks in the walls, setting the entire hall singing in dangerous resonance. What crowd was left standing at this point had their hair plastered back into the spiritual wind. Even Hesslik had fumbled on the stage, but he seemed more smug for his misstep.

"What will it be, Maiki?" Hesslik asked. The devices pressed on our necks.

"You're going to remove our threads one way or another," I sighed. "Whether it be now, tomorrow, or they day you gather the whole nation and destroy every last thread…" I said loud enough for everybody to hear. People only seemed confused, and nobody questioned it. "But, I'd rather hang on to my thread whilst I can. We'll join you."

"That's a good man," Hesslik smiled. "Now, escort them to their chambers."

Chapter 25
Changing Allegiances

Hesslik sat me down opposite him on a broad, ancient table. He allowed me my armour, just as he wore his. The walls of the dungeon were squat and thick, extending to just above our heads as we sat. He wore a smirk under his helmet as he handled my paraphernalia. He let the audio recorder speak again, Vestas' voice bouncing between the bricks.

"I don't see anything incriminating here," he said, sliding the recorder across to me. "You can show the world that I'm creating free power. I see that as good publicity."

"I saw the lab from my vision," I said. "It's all the connection I need."

Hesslik laughed, toying with the camera now. "Tell me again, what deranged plan do you think I'm up to?"

"You're going to put the thread-removal signal into your energy machine. You're going to kill all of the threads."

"Madness," Hesslik chuffed. "Even if you saw the place of your vision, how do you prove intentions with a daydream?"

"I saw the burn-mark that you left in the floor when you intimidated Vestas. I know that the vision's events occurred."

"I burn mark?" Hesslik hummed. "It's a long stretch to attribute a burn mark to a series of imagined events." He dismantled the camera, pulling out the film roll. With a click of his fingers, an arc coursed through the roll, bringing it to instant flames. "Better to be safe, though." And he slid the camera back to me.

"Look, what do you want me to do?" I tried to move the conversation along. I didn't particularly care to face the fickleness of my vision – a 'daydream' which had changed the course of my life. "What is *working for Hesslik?*"

"Down to business straight away? That's the spirit I need," Hesslik smiled, leaning across the table. "You…" He tapped the table, cracking a charge into it, "are going to be useful to me doing exactly what you're doing now, with a few behavioural tweaks."

"What does that mean?"

"You're going to find me the other Legendaries," Hesslik smiled. "Your group has a proclivity for it, being the first to do so since Masalik Vinavek."

"Thanks…" I sighed to the compliment.

"*And* you're going to stop putting your faith in grand delusions. You're going to stop trying to defame me. Although I must say, your antagonism has proven a marketing success…"

"That's it?" I frowned.

"That's it," Hesslik smiled. "Not a hard request, hey? You get to achieve *Sunasera* on the way, follow *Na Kitos Keroseva*, use my connections to stay around the world. It's a good gig."

"It's not bad," I hummed. I, however, couldn't believe Hesslik. I didn't care that my evidence might have been fleeting, I *knew* that it was correct. I was *compelled* to believe so, and I had faith in destiny, in the directions of the greater powers. Hesslik would end the Suneva, and I would have to fight him.

But maybe that could wait. At least until there weren't thread-removers aimed at my neck.

"I guess I have to accept," I said.

"Oh, well, you have no other option," Hesslik chuffed, slapping the table. At that moment, a squat figure bustled through the door behind me – a small Suneva clad in navy armour.

"*Mina Fara,*" they addressed Hesslik as they shuffled in their urgency. Hesslik leaned back in his chair, lazily waving them over to his ear. They whispered into it, and Hesslik tensed.

"Maiki, head back to your chambers, would you?" He said. "Something has come up."

"If you order it…" I frowned, standing. Hesslik had us escorted around the castle by guards, as he didn't trust us to stay in one place. As I stood, the guard, who had been in the corner, approached. They grabbed me by the shoulder, thread remover in the same hand, and led me away. The device dangled around my face as he led me away, through the long halls and courtyards of the Empire base. He took me finally into a clerestory under the moonlight, where we descended through a doorway in the central garden into a basement lockup. This was a different place to where I was held before I'd talked with Hesslik.

We walked down several flights of stairs, under layers of stone and brick, into candle-lit darkness. We came to a set of cells divided by metal bars – a metal not containing carbon, I could feel – and the guard pushed me inside. He locked the door and stepped away, ascending back out into the night. I dropped my alis, sitting on the closest bench.

Natalie shifted in the cell next to me, perched up on the bed she had, and huffed when I noticed her, turning away.

"Has Hesslik talked to you, yet?" I asked, and she peered back, rolling her eyes.

"He's certainly been talking to *you,*" she noted.

I sighed, stopping myself from running red.

"Natalie, he approached *me,*" I enunciated. "Only twice, might I add."

"And you entertained him," she chuffed. After everything today, after all of my stress, my destroyed revelations, my quick and effective destruction of our plan, the last thread of my composition twanged. My eye twitched.

"What was I meant to do, Natalie?" I growled, and she stumbled back to me energy. "If I didn't obey him, if I didn't just sit and *listen* and nod along to his shit, and instead ran, he would have followed me back to our group. It was a pretty simple decision Nat. I talked to him to save us."

"I…uh…" She stumbled.

"I had to put a *little* bit of trust in the guy that he wouldn't just follow me anyway. But look, he didn't! I don't know what his game was, because he didn't come with backup, he didn't send Boekidin straight after, he just wanted to tell me I was worth something. It's something that I haven't gotten from *you* or *anybody else* in our group until you put trust in me today. Even then I ruined it!"

I summoned my staff and swung it at the wall. The blade barely made a dint. Rather, it bounced off. Whatever Hesslik had made this place of, it was stronger than a thin diamond blade. I growled.

Natalie sat shocked, although after watching the dust fall from the stone, she had something to say.

"Fine, that's fine. You did well," Natalie said, gathering herself. "But why wouldn't you tell us after the fact? Why leave it for Hesslik to say?"

"If I'm honest Natalie, I don't know," I laughed, dragging my blade tip across the ground. "Maybe I knew you'd react as if I'd betrayed everybody. Maybe it was worth hoping that nobody found out, because nothing was said that was worth repeating."

She nodded, settling into her cell comfortably, finally. "I'm sorry to be harsh, James," she said. "I know I've changed from when we first met. I can't help it, and I hate it."

"What?" I hummed.

"I've gotten so…cold?" She clarified, shifting her head to her hands. "It's all of this *connection*. It does strange things."

"Like what?"

"There are certain things, James, that I'll have to work through if I'm going to find my peace as a Suneva. Many personal things."

"Hesslik said he could solve your problems," I added, remembering his bite last night. "How does he know you? Can we help?"

"He was taking a blind, unguided jab. Boekidin probably knows all of our insecurities," Natalie explained. "But I don't want to talk about my personal issues James, no offence. I'm not as open as you all might be, and I think that should be okay."

"Sure, that's okay," I nodded along.,"as long as you're happy."

She smiled.

"Because I do care about you. We all do. But it was you and me in this together form the start."

"We got ourselves in way deeper than we ever thought," Natalie chuckled. "What a mess."

"It's a mess," I laughed along. "But do let me know if you need a hand. Anything, I'm a friend."

"Of course," she smiled, then turned with terror towards my door.

It slammed open.

I barely had time to gasp before my body was thrown against the back stones of the cell. It was crushed there, *pushed* up against the rock as if a great weight rode my body. Through the door sauntered the distinctive zebra-plating of Vectra, her hammer aimed at my chest. The face behind her helmet held a sinister grin.

Natalie threw her hand up and fired a bolt of bright orange quatra. Vectra dropped her hold on me, and I crashed to my feet as the bolt of quatra was repelled away from Vectra, flying into the light above and causing its glass to rain down. The cell was in blackness.

"Next bolt goes into him," Vectra warned, and my weight shifted again. Vectra stepped around me, the weight of her power crushing me against the wall, then sliding me along it. I scraped my back across the stones, grinding into the corner a shared with Natalie's cell.

"Why are you doing this?" I went to ask, but I couldn't get any air into my body. I realised I was suffocating, and my eyes bulged. I tried to move my hands, to *force* the air into my lungs, but they were pinned to the stones.

"Why are you doing this?" Natalie asked, somehow using my exact words.

"Hesslik told me to keep an eye on you. Personally, I'm not fond of traitors to the Suneva. This is punishment."

"What the hell are you on about?" Natalie growled, flicking her wrists to summon her twin cutlasses. "What did Hesslik do to you?"

Altered her brain! It came to mind immediately. He'd done it to Vestas, this was the evidence I needed. I stared to Natalie with horror, but she wasn't a *Kidin*, she couldn't understand me. Before we'd even locked eyes, Natalie's body was flung backwards. She crashed against the stones on the opposite side of her cell, crying with pain.

That sparked my rage. My connections forced their presence in my mind, amplifying my senses. The air was thin in the room, and everywhere except my lungs. Carbon was thinly spread, almost nowhere except for a cluster in Vectra's neck, glowing with the blinding light of a sunset. It was *under* her armour, something so strange I thought it was impossible.

I grappled with the cluster in my fingertips. They could hardly move, but I had connected to it. If I altered that clump, maybe I could save us. I jerked my fingers the motion which they were allowed, and I knew the atoms were shifting to my command. Still, it wasn't enough. Stars blitzed white across my vision. Blackness was coming from the edges of my sight, drawing in. As my world was engulfed by black, I was left only with the carbon imprint on my mind's eye. I accepted my fate as it came, my body passing out.

Then I hit the floor, my body gasping a full breath of air. As the blood rushed my ears I could hear the chaos unfolding around, and then I could see it. Celeste stood in my cell, her purple flames flying overhead, threating to melt the stones. Her sister dodged the attack, swinging her hammer at the intruder and throwing Celeste out of the door. Free to move, I grasped at the carbon still sitting at the end of my soul's grip, and *ripped* it from Vectra's armour.

She screamed a harrowing Suneva howl – the dead scream of a truly accomplished Witch, before the light of her quatra eyes dimmed, her armour retracted, and the limp body of Amalie fell to the floor.

Celeste jogged back into the room, rushing over to me, her eyes wide with concern that I wasn't expecting. Grappling at my underarms, she hauled my still-limp body from the floor, holding it tight against hers. I felt giddy, even for the dizziness, to be held close to her.

"Are you alright?" She asked. "I thought you just died." I could feel her heart beating against mine, and I could barely respond.

"Celeste?" Natalie rasped from her slump on the floor.

"Natalie?" Celeste exclaimed, and then blushed to be caught holding me, retracting herself. "Try to stay standing." She instructed, and fell to the floor to kneel by her sister. Even the two braincells I had present at the time took Celeste's embarrassment as a hint. And after she'd danced with Yvon over me? I was confused, and without the oxygen to think it through.

"Boekidin's agents captured my sister," Celeste explained, almost to fill the silence as Natalie crawled to the dividing bars. Celeste picked up some disintegrated part from near Amalie's shoulder. Next to it was a diamond, formed in my asphyxiated state. "They were clearly controlling her with this – whatever's left of it."

"You're a life saver," I gawked, finally having the energy to speak.

"I didn't know you two were here," Celeste admitted. "I came for Amalie. This is coincidence – *destiny*, rather."

"What happened to your father?" Natalie asked. "Hesslik had his helmet on stage."

"His thread was removed. I was out of the house when everything happened. I only saw the aftermath." Celeste grumbled.

"So, he's not dead?" I sighed relief.

"Veritas, no!" Celeste held her heart. "Now, come on, let's go. This place is guarded."

Celeste and I tore down the bars to Natalie's cell, then the three of us dragged the unconscious Amalie out into the hall. We tried to stay low, but the dragging of feet against stones would have given us away. By the time Natalie located Chad's thread in the subterranean labyrinth, Amalie was awake, and without her memory of where she was. We didn't have the luxury of discussing it, however. We rescued Chad from his earth-less, iron-less prison, and backtracked to the way Celeste had come, emerging into the cloisters.

We ran through the castle, crossing the lobby with the giant statue of *Na Kafma Nas Sun*. As we toed down the adjacent hallway, Chad hushed us, hearing a conversation from a doorway in front of us. The girls urged us on, but Chad was insistent on eavesdropping, sensing the anxiety radiating through the stones. He planted himself by the door, and I listened with him.

"I just don't believe that's possible," Hesslik rumbled through the rock. "The systems here aren't even conventional computers. They don't have transistors in the access chips – you need control over electricity to even access the files – it's fully manual password entry. That's without the failsafe override just to access files of any type."

"Yes, but *Mina Fara*, that doesn't change the fact that the entirety of our documents were copied." A meek voice asserted.

"How can you tell?"

"In our systems, copying registers as a modification. Either everything was changed slightly, or they took it all."

There was a long sigh from Hesslik.

"So, all of our documents are out there somewhere, in somebody else's hands?"

"I'm afraid so."

"I wish you would have waited till the morning to tell me," Hesslik whined, and there was a crack of electricity. "I'll never get back to sleep after this. I just can't even comprehend it. It's the most secure system in the entire world…we're not even on a network! It's a single god-damn machine!" He smashed something with his fist. The sound caused Chad and I to jump.

"Clearly we're dealing with an enemy Liktas. Related to Maiki and the other terrorists, no doubt?" The other Suneva suggested.

"No." Said Hesslik. "They don't have any Liktas allies that I know of. Somebody else orchestrated this. We have more Suneva enemies than I'd have assumed."

***

"So, he's not dead?" Chad asked Celeste as our crap-box rental car bumbled up the hill, coming to the valley of Athens city.

"Worse than death, I'm afraid," Celeste hummed from behind the steering wheel. "His thread was removed."

Amalie gasped and covered her mouth, but Chad chuffed.

"That's worse than death?" He snorted.

"For a man who dedicated his life to his Suneva identity, certainly. He said that the blandness of life is worse than death itself."

"Gosh," Chad hummed, turning to look out the window, "I can't imagine."

"You can't," Celeste asserted.

"But a thread *has* been removed," I said, and laughed even. "It's the first. It proves that the devices work. It affirms one piece of the puzzle."

"You didn't find any proper evidence?" Celeste squinted.

"I...no," I admitted. "Hesslik let me keep a tape recorder but he destroyed my photos. The only thing I could find affirming the vision was a scorch mark in the ground from where he cornered Vestas. Otherwise, I can prove that the power-transfer machine is being built."

Everybody in the car immediately frowned. The weight of the mission's failure pushed me into the car door. I'd risked everyone's lives for nothing, and Adam Leroux had lost his thread because of it.

"For what it's worth, I believe you anyway," Chad smiled.

"Oh, so do I," Celeste said. "We'd all have to by now. I wouldn't have followed you to Europe if I didn't."

I sighed my relief, although was acutely aware that my friends' belief wouldn't convince anybody else. We'd need stronger evidence, or more Legendaries, to sway the populace.

"I'm looking forward to seeing a detached thread," Natalie broke the silence with strange optimism. "I wonder what happens to the Suneva and the connection."

"That's morbid," Chad chuckled.

"What are we going to do now, anyway?" Celeste steered the conversation away. "It's too dangerous to hang around my house. We need to pack our bags and leave."

"We need to follow our conflicts and resolve them," Natalie said. "Just like the Code says we should. It helped us find Amalie, and it helped you strengthen your connections, Celeste."

"It did," Celeste affirmed. "And I've been feeling much more *complete*."

"I know that I want to go home to Melbourne if I'm going to grow. I suspect that's where you're needed too, James?"

I hummed on the thought – what were my conflicts? The first thing that came to mind was my Sunevahood conflicting with my relationships – those with my sister Simone, my friend Tom, my mother. But were those enough? What else was hindering me.

"That's true," Celeste hummed. "I mean it's clear, James, that you're fed up of living in your father's shadow."

"What?" I burst, but nobody seemed surprised.

"His name has come up everywhere we go, and all it does is put a sour look on your face."

"What sour look?" I urged.

"The one you're pulling right now," Celeste giggled, and Chad couldn't help but peer over and chuckle to himself. I blushed beet red, falling into the seat of the tiny car.

"I don't think I'm living in my dad's shadow…" I retorted, but maybe it was true. I did have unresolved issues with my father. Just bringing the man to mind, I could feel his last breath sliding between my fingertips. What were my last words to him? How did he leave this earth?

"Fine," I grumbled. "I've got dead-dad issues. Let's go home."

"That's the spirit," Chad reached his long arm across the car to pat my shoulder. "Back to Melbourne, we've got issues to solve."

***

The Leroux house was missing something. Adam had spent time moving his furniture back into place, but he'd missed something unseeable, untouchable. Footfalls riding the staircase fell dead. Cheerful voices were strangled before they could reach their target. Dust hung ominously in the skylight. The house was missing the essence which made it a home. It was missing its *soul.*

"Definitely a disturbance in the quatra field here," Natalie noted as she circled the entrance. She sharply whiffed the dead air as she held her hands to the peace-sign pose. "Where did it happen Mr. Leroux. And how?" She asked Celeste and Amalie's father, who descended the stairway.

"Well, in the house…" He mumbled, his voice drained.

"Yes, but I mean the exact spot," Natalie clarified.

"Oh. I'll…I'll take you," he groaned. Adam's eyes sat in dark bags, exemplifying his weariness. He gestured us up the stairs, taking us to his private study.

"It was those agents who ambushed you in the catacombs," Adam told us as Natalie stalked into the room. She worked at the quatra field like a dog in a flower patch, her hands taking to every whiff they caught. This room was endowed in seventies wooden-chic, as opposed to the black-and-white modernism engulfing the rest of the abode. This was an office befitting a lawyer. "They were powerful enough to subdue Amalie, the Legendary Suneva of gravity."

"They're not to be underestimated," Chad said.

"I know that now," he sighed,."That Liktas was simply incredible, more powerful than any I'd ever seen..." He noted and pointed to a charred hole in the wall, "and the witch was truly terrifying. I've seen and worked with many incredibly powerful Suneva, including the previous White Witch Lilawelle, but even the *Ocras Quatrona* was no match for this witch. It's almost as if they could *see* in quatra. Their skill with the energy was indescribable."

"They are very powerful," Celeste agreed. Adam pulled up his chair and slumped despondently into it.

"Is this the spot?" Natalie asked before Mr. Leroux could point it out.

"Yes," he said. "How can you tell?"

"This is remarkable," Natalie didn't answer his question, instead her attention was focussed on the corner of the room above the computer. "Tell me, Mr. Leroux, can you still sense quatra?"

"I must admit that I never really mastered witchcraft..."

Natalie spun in a heartbeat and shot a bolt of quatra at him. Without thinking, he put his body on the line and accepted the quatra in his left hand. He pointed his right hand towards the ground, and the orange bolt burst out of its palm and into the floor.

"Look here kid, this isn't easy to deal with at all. I take you in my household as a guest despite the danger you present, I..."

"I knew you'd be safe, I just needed to prove it," Natalie cut off Leroux. He didn't know how to respond. He was searching for the energy within himself, but clearly could not find it. "Hesslik didn't think of everything. Your biology is in-tact, which means you have a chance to be a Suneva again."

"How?" he asked, shuffling closer to the witch.

"Your *thrid* didn't disappear. It's right here, right where it was severed. Like a string hanging from the ceiling. I don't know how to touch it, or move it, or attach it, but I can feel it. It's the same colour and scent of quatra that I sensed when I first met you. There is hope, *Tano Argol*. I'll find a way to reattach your thread."

***

Hours later, I returned from the local photo shop in time for dinner at the Argol household. Our tickets home had been booked for tomorrow morning, and we all sat on edge in the city of Marsielle. We had decided to stay in a hostel on the other side of the city, thinking it would keep us slightly more hidden. Amalie had decided she would flee on her own path in the night. Her nomadic life would return, at least until the issues with Hesslik had been resolved.

Natalie, Chad, Celeste and I gathered in Celeste and Amalie's room to review my evidence after the meal. Hesslik had destroyed my photo reel, but that didn't stop me from attempting to develop it. The pictures I had received were destroyed in parts, but one crucial detail came through.

The scorch mark was there in all of its glory.

"A weak link," Celeste admitted. "But it could do."

"I'm glad this wasn't all for nothing," I sighed. "Your dad lost his thread because of me."

"Something tells me that we *all* would have lost our threads if we were here instead," Natalie hummed. "Don't jump to conclusions."

"What about your 'meetings' with Hesslik," Chad asked. "What did you learn from those? What was that about?"

"I told Natalie," I chuckled nervously. Celeste hadn't reacted well to hearing of my rendezvous with the Fara either, but was willing to hear me out on it now. "But there was nothing important. He ambushed me twice, and really just *talked* to me about my progress with the code. The only thing of note was that he knew Iva was lying, because she'd altered her sword. Apparently, that's a sign that a Suneva is hiding their true identity."

Celeste now blushed, as I'd inadvertently shifted the shame onto her. I cringed, and tried to backtrack, but Natalie interrupted.

"Useful at the time, maybe," she saved me. "I just think it's important that, with everything that is revealed in all this soul searching, we're all totally honest with each other. Nobody wants to feel deceived."

We each nodded around the circle, and I sweated my relief at my friends' acceptance of my circumstances.

"Does anybody have anything to share?" Natalie asked, but nobody came forward.

"Apart from that," Celeste steered the discussion. "Hesslik has another enemy, it seems. Some hacker."

"Somebody with all of his files." Chad noted. "If we needed better evidence of Hesslik's plans, I bet there's something in that cache."

"Huh…" I quizzed, I had barely thought of that. Hesslik knew his files were secure. He probably even had a *super secret* file that only he knew how to access. It could detail everything he planned to do. With that, we could out him to the world.

"His plans could be fully detailed," I agreed, nodding along. "And that means that they can be replicated." I realised, my expression growing grave. "So, anybody can now build a giant thread destroying device. Hesslik is no longer the only threat."

I gulped on my realisation, although Natalie was quick to react.

"Let's not think about that right now," she said. "This hacker doesn't have to be an enemy. They could be a powerful ally, if we can connect to them."

"Powerful alright," Celeste noted. "Hesslik has some kind of passive mind-control device, too, it seems. Think of what this hacker might achieve if they *don't* destroy the threads."

"Yes, frightening," Chad hummed. "But somehow, I feel that we will solve all of these issues, just if we follow the Code."

"I feel that too," I said, only to agree with him and push the impending danger further away. "I'm looking forward to going home. I want to feel my peace. It's so close."

Episode 5

The Day I Lost My Identity

Comparatively much worse than the fear of being followed by Boekidin around the Mediterranean was having to answer the barrage of questions from every acquaintance I bumped into back home. A simple walk to the shops would transpire into a long recollection of a story which had more omissions than facts. The constant lies summoned my guilt – if I couldn't be truthful about myself and my experiences, and wouldn't ever find peace as a Suneva, would I?

Mum, ever savvy to my obvious mistruths, was quick to interrogate me on my experiences when I first arrived home.

"Why did you come back so soon?" She asked as I hovered in her kitchen, only just after asking if I'd had fun. "You were only gone for a month. Weren't you guys planning to spend the whole summer over there?"

"Eh, who wants to be stuck in the cold?" I set aside addressing the question. "Sun's much nicer."

"Was it money?" Mum prodded. "I could have helped you out. *Damn*, I knew I should have run you through some proper holiday budgeting…"

"It wasn't money."

"Well it certainly wasn't the bloody sun," Mum objected, stirring her pot. "I swear James, I thought you said you'd be honest with me."

By all accounts, my face hadn't faltered. I had to wonder what source Mum's lie-detecting magic had. The jab had ignited my shame, and I realised that peace wouldn't come by layering the fictional tales and reasons.

"It was…" I was about to say quite loudly *Suneva business*, but my mind had thankfully jumped to Simone, the one person who had, perhaps rightfully, been deceived to my true nature. "Is Simone home?" I asked, before realising that I knew she wasn't.

"It's got to do with Simone?" Mum quizzed.

"No, but…" I knew that I would have to tell Simone, but the speech would need planning. She couldn't just eavesdrop a casual conversation about my Suneva abilities. "It was Suneva stuff, Mum." I admitted. Mum sighed, a sigh deep enough to expel her whole soul. She shook her head and smiled to herself.

"I knew it. James, I trusted you to keep doing this thing that you love…"

"I know you did, and I appreciate it, but…"

"What I didn't want was for this to take over your whole god-damned life!" She snapped, banging the spoon against the pot. I jumped in fright. "Whatever it is that you're doing – these stupid adventures that you clearly can't handle – you need to stop and re-evaluate."

"But I'm one of the only people who can save the Suneva!" I burst, and Mum's eyes almost burst from her head. I cringed for the onslaught to come.

"James, you're eighteen *fucking* years old. No world-altering bullshit will fall on your shoulders! Christ, get a grip."

"But is has, I've got to deal with it," I protested.

"Oh, do you now?" She mocked. "James, is it too much to ask that you pick a hobby that won't kill you? Can you pick something that doesn't change who you are as a person? My lord, your whole life you were too scared to go into flower fields because you thought one-hundred bees would be enough to kill you."

"Hey, c'mon!"

"No," Mum growled. "What the hell has happened to you? You know, it happened to your dad, too. He got involved with these Argols, knew about them, thought he was invincible, and now he's dead."

"Dad *always* believed he was invincible."

"And you're sure sounding like the man, James," Mum pointed. "The apple hasn't fallen far from the tree. Let's just hope you miss the part where it kills you."

"I…" I was at a loss of things to say. This conversation had no peaceful resolution unless I abandoned everything I'd spent the last year working towards. Had I really changed that much? I thought in become braver, or foolhardier really, that I was turning into a better, more determined person. I liked the James Grey that Maiki brought forth, didn't I? "What if I just told you everything?"

"James, I don't want to know everything."

"What if I told you exactly what my intentions were. What if I never omitted a detail on where I'm going."

"I couldn't stop you from going, even if I didn't like it," Mum whined. "You could just jump over my head."

"That's true…" I frowned. I couldn't see this getting better.

"Just, *God*, James," Mum tried to gather herself. I could see tears forming in her eyes, and I wasn't sure what they were for. I stood awkwardly stiff, waiting for her punishment. "Just don't break my heart, James," she said. "I lost my husband, I'm not losing you. I can't stop you from stumbling into dangerous situations. I'm at my rope's end, James."

"I hate this…" I went to hug her, but she pushed me off.

"Not more than you care for what you're doing." She said. "And that's the part that really gets me. I hope you know what you're doing."

"You'll have to trust me, I guess." I shrugged, not sure what else to do.

"We've had this conversation before, James." Mum wiped her face. "I don't want to go around in circles. *Let* me trust you. That's all I can ask for, for now."

"Okay," I nodded. "I will." And Mum turned around cold, back to her cooking. I was left dazed, and stumbled out of the kitchen.

***

The apple hasn't fallen far from the tree – to a boy who felt like he was crawling under a giant's shadow, this was somewhat comforting. The comparison was a guilty pleasure – shameful in that Mum used it to insult me, and it instead went to my ego. Dad was everything that encapsulated a *man*. In the old-timey sense, that was. The man who could grow a beard by felling trees and had built his house with nothing but spit, twigs, shit, and wood shavings. A person who pissed beer and told stories of arm wrestles where they broke their opponents' bones. Clearly John Grey wasn't *all* that, but his stories would lead you to believe he was.

Take a particular favourite example, one tale told over many dinners with a grin and a nod, beer sipped frugally between each gross embellishment. Dad's stories were numerous, and each as daring as the last. He took delight in telling them often, in seeing our faces at the mentions of his heroic feats.

This story takes place in Dad's fifth grade, at some point in the early sixties. Many of Dad's other, consistently exaggerated tales covered the experiences of being an immigrant child in a racist, blonde-hair-blue-eyes city suburb. This yarn deals with its consequences. See, the story begins with the understanding that John Grey, even at a young age, was a God of any sporting field. The only thing dragging him out of continual, vile punishment was his ability to outplay any opponent, to force the winning hand of any team he was a part of. It was an earned respect that transcended established social boundaries. It was respect with such a great spread, that it raised his other immigrant friends in its wake.

Although his friends were always destined to fall. Zoran, a young man with a mouth as big and rude as his head, had blabbed about the wrong boys for the last time. Retribution was on the horizon, as year-eight boys from the local Highschool combed the grounds for an idiot-mouthed Croat.

John Grey, upon hearing of the impending doom, found his rude friend and urged them home. Then, stealing the boy's distinctive hat and tightening it to fit, he marched out to find the enemy. It didn't take him long before he came across the charging line – boys at least twice his size, pimples boiling with testosterone, arms wrought and ready. John Grey, the cowboy of the fifth grade, the man who would come to call himself one of the last *Old Bulls*, squared off at the enemy. He rubbed his hands, pumped his legs, stared through the turbulent souls of emasculated teen boys fuelled by peer-pressure.

And he got beat up. Bad.

That's not to say that he didn't get a few punches in. One boy was knocked out cold, another left with an eye so black that it ate sunlight. One departed with fewer teeth and a weaker bite. But John Grey left with lights out, dragged by his sisters and slopped over a bike, wheeled uphill for an hour through the freezing snow – or so that's how he told us his school commute was.

John Grey suffered punishments so that others didn't have to, and stood up for those who often deserved what came to them. John Grey always put himself on the line, no matter the cost, because he always knew what was right. Beyond that, he was loved by all, achieved all that a man could achieve, and cast a shadow longer than the tallest building in a sunset.

That was why when Mum said that my apple hadn't fallen far from his tree, I had lit with glee.

I found myself squatting in the dark attic later that night before the open chest of his belongings. Only a circle of light pierced the strange blackness of the dank setting. After Boekidin's mum's words at Hesslik's party, I even found this blackness comforting, now. It was an embodiment of truth – the acceptance and radiance of pure light.

I pulled out the usual artefacts, and I wondered what I was searching for. I had Mum's simile, however dire intentioned it was, to inflate my ego. But that wasn't enough. A mother could call a son handsome if their nose was a mashed potato and their face a pizza, so long as they loved them enough. My mother certainly loved me, despite her bluntness.

But there was one person who had never compared me to my father. There was one man who had almost avoided it, at every chance – who would almost deny that the apple could have been born of the tree at all.

And that was John Grey.

It was sad to seek his approval, I know. But I craved it. Maybe I would find peace without this, but all of my friends seemed to think this was a problem of mine. I needed to face it, wherever it led.

But how did one get a dead man to talk?

His artefacts had nothing I'd not seen before. His work folder seemed lighter than usual, but only contained work documents. I'd read them before, they were nothing of use. The man never kept a private diary, his clothes now just smelled like dust and held no secrets. There were no secret inscriptions in the amassed sports-star autobiographies. I palmed Baba's cook book, still wondering what it was doing here locked away. It *certainly* wouldn't have the answers, unless food revealed some great truth. I set it aside.

The thump of the book to the floorboards was met by a hand falling upon the attic doorway. I swivelled to see Simone, who was somehow always present when I was here.

But when did she come home? I hadn't heard her come in. She must have been somewhere when I was talking to Mum earlier. My face fell to horror, although hers was only sweet, albeit curious.

"You've been spending a lot of time up here," she noted.

"Have I?" I winced.

"Well, three times in half a year. It's odd – for you at least. With the amount you're home these days, it's almost like you've forgotten about your family."

I cringed, shrinking away towards the chest. Simone made the jab without a hint of sourness, a true feat.

"I'm just looking for answers."

"You're always looking for answers." Simone rolled her eyes. "Who's supplying you with all of these questions?"

Once again, I couldn't answer. Now was *not* the time to tell Simone anything. Not when I was literally backed into a corner.

"I want to know what Dad thought of me," I admitted to her, and her eyes almost rolled out of her head. "Hey, don't be like that!" I scolded. "He never gave any sort of praise. I have no idea if he was proud of me."

"He was proud of you," Simone huffed.

"And how do you know?"

"Why do you care?" She asked.

"Look, I just do," I couldn't explain it myself. "Like, I need that approval. I know it's sad."

Simone just shook her head, and before I could object, she cut me off. "I don't know why you chase his word, James. I wouldn't want his approval."

"Wait...why not?" I asked, surprised at the answer.

"He wasn't the pinnacle of manliness, you know?" She slouched her legs up onto the attic floor, sitting opposite me.

"Well, of course you wouldn't think that. You argued with him so often."

And it was true. The two of them were exactly the same. They each knew how to rile each other up, and did it on a daily basis. They got upset over the same things, and offered each other the same disrespects that triggered their mutual outbursts.

"All I'm saying, James, is that there are better role models to look up to," she grumbled. "He was an angry man who only solved problems by punching and yelling his way out of them. That's outdated, if you ask me."

And it was exactly what I could never do.

"But he was morally solid," I argued. "He always stood up for what was right."

"Did he?" Simone asked, "Or did he just justify himself later by saying so?"

I'd never considered this. I hummed.

"Look, if you really want to know what he thought, just ask people who knew him," Simone suggested. "Remember when I said that people don't die until the last memory of them fades? Somebody might have heard what you want to hear."

My eyes lit up. The idea was genius. Dad had so many connections. He knew so many people, that the possible stories could have been endless. There were his colleagues, his best friends, his hairdresser. I fidgeted at the thought. Peace could come sooner than I expected.

"Thank you, Simone!" I beamed.

"You're welcome, although I wish you didn't have to do this," she mumbled, climbing back down the ladder. "I think you're doing *you*, and that's totally fine." And she was out of sight, a pattern of beats down the hallway rug.

Of all the possible connections, there was one that my mind shot to first, strangely. Not anybody who I suspected had talked to Dad intimately, certainly not somebody who I would have to have an awkward conversation with about my insecurities as a human being.

No, this connection would have heard the man's most secret admissions, the things that one said aloud in the middle of the night to only deaf ears.

I thought of the ghost who haunted my house. My childhood torturer, and the one who could know all.

Chapter 27
Confronting Your Ghosts

"Remind me again, James," Natalie hummed, rubbing her brow with a tense finger and thumb as we walked. "Why do you want to talk to this violent ghost?"

"Come on, it makes sense, doesn't it?" I urged, pulling her along the local streets under the biting summer daylight. "Who else would have heard his most secret admissions? Who else could hear private monologues except an incorporeal beast who haunted his house?"

"That's infallible, strangely, and very in-line with your ideas, James," Natalie sighed. "But why do you need your dad's *most secret admissions*? And why do you need me here?"

I stopped dead on the path, spinning to face Natalie. She stumbled to a halt before me.

268

"You're here because you're the most powerful witch I know, and because you're my friend," I said. "I'm not ready to face this ghost without some help."

"Okay, well I appreciate the compliment," Natalie nodded with a pursed grin. "But the secrets?"

"Eh, Dad wasn't a very emotional man." I waved away the concern, turning to lead again. We were only a few houses off now. I could see the squat, red-brick fence that I used to call my house – although I never did call it *home*. "I figure that if he never gave me any affirmation, he probably wasn't saying it to his friends, or anybody else."

"Alright, that's reasonable," Natalie hummed.

"And if it doesn't work out with this ghost, I know that Kuvalik, or Olomb, or Vasilli Dimos, or Mr Finneck, or *wherever* he claims to be apparently knew my dad well – well enough that he got him to escort Celeste to Melbourne. Then there's LeGrand who might have some information also…"

"Okay, you've done some thinking, then," Natalie smiled. "Still, I agree with Simone, I don't see why you're chasing…" And she went silent, her whole body stiffening to occupy the hot pavement. Her hands were held in their searching pose, her eyes were dead ahead, twitching with her fingers. I immediately tensed with her.

"What is it?" I chattered, crouching low and backing into the fence.

"It's not the next house, is it?" Natalie asked, finally shifting to look at me.

"Yes, yes it is…" I felt my heart drop. "Is Boekidin in there? Is *Fisira?*" Dread, it dropped through my veins like ice. Why couldn't I feel the field like other Suneva. This really would kill me one day.

"No, James, but it's not a ghost either," Natalie warned. "This is a seriously dark, *nefarious* energy. There's a black void in the quatra field. I…I think your ghost is a *demon.*"

"A demon," I lost my legs. I caught the fence to stop my fall. "Isn't Fisira a demon?"

"No, James, that's a *Quatra Daemon,* that's somebody who has been possessed by a black hole because they couldn't control their thread."

"Then what's this?"

"This is a dead *Sunesca.* They suck the energy from everything to stay alive. *Amasos,* I should have known it was this severe when you told me your story.

269

Yamitse says that demons whittle you down by stealing your screams of terror, then the power of your step, the beating of your heart, the edge of your smile. Once they've torn down your opposition and you've got no more energy to give, then they take your body from you mind. This thing was trying to possess you."

"Sweet cheese." I snapped my head to the house. Strangely, the windows didn't hang with the shadow of dread like they used to. An air had lifted around the house, from wat I could feel. I wondered why I wasn't seeing the danger which Natalie could sense.

"I think we'll be okay," I said, and surprised myself.

"You do?" Natalie coughed.

"Yes," I said more strongly now. The house, as I found myself lingering towards it's gate, seemed inviting, even. I had a sense, and I wasn't sure how I felt it, that the demon knew I was here. I could almost hear his slimy, choking voice as he projected his greetings. He was welcoming an old friend.

"He's welcoming me."

"This could be dangerous."

"It could, but it won't be," I said, and stepped in through the gate.

The house had changed a lot in the years past. The vines had grown with the hedges and the grass, each working to conceal the red bricked cottage with its dated yellow trim. The house lay in the shadows of its unkempt greenery. I stepped over mossy bricks towards the door.

"Got any plan in mind?" Natalie whispered as I stepped up to the porch. "Do you know the new owners?"

"Wouldn't know them if I saw them," I admitted, picking up the metal knocker. I honestly hadn't thought about what to say. I'd forgotten that I'd need to convince a person to let me into their house to speak to a paranormal being. What a strange event to try and explain.

As I pondered this, the door opened, pulling me forward with it as I still held the knocker. I stumbled to keep myself, Natalie reaching out to grab my waist, holding me back.

I felt it now – that presence which I hadn't seen before. A rotting air danced out the doorway on a stiff breeze, a cold oily hand coming to stroke my neck, welcoming me back. I shuddered, and struggled to look at the fat, balding man leaning against the doorway.

"Hi?" He quizzed, and took a sip of his cold stubbie. His tank top was stained with something, and the smell of his breath almost let you know what the stains were from. This man was about as well kept as his garden. "What's this about? Is she okay?" He pointed with his can-laden mitt to Natalie, who was barely holding together in the presence of the demon. Her eyes had shot wide and her hands had naturally adopted the peace-sign pose.

"She's fine," I turned back to the man. "Look, I used to live here. I think I left something in a cubby hole near the kitchen, I…"

"Mate, I've been here for four years and I've found every hiding space this place has…"

I gave him a pointed look.

"Don't ask why," he grumbled. "But you haven't left anything behind, I can guarantee that."

"Can I have a look, at least?" I shrugged, but the man shook his head.

"Nah, sorry. Not interested," he grinned as he said it, and closed the door in my face.

I huffed. That went how I should have expected it to, but not how I wanted it to. I turned to Natalie.

"I think I ruined that," Natalie admitted. "I've just never felt anything as *evil* as this. I didn't even think things could be evil in Suneva terms…"

"No, you didn't ruin it," I patted her on the shoulder, and stepped past into the garden.

"You're leaving?" Natalie quizzed, and jogged to catch me.

"No," I turned into the garden, stepping through the rubble of plants to the driveway. "We asked for permission, but I don't need this guy's permission to loiter around, and I don't think an entity as evil as you're saying could be confined to *just* the house. There's another space where he haunted me."

Natalie followed me around the front corner of the house. We came to the side gate of the driveway, and I connected to the air at my palms, throwing it down to vault myself over it, and into the back yard.

"You know I can't do that," Natalie frowned, and went to grapple her way over the fence. I undid the latch before she hauled herself over, and swung the gate out. I held a hand out to pull her through the easy passage, and she rolled her eyes as she took it.

271

"Wasn't expecting you to," I said, swinging her into the back yard. It was in just as overgrown a condition as the front, and my first thought was of Dad rolling in his grave to see his beautifully tamed garden lain to waste.

Straight ahead, amidst a mess of vines and under the shade of broad leaves, was the red-bricked garden shed which had also held horrors for me.

"We'll try the shed," I said to Natalie.

"Watch the windows." She pointed to those which looked out onto our passage. I nodded, and shrunk to the ground, crawling along the bricks by the foundation. Natalie followed.

I stopped at the corner of the house. The deck area looked out onto the backyard and shed, and there was a good chance that a man with a beer was sitting out here on such a stinking hot day. I extended my palms to my side, and connected to the air and carbon in the area. My spatial sense of air didn't reveal any man-sized disturbances to the breeze here, and my carbon heat-map placed the man inside, probably watching the TV.

"We're clear," Natalie said before I could get the chance, and I noted her doing her own readings. I hummed, and toed over to the shed.

Usually a padlock kept the metal door closed, but it didn't appear as if the current owner had even bothered locking the thing. It hung loosely on the handle. I set it aside, and pushed the creaky, rusting door open just enough for us to slip in through the crack. Natalie swung herself around the door after me and shut it behind her. It creaked to a soft stop and satisfying clunk, sealing us in darkness.

There were no windows here, and a quick palm of the light switch told me that there would be no light in here at all to guide us. Still, from holes lingering in the cracked roof, bored by vines, the room was engulfed in an eerie blue hue between its twisted, black shadows. Before us was a working bench which stole most of the room's floor plan, and across the narrow walkway from it on all sides were cabinets, benches, and rack of tools. It was easy to feel claustrophobic as the walls seemed to close in.

"Cosy," Natalie commented. "Although your demon isn't in here."

"He'll come," I said, stepped past her to lean on the centre bench.

"I'll make it quicker," Natalie said. She flicked her wrists, drawing her twin cutlasses into reality. She crossed them both to the ceiling, producing an orange bolt which soared to the roof.

272

Only it never made it. It barely even lit up the space. The bolt flew, then faded out of existence, sparkling off into eternity before it could tear a hole through the sheet metal ceiling. "Huh?" I pondered, "How?"

Natalie shot another to the same effect. I watched the bolt this time, and behind it's dying form I could see the shifting of the shadows. All throughout the room, now, the darkness seemed to shift and coalesce. It slicked through the cracks in the plaster, coming to engulf the furthest edge of the room in blackness.

At the same time, the dust on the table kicked into a windless eddie – a vortex which my senses were blind to. My mind immediately ran to my tormentor in the final form I'd seen him, the swirling mass of ash and embers. I stumbled off the workbench, terror striking me. This really *was* an awful, idiotic decision. I fell into Natalie and grappled onto her as the *thing* formed in front of me. The darkness fell off the wall, exploding outwards to paint the whole shed in pure blackness. The swirling dust rose off the bench, a black ribbon swimming now amongst the debris.

I truly felt his full embrace now. He had eyes, and they were watching me, like a cold drip of water hitting my neck. His hands, or his *influence* was around me. The room was filled with this energy – this sense that at any time, you and anything in here could be sent flying. It was tense. I didn't know where to look.

"A kind witch," His oily voice came to me. It was less of a sound, even, and more of a *feeling* that the being was communicating with you. The sensation was deeply invasive, as if his tendrils pushed up against your fibres, as if he could get *inside* your ears with his mass. I shuddered, although the tone was less insidious than I had remembered. "Yes, a kind witch who knows what a lost soul like mine needs. And *you*, James. What a surprise to be visited by a friend."

"A friend..." I stumbled on words. The only action that came to me was to release Natalie and draw my staff. The artefact of my soul acted as an anchor in the ocean of blackness. I felt some bearings again against the beast's black reality. It smiled from each corner of the room as I drew my staff. I could feel its tendrils inspecting me as they swirled around my back.

"It would surprise many, James," it said, "that you became the Suneva when your father was so convinced that it would be your sister."

"What?" I quizzed. "Simone was meant to be a Suneva?"

"Did I stutter?" The beast rapped.

"No," I gripped the staff tighter – the only thing allowing me to stand tall. Even then, I was falling into this demon's strange world. "That's just quite an opening statement. I had other things to ask – but now this raises so many more questions…"

"So, you came for answers, did you?" The beast smirked. "I'm an old spirit. I don't work or talk for free."

"You want money?" I puzzled.

"Not money, James," Natalie rolled her eyes. She raised her twin swords to the sky to shot four more bolts of quatra. Again, they barely even formed before they dissipated. The demon glowed as he absorbed their power.

"Ah, the witch speaks my language," it said. "Now, what do you want to know?"

What could I even ask? I came here wanting to know if this *thing* knew of my father's opinions of me, but clearly it knew a lot of my dad's private admissions. There was too much to find out, and even information about Simone.

"How did you find out about Simone? Why did Dad think she was meant to be a Suneva?" I asked. It seemed like a better place to start.

"How did I find out?" The beast rumbled. "John Grey and I were very friendly. He was teaching her about Suneva slowly. Your father wasn't ignorant of quatra or its bearers."

"Wait…" I furrowed my brow. "Dad knew you were here for a long time, and you talked?" My memories ran. Dad had never disbelieved my claims, but he never damn-well backed me up! And I'd run into him conversing with a shadow in the kitchen, but that was only weeks before we moved. I always thought that was a once-off, the scare to make him move…

"Oh, your father and I were long time friends before you ever moved here."

"And…he *knew* that a demon lived in this house, and he moved us here?" I could feel my bones chill, and it wasn't to the demon's touch. My world was being shattered, and I couldn't decide whether I was terrifyingly angry or woeful. My face burned hot whilst my body went limp.

"He moved *because* I was here."

"Why the *fuck* would he do that!?" I yelled, naturally settling to anger.

"Because we were partners. How do you think a regular man got safely involved with Argols? How do you think he tracked them down and changed their ways? A demon is a powerful tool who will always be loyal for a price." I could feel him smirk as the tendrils of its soul wrapped the room. "I could be a silent mind to ride through the night and eavesdrop – almost undetectable to most Suneva. I could devour the quatra of his attackers, I could be his protector when he got too involved or spread too thin. I was his informant."

"His informant..." I stewed on the concept. It made me chuckle, then howl. Nothing was funny, it was just insane. "He let me suffer for all of those years because you were his partner."

"It was fun," the demon tried to make cheery of the situation. "I got to do something nice with my death, and your father got an unethical edge to his detective prowess."

"And what was your price for this loyal service? Was it me?"

"Yes, it was you," the demon said, and my legs gave way. My knees crashed to the concrete.

"*WHAT?*" I burst. "I meant that as a joke..." My dad fed me to a demon? Simone was right – Natalie was right for agreeing with her – I had too starry of eyes for John Grey. The man was much more fallible, much more of a coward than I'd ever known.

"That can't be true," Natalie dismissed, stepping forward. "That's far too evil."

"Fine, then, it's a dramatic exaggeration," the demon admitted. "Your father promised me part of himself and access to a small DC motor he had running in this shed. But you were such an easy target. He knew for a long time what I was doing, and he didn't stop it."

"But he spoke up when it was enough, right?" Natalie objected in my place. I could barely emote right now, let alone talk.

"Yes, when he moved his family away," the demon said. "He couldn't take the guilt of it all."

"Why did he let it happen?" I asked. "Why at all?"

"He thought you were strong, he knew you could take it, at least until he solved his biggest case." The demon smirked, "and there is never an inclination to dissatisfy a demon. Not even Suneva like yourselves can stand in our way."

I understood that – of course I understood that, because I suffered at the hands of this *thing* for years. I *suffered*, and my dad knew about it, and he let it happen, and he basically made it happen. "What the hell do I do with this?" I asked, on the verge of crying. "My dad sold me to a demon...where the fuck do I find peace in that? I came here to see if he thought I could fill his shadow...that doesn't even matter anymore."

"Oh, well, he never thought you'd follow in his footsteps," the demon was quick to answer. "No, he thought you were two very different people."

"I...great..." I frowned. Even if my view of him had shattered, I still wanted to be the man he *appeared* to be to everybody else. Not even John Grey thought that I could live up to his name.

"No, he expected Simone to follow him – but he also expected that she'd get a thread, so I wouldn't think too hard about his expectations."

Easy for you to say, I grumbled to myself. "Tell me more about that, then. Why Simone?"

"Oh, she was destined," the demon replied.

"And I wasn't?"

"No, not at all," the demon replied. "It's a happy accident, if you will. I wouldn't be surprised if you weren't a very skilled Suneva because of it."

"I guess you don't have to be surprised then," I deflated. Natalie tried to grab my hand, but I'd had enough. I slumped over the cabinets to the side of the room, looking up at the ribbon twirling in the dust storm.

"I actually saw the moment it happened, when you received your thread."

"You did?"

"Yes," the demon said, and the darkness of the room shone to an optimistic shade of black. It was hard not to feel influenced by the demon's energy. "You were playing footy in the back yard, you, Simone, and your dad. John kicked it, and you tackled Simone to get the ball. You threw her out of the path of a bolt from Omercronius, and you took it yourself."

"I have *her* thread?" I hummed. Surawelle was right, my thread did belong to somebody else. This was the first good revelation of the day, if one could call the affirmation of this news 'good'.

"Yes, and she went without."

I could remember the moment now. It was the first time I'd seen the two moons. I thought I got stung by a bee when my tackle went predictably wrong and Simone threw me into a flower patch. A bee-sting to the neck, it had opened my senses. I was eleven years old.

"So, she was *destined* to become a Suneva, and she didn't?" Natalie asked from the shadows. "That means that...that she's one of *you*, doesn't it?" She pointed to the demon, and the room smiled back.

"Omercronius..." I uttered. "How am I going to tell her that? Oh *Lord Cheese*."

"If she wants to learn, I am always ready to take on an apprentice," the demon glowed, "a Sunesca is rare. Even rarer is the honour of becoming a teacher."

"Yeah, I'll pitch that idea to her after I get through everything else..." I stumbled back, clambering towards the door. "I think I'm going to go now, though..." And I fumbled for the door handle. Natalie's hand was already upon it, and I gripped hers awkwardly.

"So soon?" The demon asked. "Emotions may be clouding your judgement, forcing your leave before your curiosity has been satisfied. Let me remove those for you."

"What?" I uttered, before all feeling was wiped from my mind. No distress, no heartbreak, no loss nor embarrassment. My thoughts were free, and they were just as scrambled. Gone was my motivation to search them.

"Please don't do that," I muttered.

"As you wish," the demon said, and my emotions flooded back with the force of a bus to the side of my head. I was winded, falling through the door and pulling Natalie with me. We fell onto our asses on the bricks.

"*Salak Kuul* is my name, James Grey," the demon said, "I hope to see you again, friend."

277

Chapter 28
A Break in Destiny

"You know, Eleni said this would happen," I said to Natalie as we lay across my bed. Outside, daylight was fading. Simone would soon be home, and my heart was racing for the moment. I had no idea how to confront her. "She asked if my thread was my own. She said that there was a personality that my thread expected to have – one which hates itself, or what it will become."

"If we believe the demon's story, then that sure sounds like Simone," Natalie agreed, flopping her head to face mine. "The only issue for you is whether she already hates herself, or if this hate is still in the future."

I gulped, Natalie was astute. One way or another, Simone would find out. That was, after all, destiny. Omercronius already knew Simone's outcome, so did my thread. Omercronius would know how Simone would learn of her power, and I did not.

I just had to hope that she already knew.

"It could be easy, then," I noted. "I hope it is. By *cheese* I hope it is. And I sure hope that opening Simone to her own truth will resolve the issue in my thread. I don't know how I'll possibly smooth out the conflict of having somebody else's thread if it doesn't."

"What did Eleni say happened to other Suneva with your problem in the past?"

"Nothing. There have been no reported cases," I sighed. "I'm alone."

Natalie's face dropped, and she turned herself back towards the ceiling in a hurry. "I see," she said. "I hope that helping Simone solves it too. I mean, hell, it'll solve other conflicts of yours."

"It will, you're right." I sighed. I felt a strange courage now. Telling Simone about myself, and about herself, could only help me. The immediate consequences didn't matter, really. It couldn't only make me stronger. "I think I'm ready." I said.

"Do you want me to stay?" Natalie asked. The support would have been nice, but I didn't know how Simone would react, and having a powerful witch in the house could have been to my detriment.

"No, that's fine," I said. "Probably safer if you go home. But I'll tell you how it goes."

"Okay, if you're sure." Natalie was clearly unconvinced. She went to rise, and as she did, we heard the front door open. Heavy feet shuffled on the front matt, clearly the footfalls of Simone. I pulled a frown towards Natalie, who understood.

"I'll see you later," she said. "You'll do great. If it's too much, just call for some more confidence."

"Thanks, Nat," I said, and I meant it. Natalie left my room and tracked down the hallway. She and Simone had a curt, muffled conversation before she walked through the door, leaving me in my silence and isolation. It would have been nice, actually, if I had let her stay…

I could hear Simone's fingers furiously batting at the keys of the home computer. I sucked in my nerves. Adrenaline rocked my limbs, giving me a shaky gait as I pulled myself down the hallway, towards the front door. I should have rehearsed what to say! What was the best point to bring up first? How could I ease her into this…?

I slipped through the study door, falling into the dark cavern. Simone held herself before the holy glow of the computer in the black room. I couldn't help but notice *Fairysmog's Blog* plastered at the header of the monitor – Simone was on her favourite Suneva-hate and paranormal discussion board.

Not a good time. I squirmed.

Below the header, I could see that Simone was writing a post.

I could see the clear marker on the top left of the wall of text reading *Admin.*

And next to that, there was a link in purple. It read: *Logged in as Fairysmog.*

Logged in as Fairysmog. Simone was Fairysmog.

Really not a good time… I gasped, clinching at the door to save myself from falling.

"What's not a good time?" Simone turned to me, closing the browser with lightning pace. I'd seen it all.

"I said that aloud?"

"Yes."

"I feel sick, is all," I burst, and I really did. Dizziness bubbled in my skull. Adrenaline ran flat, replaced with stone blood. I couldn't confront Simone. This would be impossible.

279

"James, you're white!" Simone stood.

"All of that privilege, right?" I slurred, unable to talk. "I'll talk in a bit…" And I fell back out of the door, stumbling from all fours to run towards my room. I skidded the corners, launching myself off jets off air to dive onto my bed. My heavy body rained on the mattress like a sack of bricks. I dreaded the next moment.

"James, you're not okay," Simone entered just as I lay there. "Do you need water? Or food?"

Not without dramatic flare, I toiled to roll my laden body over. I still couldn't face her, so I looked to the ceiling.

"I *need* to tell you something," I said.

"That's…not what I expected," she hummed, and flung clothes off my seat to take their place. "What's got you *that* concerned."

"I…well…" words would not come. Words could not help me now. If only I could just *connect* to her, like that strange Demon seemed to do. Talking in feelings rather than words would be great, wouldn't it? No misreading people's intentions, fast, instantaneous transfer of information. Imagine being telepathic, it would be marvellous! Surely…

"*James,*" Simone urged. She was right, I was stalling.

"You once told me…" I paused, trying to gather the order of thoughts. No order of information here would make the delivery any better. "You once told me that if a friend of yours turned out to be a Suneva, you'd no longer be their friend."

"Yes, I probably said that," Simone nodded.

"And I know that you hate Suneva because they have power, and they're dangerous, and they could subjugate all others in society by force if they gathered en-masse and decided to do so, I get that. It makes sense.

"But Simone, would you still be my sister?" I asked. *Lord Cheese*, this was a terrible way to introduce it.

"I…" She stammered.

"Simone, I'm a Suneva," I said, and then I said it louder again before she could respond. "I'm a Suneva! And you are *Fairysmog*. But you were meant to be a Suneva too—"

"Hold up— "

280

"But I stole your thread. You were meant to receive one, and I tackled you out of the way."

"James!" Simone barked, halting my slurred babbling. I didn't dare look at her eyes or face, I couldn't bare the scorn held in them. "James, for Christ's sake, I *know* that your friends are Suneva."

"You…what?"

"But you? I couldn't see it."

"How did you know?" I finally rolled over to see her face, and there was a certain desperateness captured within, eyes that pleaded. I hadn't expected this.

"Because I can see quatra, James. I can see it, but I can't feel it, and I don't have connections. I'm *not* a Suneva."

"No, you're not," I agreed.

"I thought I was meant to be everybody's saviour. I could see the danger, I could warn everybody."

"Noble of you."

"But I'm not human. James, you have to help me. I haven't found any answers anywhere. You *have to* help me…" And tears started to coalesce on her face, tears that I certainly hadn't expected. I wanted to throw myself up to comfort her, but I found that I was stuck to the bed, rising through thick, immovable air. There was no way now that I could move, and a breeze kicked through my hair and the room – one which I could not perceive in my palms.

"Ah!" Simone yelped, swatting at something invisible between us. "They're attacking again. James, I'm insane!"

"What's attacking?" I managed to say.

"The red ribbons. What the hell is this?"

"Calm down, let it happen," I advised, although I had no idea what I was doing or what she was talking about. I was now less certain of what Simone was – nobody had ever mentioned ribbons and Sunesca in the same sentence. "Just stop doing anything. You're connecting to something, creating a whirlwind."

"That's me?" She sobbed. "I knew it. I knew that wasn't random."

"Simone, I know what you are," I said, even though I could have been wrong. "But you're going to have to promise to accept yourself for who you are. It's not the way that you were *meant* to be – not that being a Suneva would have been any easier to deal with."

"What am I?" She pleaded.

"You're a Sunesca, Simone. I've barely heard of them, and only seen one before."

"What does that mean?"

"You steal energy, and you turn that into your soul connections. You were so destined to receive your thread, that somehow missing it allowed you to draw soul energy from the world somehow. I don't know how it works, but you were meant to be *Maiki*, not me."

Finally, Simone calmed. She stared at her hands, and I was launched off the bed by the sudden power of my muscles. I vaulted through the air and faceplanted onto the floor with a thud. Slowly, I peeled myself up.

"I know who can help you, too," I said. "But it may be even harder to face him than it is to face yourself."

"Wait, hold-up," she shook her head, coming to what I'd said. "You're Maiki?"

"You know Maiki?"

"Of course I know Maiki. James, I'm *Fairysmog*. You just said that before."

"Oh, right…" I hummed. Then my face furled. "You're taking this awfully well for the leading force of hate in the Suneva world."

"It's nice to have an answer. Let's see how well I'm doing when I figure out what any of this actually means," she frowned.

"Right." I fell back into the bed.

"So if you're Maiki, then your friends, they're Iva Argol, Ferrad, and Zamelle."

"You're really keeping up with the Jones', aren't you?" I mumbled. "Yes, that's us. What awful thoughts do you have about us?"

"None at all," Simone cheerily admitted. "Terrible thoughts about a band of radical activists working mysteriously to destroy Hesslik's Empire? I've been following you guys for a while." She smiled, then scratched her head. "Probably should have put the pieces together, though. Boekidin's reports said that you were in all the places that you mentioned on the postcards you sent. Should have been easier to guess."

"Alright Sherlock Holmes," I sat up again. "I hate to disappoint you, but bringing down Hesslik isn't what the great *Fairysmog* would want. I'm glad that you've liked my adventures, but Hesslik is the one who's bringing the end to the Suneva. We're trying to stop him."

"Really?" Simone huffed. "That doesn't seem right. How has he hidden that so well?"

"No idea," I said. "Really, I have no idea. But he's going to put the thread-killer wave in his global energy device…"

"Oh, that makes sense!"

"And yeah, that'll be the end," I said. "Which side are you on?"

Simone laughed, and sat back in the chair, letting it spin about. She chuckled the whole way around, teetering on the edge of her sanity – regarding questions she'd never dreamed of asking herself. When she finally turned back to me, she gave a politician's conclusion.

"Show me this teacher guy first," she said. "I'll have to decide from there. Once I know what *this* all means." She gestured to her hands, and whatever else it was she could see.

"Wise," I noted solemnly.

***

I fired three bolts of my green quatra towards the roof of the dingy shed. The shadows darted between the racks of tools and boxes, the dust on the table swirling and waning. The energy I used to think of as deeply evil formed somewhere in the room, hanging in a soot cloud with its dancing ribbon.

"Back again so soon, friend," the demon, *Salak Kuul* greeted in his oily, deep voice. Simone backed herself against the door, struggling to fight her instincts to run. "And with Simone, the one whom I had been expecting."

"James…James…it's him, right?" Simone stuttered. I could see her chest straining to catch up with her breaths. I'd forgotten the fear, somewhat, of seeing a ghost. The paranormal was real and explained for me now. Ghosts existed, this was reality. Simone had been living in a world that, until only a few months ago, these elements she obsessed over might not have existed, and there was a thrill to that. There was *everything* scary about seeing the dead talk, especially when you only had a half-conviction that it ever could have existed.

"It's him," I nodded. "Dad's partner in crime, *Salak Kuul*. This demon…"

"*Demon?*"

"This *Demon* worked for Dad. They helped Dad on the Argol cases."

"That's insane," Simone muttered. "I *knew* those case files were fishy."

"Insane, but true," Salak Kuul smiled. "Now, you didn't come here to say hello. What are you here for?" They asked, and I could feel that the question was directed towards Simone. She glanced to me, searching for her answers, before steeling herself. She stepped forwards, right up to the ribbon and soot-swarm.

"You can teach me to be a Sunesca?" She asked.

"For a price," the demon smiled. "And double. You need energy, and I need it too."

"Quatra?" I asked. "I can shoot the stuff until my arms fall off."

"Won't work, not for her." Kuul shook his being.

"Why not?" I threw my arms up.

"Only the dead can transform quatra," he explained. "You have to be dead, near the brink of conscious extinction, to understand the mechanics of transforming that energy. It's a talent only forged by desperation, and only possible without human sight to limit your scope. I could blind your sister and take her to near death if you'd like."

"No, that's fine," I squirmed. I could feel his dark tendrils caress my body. They ran down my back.

"Then you are today's sacrifice," it declared. "I hope you had a good breakfast. Next lesson, bring an electric motor."

"James, you don't have to…" Simone said, but I cut her off.

"No, it's okay," I prepared myself. "Let's see what you can learn."

"Perfect," the dancing ribbon of the demon smiled. "Now, my apprentice. Let us begin."

Chapter 29
What Would Your Mother Say?

Tom, David and I had organised to go out later that night, to some bar that David knew. From his underground, insider information, it would be groovy – maybe even too cool for Tom and I. The instruction was to dress down, look uninspired, and for the love of all things holy, memorise the DJ's names.

It would be the first time that I'd seen Tom and David since I'd come back, and I knew what had to be said here. I had to tell them the truth about who I was, especially Tom, who had seen Suneva in action and been advised against them by the late *Fairysmog*. I dreaded telling him. Who knew what new opinions he'd formed in my time away?

I knocked on Tom's door. His iconic, shuffling half-steps roared down his carpeted hallway.

"Jimmy Grey!" He announced as the door swung out. He walked into me with open arms and locked me into a hug. "Boy, is it good to see you here and alive. I got all of your postcards." He let me go and gestured me inside. I couldn't help but notice the shaved-head he had. In only a month and a bit he'd destroyed his fiery afro. It worked with the scaled down dark shirt and black pants, but it was a surprise. It took me a moment to catch myself.

"Yeah man, very good to see you too again," I smiled and walked in. "What's news? What's been happening?" The house, on the other hand, was just as it always was – one wooden hallway leading to a tiled kitchen, and carpeted lounge room, dining room and pool room. On his kitchen table lay some new gadget he had half open, soldering iron laid beside a dissected circuit board. I bypassed asking what this new project was to put my beers in the fridge.

"Not much has been happening. I mean, you left, I kept on working like normal and went out a few times. I started some new electronics projects, simple hacks. What else? Christmas was good, going out has been fun. David's good with places, you know. I'm excited for tonight." He sat down on the couch, tearing open a massive packet of chips.

"Electronics projects…" I hummed, pulling out a beer for myself. "What does that entail?"

"Simple programming," he said. "I'll show you, come on." And he rose just as soon as he'd sat, leading me through the side hallway of the house, into his study. The work bench in this small room was a wasteland of wires and metal. A battlefield of rotting, plastic corpses, cut for their guys, lain to waste and death. In their wake, some new components rose. Tom stepped over to the computer – of a much better model and make than anybody else would reasonably own – and whirred it to life.

"Like, look at this," Tom said, grappling with a long arm for a Frankenstein chipboard. He plugged it in to the monitor. An application opened, and into its command box he typed *door*. "And when I hit enter…" he said, then pointed towards the front of the house. I heard the distinctive whirr and grind of his garage door.

"Amazing," I said.

"And there's this too," Tom typed *bell* this time, and his doorbell sounded.

"Very neat," I nodded, genuinely impressed.

"The next thing though, I think your sister would like this one…" he smiled, reaching into a draw, and my heart fell into a void. What device could he have made to please Simone that *didn't* revolve around the paranormal – that *wouldn't* threaten me. I waited with wide eyes as he produced a watch from a low drawer. He strapped it to his wrist.

"Why would Simone like that watch?" I blurted nervously. Tom didn't seem to notice my sudden sweating.

"It's a *Suneva Spotter*," he declared with a grin. "Bet you could have used one of these in Europe."

Would have actually been handy… "Nah, didn't run into trouble, actually," I said. "A Suneva even gave us accommodation for a few nights. Really nice guy…"

Tom shot me a quizzical glance, but turned the device on anyway. Like a metronome, it began to pulse with rhythmic, dull clicks.

"How does it work?" I hushed. Tom panned the device around the room, searching for something with intent eyes. There was a moving image on the watch's display, an arrow shaking in its direction to accompany the beeping. I stiffened as he brought the device close to me.

"It should be able to sense passive quatra. A whole bunch of quatra-science got leaked at New Years. Apparently, the energy emits in the IR and UV spectrums…"

"Oh, how interesting," I clenched, eyes wide. Well, in any case, it would be easier to be discovered now than to have to explain myself. A coward's way out was always a blessing. As his wrist scanned over to me, sweat pooling on my brow, the device did not sound.

"Not expecting much in here," he laughed, lowering his arm. "But you know, it will work somewhere."

"Ha ha!" I burst nervously. "Yes, yes, I'm sure it will," I smiled and nodded. At that moment, much to my delight, the doorbell rang. That would be David. I leapt from the room to answer it.

With David in Tom's abode, we got to work playing pool, drinking beers and telling stories of what happened over the past month and a bit since I went away. David was telling stories of some of his more alternative and trendy friends, of going to concerts, bars, and breweries. I noticed his new clothes and blonde-streaked hair to match his new friends. He certainly held himself taller, his discerning eyes not daring to focus too hard on anything, making sure not to give approval to any one thing.

I told my tale of our adventure through the Peleponese, the trip to Sparta to meet family, the spooky catacomb tours, and having Christmas in Marseille with Celeste's family.

"Wait, so Celeste isn't an orphan?" David asked, and proceeded to screw up his pot shot.

"No, apparently not," I hummed. I'd forgotten that story of hers by now. *Lord Cheese*, she lied a lot, didn't she?

"Bit of a strange lie," Tom mumbled. "Did that shatter your lust for her?"

"No, not really," I grumbled. Celeste really had gotten away with a lot, hadn't she? "I swear she's been leading me on, or maybe I just don't know what a hint is these days…"

"No, man, she was being *really* close to you at school," Tom nodded along.

"Right?" I laughed. "And she was getting all close and throwing me signs right along the whole trip. We almost kissed, but right in the moment she just skipped off and danced with this other dude who she'd introduced me to."

"Rude," David shook his head.

"And then I swear she still must like me. She gave me one serious hug with pretty eyes right after the new-years party. I just don't know what she wants from me."

"Maybe you have to decide what you want – and it's not her," Tom said. "There's plenty of girls who'd go crazy for a taste of Jimmy Grey…"

"Not true," I interrupted.

"…and plenty of girls who will respect you. You're getting no respect from her, give her up."

"Sure I am," I objected, although I couldn't devise any examples without their Suneva story elements. Even then, was she respecting me? "I mean, she's beautiful, right?"

"Fine, change of tactic…" Tom paused, rummaging through his brain. "You dislike how you can't read her intentions, or what she wants. But what do you *like* about her? What's got you following her on this goose chase?"

"I…well…" What did I like about Celeste? It was hard to think of when instructed. "She's nice, I guess. But she has lied about a lot, and I have a hard time making her laugh. I don't really know how she'll react."

"James, what do you *like*?" Tom asked again, and I felt stupid.

"I mean, she's hot," I shrugged. "And she gives me attention…sometimes. The way she does it is hot."

"Lust," Tom said. "That's just lust. If it's gone nowhere by now, eight months into her leading you around, it won't go anywhere."

"That's a rough assessment," I hummed.

"It's a fair one," he insisted. "Let her go, you'll be happier for it."

"I probably will," I could feel myself agreeing.

"Now, in the meantime, you just stay under Uncle-Tom's wing tonight. I'll find you a nice woman, don't you worry about that Jimmy."

***

The bar David led us to was a cool warehouse get-up in the city's surroundings. Dressing down was a good move, as the people here exuded cool just by their eyes. Here non-chalance transmitted between dead, uninterested gazes, under the supervision of alternative tune. *This* was cool? Strange. David went to find some of his mates and left Tom and I to find the bar.

"I'm glad we drank enough before we came," Tom said, leaning over the counter. "Because this is expensive as!"

I peered over him to the blackboard menu, then immediately turned away with a long face.

"Yeah, I spent all of my money, too."

We clung to the bar, leaning on it to leer over the amassed crowd. Tom nodded as he gazed, intent on something as a grin formed on his face. I, myself, searched the crowd for Suneva. I couldn't sense them in the field – and I wouldn't dare make a peace sign pose next to a learned dissident – but a Suneva could be picked for their walk, or so Amalie said. Either way, I was sure no others were here.

"I've got an idea," Tom finally chose his scheme, grabbing my arm. "Follow my lead."

"Oh god, what's the idea?" I asked.

"We're talking to those two girls over there, on the edge of the other bar," He pointed across the room. "You see, they're scanning the room too. They're open to conversation."

"Oh, gee, man. Are you sure?" I choked on myself as Tom yanked me through the crowd. "Like, why would they want to talk to *me*?" How was it, I wandered, that I'd managed to throw myself in Argol's throne-room, that I'd managed to talk with Hesslik himself, that I'd managed to mingle with some of the other most important Suneva of the current paradigm, and yet I couldn't approach two girls in a bar?

"Because you're James Grey, that's why they want to talk to you," Tom tugged me along. Maybe James Grey just wasn't as interesting as Maiki. I saw Boekidin's dilemma here. If only the two could be one and it could be normal.

Or maybe I just had to borrow some confidence from myself. I'd grown.

Tom and I pierced the crowd, coming to the neck of the opposite bar. At its stools sat these two girls who, upon closer inspection, just appeared to be waiting rather than scanning the crowd. Tom went to move forward, but I held him back.

Instead I threw myself forward of his weight, coming to land an elbow atop the bar next to one of the girls. She barely flinched to notice me.

"Weird place this is, yeah?" I asked to the aether, hoping for the question to drop onto this girl's ear. She peered over to me, looked me up and down with a roll of the eye, then with a grunt shuffled her friend along. With a guilty smile, I turned to Tom and laughed.

"Wasn't expecting that out of you," Tom laughed along, strutting up next to me. "Good work, my man."

"Any other bright ideas?" I asked him, scanning crowd from this new vantage.

"Oh, I've got one," he nodded, and leaned in close. "Two o'clock, two girls in the floor centre, looking bored on a dance floor. I know one man who could make anybody dance."

Dancing? This was my kind of idea. I nodded to Tom, and he parted the sea of revellers, shouldering his way to the floor's centre, snaking through the boogie. I lost him as a long line of hand-holding friends severed us. I saw him fall into the centre clearing where the two girls stood. He introduced himself with a whisper into an ear, made a corny dance gesture, and was immediately dancing with one of the women. It was *that easy?* I was struck by his confidence, and managed to force my way into the floor's centre just in time to catch him and this woman grinding up to the all-too-tame music.

It was now just myself and this girl's friend standing in the dance centre. She didn't seem to see me as I burst in, too busy with a mobile phone. *Rich...* I hummed to myself, and tried to strike something up.

"Music's not right for those kinds of moves, hey?" I said. The girl peered to me disinterestedly, chewing a piece of gum between her disdainful lips.

"Sure," She shrugged.

Cool. "So, you guys come here often?"

Her eyes almost rolled out of her skull. "First time," she drawled.

Cool. "Oh, nice," I sighed. "What brings you out here?"

"Her boyfriend likes the DJ," she sighed, pointing over to the first bar Tom and I had been at.

"Her *boyfriend*," I ummed, my eyes floating past Tom and the girl he was now kissing, following this girl's pointed hand to the figure leaned over the bar's counter. They glared at Tom through the eyebrow-rings dangling over their vision. Greasy, dreaded hair hung from a beanie, flowing over their loose black jumper which failed to disguise their inordinate physique. It was at that moment that the hulk of delinquent caught up with Tom's act. They forced aside the crowd, followed by friends of equally terrifying appearance.

Fear spiked, my brain running wired. Air was all around me, hot and sweaty in the dance floor. It twirled on my palms, yearning to be used. My staff was thick in my arm, throbbing with the ice of adrenaline.

I had to throw my urges aside, instead pouncing on Tom.

"Mate, we've got to bounce!" I ordered.

"Huh?" He pulled from the woman. "James, this is no time to…"

A hand grabbed me, throwing me aside. I was bowled into the innocent crowd, and threw down a cushion of air in my wake. I bounced back to my feet, but Tom was already surrounded, meaty hands grabbing him by the shirt. I could feel the tension writhing in each held fist, and there was nothing I could do here. I hadn't felt *helpless* in a long time.

Tom was pulled up by the scruff and thrust high into the air. I watched his face melt to pure horror, straining purple. Collecting my own icy blood, I shouldered aside two brutes who guarded the boyfriend.

"Put him down, your girl didn't even say she was taken," I ordered, although my last few words reigned only as squeaks when the eyes turned to me. Just as the dreadlocked boy dropped Tom, a giant hand wrapped about my chest to pull me aside.

"Alright, all of you, break it up," a deep voice boomed. The bouncer waddled into the circle's centre, repelling all parties with his girth. "Loverboy, you're out. Nose ring and pals, you're coming with me."

"Kicked out?" Tom whined, but the bouncer threw him such a stare that he straight away complied.

"I'll find David," I told him, and I went searching through the drinking field.

A few short songs and a brisk argument later, and I was towing a disgruntled David down the stairs of shame, out onto the street level. He mumbled something too quiet to hear past the ringing in my ears.

"There'll be other nights," I said to him, hoping I caught the gist of his complaint.

"But I liked that DJ," he moaned. "I've been waiting so long for this night. These guys invited me ages ago, and…"

I paused in the staircase, a vessel in my head pressurised to bursting. David rammed into the back of me, but I caught us both as I turned to him.

"Well then, mate, *stay*," I broke. David's face puckered.

"No, no, it's fine, I…"

"I'm pissed off too," I cut him off. "You've got friends here, stay. I'll take Tom to somewhere more basic." I gave my frustrated and earnest offer. David, now wanting to take a high ground, declined.

"No, really. I said I'd spend the night with you boys."

"And yet you were here for the DJ," I raised an eyebrow. David shrunk into his shell, his façade of cool fading away. "We should have just agreed on a different night. It's not like good nights are running out."

"Yeah, true," he squeaked.

"Hey, you can't just stand on the stairs," a gruff, deep voice boomed at us from the door. "Are you in or out?"

David peered to the bouncer, then back to me, seeking my final confirmation.

"Get back up those stairs," I instructed. "Have your night, I'll keep Tom out of trouble."

"Alright," he nodded in earnest. "Thanks."

"It's alright. I'll catch you around." And I shook his hand, throwing it back as we released to propel him up the stairs. He was soon out of sight, and I retreated, falling out the door and onto the street outside.

"Tom?" I called as I swung around. This wasn't the way we'd even come in. The bouncer on the top level had directed me to this door, and it seemed he'd thrown Tom and I down the back exit. I was in a hot alley, roasting in the warm summer moonlight, squashed between the drifting beats of two opposing clubs.

There was a commotion to my left. Down the alley, between a set of bins, men were throwing themselves at something. A group, maybe four or five dark figures brawled under the moonlight.

I had a compulsion. In this familiar situation, this time facing it alone, I knew that I had to investigate the fighting. And I knew exactly why.

"Tom!?" I called down the way. I found myself running, my fingers begging to be one with the warm night's air. As I approached, I saw him under the clasp of too many hands, thrust against the brick wall. Spittle from enraged cries flew in his face. Once again, fists here were balled with tension. It was a tension which had not yet snapped, but was being drawn tight.

"Mate, mate, I swear, I *swear*, I had no idea" Tom winced. He squirmed against the wall, as if only the hands holding him kept him from phasing through it.

This situation was dangerous. Fighting one man was well beyond my ability. Fighting four larger men was such an impossibility that it wasn't even worth considering – like the difference between one lion and one-hundred lions, death was included in the package either way.

My *quatran* pleaded with me. Carbon was screaming from every corner. Air thrust at my senses. I could grasp at the carbon in the aggressor's muscles, in their *brain* – ending them was *that* easy.

I was disgusted at my own thoughts. The Suneva had rules for this reason. I remembered Kuvalik's voice, his ghostly head repeating them as it flew around my mind's eye. *One must not to use quatra, or quatra abilities against a person,* He said, *unless you are met with a threat. You may retaliate only with power equal to the threat. Even then, quatra must only be used defensively. You should never attack anybody.*

What classified as defence? Did I have to get hit first? How did I rate the power of a punch? This was all too much. One accidental blast of quatra and I'd paint the alleyway in brains and guts – humans just weren't built to stand up to a Suneva. Simone *used* to be right, and Tom *was* right for having animosity towards us.

A circle of thoughts, and precious moments had passed. A hand thrust itself into Tom's front pocket and drew out a scrunched note. The figure, who I could now see was the dreaded boyfriend, firmly eyed the scrawl. "Her phone number," he rambled. "You're a cheeky fuck, aren't you?"

Tension broken. A fist was swinging – a force to meet Tom's gut against a brick wall.

"Hold up!" I called, and heads snapped to me. The fist collided, undeterred, and reamed Tom's stomach flat into the stones. To the credit of his muster, Tom only winced and coughed, managing much better than I would have.

The boyfriend grunted in my direction. "It's your Butt-buddy," he growled to Tom. "You want to be a hero today, kid?" They asked me. "Didn't Mummy tell you not to get into fights?"

My mind zapped to my mother. She'd be sleeping peacefully in bed, meanwhile I stood here disobeying every directive she'd given me to stay safe and to keep our trust – to stick to situations which I could handle. I gagged on an answer, but I needed to say something – *anything* to get him to punch me. I needed an excuse to punch back.

This was such a stupid plan.

"I don't know," I steeled myself, growing a shit-eater grin. "Your mum didn't say much to me last time I was in her bed. She was too busy screaming my name."

You could map each man's comprehension speed by the dropping of his jaw. Tom, who was already frightened yet resigned to a certain level of punishment, started to twitch, comprehending just how much worse this was going to be.

To my surprise, two of the boys restraining Tom howled into laughter. I chuckled along in the dilated calm between each heartbeat, until I realised they weren't laughing for the joke.

I didn't even get a 'you're dead' before a fist was flying for my face. Blood in my cheeks, I had only primal instincts now. I blasted air from my palms, throwing myself backwards and in an arc through the air. I flipped in my jump, landing acrest a dumpster bin. I was met with stunned stares.

"What are you, Bruce Lee?" One of the cronies asked. I shrugged.

"I think I claimed to be his dad, didn't I?" I ran with the flat joke, pointing to the boyfriend. The dreaded man rushed on me, sprinting to throw himself at the bin. I launched off the tip, flying over his head to latch onto the club's wall, then jumping to land by Tom. Now amidst the attacker's three friends, I found that they were uncertain what to do.

"Let him go?" I suggested. The boyfriend, growling in his frustration, roared at his men.

"Tear that idiot's face off!" He ordered, and charged again. The friends looked almost guilty as they released Tom. They pounced on me.

I rushed air at the wall, smacking the boys into it and launching me out onto the opposite building. Tom was left dazed too, and I was in a prickly situation. I didn't want to hurt anybody, and I couldn't break these friends' loyalty with terrible jokes, so I had to try something else.

I had to threaten.

The boyfriend sprinted for me, and I satisfied an urge, and itch deep in my arm. I thrust my staff into existence, it's long green blade glowing with pulsating quatra energy. The staff grew long in my hand, and I held its cutting blade towards the enraged degenerate.

His eyes grew, and I drew from their fear. I howled, pulling the scream from somewhere independent of my lungs and breath, from a place of the soul. It was a thrilling cry, a Suneva howl which compared to Natalie's as a cat's hiss to a lion's roar, but it did the job. The rushing man skidded on his skater shoes, pulling up feet early of my blades edge. His friends joined Tom, pinning themselves against the wall, fright engulfing them.

Carbon was calling to me from the blade's tip – a whole bin's worth of it. These boys were on the edge of shitting themselves, and I was going to force them over that cliff. I grappled at the element with my free hand, then constricted my claw. The bin exploded into liquid flame as the carbon was torn from its rubbish, a diamond forming at its centre.

There were no words, only actions. Men dropped their anger, they dropped their loads, and they certainly dropped any camaraderie they gained through my joking. They ran screaming into the street, just as the fireball died into a petering splutter. Tom sat, pinning himself against the wall, the fire's embers reflecting off the fright in his eyes. I dissolved my weapon and raised my hands to the sky.

"Tom, I'm sorry," I said, and stood entirely still, my surrender. This was *not* how I wanted the man to find out. The silence between us was broken by a robotic beeping. Slowly, Tom lowered his arm, inspecting his Suneva-finding watch which rang its alarm in my direction. He peered between its dial and my face.

"It works, I guess," I shrugged.

"It works…" his bewilderment was broken for a mad chuckle.

"I'm sorry, man," I repeated, wanting to drive this conversation. "I wanted to tell you for a long time. I never had the guts for it."

Tom was silent, only making noise to breathe. I stared at my toes, sure I'd lost him, when he tore himself from the wall.

"You just saved me, man," he said, nodding rhythmically.

"I didn't save your stomach," I said, but he chuckled. With the chuckle came a tear.

"I was sure you were about to get me killed, too," Tom laughed, wiping his face. "I was sure after that mum-joke he was going to tear my neck open. I had no idea what you had up your sleeve." And he howled in laughter, falling to his knees. "I thought it was just *you*, mate, James Grey. The man who cried from a balloon, the man who can physically feel the punch from rejection. James *goddamned*

Grey." And I wanted to talk, but he didn't leave me room. "I thought you were going to have our heads taken off, you idiot." He laughed his mouth dry, falling to his palms now as the adrenaline faded off. "I thought you were an absolute idiot. But you saved me!" Tom glared up to meet my eyes. He was surprised by the sorrow I held.

"Man, I'm so sorry" I said, and I couldn't help but apologise. "I mean, I saved you, but I've been lying to you. I've been hiding a *lot* from you."

"Dude…" Tom coughed. He struggled to bring himself back to a stand, so I jogged over to haul him up. Once standing, he fell into an embrace, hugging me tightly. Tom had never done this before. "Dude, I know why you didn't tell me," he said, and squeezed. "But man…you saved me."

"Can you accept me for who I am?" I asked him. Tom pulled away, holding me at an arm's length. He nodded, taking his time to think about it.

"I need to hear it from you, what the Suneva are all about," he strung his sentence together. "You were scary. It was *awesome*, but scary. But I love you." And he grappled me in again.

***

I spent the cab ride home explaining the Suneva to Tom. He had found strange tales in the city library when he started his own research, just after the fight with the Umbrella Lady, which described the Suneva as a warring people, concerned only in advantage and death. Conferring with Simone hadn't deterred these assumptions. I advised him otherwise, telling him of Kuvalik's words, of ethics, how my actions in the alleyway withheld them, and I told him what I'd really been doing in Europe.

When he stumbled out of the cab, I had his word that he was okay with everything, that he could accept who I was. But the words felt empty, and I wasn't sure if they would hold true. As he left the car, it felt almost like a breakup. Our friendship was there, undoubtedly stronger than ever, but it had lost some aspect – some connection which couldn't be explained, only witnessed. He saw me differently, and things between us would change because of it.

I accepted this, and in it I found peace. All would be for the better, now.

Chapter 30
You Can't Sit with Us

Natalie was going to leave us for a week, off to handle her own adventures of finding peace on a trip with her Yamitse. The old White Witch would surely teach her well, and we respected Natalie's choice of company, although I wished I could have been invited.

Still, on the last day she had, just the Monday after Tom and I had our misadventure, Kuvalik organised for us all to meet at his house. Celeste and Chad, who had been living in the house again in these past two weeks, had Kuvalik confirm the story of his suspected identities. The ghost was the living thread of Kuvalik, which belonged to the man of the moniker Kyros Orion Olomb, born Vasilli Dimos some five-hundred years ago. The ghost wanted to explain his situation, and talk to us each individually. I planned to bring my father up to Kuvalik – the ghost was on my list of spirits to talk to about the man. Although I was reluctant to uncover anything more after Salak Kuul's revelations, I still hadn't found peace. I had more questions now than answers.

I also planned to hijack today's meeting to introduce Simone to the group. She hadn't returned home when I had to leave, but this was somewhat expected, she was training with Salak Kuul this morning. When I heard the knock on Kuvalik's door, I would have to introduce her formally to the group. I had no idea how this would go, and I decided that a surprise introduction would be easier and less worrisome than some calculated effort to introduce the idea of a Sunesca joining us.

I mean, it was certainly less effort for me.

When I entered the house, Natalie, Celeste and Chad were already waiting with tea on the table. The ghost of Kuvalik floated behind, blending into the house's natural darkness. I sat upon an empty chair by the coffee table, claiming the tea which was mine.

***

The little DC motor hummed away under the dark gloom of the shed. Simone focussed on the red ribbon which danced from it – this was its energy, hanging, ready to be taken. Simone could *feel* the writhing tendril more than she could see it. Always humming on her peripherals.

"The goal of a Sunesca is not like the goal of a Suneva," Salak Kuul explained. Simone found it disturbing that the demon clearly had no voice with which to talk – no ribbon of sound energy sparked from his being. Somehow, he simply *communicated*. "A Suneva channels quatra to perform an ability, and they assume a Sunesca must also want to channel energy for a similar purpose. But this isn't true, you see. Whilst Suneva can only *use* energy, you have another option – exhaust. You can *waste* the energy of a source by venting it. Suneva cause things to happen, you can *stop* things from happening."

Simone felt heat on her skin as the little motor started to slow its spinning.

"I produce heat to slow the motor," Kuul explained. "The aim is not to create heat, but to hinder the motor. Try to drain the motor."

Simone hummed. She had two connections which she, Kuul, and I had discovered. One was to the air, which was obvious, and the other was to *silicon*, known as *Nikess* in liktan. Simone remembered destroying her computer chip when frightened by the dog, and that led her to experiment on the old circuit boards in this shed when we'd first met the demon. Silicon might have been useful to drain the motor, but air was everywhere, it would be easier to connect to.

Kuul had taught her the other day how to reliably draw the energy, and how to connect it to her abilities. Energy granted her an extension of will, which let her tug at the universe through her brief *Soul Connection*. Simone reached for the ribbon, beckoning it to her. Like a curious dancer, the energy was charmed. It tangled towards her body, then lunged, plunging into her chest. Simone quickly grappled at the air, causing a blast that threw her balance and broke her concentration.

"Draw through the elbows," Kuul instructed, "it's less of a shock, you could have kept going."

"Kept going?" Simone inquired. "I…I don't know how to make the blast longer than that." Simone didn't have a feel for what was possible yet, and the fickleness of her connection stopped her from exploring her powers.

"It's not a blast," Kuul hummed, "it's *exhaust*. Long and steady."

"How do I do that?" Simone asked. "How do I connect to make that happen?"

"Think less," The demon unhelpfully instructed. "The most basic connection is passive exhaust. Focus more on drawing the energy. Feel what *creates* the energy as it flows through you. Give little thought to the product of the energy. It will go *somewhere* if you keep taking it."

Well, then made sense – energy had to be conserved, after all. Simone reached out for the dancing, red ribbon. When she focussed on it, the head of the ribbon centred on her chest, magnetised to her calling, flailing for her. She commanded it towards her, into her elbows. The poor ribbon ripped in two, streaming to her arms. *Connection*, she reached for the air, and shifted her focus.

An eddie formed in her palms, but Simone didn't pay it attention. She searched down the ribbon. She could feel the mass of the motor as it turned, she could feel the inertia which she drained from this, almost as if she held the spindle between her finger and thumb. She could feel the motor's struggle to fight her, throwing its mass savagely.

And the eddies kept circulating between her digits.

"Yes, very good," Salak Kuul smiled. "Now, *drain it*. Take it all."

The motor fought her so valiantly and with such determination that Simone felt bad stealing from it, but she found it so easy. With her arms by her side, she wore down all the resistance that the motor had. The eddies of air kicked into whirlwinds, spinning dust about the small room. The red ribbon of energy stretched in her grasp, drawn longer and longer, elastically resisting her pull until...

The ribbon snapped. A shock drove through Simone, zapping her in retaliation for her greed. She stumbled to her knees in the sudden pain of it. It felt as if she'd been electrocuted. The motor whirred back into full life, revving with joy, leaving Simone to wretch herself to her feet.

"That's the *limit*," Salak Kuul warned. "It's better to learn that sensation by feeling it."

"Yeah, thanks," Simone mumbled.

"When you draw every bit of an energy, you stop the chain of conversion. You can't draw from *potential* energy, so you feel the snap as you are removed from the system."

"What energy *can* I take, then?"

"*Active* energies," Salak Kuul said. "And there is an order in which you will learn them, because they become increasingly harder to draw from. First is kinetic, then sound, then heat, and finally light. Although I would never depend on light. The sun is too far away to pull ribbons from, and incident reflected light has such little energy…"

"Sounds like a lot of time spent in this shed to learn it all," Simone hummed.

"Oh, no. Salak teachers don't hold on to students," Salak Kuul laughed. "I will teach you what I can, but most of the journey to power is self-motivated, and by your own feelings."

"So, is this the stuff James mentioned?" Simone chuckled, "about inner peace and connection to the universe?"

"Don't listen too hard to Suneva," the demon's tone shifted. His shadow and soot spread across the room, the light fading out. "Peace is not the path of a Sunesca. We are not pawns to the black holes like Suneva are. They call us *evil* because we take energy from the world. We were denied holy gifts and so we have, in turn, become our own Gods, with our own free will and influence. We do not need peace to find our connection to the world, because we are our own connection. You are truly *free*, and your *freedom* from control is what grants you connection to the universe. Thank your brother one day, because he allowed you to be removed from the tyranny of the black holes."

"Freedom…" Simone pondered. "I don't mean any offence, *Salak Kuul*, but you don't seem very free. You've been trapped in this house for years."

"Yes, but by my own accord. I could leave, but it is safe here. By transcending destiny, I have become my own ruler. I have been granted the choice, not merely the privilege, to live beyond my bodily death. The Suneva call the way demons selfish and evil, but the need for sustaining one's life is an inevitable part of human nature. I am free to live and do as I please, and no Suneva can harm me, so destiny will not touch me. This is freedom, and it is *powerful*."

Salak Kuul drew a long breath. With it, the room plunged into a total darkness, engulfing Simone in the infinite black void. Simone could see nothing.

"To signify your journey into freedom, my apprentice, you will choose your name. The title of *Salak* is not given to you by destiny, but by your own creation. Make your first free choice, my pupil."

Simone glared into the blackness before her. With no light to touch the eye in any direction, there was nothing to guide her, and no sense of time's passage.

She listened and squinted, expecting a vision or a mirage to appear and guide her in her choice like I said had happened to me, but there were no signs. She was alone in her thoughts. Nobody, no *thing* could influence this choice now, because it was hers alone and she was *free*.

"I am *Salak Nera*."

***

"You're bringing Simone into the group?" Celeste quizzed, perplexed. Natalie and Chad sat into the couch opposite, but Celeste had joined me on my one-man bean bag. Her closeness, which I would have welcomed before, now had me set on edge. I'd stick to my guns and refuse to believe she was flirting with me, wouldn't I?

"Yes, essentially," I nodded. Celeste was still confused.

"James, she hates Suneva," she reminded me.

"But she likes *us*. She's read all about us."

"Good," Celeste rolled her eyes, shifting away.

"Doesn't this seem a little dangerous to you?" Chad asked. "We're already in enough danger as it is, and we're Suneva."

"Wait," Natalie narrowed her eyes at me. "She *is* a Sunesca, isn't she? The conversation worked."

"Sunesca?" Celeste gasped her surprise.

"This is a good advantage," Natalie nodded along to my thinking. "But Chad's right, it could be dangerous for her, especially since she's new to herself."

"A great advantage, I know," I smiled along. "We had no idea how to face that Sunesca in Paris – imagine if we had one on our side."

"You all think this is a good idea?" Celeste interrupted, searching for reason in the group, but she found none to side with her.

"You think it's bad?" Chad asked. Celeste huffed, throwing her arms up.

"None of you have read the old stories? None of you have engaged in *tradition*?" She pleaded, but none of us had. We exchanged confused stares. "Sunesca are *thieves* without destiny. Involving them in any plan is a huge gamble. Any action they commit will change the pre-planned course of things. You can destroy divine intentions just by pushing Sunesca into their path."

301

"There's certainly some plans we'd like to destroy," I pointed out, but Celeste just growled.

"You think Hesslik is destined to win?" She jabbed at me. "Your sister hates the Suneva, I wouldn't be surprised to see that she joined us as a *Salak* just to destroy our cause. You don't really know how long she's been aware of her condition. Suneva can't sense Sunesca."

I puckered my lips. Celeste was right, but I *knew* that Simone wouldn't be lying to me about this. There was one other important fact, too, that I shouldn't have dared to bring up, but I had to.

"That's true," I said. "And I'll have to disclose this, not that it helps… but Simone was *Fairysmog*…"

I cringed as a unison "*James!*" rose with the collective thrown hands of everybody in the room, Kuvalik included.

"You invited *Fairysmog* into our chats?" Natalie huffed, now furiously against me. "James, what a terrible idea! By Amasos, you should have *at least* consulted us."

"She's good, I swear," I held my hands up in surrender. "Plus, do you know how much knowledge she has about Hesslik and his politics? Do you know how many *connections* she…?" There was a rapping at the door. All the eyes which had fallen on me now glared with intensity. I made my way up hastily, stumbling towards the door before I met resistance.

Simone stood there, nervous as a wet kitten, held only at half her height. She could barely look at me.

"This could be rough," was all I said before dragging her inside. There, by the couches, she was met with four dissatisfied yet polite stares.

"Oh my God, is that a ghost?" Simone gasped, pointing at Kuvalik as her knees wobbled beneath her.

"That guy lived to over five-hundred years old. Last *Fara* of the Electric Nation," Chad pointed to the spirit with a thumb.

"That's Olomb?" Simone coughed a laugh of disbelief. "My God, I was not prepared to be surrounded by so many celebrities." She gawked as she pushed herself over to a bean bag, slumping into a seat. Not even the power of gazes could repel her.

"So, Simone," Natalie leaned forward, "as Fairysmog, what do you know about us? What do you know about *everything?*"

"As Fairysmog..." Simone chuckled, nervous, and eyed me. I nodded that my friends knew, and she sighed, turning back to the circle. "As Fairysmog, I idolised this group. I reported on your whereabouts, and on your activities. I had insiders collecting information from Hesslik's secret channels, I had dedicated fans providing me sources. I believed that your group was intent on stopping Hesslik because you were following some accusation – although nobody could pin down what it was. I now know that you're trying to stop him from destroying the Suneva."

"And how do you feel about that?" Celeste snapped at my sister. "You know, as the largest force of Suneva hatred in this world."

Simone blushed, falling into her shell. Celeste was cold, and Simone wasn't expecting such animosity.

"I spent years hating a community on a global scale because I thought I was some saviour given quatra-vision to defend humanity. Really, I was denying that I *knew* I was something that nobody in either my or your community could explain to me. As *Fairysmog*, I would have lumped my abilities under the umbrella of Suneva, so I guess Suneva problems are now my problems too. In discovering who I am, I've been given *freedom*, apparently, and I want to use it to save the community who I ostracised and robbed of peace on a global scale. I need to give back, and I want to. This is my community now, too."

Simone's speech was met only with silence. Even Celeste was too stunned – too enamoured – to give any cynical feedback.

"I don't mean to ruin your change of heart, and I really mean that," Celeste said, softly, "but the Sunesca aren't widely trusted amongst the Suneva. This might not be the community you were hoping it is."

"I've been warned," Simone nodded, "but if I help you all, and we succeed, maybe I can change that."

Celeste bit her tongue from further comment, not daring to admit her own personal animosities. I could see the girl supress them in her flushed red face.

"I think your heart is good," Natalie said. "I was definitely unsure there, for a minute..."

"And you've got great connections, it seems," Chad said. "I've got to admit, I was always impressed by how much you knew. There's not much publicly available information on Suneva. Your connections will be an asset."

"Thanks," Simone smiled a wide, unbelieving grin.

Natalie nodded. "I think if you're truly reformed, we'd love to have you around. A Sunesca can only be useful. As long as you have only been truthful," Natalie emphasised. Her glare to Simone projected the scorn written in her statement. Simone shied from it, scared as anybody should be.

"I know it might be hard to believe, but it's the truth," Simone stammered against the stare. "I want to help. I want to protect the Suneva community. I finally want to *fit in*, damnit."

Natalie and Chad nodded, and then we all turned to Celeste. The French girl sat tensely atop the bean bag, but gave her verdict.

"I don't want to deny you the opportunity to finally be yourself, or the opportunity to help us." Celeste prefaced, then sighed. "But my trust is hard to gain, Simone. I'm saying yes to let you join in, but I'll be watching you."

***

"There is something I must tell you, James," the ghost said as the door clicked closed. He had led me into his room for a private discussion. His apparition smoked with a blackness of concern I hadn't seen before. It set me on edge. "And you must promise to listen."

"I will," I said, "although I have questions of my own." I fell onto the bed, pulled down into the blankets. I wanted to ask him about my father. I hadn't found any peace in Salak Kuul's interpretation of my dad. Kuvalik knew him too, or so Celeste's stories said. What else could he tell me about the dubious man.

"I...okay," the ghost hummed, and wafted by the cupboard. "You should ask first. What I have to say will beg more answers than it resolves. I wouldn't want you to lose your thoughts."

Ominous. I coughed, but continued. "One of your alter-egos knew my father, right?" I asked. The ghost chuckled.

"I wasn't expecting *that*," he snorted. "Yes, John Grey knew me. In fact, he knew me as Roger Finneck, Vasilli Dimos, Olomb, and Kuvalik."

"He knew *that* much?" I quizzed, surprised by this answer.

"John Grey was instrumental in creating relations between the Argols and my Electric Empire. He and Salak Kuul became a cornerstone of my plans in their conversion of local gang members," he said, then paused. "How is Salak Kuul?"

"Kuvalik, my dad *sold* me to the demon," I said. "Did you know about that?"

Kuvalik's smoke dropped, his frown wafting closer to the floor. "Kuul told you that much?" He asked.

"Salak Kuul held no bars," I said.

I could see Kuvalik's grimace. He sighed, "I told your father to let it happen."

"What?" I coughed, before the fact had really settled in. "I mean, *what?*"

"Simone was meant to be Maiki," Kuvalik blurted. "Your dad knew that, I knew that, Kuul knew that. I needed her for my plans. She was meant to be where you are right now, having met the same friends, having made some adventure. We couldn't have scared her off the path by letting a demon be her introduction to the Suneva."

"So, you let a demon drain me?"

"You were strong – your dad always said that…"

"He did?" I felt elation in the fact, and I wished that I didn't. That soured me immediately.

"…and I didn't know that Kuul would be so cruel. I've known him for five hundred years. He trained me."

"What?" I quizzed, perplexed at the complexity of these mundane relationships.

"It was your dad who stopped Kuul. Please don't think ill of John for my actions."

"I…I won't," I said, "but *you* on the other hand. I can't believe you'd do that."

"Salak Kuul needed more energy to help John in my plans. Your father offered himself, but the demon couldn't get everything he needed from him. John suffered for *years* alongside you, too. I didn't think it would be so bad for you. James, I am truly sorry. Some of the decisions I've had to make in the past five hundred years have been deplorable, but all towards what is right."

305

I sat silently. Kuul hadn't mentioned Dad's suffering. Dad had never mentioned his own suffering, but in my memory now I saw the desperation in his eyes when I mentioned the supernatural tormentor. He endured it with me, and I never knew.

"What are these *plans*, Kuvalik?" I asked. "We wondered about this on our time away, when the pieces came together."

"That's what I wanted to talk to you about, James," the ghost said, floating off the floor. "Although I never intended on making this speech when I had so soured my image for you."

I didn't give a response, and the ghost simply drew his lip as if he was expecting that much. He wafted towards the window, where he peered out over the sunny side-yard.

"When I was a young man, James, I was handed a powerful destiny," Kuvalik started, and I had to wonder where this was going.

"Handed?" I quizzed.

"Yes. I was a young *Zalach* as the Kiin called them, a Sunesca training under Salak Kuul. I was *Salak Nolver…*"

"The guy who wrote that Suneva history book?" I remembered that book Kuvalik had forced Celeste and I to recover from Vestas' base. He had called it 'his' book, I never pictured that he was the author.

"That was me, yes. Although now I feel like that identity has left me," he admitted. "It is from my Salak title that I coined the name Kyros Orion Olomb as my moniker…" He shook his head, grumbling. "Sorry, I'm getting distracted. The ghost Kuvalik, of a long passed Electric King, had a destiny to fulfil. A ghost is only preserved when they are yet to fulfil their purpose, and in his death, he felt like he could no longer do it. He chose me to hand this destiny to, and I have since carried it."

"Wait," I threw my hands up. "So, you're *not* even Kuvalik, then?"

"I am, and I'm not," the ghost said. "Giving me his destiny, he…*imbued* me with an essence of himself. His experiences guided me, in a way. Although close to five-hundred years on, it's hard to say who I was originally.

"But the time has come, James, that I feel the same way as the old ghost once did. Being dead for so long now, and with John Grey also passed, I no longer have a strong enough foothold in this world to influence it. Years ago, I led Hesslik

306

to power to enact my plans, but it was ultimately their selfish impatience which led me here. And it's strange to think that everything I've done in my life, everything I have done in chasing my purpose, has led me to uniting you and your friends, and has led me to you, right here and now.

"And when I met you James, I knew that it was you who I would pass this destiny on to. And I know that this is the moment when I will do it. I know you can do this destiny justice."

I stood quickly, hands raised for a surrender. I stepped away from the ghost. "I don't understand," I said, backing myself right up to the far wall, "you want me to continue your destiny."

"Yes. I know that *you* are the Suneva who will protect it best."

"But...but I'm a terrible Suneva," I spluttered. "Why not choose Natalie? Or Celeste?" I searched for excuses. It wasn't that I was too flattered to take the honour – rather, I could see the pain in the ghost's eyes, that regret of a life lived. He didn't have a lot of peace in these moments – what would this destiny subject me to?

"You, James, have such a peculiar connection to destiny," he said, advancing towards me. "You *see* your future, where others only know compulsion. You will know the path better than anybody else."

"Okay, then...what about Simone?" I fretted. He drew closer, and I slipped towards the door. "She could use a destiny."

"I learned, James, from my own experience, that the freedom of the Salaks is something to be preserved." He wafted towards me. I jiggled at the handle, but my sweaty hands slipped on the rusty knob. "You are the best choice for this. I've lived for five-hundred years, James, and I've never been so personally sure as I am now."

"How does transferring destiny work?" I eeked, flicking my sword into existence.

The ghost simply eyed me. "Goodbye, James." He said.

The smoke of his body exploded, plunging the room into darkness. The purple orb of his soul broke the black, zipping towards my chest. It slammed through my body, throwing me up against the door, smacking my head solidly against it. My eyes rolled into my skull, and in the void there I could see a light – a halo shining in a night sky, *Omercronius*. The eclipse of the moon was overpowered,

307

however, by a bright snap. The sky exploded into the blue of daylight, and in the haze of returning night, I noticed now *two* halos hanging in my mind. Two threads.
Kuvalik.

Chapter 31
Identity

"Remember, Hesslik," I said, "quatra flows with the pulse of your nerves. Feel the electricity which controls your body and use it to guide the quatra through you. Then you can guide your own charge."

"Yes, Master," the young Suneva replied. They knelt over the squat table in front of my couch, concentrating on a small light globe I'd placed there. It was turning to dusk, setting the room in the glow of our eyes. I sipped on my tea through my helmet. English breakfast – not my favourite, but I didn't care anymore. Whatever John gave me, I drank.

The young Suneva held their armoured arms before them, one to each side of the globe's prongs. Holding their hands in the *Serebe* stance, known to young Suneva now as the 'peace-sign-pose', they concentrated.

Drawing quatra, their metallic, purple fingers twitched, the cyan in their eyes glowed hot, and an arc of blue charge ignited between the index fingers of their right hand and the bulb. The light screamed with intensity, blinding us, before shattering in our faces. The room returned to sullen black.

"That's why we wear armour when learning this," I chuckled to my student, patting their shoulder.

"I don't think I can do it, Kuvalik," Hesslik complained to my joke, "they just keep exploding."

"Well, you have so far mastered aim and control separately," I said, squatting to their eye level. "Using the two together is an important step. It is difficult, but important. You've already done the two hardest parts."

Hesslik pinched their lips, nodding reluctantly. "Okay Kuvalik, I'll try again."

I smiled, replacing the spent globe with a fresh one from a pile to my side. "Remember to think of your soul. Extend it into the current, and *control* your extension." I told my student.

308

Hesslik sighed their nod, preparing themselves again.

They outstretched their hand to the fresh bulb, groaning with concentration. With a growl, a bolt of electricity flashed from both of their palms and into the bulb's base. The light flickered on, buzzing and moaning, but it settled. Hesslik strained with their power, fighting to keep *just enough* charge running from their hands. The light dimmed and waned, then flared, and it cycled like this as my grin grew bigger.

"Very good Hesslik," I smiled. "That's enough."

Hesslik threw their hands to the table, panting from the effort. "Thank you," they wheezed. Thank you for teaching me."

"Somebody has to develop young, responsible Suneva," I hummed. "I'm simply fulfilling my promises to this world."

I awoke, despite already being a wake, sucking in a deep, powerful breath. I was on a bed – but whose bed was this? I tried to place how I'd gotten here, but my mind only ran blank, I was just teaching my student. I noticed the air which spun in my room, and the weight which sat on my lap. I finally cared to focus, pulling my attention from my mind and into my house.

Celeste was straddling me. She, and the room beyond, glowed in a flickering, purple awe. We were both sweating, both half naked, as she gripped into my shoulders, staring into my soul.

"James, you're back!" She smiled, relieved, and crumbled against my body. I stiffened. I was James Grey, this was *my* room. Celeste was not four-hundred-some years younger than me. I also had no idea how to respond to her affection, or this situation. "What happened?" She asked, pulling back.

"What *has* happened?" I asked, throwing my eyes about the room. Clothes lay on the floor, my bed was a mess, red lipstick marks ran down my chest, and now lay smudged on Celeste's.

"What do you mean?" She quizzed me, hands on my shoulders again. I felt bad that I left mine rigid by my hips, but I had no idea where to place them. "You were having a great time up until now."

"I don't doubt that…" I coughed. "I mean that the last memory I have is…" I pondered, but all that came to mind before the *vision* was the blackness of nothing. "What day is it?"

"The day?" Celeste raised an eyebrow, "it's Friday."

"Friday…" I hummed. Yesterday was Thursday, and yesterday I'd gone to see Kuvalik, and shown my sister to the group. "Right, I'm only missing a full day."

"Missing a full day? Where'd it go?" Celeste asked.

"I don't know," I said. "I just had a dream, or a vision…" But was 'vision' the right term, especially since the dissociation lingered? "…or *something* that I was Kuvalik, teaching Hesslik to control electricity."

"And before that?" She asked.

"Well…I guess the last thing I can really remember before that was giving my soul over to James," I said, then paused, realising what I'd said. My face dropped. "Oh no…what's happening?"

"This is insane," Celeste gasped. She cupped my jaw with her hands and locked my eyes to hers. "You are *James Grey*," she instructed.

"James Grey," I pondered, "yes, I know that. I don't know how I'm slipping with it. But I hardly believe that *I*, James Grey, am here with you." I gestured to the bed, and the clothes, and our bodies again. Celeste blushed. I was acutely aware of the pact I'd made with Tom – that I'd stop fawning over Celeste, because she was being so uncertain and unclear, and it was driving me nuts. What happened to that conviction whilst I was away? "How did this end up happening? I've never had a chance with you; you've only ever implied your disinterest."

To this comment Celeste recoiled with genuine confusion, she huffed a chuckle. "James, haven't I been the one reaching for your hand all the time?"

Riding through the mountains, confronting her father, dancing in her room. Celeste had been forward, but never *direct*. She'd never indicated interest through these actions.

"Sure, but…"

"I don't believe you've ever shown me affection first. You comfort me when I want it, but maybe you were just going along with it awkwardly this whole time." Yes, that sounded *exactly* how me, a man scared of making any move, might have come across. "I've had no idea what you might want. It always seemed like you were interested, but you never let me know."

"What happened this time, then?" I asked.

"You let me know," she said, her voice sultry, her eyes sparkling into mine. I could feel her sweet breath on her face as she whispered the words. I could feel my bones melt with her flutter of the heart, throwing me into a giddy spin.

But *no*, I said to Tom that I'd stay away from her, from *this*. I said it to *myself*, too. I didn't want to play her games – the kind where she holds me close then dances with Yvon. I had better conviction than this, didn't I?

"I think I might have been wrong, then," I used every ounce of willpower to say, and squirmed from under her hips, "I don't know if I want this."

"Let it happen just this once," Celeste said, and before I could respond, she had lunged, and her lips were wrapped around mine.

It was ecstasy. I melted into the bed, into her embrace, pulling her close to me. Maybe one time wouldn't hurt.

***

When I woke the next morning, her arms were still limply wrapped about my body, holding me tight in the sweaty heat of summer. Being held carried an empty feeling that I couldn't gauge mid identity-crisis. I wanted Celeste's attention, and her body, but I didn't want *her*. I felt dirty, almost as if *I'd* initiated this romance to her protest, rather than the other way around.

I made us breakfast in the kitchen. Simone and Mum eyed Celeste and I, and our bed hair, with drawn, supressed grins, telecommunicating between their glances like women seemed to be able to do. Once our affair of toast and judgement was over, I led Celeste to my room.

"I don't think I want to do this again," I said plainly, and the weight of my dirtiness began to lift.

"Really?" Celeste asked. Her voice was more hurt than understanding.

"Look, I think we're good friends. Maybe we have chemistry…although it never felt like that, really…" I rambled, and shook my head. "I just…don't feel right being intimate with you. I don't know why." This was a half-truth, more to save her feelings than anything else.

"That's okay, James," she smiled and kissed my cheek. My face flushed red, and I saw her grin inflect to that. Still, she accepted my feelings, gathered her things, and was soon gone.

It was then that I turned to Simone, who was, for a change, in the back yard, painting her nails as the dog ran laps of the garden.

"What the hell happened last night?" I coughed, sitting beside her.

"Hey, I don't even want to know," Simone recoiled sharply. "Did you know how creaky your bed springs are? I can only ignore so much – and Mum's never been a fan of Celeste, have fun explaining your shenanigans to her."

"No, cheese, not *that*," I cringed. "I mean, before that. Where was I last night?"

"Is this some sort of quiz?"

"Yes, it is," I stressed. "I have no memory between being in Kuvalik's house to waking up this morning. All gone in some mad vision."

Simone turned to me, stumped, "James, that's serious. Maybe you should go to a hospital…"

"Not required!" I interjected immediately to her surprise. "No, it's some effect of having another man's *soul* inside my body, I think. Kuvalik had, like, five alter egos…maybe this is how he got them."

Simone grunted, frowning. "I'd still go to a doctor, at least," she chimed, rolling her eyes. "But you were with Tom and some others. Maybe he can tell you what happened."

"Okay, will do. Thanks," I said, and sprung to life.

"But there is something you might not know!" Simone yelled up to me, and I paused. "You're going to America in, like, two weeks."

"What?" I coughed. This was new, and I couldn't imagine why.

"For Chad's *spiritual* journey. I think Chad is finding some tickets for you all."

Well, that made sense, although was sooner than I expected. "Right," I hummed. "Are you coming?"

"Natalie said that it might be too dangerous, given I haven't trained much. I think it's better that I learn a bit more before I come along."

"You're fine with that?" I quizzed. "Didn't want to learn on the job?"

"No, I'll stay," Simone said. "I haven't told Mum yet about, you know…what I am…" She gestured to herself. "I think she'll lose her head if we both suddenly go on some dangerous, magical holiday."

I nodded. "You should tell her about yourself, though. She was fine with me – although she was ready to murder me after the Europe trip. I don't know how I'll break *another* Suneva holiday to her."

"She knew about you?" Simone asked.

"I made her keep it from you. I thought *you* would kill me, not *her.*"

Simone chuckled. "You were probably right. I'm only now seeing how bad I was being…"

"Don't get hung up on it," I said, the turned to leave. "I'll be back later, though. Now, I've got questions to ask."

***

Tom answered his door as I knocked in no more than his pyjamas. I glanced at my watch, seeing that it was almost midday.

"I just woke up," he felt the need to inform me. "I didn't expect you to be awake yet, though. You didn't go home alone…" He winked, and I blushed, falling into myself.

"No, I didn't," I cringed.

"Come in, man, I want the gossip," he pulled me inside and threw me towards his couch. The kettle whirred in the background. Tom leaned over the counter, ears alert.

"I thought you'd hate this turn of events," I mumbled. "Didn't we just agree that she was bad news?"

"Sure, but that was *before* you took her home," he laughed. "Doesn't really matter now, does it?"

I guess not. I thought, although I wasn't satisfied by that. I wanted to stick to my own convictions. "What even happened last night?" I asked. "I think I hit my head, I just woke up with her in my bed thinking it was Friday morning."

"Uh, *dude,*" Tom eyed me, shocked. "Did you go to a doctor?"

"Yes, yes, I'm all fine," I lied. "I didn't want to ask Celeste about details though."

"Right…sure," Tom quizzed, pouring boiled water into coffee cups. "Well, we went bowling. You, me, Celeste, David, Chad. Then we came back here

313

for drinks." After Tom said that, I noticed the evidence. A few bottles sat by the bin, and there were still red cups stacked by the T.V.

"I didn't feel groggy this morning," I pondered aloud.

"We didn't drink *much*. Only Chad and I, really," Tom clarified. "You know, he actually is a good bloke. Plus, he can down a drink."

"I do know that," I nodded. "So, I was sober..." and then the pivotal question came to mind. "What did I do to impress Celeste?"

Tom handed me my coffee as he sank into his couch, shrugging. "No idea, man. You just had a different energy about you last night..."

"Oh, I'm sure," I grumbled, concerned that Kuvalik had proven smoother than I had ever been.

"It's a shame you missed it."

"Big shame," I agreed, sipping my coffee.

We continued chatting right into the afternoon, cleaning the house just in time for his parents to come home.

Chapter 32
Target Practise

I stood in Natalie's backyard. With our tickets organised, it was just a week until we would fly to America, and it had been just a few days since Natalie had left on her own, lone journey. On her return, she called me and told me to swing by – apparently, she needed my help. Keen to return a favour after she'd helped me confront a literal demon, I slotted her into my schedule.

Just this morning I had gone to visit Chad and Celeste at Kuvalik's old house. Chad wanted some confirmation on the tickets he was buying, and my cash too, so he needed me to visit. I'd skipped through the underpass and down Kuvalik's street. Today, just past mid-January, the sun was full and hot in the sky. Even the effort of walking stirred a sweat, but I was glad to be baked in the heat, compared to the cold of Europe we'd just had, and the cold of America I would soon face.

I stepped up to the front gate of Old Finneck's house and pushed through onto the brick trail. With the house recently renovated, it glistened in the roaring sunlight, and a compelling case of déjà vu struck me. I pondered, and a memory came. John Grey had been standing in my garden, sweating from his labour, rising tall by the blossom tree with a hand full of weeds. He followed my eyesight to watch me admiring the house, and smiled.

"Paint looks good, Vas," John nodded. "Surprised you didn't insist on doing it yourself."

"Oh, old age makes it hard. I know my limits," I shrugged. "But thank you for today. I appreciate having a friend like you only around the corner."

"Hey, any time, Vas," John said, tossing the weeds in the bucket. He squatted again, disappearing behind the hedge to pluck at more. "I'm always on call – as long as you haven't also got me chasing Argols."

John was joking, but I had accidentally called his house once while he was on a mission. I couldn't remember what the situation was at all, but I had the strong inclination that it was a hilarious anecdote.

"Have you still got the *Vatje na Vochduh*?" I asked him. Even though I said the words, I didn't know their meaning past some emotional association of *importance*. Trying to draw on the meaning of *Vatje* and *Vochduh* only pulled up blanks.

"What, my translation of it?" John asked.

"The translation was Muhrakiin's, wasn't it?"

John grinned, shaking his head, "Muhrakiin found it, I translated it. Wouldn't trust an old Vochduh to translate truthfully, would you?"

I laughed, although I couldn't know why, because I still didn't know what a *Vochduh* was.

It was this confusion that tore me from the daydream, and threw me into a grumbling mess as I realised what had happened.

"Kuvalik again…" I cursed, trudging forward to the front door. "I am *James Grey*."

It was insane that I needed to stamp my own identity into my brain, but I had to do it if I was going to walk into this house without slip ups. Chad soon opened the door, and led me through to the living room, where he and Celeste had the proposed tickets laid across our meeting table. Celeste smiled her hello with eyes that knew all too much about my body. I wanted to hate that look coming from her, I wanted it to feel uncomfortable, but it didn't. Now *I* was the one with

315

no idea what I wanted. I frowned at this, but still sat right next to her, allowing her to scooch closer.

"This Saturday, we leave here at nine in the morning, and we're flying to Portland," Chad explained, handing me an itinerary. "Then we rent a car and head inland." He was expecting some argument or affirmation from me, but I had nothing.

"Sure, man," I shrugged. "You know the land the best."

"There are other options…" he suggested, pulling forth at least five other options, all made with love.

"This one is the best though, right?" I asked.

"Sure," Chad agreed. "This is the one Natalie thought was the best."

"Then it probably is," I said, trusting Natalie's prudence to properly scan and analyse any documents presented to her. "Let's do it."

"Good choice," Chad nodded. He pointed out the price, and I handed over the cash.

"I hope this ends up worth it," I said. "There's still two more Legendaries, and you're the only one left to solve their conflicts. We need to find at least one Legendary whilst we're away."

"You know James," Chad rested a palm on my shoulder. "I'm sure everything will be just fine for us. You just follow me for a change and see."

"Alright," I smiled. "As long as you're ready to face everything you need to."

To this Chad gulped, then laughed nervously. "Oh, I'm not," he chuckled. "But I'll have to be."

"Well, if there's something you never run out of, it's courage." I said, and stood. "Thanks for putting everything together though…"

"You're welcome."

"…but I've got to help Natalie with something of hers. I'll see you later."

And with that I left, to find myself positioned in Natalie's backyard under the shade of her wide trees. We stood opposite each other on the strip of grass, like two cowboys under the midday light.

"I need you to shoot quatra at me," Natalie clarified the instructions, standing stiffly in front of me. "Not *at* me, but near me."

"Was this what you covered in your *self-discovery*?" I quizzed, drawing my weapon. "How were your three days away? You really could have taken more time…"

"Didn't need it," she quickly retorted. "All I had to do was talk to my mum and my Yamitse. I know what I have to work on now."

"Okay, fair enough," I sighed. "I'm just glad to be involved."

"Don't feel too blessed," she chuckled, and it was nice to see her crack a laugh. "I just need to practice some quatra-control skills. For all intents and purposes, you're just a quatra gun."

"Right," I smiled. "Be one with the inner gun. Got it. Just don't shoot directly *at* you."

"Exactly," Natalie smiled. She gauged the distance between us with an out-stuck tongue, and stepped back to some arbitrary line she'd decided upon.

"And the purpose of this is?"

"You'll see," Natalie hummed, and readied herself, drawing her twin swords. "Okay, shoot."

I lined my shot, then misaligned it, blasting a green bolt from my staff-end off to Natalie's right. Before I'd even drawn the bolt into my arm, Natalie's eyes locked to the energy. She raised her staff to meet mine and we each produced our bolts in unison. Her orange bolt of energy flew directly into mine, and the two absorbed each other, destructively imploding with a crack of space and time. I gaped at my friend, not believing what I'd just seen.

"You learned to do *that*?" I awed. "Your self-discovery was becoming Fisira?"

I could tell that I'd struck a chord in my wording. Natalie frowned, her swords drooping as she composed an answer. "The opposite is my intention," she said, her eyes rising to meet me. "Fisira is a Suneva possessed by their quatra use, like my cousin Christina."

"Eh…" I cringed, remembering plunging into Christina's grey, dead eye, and facing the terrible vision therein.

"Being a powerful witch allows you to do things like predict bolts, but it may cost you some autonomy if you don't learn to control the quatra as it gives itself to you. I am powerful, and now I have to learn to control the power. I'm trying very hard *not* to be like Fisira by practicing this kind of concentration."

"Right, I see," I blushed. "I'm sorry for making that simile…"

"It's fine James, I know you didn't mean it seriously. In fact, barely anything you say is meant to be taken seriously," she smiled, and I laughed along. "Plus, Fisira can only cancel bolts because she's so lost to her black hole that she's basically a vessel for destiny. It's not impressive that she can cancel bolts, but it's *very* impressive that I can – if I'm allowed to say that."

"I think you've earned the right, Natalie," I chuckled. "Can I see it again?"

"About one hundred more times, sure," she chuckled along, readying herself. I chose another spot now, moving my arm just as I went to fire, and amazingly Natalie predicted it, and intercepted the bolt. And she did this ten more times, then twenty times, then more times than I was prepared to count, only missing the odd shot which soared past the broad trees that we stood under. Somehow, she even seemed to hit the bolt I fired from my hand after faking-out with my staff – she never even thought that it would come from the wrong limb. Her eyes snapped only to the flow of quatra in my body.

"This is nuts," I marvelled. "I can't believe you can just learn to do this. You're amazing."

Natalie chirped, her lips taught. "It's what I have to do to control it all," she said, then smirked. "But you won't believe the next exercise." She pulled a bandana from her rear pocket, and slopped it over her face. Natalie then reached around the back of her head with it, tying it into a blind fold over her eyes.

"Blindfolded?" I scoffed. "Isn't that ambitious."

"It's *required*," she insisted. "Try me."

And so I did. I summoned the quatra to fire a bolt. It came down from my thread and it entered my body at the neck. As soon as the energy came into my veins, Natalie locked onto it. Her head turned, her hands pointed towards me, and a burning hot bolt of orange quatra erupted from her hand towards mine. I didn't even get to aim the bolt. I flailed my arm and let the quatra fire itself as I rolled out of the way, afraid that she'd miss. Even so, Natalie's bright orange bolt collided with my green one a just a foot from my hand. They combined, flashed white, and collapsed into nothing as I hit the grass. I pushed myself off the dirt with a gust of air and stood still.

I couldn't believe it, and I stood in shock until Natalie raised her blindfold. "I got it, right?" She asked.

"Yes, Nat. You got it," I coughed.

"Well, come on *gun*, keep going," she insisted, and I did. I laid a volley in her direction, bolts flying to any which side of her body, whizzing about the shaded garden in the hot summer sun. To each of my calls Natalie had a flying, orange reply, fired just as I drew the energy for its bolt. Her swords were dancers, her body a receiver, reading the impossible depths of the field. Shocks rung off the house like artillery, one for each interception.

Only one bolt was missed, and Natalie had to run to threw water on it's landing spot as her dad's shed started to singe.

We stared at the tiny spot of charred wood together, laughing as it smothered to smoke.

"Natalie," I turned to her, "you're incredible."

Episode 6

The Cowboy Rides into Town

Chapter 34
Under the Spire

There is a river which runs between this world and the void. The river is thick, and flows with the strong current of pure quatra. This is the realm that the *soul men* draw their power from – explained Chad as we soared thirty-six thousand feet in the air.

In Western Suneva understanding, there is the soul, and there is the soul's influence. The power for the soul to influence comes from quatra, the energy source given by the Gods. The Gods can guide Suneva through the use of quatra, and they direct destiny. For the *Liktan* Philosophies, destiny is seen as a duty, and a blessing of purpose. To the Native American Suneva, the direction of the void's river was the way of the Earth, and seen as an inevitable flow, just like water from the mountains to the seas. It would always happen just as it did, and its path would shape life and lifetimes.

To these people, quatran were not important, and quatra abilities were not categorised. Instead, the *soul men* gained understanding of themselves through the influence that the current of the river had on them.

In the continual stream between here and the void, you could be *grounded* or you could be *spiritual*.

To be *grounded* was to walk with your feet in the riverbed. The magnitude of the current would only allow you to walk in one direction – the way of everything – but you could resist it. Resisting the flow of change would wear down on your soul, like a river would wear down rocks from jagged to smooth. A grounded Suneva could not be easily influenced by quatra and its flow, nor seduced by its power, but was still subject to the current. They had control, but at the cost of their soul.

To be *spiritual* was to swim on the surface of the river of quatra. Spiritual Suneva could always see into the void, and were subject to images of the afterlife. They could see the future flow of the river, and gain insight into what was to come. They could look up to the stars, and view the alternate realities. For this, their cost was being controllable. They could in no way resist the flow of the river as it carried them away into their lives. They had the illusion of purpose, and were gifted powers and visions, but could not fight for their free will to use them how they wished.

To be grounded was to experience none of the spirituality of Sunevahood, but to have control over oneself. To be spiritual was to connect with the plan of the universe, but have no control as to what you saw nor how you used it. A legendary Suneva, for these people, was one who could dive down from the river's surface, plant his feet in the mud, then swim back up. It was true that most Suneva rested in between *grounded* and *spiritual*, but to traverse your position on the gradient of spirituality was the ultimate connection.

Chad explained that I, with my propensity to strange visions and the pull of destiny, was clearly spiritual. He, with his inability to be tugged by the tide or be pulled into the supernatural, was grounded. Natalie and Celeste were somewhere in between.

We arrived in Chad's home town at noon, having traversed the sleepy, winding mountain roads to get here. Our car spluttered and jerked along the whole journey, a tiny red hatchback which groaned through each corner, just managing to hold itself together as we rounded the curve into the town's lines.

Frosty sunlight teased the high settlement, which sat gleaming in the forested saddle of two giant's peaks. The church spire, visible even above the tall reaching fingers of the farthest spruce trees, had guided us into the main strip of shops. The colossal tower cast its cold, midday shadow over the town square, which reached right to the farthest shop. We drove there, hoping to get a snack before finding the motel.

Chad stayed in the car, ordering a cola from me. 'Don't want to be seen just yet' was his excuse – although the car, bright red and decrepit, was an easy stand-out on its own. Still, we made quick work of raiding the corner store for its treats, and Chad kept us moving, on to the one motel in town.

Just five minutes down the road from the main drag the motel lay – moss and mould lining the grout of its brickwork, it's neon sign reading 'M-TE-' in a dazzling, flashing green. The room we were handed was in no better state of maintenance, but it had a roof and walls at the least. It comprised of an eclectic mix of furniture – clearly whatever was found in the local garage sales of the last twenty years, each object clashing perfectly with every other. Of the 'new' items were the double and single bed in the main room, and the single bed in the private, forest-facing room at the back. Still, despite the disrepair of it all, there was a hopefully-operational TV at the double bed's foot, and a trusty bible for the nightstand.

"Home sweet home," Chad wheezed as he flung his bags over the single bed in the main room.

"Didn't want the double bed?" I asked, pointing to it. "It is your week, after all."

"What, you wanted to share it with me, did you?" He grinned, flexing his eyebrows. I chuckled, only to see Natalie claim the second single bed, and Celeste throw her bags onto the double. I glanced between her and the last remaining spot.

"What's on the agenda today, then?" I prolonged my decision. "We've still got about half of it left."

"I'm waiting till night to make my first move," Chad said as he was absorbed into the soft bed. "Don't want to be seen in daylight yet."

"Wait, really?" I asked. "No friends to surprise."

"Sure, totally. But it wouldn't be a good move," Chad sighed, sitting up. "You've never lived in a small town, have you?"

"I…" I wasn't sure how this was relevant. "No, I haven't."

"News spreads," Chad explained, "even without people intending it, it spreads. Did you see that spire in the town today? That really tall one?"

"Yeah, the church?" I quizzed.

"Gossip centre," Chad corrected. "That spire is visible from every corner of the town – it controls everything here. If I was seen in daylight, then people would start talking about it in the church café, suddenly there'd be a witch hunt. And I mean that in the most literal sense, too," he clarified, sitting stiff and pale. "The people here would believe that I'm a witch. They'd have to have heard what I did."

"I'd take it that people here aren't too fond of witches, then," Natalie hummed, emerging from the private room. "Otherwise you wouldn't have run away, right?"

"The church-types never are a witch's friend," Celeste grumbled.

"I wouldn't make generalisations like that," Chad shied away from agreeing with Celeste. "But the preacher at the church here…he's a little *enthusiastic*, to put it lightly. The people of this town are *strong* believers in God's word."

"Is it safe for us to walk around, then?" I asked. "I wanted to walk into town if we were making nothing of the afternoon."

"It's safe," Chad nodded. "But no *Suneva stuff* of any kind. And you'll especially have to watch out for the Sheriff, Stan Johnson. If he thinks you're 'strange' in any way, he will treat you differently."

"Noted," I gulped. "Anybody keen for a walk after that warning?"

"I'm coming," Celeste said. She hopped up, grabbing my bag from my hand and throwing it onto the bed beside her own. "Too nice of a day to stay here. Will you come, Natalie?" She asked, but Natalie shook her head.

"I don't want to leave Chad alone, not when this town is apparently out to get him," she said, taking a seat on the end of his bed. "Plus, there's only a few hours of daylight left, and we don't know if there are other Suneva in the town. I'd like to read the field here before venturing out."

"That's astutely cautious," I nodded.

"Natalie always has her head in the right places," Chad smiled. "I've got cards, we've got a table, time will pass here. Go enjoy the town." He waved Celeste and I off, and we obliged him.

We walked together on the roadside grass towards the main town. Even with the town a mile away, and cut from view by the sky-reaching conifers, that church's dark spire still peeked into view. We strolled towards it.

Birds sang to our step, the golden light of a fading afternoon painting our cold faces. I could feel the biting winter even through my gloves. I turned to Celeste, who braved the chill in just a red skirt, thermals, and a tight pullover. She caught my eyes just as I gazed at her body, and her lip cracked a grin to the implication.

"Here," she said, grabbing my hand firmly in both of hers. Her uncovered fingers were red hot – pinker than my blush – they threatened to melt my gloves.

"*Cheese*, you're warm!" I coughed.

"*Ivaer*, James," she reminded me, "we can do things like this. Winters are nothing."

"Right," I puzzled. "I didn't know you could create heat. I thought it was just fire."

"It's ill-defined. Nobody really knows what *Ivaer* is," Celeste mumbled. "Quatra moves with the heat of the body, but I'm putting quatra into my heat, if that makes sense."

I wasn't sure if that made sense. Quatra moved with my breath, so could I put quatra into my breath? I didn't know what that might do. Still, I was glad that Celeste had figured this reversal out – her heat was bringing me back to comfort.

It was then that she grabbed my arm by the elbow, and threaded hers through mine, pressing her body against me as we walked. I couldn't ignore her gesture now.

"What do you want from...us?" I asked her. I could only be sure that I'd really asked it by the mist rising from my mouth. She hummed to the question, squeezing at my hand. "Because I hadn't given anything much thought. I don't know where I stand."

"Why does it have to be anything?" Celeste asked me, tugging me along. I was surprised by this response, but even more surprised by my reaction. I felt a small pit open in my stomach, as if I'd already lost some secure ground that I didn't even know I had. I assumed she liked me, based on our actions on my bed, but maybe she didn't.

What *did* she want, then?

"What do you mean?" I asked.

"Why do we have to make something out of this?" She asked me again. "Isn't it nice just to be held?"

"Yes." It was nice to have her arm locked in mine. It was magical, really. There was some deep part of your brain, some caveman, locked away in a cage, yelling that a woman on your arm is the key to happiness, and he was throwing dopamine into my dizzy blood in buckets.

"So, why make something of it?" She asked again. "I mean, I don't know if I *like* you, James, like that. But I *want* you. Does that make sense?"

This made clear sense. I nodded to my own feelings, grunting with the caveman who was suddenly growing more excited.

"So then, why not keep *us* casual? Act on desire. Things don't always have to be serious, you know."

"I guess they don't," I agreed, riding the wave. Celeste really did have a way with words, I was convinced. Why involve muddy emotions into what could be nice, physical gratification. I had thought myself that I didn't want *her*, just her body. I nodded along, satisfied and dizzy in a strange flood of giddy. "Let's keep it casual."

"I'm glad you see it my way," Celeste grinned, and she stopped me with a tug of my arm. She caught me as I spun, and nailed a hot, passionate kiss to my lips. I gripped her in her hot embrace.

When we finally walked into the town centre, hand in hand, the town was gathering slowly to the church. Shops appeared to be shutting all around the spire as locals, dressed in black, hung to the shaded courtyard. On each side of the church, I could see now, rose impressive buildings in roman style – the town hall and the library.

"Good thing Chad didn't come with us. The whole town is here," I said to Celeste, and she hummed along.

"It's a funeral," she mused, pointing to the letterboard next to the church door. *Funeral Service: Reverend Robert Brand* it read.

"For the Reverend," I said aloud. "I wonder if that's the preacher Chad was talking about."

"Knowing hateful preachers, I can only hope so." Celeste said. She tugged me away from the court. From the crowd in black, solemn with hung heads, we garnered no attention.

We walked onwards through the town, tracking back the way we'd driven through it. Cosy shops abutted each other along the main road, a town hall rising on the far end, right at the town gates. We walked aimlessly towards it, enjoying the sun, but without any idea what do to. All around, shops were closed – blacked out to respect the large funeral.

"It'd be a good day for a picnic," Celeste suggested. "It's sunny enough for one."

"But where would we get food?" I asked, gesturing to the shut stores. She pointed directly across the road, to a grocer that was dark enough to appear closed, but had some customers slipping between its aisles.

"That's why I thought of it. Only thing I saw open." She shrugged, and skipped across the road, losing my hand. I paused at the street, still disturbed by the cars driving the wrong way, the jogged to catch her.

A little bell chimed as we passed through the front door. An older lady peered up from behind the register with a face painted dull in years of monotony. To see strange guests made it light up, once the gears turned.

"Howdy, strangers," she sparked. "Just get into town?"

"Just this morning," I nodded, and followed Celeste who slipped further into the aisles. Inside we found a French stick, some cheeses, and a cucumber. It wasn't much, but it would do the job when nothing else was open. I let Celeste ring the items through, giving the teller the kick of having a French woman buy a French stick.

"Canadian?" The woman asked as Celeste spoke.

"French, actually," Celeste curtsied.

As she finished, the door's bell chimed again, accompanied by the heavy toll and tambourine of a spurred boot. I glanced to the disturbance, to find a walking barrel of a man occupying the height of the door. His face was hidden down to the chiselled jaw by the shade of a broad brimmed hat. A moustache twiddled under an upturned nose in that darkness.

The woman peered over Celeste to see the newcomer, and she bit her lip. "Sheriff Johnson," she greeted.

Stan Johnson. I heard Chad's voice in my head. The hulking figure of a man seemed to have more bite against the light of day. It strode further into the store.

"Hi Marissa," his voice boomed from a broad, deep chest. He then turned to Celeste and myself, who had found ourselves staring. "Young man. Miss," he greeted, tipping his hat to us.

"G'day," I wheezed, my face flushing pale. "How's it going?"

The Sheriff glared his sudden disapproval. The force of his stare crushed me into the counter, I had no idea what I'd done wrong. His casual hand, hanging by the grip of his pistol, twitched.

"We're sorry for any *faux pas*," Celeste said sweetly, stepping between us. "It's our first day in America. We don't know the customs."

"Right," Stan Johnson huffed, his eyes still squarely locked on mine. "Well, I'll teach you a lesson boy, and ma'am. I'm not sure what kind'a manners they teach you in Canada, but here you'd do well to call your superiors *Sir*."

"Yes *Sir*," I quickly eeked, trying to recover. Stan huffed, then stepped past us to the counter.

"Just…just your usual, Sheriff Johnson?" The woman at the counter asked.

"Please," he nodded. Celeste and I took that as our chance to escape.

We escorted our bags of food down a nearby alleyway, emerging onto a dirt road and grassy flat at the foot of the forest. The sun was beating its winter tease here, and the ground was dry and clear of snow. We placed ourselves down here, unravelling the bag of food.

"Chad was right about that sherrif," Celeste said as she tore at the bread. "I hate people like that."

"Like what?"

"Like…like him," she huffed. "Bullies who thrive on the authority they give themselves. What gives him the right to shame you for a faux pas?"

"Maybe what I said really *was* offensive," I reasoned, although I didn't believe my own grounds.

"I don't think you should take being talked to like that," Celeste pouted. She smeared cheese carelessly onto the bread, taking a huge chunk which she threw into her mouth. "We're *Suneva*, we don't *have* to accept that kind of treatment."

"I don't know," I mumbled. "We're just like anybody else, right? We don't get special treatment - why doesn't anybody else stand up to him?"

"Oh, if he *knew* we were Suneva, we'd be getting special treatment, let me tell you," Celeste chuffed, almost choking herself. "I know these kinds of people. We're the only ones with the strength to show them their place. Nothing scares a bully more than power. They're cowards."

"If we're done making assumptions about a rude Sheriff…" I steered the conversation sharply away, finding relief. "Why don't we just enjoy the day?" And I grabbed her hand, staring up to the clouds and the sun. Her skin was boiling, and I flinched to hold it.

"Sure," Celeste huffed, but I could feel her pulse through her burning palm. She was agitated.

Then, as if summoned, the tambourine jangle of spurs sounded from the alleyway. Broad, military bootsteps rang across the asphalt road.

"Oh, come on," I moaned, "what now?"

Celeste restrained herself, squeezing my hand to stare straight ahead. I turned instead, to see Sheriff Johnson storming our way.

"Is there anything I can do for you, sir?" I asked, putting all of my concentration into politeness and bravery. The Sheriff snorted, stamping himself to a stop at the edge of the gravel – just long enough away to force a yelling match.

"You can't have a picnic here," he stated, and I was floored.

"Oh, why not?" I asked form instinct, but immediately cringed as his face folded.

"Because having picnic here contravenes the seventh subsection of the third section of the town's forest protection charter."

Forest protection? I wondered, noting that the forest was still a few metres away from where we sat. As I glanced about, I caught Celeste's hand as her fingers twisted and griped about her palm. She faced the Sheriff now, her face blank.

"We're sorry, sir," she said, her voice snow cold, "we hadn't read the town's specific rules before deciding to eat lunch. What exactly does this law forbid, if I may ask?"

The sass dripped from her mouth in place of her regular purple flames. I could feel her heat now, and I could sense her quatra. Behind the Sheriff's head, I noticed a glob of white mass forming, growing in the air.

"I can take you to my Deputy's office if you want the rules explained to you," he said, and it was a threat. My eyes went small in my skull. This man was intent on landing us in trouble, and I didn't know how to talk us out of it. "Otherwise, you'd do well not to talk back."

"Where would be better?" I asked. "We don't want to break any more rules."

"Well maybe you could look up the *laws* of a place before you just stroll into it," Stan Johnson proclaimed, jiggling at his belt. I nodded, waiting for further instruction, such as *go get on your way*, or, *pack it up now*, but instead Celeste chose to open her mouth.

"Maybe you could do to treat others with respect," she snarled, and my legs went weak. My head would have fallen of my neck and run away if it weren't for my spine. I could see that glob of white still growing behind Stan's head. *What are you doing, Celeste?* I screamed in my skull. "I think you'd get more people obeying your *rules* then."

I'd never seen a man's face more enveloped with disgust. It turned fully green and red at the same time. His fists balled tight, tighter than his foul stare. He ponied up, stomping towards us.

"That's it young miss, I…" and then he couldn't help but fall over. His eyes rolled back in his head, and his body pitched forward into the snow and mud. The tight white glob dispersed.

"What was that?!" I shrieked, not sure to which action in that series of events I was referring.

"Oxygen deprivation," she answered grabbing my hand. "Lets go!" She urged me along. I stood planted, anchoring us as I watched over the passed-out Sheriff. His fingers twitched against his closed, flat face. He might get up at any moment.

"Yeah…let's go," I finally said, and kicked into a run.

***

"Well, that was risky," Chad appraised the situation when we were finally back in the motel room, after an hour of trekking just in the forests' line of shadow. Celeste and I had ducked behind trees to avoid cars, and sleuthed the two-mile walk. "You shouldn't be seen again in the town centre. The Sheriff is ruthless."

"I'm glad I put him in his place," Celeste grinned with gritted teeth. "Nobody needs to take orders from a coward riding their authority."

"Sadly, that's how this town is built," Chad said. All throughout our recount, his muscles at been drawn tense and his face in knots. "Although I think suffocating the guy is a bit on the nose. If he suspects that you're Suneva…"

"He probably won't have remembered the encounter," Celeste huffed. "Oxygen deprivation does that. He thought he could take our rights, I took his ability to enforce that."

"You've never used your connections like this before," Natalie hummed, chiming in. "It seems a little…violent. I mean, very useful too, but maybe a little *much.*"

"Some people need that to wake up to reality," Celeste wouldn't back down, grappling my hand tighter. As much as I disagreed with her methods, I didn't want to speak against her and corner her here. I didn't back up anybody.

"Well, I wouldn't worry about the Sheriff picking up that we're Suneva, anyway," Natalie said, shifting the conversation along. "There's two Suneva in town, and he hasn't noticed them."

"You mean us?" I asked.

"No, James. Besides you," Natalie smiled, shaking her head. "They're not anybody that we know, but they're here. I can sense them in the town."

"I'm not taking that as an excuse to get away with Suneva nonsense," Chad said, his voice growing deep. "We need to be careful still."

"I agree. We don't know who these other Suneva might be," Natalie nodded.

Chad smiled, finally. I could see his tension replaced with anxiety as he paced towards the window. It was nearing dusk now, the sun almost setting through the forest.

"Are you ready James?" He asked me. "It's getting dark. It's about time we left."

"If you're ready," I said.

Chapter 35
Coming Home

Chad and I pulled our rental to the gutter, the tiny red car spluttering to the curb in a mess of hot oil. It curled up to rest just one street from his childhood home, on the border of a swathe of forest.

This section of thick woods connected the houses on this side of town. The sun was coming down over the mountains to the west, but not even the pink light of sunset could penetrate the canopy just before me. The ground under the pines was a permanent blackness.

I noticed how dark and chilly it was when we stepped out of the car. Pine needles rustled in the stiff January wind. I pulled up my hoodie to protect my ears, but the breeze was icy and swirled around my face in eddies. I used my power over *kiin* to lessen the effect.

Chad walked wordlessly into the grey, damp forest, and so I reluctantly followed.

Needles and twigs crunched underfoot. The soil was saturated and muddy, and I almost fell on my face trying to keep up. Having stepped into the dense swath of tall trees, I could not see any edge to the woods. They endlessly extended into all directions – the only indication that I was still near the town being the pink-turning sky above my head, and the knelling of the church's bells.

Chad led me to a small and fast flowing creek. There was a single sturdy log which crossed over the wide stream. It was secured to the soft ground with rusty, old railroad spikes and roped onto nearby trees.

"I made this, you know," Chad pulled down his wool mask and pointed to the structure. "Didn't know it would last this long. We're close to my house now, anyway."

"It's neat," I smiled, "but is it safe?"

"Send the *Kiin* across first?" Chad chuckled. "You've got lighter feet than me."

I nodded and pulled my face warmer back over my nose and mouth.

I took a cautious step onto the rotting log. It twisted slightly, and for the brief second, I saw myself plummeting into the icy water, but it steadied. I took a deep breath and kept walking across, one foot at a time.

The old, dead wood moaned as I stepped across it, and despite its threats of throwing me into the cold drink, I remained dry on the other side. I gave the thumbs up to Chad and he embarked on the tightrope himself.

In the near distance, visible through the screen of gangly tree trunks was a peaked roof and a patch of grass. We stalked towards it. Soon a whole house became visible on the edge of the woods. The land sloped up to meet its back yard, which was just a field of frosty grass with a totem tennis pole nailed into it. On the perimeter of the double storey house was a small hedge guarded by garden gnomes. Through the visible doors and windows were closed curtains. Not a light flickered through.

Chad pulled me close behind a tree for cover.

"Have you ever read a bible?" He asked me. I coughed in surprise.

"Like, the whole way through?" I asked, and he nodded. "Never. I've barely read a chapter."

"A bible doesn't have chapters..." Chad sighed, and peered around the tree at the house. "Fine. It'll be fine. Just...you might have trouble interacting with anybody we might meet. Not that you'll be doing the talking. Not that they'll be interested in you past me...not that..."

"Dude, you're nervous," I grabbed him arm and pulled him back to face me. His face was pink – flushed white in nerves and red in adrenaline. He nodded slowly, trying to shake his feelings.

"I'm being *pulled* towards the house," Chad said. "I never feel the pull like this. And when I do, I usually avoid it. I don't know what will be in there. I don't want to run into my family just yet."

"Wait, you don't?" I quizzed.

"No. Lord no. I'm not ready for that," he laughed uneasily. "I just feel that going into the house is my first step. I need to see my room. I need to see what happened."

"Alright, I'll respect that," I hummed along, knowing that whatever intentions he was hiding would be soon revealed.

"Meeting my mother is something I'd rather not put you through," Chad gulped, following his own train of thought. "Have you ever met a narcissist?"

"What's that?" I asked.

"Be glad you don't know," he chuckled, patting me on the shoulder. "Now, back to the mission. I've got artefacts to recover..." And he peered back around the trunk of the tree, eyeing the house.

"Best way in?" I asked.

"There's a key by the back door – or there should be," Chad said. "But do you see that window there, right by the garage..." he pointed to a window on the rightmost end of the second storey. Below it sat a pitch of roof for the adjutting ground floor. I nodded. "That's my room. That's primarily where I want to end up."

I could see a clear path from ground to that window – I could leap onto that small eave of roof easily, then shimmy along to the window and slide a diamond blade in to unlock it. This was an easy entry.

"Got it," I said. Chad left the shade of the tree, stalking towards the house. I sleuthed in his wake, up the muddy bank and into the house's back yard. Chad led us to the back door, where he upturned the gnome sitting sentry by it. Nothing was beneath. He hummed, "changed the spot, I see," and upturned the next gnome. I turned away, drawn to his window. The jump to the awning was so easy, that it was impossible not to attempt. I extended my soul to the air around me, and forced it down as I leaped from the ground. I soared high, somersaulting in the air to land on the black slate tiles on two sure feet. Chad's head snapped to me, his face of horror.

"Didn't I say *no quatran* in this town? I know that it's lost on Celeste, but…"

"There's nobody around," I said. "We don't need to hide our true natures right now."

Chad went to rebut, but found himself pouting, lowering his objecting finger. "There's still two unknown Suneva in town, even if there's no towns folk to see you not fearing their God."

"That's true, but this will only take a second," I said, and pulled at the carbon in my surroundings. From the coalesced black mass I formed a diamond blade, and used it to cut at the deadbolt locking the window. I quietly palmed the pane, lifting it without a creak. I turned to Chad.

"I'll pull you up," I said, squatting down on the awning. Chad refused, swatting my hand away.

"I don't need to hide who I am. You're right about that," he grappled at his element and heaved upwards, forming a step from the wet earth. He used it to grab at the gutter, and with minimal effort pulled his muscular body onto the eave. "Why would I come back here if I wasn't ready to show these people who I am?" He asked as he shimmied by me, ducking through the window. I smiled as I joined him, falling into the room with my muddy boots.

Chad froze as he landed, and I stumbled into his stone-frozen body.

"What's up?" I asked him, and his eyes glared about the bare, stripped room before us. Nothing was in sight apart from a computer on a desk and a photo in a frame. The walls were littered with remnants of an old wallpaper that once was, the cupboards scraped of their stickers, with residue left behind, clinging.

"They got rid of everything," he uttered, laughing to himself.

I wasn't sure what to say to this. Instead, I tracked my muddy feet further into the room, standing there stupidly. "I mean, it has been two years, right?" I asked him. "You've been missing a while. Some people give up sooner than others."

"This wasn't giving up." Chad noted, stepping over to the computer and its desk. He inspected the framed photograph, then showed it to me. In the picture was a man and a woman, with another photo inserted over the bottom half of the frame, clearly covering Chad. I cringed audibly. "They've even blocked me out of their photos," he said. "And I expected all of this... so why does it sting?"

"I'm not going to pretend that I know how this feels," I said, grabbing for the office chair. I sat myself into it, trying to think of *anything* to say. "I mean, I guess you're still on their mind if they go out of their way to cover you up instead of removing the photo. It's a level of pettiness that represents care, right?"

"Sure," Chad chuckled, putting the photo face down on the desk. He lumbered over to the closet now, and I followed, rolling in the chair behind him. I wanted to ask what he was searching for in this room, but I got the idea that he wasn't looking for any items, just truths.

"What else do you need to see?" I asked him instead.

"I think I want to reminisce," Chad said simply, opening the closet. "In the catacombs, I had a vision that suggested I'm still the same kid I always used to be, stumbling with the same *assumption*. Truth is, I forgot who that kid was."

In the closet were stacks of dusty tubs. He scraped them across the floor, clearing a space at the back of the closet which he crawled into. I, instead, took the box from the top of the stack and opened it up.

"What did you forget, then?" I asked. In this box were stacks of photos, all of music, musicians, concerts. Each shot was authentically amateur, with smoke hanging before smiling faces in flash lighting. Chad appeared in some of these photos as I flicked through them.

"Well, for a start, I've been lying about who I was. I lied to you guys. I was too afraid to admit that to Natalie." Chad admitted, his voice growing small.

"How big of lies?" I coughed, my concern growing.

"Oh, like, I never played football," he said. "I never liked sports, or weights, or...well anything cool."

"That's not a heavy lie," I sighed, relieved it wasn't anything more. "Why hide that from us?" And then I overturned the next photo. A tall, chubby child with a jet-black mop of hair obscuring their excited face stood in the shadow of a crowd before a concert. Black, studded clothes embroidered with skulls shone in the red haze of the flash-soaked view. The face was Chad's, clearly.

"This was *you*?" I turned the photo to him, jaw open in disbelief.

"That was me," Chad nodded, shuddering. "Yep, that was me." And he turned his attention back to the cupboard's rear, shoving his arm deep in it.

"Not what I was expecting. When did you glow-up?"

"Kuvalik did it to me," Chad said, his voice bouncing off the back wall to reach me. "That photo was just a month out from the prom. Kuvalik scraped my fat, greasy-haired ass off the side of the road and trained me up. He worked me hard all winter, grinding me into the earth to train my connections. Come to think of it, you might remember the details."

I turned the next image, and was met again with a smiling, chubby boy with his jet-black hair. This picture, up close and under the white light of the stage, showed the blonde regrowth through the black mop.

I remembered then, seeing that hair grown out, seeing its black ends waving in the smoke of a campfire, embers circling in the eddy of the night. Men chanted in a circle about the blaze, tanned of skin and with intricate feathered headwear. I held my blade to Chad's hair in a trembling, wrinkled hand, and I cut the black from his head.

"I remember," I said, not annoyed at the intrusion. "I cut your hair the day you became a man." What did that mean? I didn't even know as I said it. Chad just hummed along, then hollered with glee.

"I knew it!" He said, excited. "Mom never found my stash." And he thrust his arm deep into a hole in the wall, pulling out a handful of music CDs in cases and a wad of cash. He fanned the stash before his face, his smile immeasurable. "Man, it's been so long since I got to listen to these. I barely even got to play them when I lived here." The covers were all intricately designed, showing painted artwork of gory scenes.

"Metal?" I quizzed.

"Yeah, only the best stuff," Chad nodded. "That photo you've got, that one was from the *Steel Mistress* concert. I remember sneaking out to go there – Mom almost burned the tickets, told me she was 'scared for my soul' that I was into the 'devil's music'. She never grabbed me harder than when she dragged me into church the next day…" He laughed the memory off. I cringed away, not sure how to react.

"What's with the money?" I asked. "Didn't have a wallet?"

"Oh, no, the wallet was for money I didn't care about," Chad explained. "Mom would take money from my wallet, claimed I was too young to need it. How else do you think I bought concert tickets without a stash?"

"How else?!" I stuttered, barely believing what he'd told me. "With the money you *own*. What do you mean she just *took* your money?"

"Yeah. She just *took* it. Her house, her rules. I didn't need luxuries, according to her," he shrugged off my response, then pointed to the wad in his hand. "Can't tax what she can't see though, right? I wonder if my headphones are still where I left them. Paid a lot for those, only way I could listen to my music…" and he stood tall, walking over me towards the room's door.

"You are aware that's madness, right?"

"Oh, totally," Chad said. "But you live with what you have to, I guess. It made running away an easier choice."

"I bet…" I followed him as he went for the door. At the foot of it, he knelt, pressing his bare arms to the floor and the metal strip which lay there.

"Nobody's home," he declared, pushing the door open and rising. "I've just got to check out the attic. If I find my headphones, I think my life will be complete."

"The *Legendary* headphones," I joked. "Must be the goal of your realisation."

"I hope so," he smiled, and led me to the left.

Chad's room opened into a hallway which ran the width of the house's top floor. At its centre, the hall opened into a mezzanine, the right wall disappearing for a balustrade. Chad stalked into the open section uneasily, reaching for a piece of string dangling from an ominous attic door. I followed him into the opening, finding that it looked over the house's entrance and grand front door.

Shadows amassed at the door's windows, announced by sharp footsteps.

Chad froze, his meaty grip having clenched around the attic drawstring. I latched onto the air in front of me and threw it forward, sending myself crashing back into the closed section of hallway. Chad still did not move.

"Man, move!" I croaked, but Chad defied me. I saw his face shift, melting, firing stoically. He dropped his hold on the string, instead leaning onto the balustrade, sighing deeply over the entrance space. I crawled to him, as if I could grapple at his ankle to pull him away.

The door opened just as I crawled into sight.

A stout woman and a lanky man bustled in from the darkness, the lady turning quickly to stow her coat on a rack. They were both dressed in black.

"You see, Marty, I told you…" she said, although Marty's attention was elsewhere. He stared at Chad, his eyes gaping. When the woman turned slowly to meet the object of his gaze, she cried in a fit.

"Ah!" She wailed, reaching for the wall and ripping a metal Jesus-laden-cross from it, then thrust the other hand into her purse. "When the dead live…" she threatened, but Chad cut her off.

"Surprised to see me, Carol?" He asked, a smirk coming to light his face. I wasn't sure where this confidence had come from, and I didn't know whether to entertain it. "I'm surprised to be here, really." And then he turned his gaze to the man. "Hi Dad."

"Hi Chad," they nodded, although were on the verge of fainting, their face white.

The stout woman, Carol, tore her fumbling hands from her purse. They emerged only with the same cross which they delved in with, and she thrust it into the air, holding it between herself and Chad with a mean grin.

And then nothing happened. The chaos fell to silence, until Chad coughed.

"Oh, sorry," he laughed, "my bad, my bad." He grappled his chest over his heart, falling to his knees against the mezzanine balustrade. "Oh no, the Christian cross, my only weakness!" He wailed condescendingly, clutching at his body. "Ah, my weakness, Mother, you know it! Oh, my devilry…" and he collapsed onto the floor.

I wasn't sure what to make of this scene. How had Chad's mood flipped so suddenly? Were these people still a threat?

"Don't you dare mock God in this household," Carol hissed, holding the cross with dangerous intent, arm tensed to the point of snapping itself. Chad slowly rose, chuckling the entire length of pulling himself up. Once he dusted himself off, he threw his right hand towards his mother and yanked at his soul connections. The cross threw itself towards him, pulling Carol off her footing and sending her to her knees. Chad caught the cross and set it gently aside.

"I didn't come here to bow to you, Carol," he said. "Although, I expected no less from you."

"Please, forgive your mom. It's been a long day," Marty spoke. "This is just…well…impossible. It's impossible that you're here."

338

"Why?" I asked aloud, before realising that I should have shut up. I covered my mouth.

"Who is that?" Carol barked.

"Emotional support," Chad quipped. "Now, are we going to talk like adults, or have you got more crosses to show me?"

Marty glanced at Carol, and seeing the pace of her rise, spoke before she could. "I'll get the kitchen ready," he said, and dashed past his wife.

***

The kitchen was the oldest part of the house, and the least maintained. It was a small square room built around an ancient, round table. In the back wall, over the sink, was a singular window which looked out onto the forest. The cabinets which ran along the tops and bottoms of the walls were all finished in varnished wood with wooden benchtops. The oven looked as old as the house, and there wasn't even a dishwasher. A singular lamp hung uneasily from the ceiling, and spewed a pool of dirty, orange light over the old table. Outside it rained now, and the night marched on the tin roof like a running army.

I leaned up against the sink's benchtop, standing next to Chad's dad, Marty. He leaned back with me, pulling a cigarette whose smoke danced under the gross lamplight. Chad and his mother sat opposite each other on the little round table. Their gazes cut like glass, their mouths silent.

Marty had fetched a box from the attic in preparing the kitchen, leaving me to stand between the opposing parties in their silence. Chad had tried to engage his mother, but she scoffed at the movement of his lips, turning from him in huffs. The box Marty had placed in the table's centre had Chad's school photo glued to its lid.

Marty handed Chad a piece of paper from the box – under which letters and photos had been piled in. Held in Chad's hands, the paper's header read 'Euology'.

"I see," Chad nodded, frowning.

"Ah…" I joined, just reading the title myself over his shoulder.

"How'd you do it?" Carol asked as Chad placed the letter down. I wasn't sure if it was restraint or fear which kept him from reading the celebration of his own death. He simply gave his mother a quizzical stare.

"How did I do what, Carol?"

"How did you come back from the dead?" She asked, leaning over the table, into him. Chad huffed, throwing a lazy arm over the back of his chair. He shook his head, trying to speak with some sense.

"There's a simple answer here, Carol," Chad scoffed. "It's that I didn't die."

"Bullshit," Carol hissed. "The Sheriff pulled your body out of the quarry and it was your…"

"Pulled *my* body?"

"*Your* body," Carol hissed. "No head, but *your* body alright."

"Okay," Chad chuckled, shaking his head.

"It had your damn wallet in the pocket. It had that stupid wallet with the chain, and your license."

"It's true," Marty backed his wife.

"And I'm here now, so doesn't that blow your theory away?" Chad scoffed, although his mother's face didn't lift. It furrowed in its intensity, standing firmer. She then smirked, an idea crossing her face. Her eyes twitched to follow it.

"I always knew that damn devil's music would corrupt you one day. I knew it had to be true," she cackled.

"Excuse me?" Chad quizzed.

"It's a gateway to the devil, to *witchcraft*. You start listening, you *disobey my rules* to go to those awful concerts, and then you're beating up the Sheriff's poor daughter and her friends with magic."

Chad raised his hand to air a response, but he stiffened himself instead as his mother continued over the objection. "Then you die, but you weren't dead, you planted your *evil* blood sacrifice and came back here just in time to kill the Pastor and do witchcraft on my cross from the Lord." She stood suddenly, throwing a finger to Chad's face. "You're a sick and twisted boy," she snarked. "You've lost your way to the devil, and I *saw* it coming."

Chad held his lips in his disbelief. He craned his neck to peer at his father, who simply shrugged, offering no support or accusation. Chad then cracked his fingers, huffing loudly.

"It's an interesting story, Carol," Chad said, "but…"

"It's a true story! I've seen the witchcraft. You can't deny it!"

"I can't deny what I am," he enunciated calmly. "But I'm not a servant of the devil or whatever bullshit you're thinking. I'm…"

"There's no repenting now! I can't have you in this house of the Lord, get…"

"For *fuck's* sake Carol, shut up!" He roared to a stand, gritting his teeth into her smug, fat face. The woman struggled to hold her stiff lip as the iron in her earrings tugged at her ears. The two had come to a standstill, and only as Chad moved to sit again did Carol join. "I'm not a servant of the devil – the devil isn't even real. A singular God isn't real either. I'm connected to one of the *real* Gods…"

"So you're a Pagan, then!"

"I'm a *Suneva*," he barked. "My God. There's no blood sacrifice, no indoctrination by metal. What I did to Stacy and her asshole friends was in self defence as they *drowned* me in her pool. I don't know whose body had my wallet on it because I didn't even take my wallet to the prom! I ran straight from there. I ran away because I knew you'd do *this*."

"You're damn right I'd disown a dissenter of the Lord."

"I knew you'd never accept me! You never have, you never did!" He cried it, and was out of breath, huffing in his seat. "*Nerios*, this isn't about the fucking bible, Carol. It's about you and me."

"You killed the Pastor." Was her fast response. I could feel the blood boil in Chad's eyes. The knob on the drawer behind me rattled, then settled as Chad calmed.

"He was an old, bigoted *bastard*, Carol. Look at all of the hate you have and blame it on him, but I didn't murder the idiot. Stop deflecting the real issues here."

Carol took the vitriol with a smug and dissatisfied, static expression. She waited for the dust and silence to settle, all leaning in on her eventual response.

It came in a meek, mousy voice. "Don't speak ill of the dead," she said.

Chad blinked, barely holding his frustrations, but his laugh was his release. He burst into a crazed chuckling, leaning all the way back on his chair, running taught, thick hands through his blonde hair. "You're a *master* at this, Carol. It's a pity you never became a politician."

She stared at him blankly.

"Really, Carol. In all of my journeys, in dealing with heads of the Suneva state, high-level gangsters, and prolific business people, I've never met anybody with such skills of distraction. I've never met a single other person so opposed to self-introspection and critical thinking, so *static* in their idiotic mind, that they were so incapable of empathy. You call me a monster Carol, *you* truly are the devil."

"I'm honest and holy, it's more than you can say."

"Religious scripts aren't a personality, darling, and they're certainly not a reason to be as big of an asshole as you are. Let's dip in to your cognition, shall we?"

"I'd like you to leave my house," she said suddenly, standing.

"Oh no, not yet," Chad smirked, still leaning all the way back. "We're going to dive into the depths of that peanut you call a brain. Let's find out where your empathy went."

Carol slammed her hands down, urging the immovable Chad, to no avail. "You want empathy?" She demanded. "How about some empathy for me? You disgraced our name with everything you did. All of that devil…Pagan…whatever-you-call-it crap. I've been ostracised for years because of your behaviour, young man. Then when you finally used those *unholy* powers of yours, that was it. We were lucky they didn't close the church on us, we barely scraped in!"

I could see Marty nodding to my side, and suddenly I felt truly uncomfortable. Chad, meanwhile, maintained his stoic flippancy.

"Do you know what that means in a small town, Chad? We don't have the money to move, to establish ourselves elsewhere, and yet you always *selfishly* chose to isolate us. I tried to steer you on the right path, by taking your money so you wouldn't spend it on stupid shit, but you always found a way to humiliate and ruin me. Are you sure that *I'm* the monster?"

Chad straightened his chair now, level to stare his mother in the eyes. Silence fell under the orange lamp light, and Chad opened his mouth a few times to speak, with each failed attempt his mother's lips growing smugger.

"You can't just be whatever you want to be in a town like this, Chad. It's not like the movies, or the TV. If you don't fit in, you get left behind. I wanted you to succeed, but you betrayed me and everybody."

Chad stewed on that line, all tension leaving him. I felt black in my gut, unsure of where to look.

"Were you happier with me dead?" He asked.

"It's hard to say," Carol answered. "I thought I'd be happier, but the isolation continued until recently."

"You never loved me then, did you?"

"No," She said, all too easily.

"And there it is," Chad sighed. "I guess I could have asked you to defend me when I was young – to stand up for my differences and support me – but you can only do that for somebody you love. I understand, now." And he rose from the seat, pulling it out as if to leave.

"Hold up," I interrupted, and the room turned to me. "You're going to take that? You're not going to stand up to this blatant narcissism?"

"No point," he said, calm. There was no disappointment in his eyes. No hate nor resentment. "I got my answer. I only have to understand – not accept, nor demand."

"But you shouldn't have been treated like that for a phase as a child. Where's the support?"

"James, that's been answered," he said to me, and placed a meaty palm upon my shoulder. I didn't get it – what happened to his rage? How could he stand to be told that he wasn't loved? How could he let this woman get away with that?

"I think it's best that you leave," Marty said finally. "I'm glad to see you Chad, but…"

"I know, Dad," he nodded, then said to me, "come on, James."

"Okay…if you're sure," I quizzed, being turned away and towards the door.

"I'm going to tell Sheriff Johnson that you're in town," Carol called to us as we left. "You're still up for the assault of those kids."

"I'm sure he already knows that I'm here," Chad called back, and pushed me to the front door. He opened it calmly, ushering me out and under the awning. The violent rain obscured all sight, turning the ground to a thick mud. I stood deflated next to Chad, who seemed to hold himself higher now. He smiled, even.

"Are you sure you're satisfied?" I asked him. "You didn't want to tell that woman off? I mean, sure, she recons that you screwed up her life, but you were her kid. She can't just abandon you for your personality."

343

"But she did. It doesn't matter that she shouldn't have." Chad said, staring into the rain. "She hated me, and I never really understood why. Now I do, and there's peace in that, James. I feel like I finally connected to her."

"Do you believe that you wronged her?"

"No, not really," he said. "But she is a selfish woman, and maybe I lacked a bit of perspective too. I have always been stubborn, exactly like her. I also *assumed* too much about why she treated me awfully. Now I asked, and I know why she did it. I can move on."

"You're not delusional in your stubbornness, though."

"Maybe I'm not, but it doesn't hurt to be humble."

"Alright, then," I hummed, joining Chad's gaze. The weather was insane, the landscape invisible. All but for the light on the church spire.

"Settle in," Chad said, and took a seat on the doormat. "It's a peaceful night, don't you think?"

I took a seat next to him, unsure of the statement. This certainly was a strange thing to call peace, what with all of the chaos before us.

"It's a bit chaotic, isn't it?"

"Peace looks different to everybody, then," Chad said. "I think I see the peace in chaos."

And so, we stared out together.

Chapter 36
Chad and Stacy

The rain continued to come down all night after Chad and I arrived back at the motel. Celeste and Natalie had the lights out and had put the double bed up to the window, watching the rain come down and waiting for the lightning to strike. The television set, an old cathode-ray thing, set out its faint glow of deadly light into the room, like a light fuzz painted over the walls and furniture. The volume was turned on low, and neither Celeste nor Natalie could tell us what was playing on it when we entered.

We sat and talked about the night, then decided to get to sleep. Celeste and I snuggled in the bed, under the cover of lights-out as Chad snored nearby. The day had been massive from start to end. *To think*, I hummed to myself as

Celeste and I kissed and danced between the sheets, *that I haven't slept since I was on the plane...*

Soon after, I was dead asleep.

A faint screeching woke me up. Chad warned me that racoons and opossums make noises at night, so after a moment of dead silence I turned myself over and tried to fall back to sleep.

It came again. It was the sound of a dying possum's nails being dragged down a chalkboard. I sat bolt upright in the bed and waited to hear it again - I could have just hallucinated it on my way to dreamland.

But there it was, louder again, whining with a moan underscoring it, from inside the room, some animal dying in pain. I staggered up, Celeste and Chad still asleep, and the moan whirred again, screeching from the bathroom. I stalked towards it.

The shriek squealed, now in split tones. I froze up in place, expecting to find a demon in the toilet. My eyes darted to all of the shadows. The animal laughed at my panic, the deep bellow of a gorilla thrown towards me from behind the closed door. Neither Celeste nor Chad seemed phased by the haunting ruckus, and I had to believe I was dreaming this all.

Then it died, the scream pausing. Catching my breath, I bravely marched towards the bathroom door. Hand on the knob, I twisted slowly and creaked it open, just enough to thrust my arm in and flick on the lights.

Lights on, I swung the door open, eyes wide and nerves racing. The room was empty, even past the light blinding me. A faint moan grumbled again, but it was coming from the next room over. Behind that wall, Natalie slept.

Natalie?

I sidled up to her door, edging it open and peering in. Natalie sat bolt upright in the bed, her mouth agape and her eyes glowing as screens of orange quatra. Her hands clutched at the bed covers with a death-grip, and the Suneva howl of the departed coursed from her lips.

"Oh cheese, *Natalie!*" I ran into the room and grabbed the girl by her arms. "What the hell is happening to you?" I throttled her by the shoulders, but her head simply bounced around on her neck. Her eyes glowed to spite me, her howl lifting its pitch.

I slapped her face, because it was the only thing I thought to do.

345

"Come on Natalie! Wake up!" I yelled, and shook her again, making sure to hold her head. The orange in her eyes continued to glow.

"James, step back," Chad said from behind me. For whatever reason, my body refused to move. Chad pried me from the girl, squeezing himself between Natalie and I, and throwing me into Celeste, who now also crowded the room.

"You've got to wake a witch in *Liktan*," he said, and leaned down by her ear. "*Sara-sera, Natalie.*" He whispered '*good morning*' warmly into the shrieking girl's head. "*Sara-sera, Zamelle.*"

Natalie's hands ripped at the sheets, tearing a hole in them. She cried in anguish.

"*Sara-sera, Zamelle. Di yesalka se quatra naffos!*" Chad remained calm. He held the girl's face as her body turned to spasms. "*Sara-sera, Zamelle,*" Chad said for a final time. The moaning stopped, to be replaced by heavy breathing. The orange drained from her eyes in tears. Her hands slammed down on the bed and she absorbed the room in a dazed panic.

When she realised where she was, with all of us in this room with her, Natalie burst into tears. She curled up, covered her face with her hands, and wailed into her palms.

Chad removed himself to give her space, but Natalie reached for him, pulled him in close and cried over his shoulder. Chad gestured for Celeste and I to leave, so I took Celeste's hand and led her back to bed. Natalie continued to cry as Celeste and I together fell back to sleep.

***

"Alright, I'm ready for this," Chad said as we embarked from the little red car. This time, even though it was the middle of the next day, we had not decided to park the car elsewhere and walk to our destination. "No point in hiding now. I believe my mom – she would have told Sheriff Johnson I'm here."

We had driven the car around to the other side of the forest, almost to the same street on which Chad's parents resided. We had parked in front of an ancient and tall pine hedge which bordered a hidden house. In the centre of the hedge was a wooden archway which gave channel to a gravel path wide enough for a car. On

346

all sides of the property were the tall, gangly trees of the pine woods. They watched over this place.

"Are you sure you're ready man?" I asked. "I mean, this girl, she didn't exactly treat you the best..."

"Yeah, Chad," Natalie agreed. "She doesn't sound like a good girl, why bother mending it?"

"Look, we both had our faults," Chad said as he led us through the archway. "I doted on her and never gave her a break, she was caught up in popularity. People acts all sorts of stupid ways when they're young. I'd like to see how she's grown. Maybe she's changed – but the point is I'll never be able to resolve anything unless I go in there and find out. I have to stop *assuming* reasons why people treated me poorly."

"Just don't count on her changing..." Natalie said to herself.

The house inside the hedge was unfashionable, but well kept. Each tree was prudently trimmed, each gravel stone perfectly placed within its perfect wooden boundary. The hedge was immaculately maintained and cast its shadow over the laser-green grass. Not a single paint chip was visible over the whole house, not a single smudge nor mark on any window.

"How do you know she's home?" Celeste asked as we walked across the grass. Chad paused on his way to the door, then turned to us, pondering this.

"I don't know," he said. "I didn't even question it."

"You mean, you didn't think of it?" Natalie asked.

"No, I didn't question it. I just had the feeling she'd be here today. I keep *feeling* things in this town..."

"That means you're meant to be here, then," Natalie hummed. "I'm surprised how little you feel the calling."

"I *hear* it," Chad noted, "but I don't often *feel* it like this. She's in there, I'm sure of it."

"Then is that her car?" Celeste asked, pointing to the blue hatchback parked on the gravel lot.

"No, I don't recognise it."

"It better not be mister Johnson's," Celeste clenched her fists.

"No, he drives the Sheriff's car. It's a real beauty she is – an old station wagon from back in the sixties converted into..."

"Alright, we get the picture," Celeste said. "It's not his car, that's enough. Let's get you reunited."

Chad crunched his heavy feet across the gravel lot to the front door. As we stepped closer to the house, we could hear pop music playing from one of the upstairs rooms. It blasted through the walls. Chad paused under the awning, hesitant to reach for the bell.

"Come on man, you can do it," I said. "She probably won't even hear you."

"Yeah, I know I've got this in the bag," he pulled a smile. "The significance of the whole trip just hit me all of a sudden, you know?"

"We know," Celeste said sweetly, then frowned. "Now, knock on the door."

"Yeah...right," he shied away from her sudden change in tone. Chad paused, and sweated, then all at once threw his finger to the bell.

The record player scratched, and the blaring music came screeching to a halt. The house was blanketed in silence.

"Is somebody there?" A pretty voice called out.

"Yes!" Chad yelled directly into the door from a few inches away.

"Okay, I'm coming," the girl replied in an uneasy voice. The thuds of her footsteps moved through the upper floor, then down the stairs to the door. The handle clacked, turned, and the door flung itself open.

The girl behind was, by every definition, stunning. She had long, straight blonde hair which hung messily around her face and over her shoulders. The face it framed was the stock image for cliché cheerleader, complete with pink lipstick. She wore an infectious smile, and bounced on her toes as she eyed Chad up and down.

The first time she looked was to register that there were four people at her door. The second time was to, not discretely, check out the specimen of a man who had knocked upon the door with his meaty paws. The third look was a double take once she's realised who she was looking at. Her eyes opened as wide as her skull let them.

"Hi Stacy," Chad said with a dumb smile. "I know I'm meant to be dead, but..."

"Chad Rogers…" she wheezed in her shock. "Oh my god, it's Chad *fucking* Rogers…"

"Yeah, it's me," he smiled.

"It's really him?" She looked directly into my eyes and pointed at Chad.

"Yeah, that's Chad Rogers."

"You died…my dad found your body…" She blabbered breathlessly. She kept looking between her hands and Chad, before she finally decided to ram them into Chad's cheeks. The fact that she could touch him rocked her mind like a scientific breakthrough. A smile of incomprehensible proportions streamed its way across her confused face. Tears came from her eyes.

"You're real…it's really you…" she flung her arms around him and squeezed with all her might. Chad Rogers and his mighty, muscly circumference were hardly phased by her twig arms. He laid a paw across her back.

"This wasn't the reaction I was expecting," he chortled.

"Then I don't know *what* you were expecting," she blurted between tears. "I have so much I have to say to you. This is unreal…it's a dream."

"It's real…" Chad assured her, but she continued to cry is disbelief. It took her a while to catch herself. "Please, everybody come in and sit down…"

Stacy ripped herself from the hulking body of Chad and led us through the door and to the left, into the 'sitting room'. There was an old brick fireplace on the far wall, a dead log smouldering a pathetic, smoky flame sitting in its pit. In front of the fireplace was a lovely, new coffee table, surrounded by comfortable looking couches. We each took and seat and introduced ourselves whilst Stacy grabbed us warm drinks. Celeste got up and sat on the floor by the fire with her coffee. I could see her hand twitching by her side as she played with its flames.

"I'm lucky you caught me, Chad," Stacy said as she took her seat next to him. "I'm only here for a few days. I have to head back to college soon in New York."

"Well it was more than luck," Chad smiled. "What are you doing in college?"

"Studying law…but look, that's not important. I have so much I've wanted to say to you."

Chad put his hands on his lap and sat attentive with a rosy smile, ready to listen. Stacy sighed and cleared her throat. She opened her mouth to speak, then closed it and took a few moments to think about what she was going to say. She did this three times.

"You know that I loved you, right?" She finally said. Her eyes were wide with anticipation.

"What?" Chad coughed.

"No, you don't get to say that," Natalie burst. "Not after how you treated him. Not after what you and your friends did to him."

"I know it's bad, I know," Stacy scrambled for words, "but I was told to treat you badly…"

"Oh, bullshit," Natalie eyed the girl off. "You can't palm off your actions like that. Have some responsibility."

"Let the girl speak, Natalie," Chad shushed the powerful witch. She scrunched her face and sat right back into the couch. Surprisingly, Natalie stayed quiet.

"Who told you to treat me badly?" Chad asked. His voice was so sweet, and his demeanour so caring. It was no wonder this girl felt she could open up to him.

"My dad told me that I had to stay away from you. He said we weren't allowed to hang out any more once I got into high school. I didn't want to let you down, so I tried to make you hate me. But Jesus did I go too far with it."

"Oh, gee…" Chad cringed.

"But you just kept coming back. I felt awful, and I don't know what the fuck was going on in my head. I couldn't bring myself to tell you that we weren't allowed to hang out, so I just pushed you away and I was so awful to you and it felt terrible every day but I just didn't do the logical thing …and then you *killed* yourself over it…"

Her face went wobbly fighting back the urge to cry, and she suddenly burst into tears. She shoved her head deep into Chad's muscly bosom and wrapped her arms around him. He slowly patted her on the back, but was looking with wide eyes between Natalie and Stacy.

"Yeah, but it's okay," he finally said. "You didn't kill me. I mean, you'd finally gotten me off your tail. I ran away. Plus, I was totally annoying. If anything, I couldn't take the biggest hint that you wanted to be left alone – although I'm glad that you really didn't – but still, I could have ended my own suffering. I chose not to. It's not all your fault, you tried your hardest."

"No Chad, you can't shift the responsibility," she hoisted herself up out of his chest, she was choking on the remaining tears. "I'm owning up to this. I was awful."

"And I was clingy. We were both terrible, but the main thing is that you didn't *want* to be, and to me that matters, a lot."

She smiled and wiped her eyes.

"So, you just ran away, then?"

"Yeah," he said. "I ran off down the railway. I met an old man in a Burger King bathroom who ended up being the ancient leader of an old empire. He trained me and taught me to be connected to the earth. I went on a whole *spiritual journey* and everything."

"I'm not sure what you mean, that sounds crazy," she said, "but maybe some things are just meant to happen?"

"That's the philosophy," I said.

"And what about your body?" Stacy sat up properly to ask. "I'm the one who found it. I didn't go to prom that night. I went looking for you. I found a trail and I followed it out to the quarry and I saw the body in there and it had your wallet in it and it was wearing a suit and it was you...I swear it was you..." She covered her face with her hands.

"It was a set-up," Chad said.

"We know that by now," I said, "but by whom?

Chad pondered on this.

"Stacy, did your dad give you a reason why you had to stop being my friend?"

"He...he..." she had to sniffle. "He said you were *evil*. Not, like, a bad guy, but evil against God.

"Something about witchcraft?" I asked.

"No," She hummed. "More like you were in a devil cult, and it wasn't allowed near the house."

The Sheriff and Chad's mum seemed to have the same opinion of Chad. I had to wonder if there was something bigger going on here.

"Well, neither of them picked it exactly, although they saw it coming," Chad chuckled.

"Wait," Stacy pulled herself up. "You *do* worship the devil? I thought you just liked metal music." Then, in her panic, she stared down the rest of us, drawing dots between us. "Are you all cultists?" And her face drew white.

"No, no, it's not a devil cult," Chad laughed. "Well, not *exactly* – but you saw what I did."

"I did…" Stacy grabbed her neck, suddenly remembering. Her eyes shifted about the room. "Jimmy told us that he spiked the brownies, that nothing happened that day. But it did, didn't it? Those weren't *God* given powers…those things don't exist…but the Devil's powers…"

"None of it is in Christian terms," Celeste huffed. "All the Catholics at home would call us the devil too. They used to tell us that we sold our soul to drink the devil's juice, or the devil's wine depending on which idiot you asked. It's hard to argue with them when we hold the power of fire." She clicked her fingers and a bright purple flame appeared in her palm. The wood-fire burst into purple flames behind her. "We're *Suneva*. We channel the energy of Gods to extend our soul into elements beyond our body. The fire is an expression of my soul, not some black, God-hating magic."

"Oh. My. God." Stacy uttered. "What the hell just happened."

"We're Suneva," Chad said again. "We have a connection to the world that we can act on. I control the ground, James controls the air, Celeste controls fire and Natalie controls water."

"That's…that's insane," Stacy said with wide eyes. She was clearly caught between what to think, and had no idea which of her senses to believe any more. "This really is a dream, isn't it?"

"No, it's all real," I said. "There's more to this world than you've been taught."

"And you're *not* evil?" She asked again. "Not associated with the Devil?"

"No," Celeste rolled her eyes.

"Then why do they call your juice the *Devil's juice*?"

"Because *quatra* – the Suneva energy - *is* the devil's juice." Natalie said, and we each turned to her in surprise. She sat taller in the couch, breathing our disbelief. "You do sell your soul to use it. You might not realise it, but the first

352

quatra you pull consumes you. It grants you power, great power and perception. You can feel the world at your fingertips like never before, and understand it in ways you'd never be granted as a person. It's the ultimate temptation. The more you sell your soul to the energy, the more power you can receive from it.

"Quatra tears at your humanity and your sanity. The more you use it, the more you lose your ability to operate as a human. When the black hole eats at what makes you human, you shriek a demonic cry. My cousin was taken by black hole and it haunts me how departed she is. She can no longer speak or communicate. She sits still, doesn't eat, just walks, yet has the whole universe in her mind, I'm sure of it. My grandmother, once the most powerful witch on the planet, couldn't fight the night terrors and screaming caused by the corruption of her humanity. I've already fallen to the terrors, and no matter how many you have, there is nothing scarier than regaining your humanity and knowing that you have no control over it. It's too much power for humans and we don't know yet how to properly control it, we can only *try*.

"Above that, there's no incentive to stop using power. It feels too good to just abuse the world around you if knowledge, connection and enlightenment aren't what you seek. You sign your soul and become a pawn in the universe for Gods who we do not know to be good or evil. That is why religions fear us. That is why it's called the Devil's juice."

A blanket of silence came over the sitting room. Only the light crackling of the purple-flamed fireplace broke the ambient buzz.

"Uh, Natalie…are you okay?" I asked.

"No," she said. "I haven't been okay for a while."

"You know you can talk to us, right?" Chad stepped in. "I mean, we're all friends here. We're all going on the same journey. We all agreed to be open and honest."

"We're *not* on the same journey, Chad," she snapped, but calmed herself. "Look, I've had to be strong. I wasn't going to worry anybody by feeling sorry for myself."

"It's not feeling sorry for yourself," Celeste said. "It's about opening up and accepting advice. You taught me how good it feels to open up and by honest."

"We didn't come here to talk about my issues – and I don't want to talk," she said. "I've just taken away from Chad's journey. Chad, Stacy, get back to making up with each other. Maybe make out, I don't know."

Chad and Stacy eyed each other awkwardly, then turned to Natalie, who had closed her eyes to lie back on the couch.

"I don't think it's worth abandoning this conversation, Natalie," I said. "If you want to…"

She flung herself forward and drew her twin swords. They swished into reality from the depths of her soul with a shimmer and a clang of metal.

"Oh my Gosh!" Stacy screamed, scrambling for Chad's body.

"Jesus…okay…I'll leave it," I shuffled further into the couch, away from the madwoman.

"Shush!" Natalie whispered, holding a finger and a sword to her lips. She tried to edge her line of sight around the window's drawn curtain. I craned my neck to the house's front to follow her gaze. Natalie rose, stalking from the couch towards the window, leaving us to wonder what was going on.

"There's another Suneva coming," she said, "They're close. Does anybody else feel them?"

"N…no," Chad said. "Should we?"

The low, heavy rumble of an old engine vibrated throughout the house. We could hear a car coming down the street and slowing by the front archway. Gravel crunched and asphalt squealed as it turned into the rocky drive. Natalie shut the curtain fully, freezing.

"I can feel them now," Chad said. "They've got a strong thread."

"And aura," Celeste noted.

"Ha, ha, yeah," I nodded along, feeling nothing, like usual.

"They're no ordinary Suneva," Natalie agreed. "I've never felt quatra like this."

"Native-American Suneva have a totally different experience of the soul," Chad noted. "They could be native."

"It's not *that* different," Natalie dissolved her weapons. "It's just powerful in a way I've never sensed before." She returned to the curtain, making a gap to peek out once more.

"What car is it?" Stacy asked. "Who the hell is a *Suneva* that's coming here?"

"It's an old, black car," Natalie said, then hummed. "There's a young man stepping out. He's trying to grab too many bags at once…" Then she turned to examine Chad and myself. "Such a *boy* thing." She shook her head. "Just get what you can pick up and go back for more, what's wrong with that?"

"They don't look like a threat?" I asked.

"I think it's just my brother," Stacy frowned.

"No," Natalie replied to me, voice muffled by the curtain. "Although they are in an *incredible* hurry…"

Natalie was interrupted by a key being thrust into the front door's lock. The entire couch jumped with the surprise of everybody on it. Chad and I turned to face the door as its tumblers clanked. The whole thing was thrown open, making room for a lanky, dark-featured boy to stumble in with a cough and yelp. His bags hit the floor before his clumsy feet found themselves. Despite his rushed incoordination, his flailing was super-smooth, as if my eyes played his image too fast. Bags fell as if they were magnetised to the floor.

"Chad Rogers…" the young man panted as he caught himself. "You're here. I knew you'd be here." And they dropped everything that they hadn't already, running over to the couch.

"Nick!" Chad rose to face the boy. "You don't think I'm dead?"

"I didn't believe that for a second. The body clearly wasn't yours, everybody was dumb for believing it."

"*Hey!*" Stacy protested.

"That said, I'm not sure *this* body is yours either," he stopped himself just short of the couch, eye scanning Chad. "When did you get hot?"

"All in the journey, man," Chad chuffed.

"Sure, it's been years," Nick nodded, "but look, you're in danger, it's why I raced over here."

"How'd you know I was here?"

"Quatra," Nick said. "It's how I knew you weren't dead – your trail was still out there."

"You mean that you knew about all of this too?" Stacy whined. "Why am I the odd one out?"

355

"Because you never listened to metal and joined a witch cult," Nick rebutted. "Anyway, look, that's not important. What *is*, is that Dad knows you're alive, and he's coming here for your magical ass right *now*."

"Good," Chad smiled into Nick's stunned face. "I need to talk to him."

"No, no you *don't*," Nick pressed a finger into the hulking Chad's chest. "You thought Stan was bad before you left? He's a lunatic now. That reverend got into his head *real* bad. He's going to kill you Chad, I know it."

"For what?" I huffed, speaking up.

"Witchcraft, for one," Nick said. "For strangling his daughter and assaulting her friends before running away, that's the second reason. Also, just because he doesn't like Chad."

"You think we're scared of some gun-slinging policeman?" Celeste piped up, nursing a purple flame between her fingers. "I've dealt with bigger egos."

Nick, maybe only having registered Celeste now, jumped out of his skin, stumbling backwards. "Oh my word," he uttered. "You're Iva Argol." And he backed himself right up to the wall, glancing between us with peace-posed hands. His gaze lingered particularly long on Natalie.

"Yes, I'm Iva Argol," Celeste nodded, and placed her hands firmly by her side, standing down any threat.

"And then…then you're Zamelle Menas, and Maiki, and Chad's Ferrad?"

"You're up to date with the news," Celeste hummed.

"Yes, I am," Nick nodded, but stayed pinned to the wall. "I still don't think you should cross the Sheriff, I still think you should run, and I don't think I should be here when he rocks up…or be seen with the four of you." And he sleuthed towards the door, his hands and body scraping against the front wall's plaster.

"Are you sure you don't want some Suneva friends?" Chad asked, extending a hand to the young man. Nick flinched, slamming his hand into a table holding a vase and a photo. The vase wobbled precariously. "We could learn from each other, I doubt there were many good Suneva teachers around here."

"No, that's fine, *really*," Nick nodded nervously. "I shouldn't even indulge the powers. You guys really should get moving." And he stepped his way around the front of the side table, keeping his face to us, analysing us with panicked eyes.

That was when his backpack knocked the vase.

356

It fell with that hollow sound of dry ceramic, that sound that feels like chalk under your nails. It only fell over on the table itself, but it smashed there with vigour.

"Ah!" Nick gasped, his hands forming peace signs and locking onto his connections immediately. He jumped away from the table, letting us see the ceramic shards raining in reverse. As his hands were held there gripped, the smashed remains of vase flying and bouncing back into place, cracks smoothing, the vase wobbling to shift upright.

Then it held in place, Nick realising what he'd done. His body frozen solid, he eyed the room as the vase held in limbo.

"Oh no," he uttered, before dropping his concentration. The vase exploded again in real time, its shards falling just as they should have.

"You're the Legendary Suneva of Time," Natalie coughed. "That's why your thread was crazy."

My eyes widened. Another Legendary, and we weren't even expecting it.

"*Nick?*" Chad spat in surprise.

To this, Nick flicked his wrist. A long staff tore itself into the world, tipped in a glass orb sloshing with viscous liquid. He aimed it at us, pooling it with quatra and drawing back his left hand.

"Good luck fighting the Sheriff, I'm sorry I won't help."

And a shockwave erupted from the orb.

Celeste ran towards it, but her speed was no match for the force field. It consumed Chad, who was stuck midair between steps, then Stacy, and Natalie, who was still in shock.

Then it got me.

In less than a second, all of us were engulfed. Sound died, the bubble's perimeter melted into streaks of light, obscuring anything beyond its walls. All of us in the bubble were moving at the same speed, and in the bubble, it was *cold*.

"What do we do?" I asked Natalie, but she had only a blank stare to give me. By my side, Celeste nursed a flame for only a moment, then broke the barrier around her body, swirling into the void beyond.

"*That,*" Natalie answered me, and then suddenly the bubble dropped, the streaks of light swirling back to their origin, sound crashing into my ears. In the wake of the sensory overload, Celeste stood over Nick in the doorway, her hand around the rear of his neck.

"What was *that*?" I asked, joined by the voices of everybody else in the room at once. Neither Celeste nor Nick seemed to know who was being addressed, and neither did anybody else.

"Entropy," Nick said, cutting off Celeste as she opened her mouth. "It's not *time*, it's entropy. Slowing disorder stops reactions from happening at the right speed, slowing things. Reversing it *looks* like time goes backwards, but it doesn't really, it just makes things happen the wrong way."

"I was definitely asking Celeste," Chad said, pointing to the French girl. She still held onto Nick, as if he was going to spring up and leap away. "Are you a time Suneva too?"

"No, but I figured out what was happening. The slowing time made me cold, so I circulated quatra with my body heat. Then it came to me that I was *creating* heat – I didn't need a fire to create heat, I needed heat to create a fire. So, I channelled quatra straight into heat, and that gave me more entropy."

"I didn't know *Ivaer* could do that," Nick said, pushing to stand. Celeste let him, but kept her grip.

"I didn't either. I've never heard of other Ivaer talk about *heat*, but I've always been able to connect to it." And she produced a flame in her free hand. It roared pink straight from the palm. The spectacle captured the awe of all in the room.

"I thought purple was the strongest Ivaer flame," Natalie pointed.

"It was, until now," Celeste chuffed happily, before putting away her hand. She turned her attention to Nick, and all eyes followed.

"Celeste, you should probably let him go," Natalie said, and stepped over.

"So he can run away?" Celeste asked.

"If he wants to, sure."

Celeste's face wound to disgust. She regarded Nick, who only had a nervous smile for her. "Are you going to run off?" She asked.

"I think we should all be running right now, really," he squeaked. "In opposite directions would be nice."

Celeste growled at the response, her gaze burning. "Natalie, we can't just let him go, he's the Legendary of Time! He's *literally* the reason we're doing this soul-search goose-chase!"

"We let Vectra go," Natalie said.

"Yes, but we *know* Vectra. We can always find her."

"You *know* me...right?" Nick said, and Celeste huffed on her lip. "Chad can always come home. Well, *if* he runs now, because this Sheriff *will* kill him."

Celeste growled, searching for a valid rebuttal. "We've come *this* far, Natalie. I'm here to save the *Suneva people*. This is bigger than us, it's bigger than *him*, it's about everybody. I don't want to just let him run off."

"Doesn't he get any agency?" Natalie asked.

"I don't know," Celeste grumbled. "Why should he? He's got a destiny bigger than any of ours."

"Look, Nick," Chad rose, stepping over to the scene. Celeste let the boy go, and amazingly he didn't run. He stood tall to Chad's physical authority. "Why *don't* you want to come with us?"

"Because it's a big risk, and I don't personally care about the Suneva," he said, and turned to Celeste. "I'm sorry, but there's so much politics, so much danger. The four of you are being chased by Boekidin, his team, Hesslik. You're enemies in the community. I don't want to get involved. I'm sorry. All I've ever done as a Suneva is stop other Suneva from pissing off my dad... and honestly, it would all be easier if none of us were Suneva."

Celeste huffed her final complaint, letting her body slump to the floor in the doorwell.

"I just can't believe this," she said.

"It's all destiny, right?" Natalie said, causing Celeste's face to sour. "If you believe that the black holes are setting us up to find the Legendaries and stop the Suneva destruction, then this is just one step, right?"

"Sure," Celeste huffed.

"I might have grown mixed feelings about destiny, but the one thing I believe is that the black holes aren't going to give up their power of this world. We've done what we can, but *if* you believe we're the ones to stop Hesslik, then you have to know that this let-down is just one cog in the machine."

"Fine, fine," Celeste nodded, defeated.

Sirens could be heard wailing in the distance. First, they just pricked our ears, but they were screaming closer.

"Oh *shit*," Nick squeaked, kicking into life. He pushed himself past Celeste and Chad, running for the stairs. "I'm going into my room, but you guys have *got* to run. Quick!" And he vaulted up the stairs, sprinting out of site.

"Probably shouldn't have disabled his thread," I coughed, thinking of how useful a time Suneva could have been. "I don't think you want to meet the Sheriff today, Chad. Let's run."

"I agree," Chad nodded. He shuffled over to Celeste and lifted her up. "We'll have to run into the forest, they'll have our car surrounded before we can get to it."

"When do we go back for it, then?" I asked.

"We'll figure that out later," he said, the sirens growing louder behind him, shrieking their intent. Tyres screeched along the road, engines roaring. "Quickly, follow me." And he kicked off to run past us, but didn't get far before Stacy grappled him to a halt, desperately holding to his arm.

"You're not going to say bye?" She asked. "Will I ever see you again?"

"Ever again?" Chad chuckled. "Of course you will."

A car rounded the driveway, its driving tyres chewing at the gravel. Our ears were attacked by the dusty sound. Sirens blared.

"See-ya, Stacy," he nodded, and tried to leave again, but she had pulled herself onto him, her mouth lunging for the kiss. Chad avoided it, easily holding her and setting her aside. "I'm not sure that's a good idea."

"Why not?" She asked, but Chad had already started his sprint. "Come on!" He yelled, but we were already following. We flew through the house, limbs scraping drawers and walls, until we collectively piled onto, and fell out of the back door.

We landed on a deck which straddled a frozen pool. Further down, past the dog-leg of the house was a large shed, and from that shed extended a gravel driveway which cut alongside the pool and up the left side of the house. Beyond all of this, the dense woods lay, dark and damp.

Chad ran to the left, leaping from the deck and to the mud by the driveway. Where his feet were solid on the mucky ground, I sank and tripped, rolling over the mud and blasting air down to hoist myself up.

"If we get into the woods…" Chad started, still sprinting away, "we can…" But his voice was cut off from Natalie, Celeste and I. A powerful roar filled our ears, setting me dizzy. Gravel screamed behind my head, and dust wrapped around my face, forcing me to splutter. Two cars careened down the driveway next to which we ran, narrowly missing us, to drift to a halt by the large, tin garage.

Paralysed by the commotion, we each stood still as the doors of the police vehicles flung open. From them five officers leapt and hoisted their weapons to the ready, scurrying behind the cover of the vehicles to hold their aim over the roofs of their cars. I was the first to throw my hands into the sky. Quatra was frightening, but defendable. Guns were an unknown, and they were certainly deadly. Celeste flicked her wrist to draw her sword, which flushed in a helix of pink, incredible flames. Chad and Natalie did not move, waiting for the Sheriff.

Stan Johnson exited his vehicle with a slow, deliberate stamp of his boot to the earth. His spur chimed as his boot crunched the gravel. He stood slowly, his face smug, almost laughing. He leaned onto the car, tracing a finger over its top as he rounded it to our side. His hand locked to the pistol at his holster.

"Chad Rogers. If the rumours weren't true…" Stan grinned.

Chapter 37
I Shot the Sheriff

"Pretty short turn-around on a rumour, really," Chad chuckled to the Sheriff's introduction, and his joviality was met by Stan's swaggered step. He crunched his heavy, leather boots up the small hill, coming to a stop on the rise before us, in the backyard of his own house.

"It's brave of you to come back, given what you did here," Stan said, tipping his hat, "and by *brave*, I mean stupid."

"And what did I do, according to you, mister Johnson?" Chad asked sweetly. The Sheriff grinned- he liked this dumb exchange.

"Well you assaulted my daughter and her friends, then killed a man, assumed his identity and faked your own death – clearly some cultish blood sacrifice, maybe an entry ritual. Now you've come back from your cave in the woods and killed the reverend of this town. Cowardly, that. Puts a good explanation on an unexplainable murder."

"The man was old and bigoted. Surely he had enemies," Chad said.

"Not denying your input, then?" Stan huffed.

"I don't have to confirm or deny anything, Stan. I've got rights under the law." Chad stood tall and firm. I could see his hands contorting by his side, searching for a soul connection. Then Celeste huffed and grumbled.

"What are we playing games for?" She growled, her sword's flames licking at the earth as they charged, scorching it black. "Let's bypass this idiot and get moving."

"Put the sword away," Chad ordered, dismissing her. "This *is* my next point of call."

"I'm glad you see sense," Stan smiled, and this time it was genuine.

"I'm searching for my enlightenment. I should be cooperative with those who I need answers from."

Celeste kept her sword drawn, and kept the flame roaring, planting herself firmly into the earth. Guns shifted to aim at her, and she growled at them a Suneva hiss.

"Well, I'd agree that you *would* have rights, Chad," Johnson continued, ignoring Celeste.,"but you're dead. You left your rights in the grave that I dug for you." And he drew his weapon, a modified gun of sorts with a huge bore of a tip.

"You're going to charge a dead man for murder?" I quizzed. "I'm not sure that works…"

"Well, I've got to *prove* that the man is who he says he is," the Sheriff mulled. "But I see only one way that this ends, Chad. You get in my cruiser, and your cultist friends get in that little red car that they bewitched somebody to take. They'll then leave this town forever while we talk. Don't have room for any more devils here."

Natalie huffed, "you think we're going to leave our friend? We're not *devils*." An odd assertion to her previous outburst, but it was met with a throw of Stan Johnson's hand. He aimed his gun squarely at Natalie's head. She and I shrieked in unison, and Natalie ducked to the ground, covering her skull. Stan laughed.

"Your heathen Gods don't afford you bravery, that's for sure," he said. "I expect you to leave because you witch types don't belong in this town. It's a good offer, believe me, *letting* you run. You see, I'd rather you alive, just somewhere else.

362

That's the difference between you types and me – I don't want to hurt anybody or destroy anything. Unfortunately, that's what Chad has been doing his whole life, and I'm not about to let four of you run through this town of mine."

Celeste laughed, pointing her flame sword to Stan. "You throw around guns and try to preach to us about how we're dangerous. You're a hypocrite, and…"

Stan pulled his trigger, two bullets flying towards Celeste. The young *Ivaer* shrieked, pink flames erupting from her sword as she downed herself. Natalie whipped a bolt of orange quatra through the air, and it collided with the first bullet, obliterating it. The second bullet flew into the house, crashing into the wood just below the window. I followed it to see Nick's frightened eyes peeking, and he bolted further into his room.

The rear door burst open, and just as I thought with glee that the Suneva of Time might save us, Stacy emerged instead, running for Chad. "Wait, Daddy! Don't shoot!" She demanded, screeching across the deck to land in front of Chad. Chad picked her up with careful hands and set her aside, but she stepped right back in front of him. "Chad isn't evil, Daddy."

"Go back inside, sweetie," Stan swallowed, his voice growing gruff. "You don't want to get hurt."

"I won't let you take him," she demanded. "I don't want to charge assault against him. I *love* him."

The very word caused Stan to slap his own face in frustration. He shook his head. "Honest, you don't *love* him, now get back inside."

"You can't arrest him if I don't want to charge for the assault," she huffed.

"No, he's going down for more than that. Witchcraft is still illegal, and I'm seeing four active witches in front of me."

"Stacy, go inside," Chad ordered. "I've got this." And he went to move and escort her, but Stan's gun cocked and forced Chad to pause.

"You're staying there, devil boy," Stan demanded, and Chad obeyed. Stacy still stood her ground fiercely, and so I, feeling some sort of bravery, carefully toed towards her. Seeing no reaction from the Sheriff and his men, I grabbed her by the arm and led her across the snowy mud to the back door. She protested as we walked, sulking that her dad couldn't do this.

"Chad seems to agree with him, somehow." I said, before forcing her into the door. As I stepped back, a pillar of earth and rock grumbled and rose to meet the door's handle, locking it shut. Chad turned back to the Sheriff.

"What will it be, boy?" Stan asked finally, his aim still held at Chad's face.

Celeste's flame bubbled quieter, Natalie hushed her breath, leaning in. The wind seemed to stop as we waited on his verdict – although I already knew what it would be.

"I'll go with you," he said, "we have things to discuss." And Chad dropped to his knees, hands in the air. Stan grinned ear to ear and advanced on the boy.

"Glad you see the sense," he nodded.

"Chad, will you be okay?" I asked.

"I'll be fine, but you guys have to leave," he said. "I'll meet you later. Remember that town we passed through before we arrived here?" and I had some vague recollection of two houses abutting a hardware store full of rusty trash some few miles down the road, but I wasn't sure if he was thinking of that place or somewhere different.

"Maybe?" I quizzed.

Stan leant down, wrapping his cuffs around Chad's hands and then hoisting the boy uncomfortably. "That won't be necessary," he said to Chad. "Your friends are too dangerous to be left unescorted. Boys, take them in."

"What?" Celeste growled, her flames pluming and roaring. Guns levelled on us, readied with fingers on triggers. I did the only thing I saw appropriate – I dropped to my knees and thrust my hands in the air. Natalie, on the other hand, had drawn her twin swords along with Celeste, and gripped at her soul connections.

With a yank of her form, suddenly half of the pool was loose, roaring from its walls in a great wave. Gunfire started, but the water wall which raged before us slowed and misaligned the bullets, sending them as rogue metal chunks.

"James, get up!" Celeste barked. It wasn't a smart idea at all – much easier to escape from a police holding-cell with our abilities than to escape from a gun fight – but I didn't have a choice if I was the odd one out. I drew my staff from the depths of my soul, and then paused frozen, with no idea how to help next.

Gunfire roared, forcing me to leap aside behind a nearby tree. Natalie unleashed the wall of water, officers leaping from their stations as it rammed through the cars, skidding them across the loose gravel. Stan, clear of the wave, fired his gun towards Natalie. From its huge bored tip erupted a blast of pink quatra, which sailed true through the air. Natalie countered it with an orange one, and the two met by the pool's edge, exploding into nothing.

Celeste went to run, and I thought to join, crawling away from the safety of my tree, but Stan had given his officers time to rise, and the bullets started again. Celeste ripped a plume of pink flames towards them, retreating to my tree as she did so, but the wind carried the fire back away from the men. *Celeste needs a better wind – I can be a help!* I thought with glee. Celeste fell in with me.

"When I say *ivaer*, we both jump out and you do that fire again," I said just as she caught her breath. I peered around the tree, to see that Natalie had found refuge behind the pool's pump and filter. A bullet crashed into it, springing a leak with a nasty crack of plastic.

"Okay," Celeste said, and as soon as she said it, I shouted.

"*Ivaer!*"

We leapt from cover, Celeste throwing her intense flame, and I, dredging into my soul connection, backing it with a huge gust of wind. The wall of fire roared, hot and bright enough to blind. It tore at the water in the earth, the gravel shifting to a cloud of hot dust in the air, obscuring us from the officers. A ceasefire fell to the smog, and Natalie emerged from cover.

"Let's go!" She mouthed, and ran our way.

But something flew towards her. Small, white, on a thin string, blasted from the fog. Natalie didn't see it, and it landed on her back as she ran. Suddenly she lost her legs, crying and falling to the ground.

Something was coming for me.

I sensed it in the air, just as I'd started to run. A disturbance. I turned with my staff to see the same flying anomaly dragging string behind it. I wound my staff in its direction, and the little flying prong wrapped around my staff and stuck.

Too bad my staff conducts electricity.

It was a taser bud, I realised all too late, as my body flowed with liquid, electrical pain. My hand clenched uncontrollably, tying me to the staff and felling me to the muddy earth. I seized and gasped, the ripping at every muscle, taking away any sense I had.

Celeste had run off, melting the taser or avoiding it somehow, I couldn't be sure. All I saw from my spinning eyes were the footprints she left behind, as she ran with an inhuman pace. I heard Natalie scream, a deathly shriek, as if she'd been stabbed or shot. She howled and roared. I couldn't feel her next to me – her thread had been deactivated.

A pink bolt came for me next, slamming into my foot. Such a long path to the thread would have been otherwise easy to redirect, but I was powerless in my convulsions. My thread was cancelled.

***

Natalie gasped, chasing breath as the Sheriff's car rounded a bend in the road. We were bunched together, hog-tied across the backseats, watching the wintery forest pass by outside. We'd been captured, and I had no clue where we were being taken.

The colour returned to Natalie's eyes, as did horror.

"Boekidin is here," she uttered. "I can feel his witch."

"What?" I coughed, pricking to attention.

"We don't have time for this," she said. "We've got to get out of here."

"You're not going anywhere," Stan interrupted, leaning his head back. "I can't have any witches or devils running around this town, and Chad agreed fair and square to our little chat."

"Oh, you're about to have a few witches running around your town in a minute if you don't let us chase them off," Natalie threatened, snorting. "Have your little chat and let us run, we *want* to leave this place."

Stan frowned, and the tyres screeched. Our heads flew into the front seats as the car slammed to a stop, and we found ourselves jumbled in the footwell, groaning in pain.

Somebody's foot was wedged in my face, squirming by my nose, until cold air rushed into the car and it was removed. Stan had picked up the whole body cleanly, and he hauled Chad's tied body in one hand from the car, throwing the hulking young man to the roadside. The Sheriff's huge paw then came for me, grappling at the scruff of my collar. He hauled me with a hydraulic arm, flinging me from the door of his car and onto the fresh snow. I tumbled across the dirt, falling into Chad. I should have felt cold, freezing even, but my lungs and blood ran hot with gas. My palms twitched as my soul connections returned – to bad I couldn't do anything with my hands tied.

The brutish Stan took greater care with Natalie, waddling over with her to place her upright in the ditch.

"Fine," he mumbled, "this *chat*, as you insist, witch." He stepped around to Chad, bearing over the boy. "I don't care that you're a devil-boy, Chad. I don't care because as you've found out, I'm a witch myself."

"Then what's your problem?" Chad asked. "I know that you turned your daughter against me. I know that my mom, above being narcissistic, shunned who I was so that you wouldn't bully me. If it's not religious zealotry, what is it?"

"It's that I hate you, Chad Rogers," Stan seethed. "You might have turned out to be a pushover, agreeable, limp-dick like your father Marty, but you've got my chin and my eyes, and God-damned were you my greatest fuck-up."

Chad's eyes widened as this truth hit him.

"I'm your kid?" He coughed.

"You're my biggest mistake, and you befriended my daughter, and I had to look at your dumb face every day," Stan growled. He pushed a stumpy finger to Chad's chest, and used it to shove the boy back into the mud. "And as much as I didn't want to look at you, I didn't want my daughter to grow up and fuck you either. Witchcraft might be excusable, but incest just isn't right. She's your sister for fuck's sake."

"She's my sister," Chad uttered, and coughed. He eyed the man with bewilderment, before shrinking into himself. "Why is everybody so solidly intentioned, but incredibly unreasonable?" He chuckled with a furrowed brow. "Is this town full of idiots? Didn't you want to just tell me the truth?"

"Marty doesn't even know, kid," the Sheriff said. "You think I'm going to air that for your sake? No, I'd rather just make your life hell until you walk out of mine. I'm glad it worked."

Chad nodded, frowning. I was amazed by his propensity to find acceptance in these identity-altering circumstances. Still, I wasn't about to talk him out of his peace. I squirmed silently in the ditch by his side.

"Great, great," Natalie chimed with faux excitement. "Now that you've revealed your true shame to your illegitimate son, can we get going? Danger is coming."

367

Stan chuffed, not even looking Natalie's way. "Oh, I'm not done," he muttered. His hand launched at Chad's neck, and in one powerful thrust the man hoisted Chad from the ditch and slammed him high up onto the tree behind. Chad's neck was crushed against the bark so powerfully that he couldn't even gasp. On my fingertips I could feel the pitiful trickle of air seeping into his lungs. It was almost nothing.

"What are you doing?" I demanded, and was met with a hard kick to the stomach. I gagged and rolled, but was too tied to do anything more.

"This is what you did to my daughter, you uncontrollable animal," Stan barked at Chad. "I wanted to end you that night, but I was more relieved that you'd just left, fearing me anyway. I'm not making the same mistake this time. I'm going to kill you, and then your friends, and all of this will disappear with you."

Chad tried to form a response, I could feel his breath try to speak, but it was too weak. The huge boy was turning blue. Stan *could* kill him. If only I could move his breath for him – fill his lungs. It would be so easy if my hands weren't bound. I connected to the air that I could, feeling it all in my palm, and concentrated my focus to my fingertips. I wiggled them about, but it wasn't enough to move the air – my movement and its movement were tied.

If only I could *breathe* for him.

There was a flash of some memory. Four robed men sitting on the step of a temple, breathing in unison, a wind blowing. It seemed relevant, but where did it come from? I dug, and soon found the start of the sequence in my head. I stood robed, peering up a giant cliff face from the valley of a mountain range, cool air blowing by me. Almost at the cliff top ajutted a short landing, to a temple, breaking the sheer face. There were many monasteries here in Northern Greece, I recalled, but this palace was the centre of the Vochduh people – the ancient *Kiiin*, belonging to their king, the *Vochduhvlad*.

I'd come here as Salak Nolver, instead of Kuvalik. The Vochduh had a strange affliction to Sunesca, they worshipped their *freedom*.

I drew my climbing daggers, and meeting the face of the cliff, I thrust them in to climb.

I'd never imagined myself to be so brave, and I'd never imagined such poor hospitality in the face of an invitation from the Vochduhvlad himself. One king to another, this was a strange way to host a man, but it was the trial of the

Vochduh. The only Suneva worthy enough to be in the King's temple were those who could make it there.

The Vochduh were very traditional in this way. They had developed extensive and liberal codes of morality and self-introspection which laid the foundations of their monk society. It was these codes which drove my pilgrimage and conference here. I wanted to implement them with my people, and work with the Vochduhvlad to combine our empires, to unite the Suneva people under his morals. They encouraged self-introspection and cosmic understanding as the pinnacles of Suneva spirituality, rather than *knowledge* or *power*. These codes forbade fights that were not entirely evenly matched, and disgraced those who would take advantage of others. These were intelligent rules for any large-forming Suneva empire.

I eventually reached the top of my climb, hauling myself over the lip of the temple's landing and onto my feet. There I was met my four sitting monks, in their green and blue robes, eyes closed but breathing in unison. The wind moved, and it moved for them.

"How do you do that?" I asked them in their language. "How do you move their air without hands?" One monk eyed me with contempt, but his face soon fell to awe. He bowed to me.

"Great *Zalach*," he greeted from his perch. "Quatra moves with the breath, so does breath not grant the extension of the soul? Is breath not a part of the soul, ready to expand and connect to the world around? It must be, for we can move their air with it."

I snapped from the daydream. I would regularly have been mad at being convinced I *was* Kuvalik and his memories were *mine*, but this time it was useful and I didn't care. What that monk said, it was almost the same as Celeste had discovered earlier today – quatra moved with heat, heat was her soul, so she made heat? Oh *Omercronius*, it was something like that, wasn't it? Did it even matter? Chad was suffocating and I could feel it on my fingertips, but I'd have to forget that connection to establish a better one.

I sucked in a deep breath. Quatra was commanded into my body from my thread with my diaphragm. It ebbed and flowed with the air in my lungs. Was my breath part of my soul? I could feel it as it left my body. I could feel it on my lips, in my throat, and on my palms as they connected to it, but above all, yes, I *could* feel it in my soul. The breath was connected to my soul.

But were they the same?

Chad told me that he felt his soul through the earth, rather than feeling the earth through his soul – he needed to be grounded to be a Suneva at all. Maybe this was the same – feeling for my soul through my connection to the element, rather than the regular way which immediately made sense. *Cheese*, this soul searching was taking too much time. I felt for Chad's breath again, and there was none. The air in his mouth was stale, the boy was going limp, spluttering, sounds which I was deaf to in my concentration.

And then, I hadn't connected to the stale air by the soul in my palms, for they didn't tingle like they might usually. I was connecting from my core. And my breath came from my core, that's where I felt it before, so if I just *commanded* with my breath…

The air moved. I blew, and it moved. I could feel that stagnant pool of air in his lungs, and I connected it to my breath – to that extension of my soul, that which drew quatra and could therefore command it and my power – and I blew as hard as I could. The air blew out of Chad's mouth, and forced its way down his throat as I commanded it next. And I forced it again, and again. I was hyperventilating, going faint, but Chad's colour was returning, he was coming to, his lungs fighting my efforts, but they could not act alone.

"What the hell is this?" Stan uttered, then roared. "What the *hell* is this?" And he tossed his head around to the groan of my laboured breath. "It's you!" and he dropped Chad to the ground, stormed towards me before Chad's ass had even thumped to the mud. Stan wound a booted foot and drove it through my guts, throwing the wind from my stomach. The pain was awful, and I could do nothing but squirm. To preoccupied by the pain, and with my eyes closed, I had no ability to redirect the quatra bolt which soared to my thread.

Behind my closed eyes I heard another bolt fire, and then Natalie ejected an awful scream. She shrieked and cried, sobbing as her thread was closed from her soul. She lay twitching next to me when I opened my eyes.

"It's not *that* bad, grow up," Stan spat.

"You don't know about this kind of pain," Natalie sniffled. "You'll never be *this* connected."

"I've been shot, love," he tapped his temple. "I know pain. Speaking of which…" And the Sheriff turned to Chad. He squatted with a smile, and thrust his open palm over Chad's face. From it erupted a bolt of quatra, muffling Chad's sigh. Stan then stood, levelling his gun at Chad's head as he did, and he grinned.

"Any last words, Chad Rogers?"

Chad bit his lip, staring down the barrel of destiny. The black holes had to have more in store for us – more than meeting our end to some ass-backwards hack Sheriff.

"Will you write them down if I say them?" Chad asked.

"Sure, I'll write that down for you," Stan chuckled. His pistol cocked.

"You don't have to do…!" I shouted, but the trigger was pulled. The barrel flashed hot with a blinding light that lasted seconds. I screamed, Natalie screamed, and Chad screamed.

But we all kept screaming.

Chad was heaving for breath, and finally opened his eyes. I saw it when he did, the bullet as it poked its head out of the weapon's tip, like a lazy fox inspecting the twilight from its burrow. It meandered forth, still over three feet from Chad's head. The shockwave rocked the air like a hot explosion of honey, just bothering to spread as if obeying the laws of physics were a chore. The flash only just died.

"I…don't…get…it…" Chad wheezed between breaths. He sat there stunned, just watching the bullet crawl towards him – then again, I hadn't moved either.

The was an eruption of flames in my peripherals. Across the road, in the opposite ditch, a tree burst into fire. The whole plant *melted* first, parts of it so hot that they turned instantly to smoke. Then another tree met the same fate, cracking and exploding into a black cloud.

"Don't just sit there, move!" I heard Celeste shout.

"Celeste?" I shouted, craning my head around the place. She was running towards us from down the road, from a small red car which lurched over the ditches' edge. *How didn't I hear them?* "We can't move. You have to help us!" I said, and she sprinted over.

She grumbled, but leaped into the ditch, careful to make a radius around Stan and his gun. Her hands cupped Chad and flipped him over, out of the way.

371

"*Zirrus*, the *Suneva of Time* can't hold this for much longer," she warned, drawing her sword and slicing at Chad's bindings.

Nick! "Where is he? He joined you?"

"In the car," Celeste gestured over her shoulder, although the boy was out of the car by now. He had on his Suneva armour, a sleek set of purple and black coverings which formed a sharp and mechanical body. For his eyes there was only a single visor which wrapped the whole helmet. He was straining, gripping into his staff and element with every ounce of strength he had. Two more trees sublimated before my eyes. I heard them puff to dust just as Celeste flipped me over. "He had to help you escape, I made him feel bad."

"You're always good at that," I noted as my limbs were freed. I scrambled to my feet to see Chad clawing at Natalie's bindings.

"Run!" Zirrus shouted. "I can't hold this!" And entropy slipped from him slowly, the bullet kicking into gear, now a walk instead of a crawl.

"Boekidin's coming," Natalie remembered. "I don't know where to run to. I don't know what's best."

"The car!" I pointed. "Let's drive."

"What about Nick…I mean *Zirrus*?" Celeste said, making a head check to see that the Sheriff was still frozen and hadn't heard. "Boekidin can't find him."

"We drop him home, then," I urged, "and quickly, come on!" I sprinted towards the car, and soon everybody followed, climbing the ditch and running across the asphalt. That's when I saw Zirrus give up. He dropped to his knees, spent, and as he hit the ground, there was a deafening crack. Stan's bullet ripped into the tree before him, and his cackle turned to a howl.

"Where'd you go?!" He roared. I didn't dare to look, I only ran faster, urging my legs towards the car. I pounced at the rear door, throwing it aside and leaping in. "You're not getting away, Chad Rogers!" Stan yelled. Celeste and Zirrus – still in armour – piled next to me. Natalie threw herself into the passenger seat, and Chad took the wheel. He ripped at the ignition, frightening the poor, dead car into life.

I craned to stare out the back window. Behind us, Stan's eyes burned an inferno. He aimed his pistol at the car. Chad pounded at the gas, lurching the car forward, but the bullets came. Two burst into the panelling, and the third caused the car to scream. It lost all traction as the tyre blew out, sliding on its path and lodging on the edge of the ditch. It hung precariously, the wheels spinning and the motor crying as Chad slammed it in reverse. There was no budge.

"There goes the insurance deposit," he whined. Behind us, Stan Rodgers crested the ditch, an insane scowl printed on his face, his swagger gone for his sprint.

I threw my door open. "Come on, run!" I suggested, more of an order, and stumbled from the car. I rolled into the ditch, anxiously waiting for everybody to follow. Chad threw himself down with me, and then Celeste, and then Natalie. The insane footsteps of Sheriff Johnson were silenced as we piled into the ditch. Zirrus' sleek helmet bobbed above the car.

"Go!" He yelled. "I'll hold Stan for now, as much as I can. Get a head start."

"What about you?" I asked.

"I can't come with you," he said. "I'll go my own way, I'll make it home safe, I've done this routine before with Dad. Now get!"

I nodded, and I turned to run. We launched into the forest, only Celeste connected to her thread. The ground was wet, uneven, and covered in vines and bushes, but there was no room for mistakes, only speed. I cleared the terrain with lightning reflexes I didn't think I had. For each trip there was a miraculous recovery, feet landing and pressing on, but where to, I had no idea.

Then, we'd only made it a minute into the run, and I was already losing steam.

"This way," Chad puffed suddenly, veering right of our path. "We'll get back to the motel this way."

As we paused to turn, catching our collective breath, there was a frightening rumble. Through the brush, crushing the undergrowth, thundered a growling, screaming vehicle. The Sheriff's truck masterfully cut a path, as if the tall thick trees were nothing but cones on the road. It crested a ditch, catching air before ripping at the mud and scrub.

"Change of plans," Chad gawked. "*This* way." And he jogged off in the other direction, the way I'd been leading us. A bullet slammed into the tree by my head, and I jumped into action.

"We're going to die…" I said aloud, coming to the only logical conclusion. At that moment, I felt a strange relief, as if my ear had been blocked by water and

373

had just drained. It was warm, and comforting, but when I realised what it was, it only added to my fear.

Boekidin…when did he get in? I hadn't felt it, but there was no time to contemplate. We were going to die from two enemies, it didn't matter which got us first.

"Not yet," Celeste said. Fire laced her heels as she ran. It was hot enough to set alight the wet and snowy scrub, and soon a wall of flames followed us. The car still tore the forest behind us, its crushing rumble berating my ears. I ran like an animal, it was only instinct. And even then, bullets were still smacking into trees. I had no thoughts. I had nothing.

Then the gunfire stopped, and the engine faded against the trees. It seemed like we were getting away, like the Sheriff had given up. Ahead, just visible through the swathe of spruces, I could see a clearing before dense scrub which cut a line through the forest. The thick was much greener than the surrounding pines.

"There," Chad must have read my mind. "The creek. He can't cross."

I wasn't even sure that the Sheriff was following, but Chad's head was in the right place. We bounded towards it.

Then the engine grew louder.

I could hear the car coming, and craning my head I saw nothing, my eyes struggling to focus at all atop of my leaping step. Yet the engine roared and the tyres screamed, an apex predator hiding in the tall grass. Fear kicked my heart.

But the thick wall of plants and the creek were just up ahead, just beyond the next few trees, the next few roots, the next bounds of my feet.

Then I saw the car. The clearing before the creek's banks wasn't a clearing, but a service road. To our right, Stan Johnson's truck growled and pounced. I stopped running, slamming my feet to the mud and leaping behind a tree. The tyres yanked the car to a sudden stop right in our path, the ass of the truck swinging around on the loose gravel. I peered around to see Chad caught in the clearing, staring down those deadly headlights.

Stan Johnson ripped his own door off its hinges as he leaped from the cab. His eyes were insane, the pistol in his grip. No words, he fired.

Chad had at the same time gripped into his element, and before him he heaved a wall of earth. The bullets lodged themselves there, and then Chad tossed the thing. The hulking rock flew towards Johnson, but missed, slamming into the car and crumpling in the whole front end. The engine hissed in a cloud of steam.

Johnson roared. He went to fire again, but found a bolt of orange quatra coursing his way instead. He averted his attention, leaping from the path of the energy to roll back onto his feet. It was then that my thread came back to me – a searing warmth, pneumatic in my veins. With all of my connections afforded to me again, the world was clear.

I emerged from behind the tree and fired quatra on Stan's position. Two other bolts had joined mine, and the man's eyes struggled to keep up. He ducked behind his truck, but the whole beast was crunched then thrown by a column of earth which blasted up under it. Stan, eyes wild, drew his gun again, but in his hands it crumbled, its iron flying through the air and into Chad's fists.

"Surrender, Stan," Chad said. "I'm leaving. I'm never coming back, I can guarantee you that. Just let me leave."

"I don't believe you," Stan barked, although he did raise his hands for the surrender. "You came back now to haunt me, to *taunt* me."

"Uh, *guys*…" Natalie said, although she went ignored.

"I came back to see why the adults in my life had destroyed my childhood," Chad said. "I came to connect with my past. I've done that. I need nothing else from it."

"*Guys*," Natalie said louder. I turned to her, and saw the armour of Zamelle writhing over her body.

"Hey!" Stan pointed. "This is a surrender!"

"Look at me, Stan," Chad demanded, pointing to his own eyes. "We're leaving. You can too."

"Oh, you're leaving now, are you?" A new voice called. *Try it*. It said into my skull, before the familiar raven-figure tore his way through the scrub bordering the creek.

"Boekidin!" I shrieked, pointing.

Stan swung around, his eyes already falling out of his skull before he saw the black, armoured bird-man lunging at him. Boekidin's long talons wrapped around the man's neck, in one of those hands he held a small box, and it arced with electricity to the push of a button.

Stan cried out, but then his head lolled on his shoulders. I could feel the rift in the world as a soul screamed for its host but was silenced. I could feel the energy cease its flowing, and I could feel the disturbance in the quatra field which it left behind. Stan Johnson flopped into the mud and did not get up nor make a sound.

"That thread has been on Hesslik's list for a while. Little man made a name for himself, somehow." Boekidin smirked.

"What do you want, Boekidin?" Chad asked, adopting his armour to become Ferrad. I let Maiki encompass me, and could feel now the presences all around me. I couldn't read the quatra field, but I knew that right now, it was heavy.

"What I want, Ferrad, is for you to take me to the Legendary of Time."

Chapter 38
War of the Witches

Boekidin stood before us, a slumped Stan Johnson rousing quietly by his feet. Behind him, a wall of thick scrub and a lazy creek cut the forest. The air was thick with Suneva presences, I felt them pressing on my soul from all around. I just had the confidence to set my sights off Boekidin, and twirling around I could see that we were surrounded on all sides. Fisira – the Quatra Daemon, Talik, The Space-Cowboy of lightning, and Vasloka, The Magnetic Cat, closed a circle around us.

I could feel Fisira's soul impinging on mine, her energy so great and unstoppable. White, pure, straight from the black Gods. Her mechanical eye buzzed white, and I had only one thought. *Run, run, run.*

"We're as lost as you on the Legendary of Time, Boekidin," Chad said. "We've got no information to give."

"Don't lie to me. Do you know how stupid it is to lie to a *Kidin*?" Boekidin snarled. "I've seen their *alis* through Maiki's eyes. I've heard the name *Zirrus* and the name *Nick*."

"Oh no..." I mumbled.

"He wouldn't join you, I know that much too," Boekidin continued. "So don't play dumb with me. Tell me where I can find him, so I can work towards the *betterment* of the Suneva people, or I'll sit all of you terrorising ruffians down and I'll draw each thread of information from your minds. Which will it be?"

"Oh, cut the monologuing," Iva whined, "you get nothing." And she blasted Boekidin with a bolt of blue quatra. Before it had even left her sword, there was a shockwave in the universe. Something so hot and imposing that it screamed its danger at your soul. From my right, a bolt of white quatra soared from Fisira's golden staff, so fast and well-aimed, it hit Iva's blue bolt, obliterated it, and was deflected, roaring on a straight path into the top of a tall spruce. The wood simply ceased to exist. It burned white hot before sublimating on the spot, white rings of quatra emanating out from the burn mark. Branches fell and Iva had to leap to avoid them.

"Will you talk now?" Boekidin asked. Silence fell with the question, the surrounding footsteps marching closer. Ferrad, Iva, Zamelle and I converged in retreat, coming back to back in the tire-well of the dirt track.

"What do we do?" I whispered.

"Fight, of course," Iva grumbled. "We owe it to Nick."

"Do we?" I asked.

"We owe it to the Suneva people," Ferrad said. "We didn't come this far to hand over a Legendary."

That much was true, but I stood now facing the Suneva cat Vasloka, and I didn't see a way that we could defeat this pack and run off without being caught again, and again.

"Fine," I brushed off the impending cycle of doom. "Boekidin will retreat to a hiding place soon, to get in my head…"

"I'm waiting," Boekidin called. "This isn't some long deliberation, it's simple."

"Maiki, don't say what you're going to do, he's listening," Zamelle reminded me. "We'll have to do this on the fly. Pick a target, do what you do best. *Go.*"

What did I do best? There seemed no obvious answer, but all around me chaos erupted. Ferrad jerked up a clump of earth and threw it towards Talik. Iva blasted Boekidin with more of her quatra, and Fisira retaliated with her indigo bolts. Natalie, however, anticipated Fisira's attack, and met their indigo quatra with her own orange ones.

Boekidin, with many of Iva's bolts cancelled, but some still coming, leaped into the foliage. He needed a safe location to rest if he was to mind read. I wanted to chase him, but couldn't turn my back to the battlefield. I twirled about, seeing Talik to the left, Vasloka behind me, and Fisira running on Boekidin's old position out front by the creek. She would blast me if I even tried to follow, so that wasn't a good idea. A bright light consumed my vision, blinding me, and a roaring thunder tore through the earth itself, deafening me. My head rang as a tree wobbled on its destroyed, burning trunk, Talik holding his sword to aim.

Maybe I had to run.

It seemed selfish, but Boekidin needed me to stay in range if he didn't want to become *Natasvoul*, the lost soul. Somebody would have to slip off and follow me, I could reduce pressure here, giving Zamelle, Ferrad and Iva the upper hand. It was a perfect plan.

So I ran.

I vaulted off the mud, launching down a blast of air and flying for the canopy. I grappled into a nearby tree, then leaped off it for the next, downstream along the creek.

As I flew from the next tree, it exploded behind me, my eyes flashing white and my ears ringing dead. The tree was on white fire, cracked and black, its tip toppling, and far behind it the Space Cowboy smirking. As I grappled to the next, a white bolt flew my way, and I pushed off to the next tall spruce. The previous tree was obliterated too, sublimating as the white quatra bolt rocked through its bark and flesh. More white bolts had been fired too, but Zamelle had launched her orange ones into them, sending them loose into the sky. Iva and Ferrad attacked Talik, deterring his lightening. All that was left was Vasloka, the cat.

And I saw her sprinting on my tail.

Good...I think, I puffed, leaping away and farther up the canopy. Vasloka clawed into the trees behind me, gaining quickly. Now there was no time to stop and consider. From her tail she fired bolts at me, and I had to move quickly, slinging myself between branches, higher and higher, to avoid them.

Here, high in the pointed trees, I could see the spire of the town's dark Church. Another teal bolt flew at me, and I leaped from the treetop, commanding airspeed under my belly to glide off. I swooped towards the ground, tearing at the air and pulling into a soar away from the action. I had to be close to Boekidin's limits now.

And that's when Vasloka turned away.

She ran quickly, as if she'd only been entertaining me before, right back to the fray where my friends quarrelled. Her speed was insane, leaping between feet, cutting the ground on all fours. The dagger she held in her tail blasted quatra bolts, more to scatter than to hit.

The weight of Boekidin in my mind was still strong – who knew how far I'd have to run to lose him. I had three options: run out of his range and hope that my friends survived, find him and take his thread, or help my friends. From the tree on which I landed, I could see Boekidin across the creek from the fighting. He was sitting behind a thick, tall spruce, meditating. Vasloka pounced towards the action. I had to act now.

I went back for my friends.

Four of us on three of Boekidin's agents should have been a better fight. If Vasloka was occupied, and Zamelle intercepted Fisira's bolts, I could take out Talik, then we could work our way towards Boekidin. I saw the plan forming in my mind – a low swoop from behind, a surprise attack which was quick enough to avoid his retaliation. I just had to get there.

I diverted my path, leaping onto a next tree away from the creek, further from Boekidin. I vaulted to the next, and scrambled as high as I could hold on, before blasting off from its tip and riding the wind towards the ground. I gained frightening speed, ripping at the air beneath me to force my swoop and glide. I was a bullet shooting between the trees, dodging the branches and trucks as they came with blasts to either side. I arched up just before losing speed, pulling vertically to latch onto the next tree and clamber up its trunk. I was even with Vasloka now, making a wide berth to the fighting ahead.

Zamelle and Fisira were separated, chasing each other about the edges of the clearing as another battle ensued between them. Iva, Ferrad and Talik were locked in a stalemate of elemental attacks. Ferrad had barricaded himself and Iva behind a wall of earthen mud. A stunning crack of lightning threw itself from Talik's swords towards them, but Ferrad grappled at the dirt with all of his might and held it to the onslaught. Iva cut through the stone with her sword, firing a bolt of quatra to their attacker. Immediately Fisira drew her own quatra to counter it, and Zamelle fired a bolt to counter that one. Iva threw a bolt of quatra at Fisira, seeing her distracted, but Fisira immediately retaliated, and Zamelle engaged that bolt too. Numerous bolts collided, sending shockwaves across the forest. In the end, quatra seemed to land *somewhere*, but I couldn't be sure where.

This was a stalemate that I needed to end.

Vasloka entered from Zamelle's flank. She fired on Zamelle, diverting the witch's attention, giving Fisira an opportunity to strike. The Daemonic Witch hailed a frenzy towards Ferrad and Iva. Ferrad gripped into the earth, throwing first a wall to the barrage, then tearing at the ground under Fisira's feet. His lack of concentration gave Talik an opportunity however, and suddenly things were looking dire.

No more time to lose, I threw myself from my perch, swooping to the ground and blasting from it to reach higher on the next tree, and then the next, and the next, encircling the battle field.

White quatra singed my tail and I hadn't expected it. I grappled the next tree and dug my claws into it to stop myself screaming from fright. Zamelle, now close to the creek, diverted the next white bolt with her own orange one and drew from the waters of the stream, summoning a wave to breach the banks. I didn't get to see the result of it, instead I made my final leap, flying into and away from the ground, onto the tree behind Talik, behind the battle.

Fisira had been washed over. Zamelle drew the water back from the mud, raising the wave to fight again. Iva and Ferrad had backed Talik towards my tree, the Suneva trying to shock them with electricity that was grounded by Chad's iron axe. I could see my flight path – down onto the man's head to fire quatra, then a pull up to land on *that* tree across the way, the stubby one. It was dangerous.

Hang on – where was Vasloka?

A crunch pricked my ear. I turned, to see the cat on the tree behind, grin wide, ready to pounce.

And she leaped.

I dove off my perch, falling like a stone, fast and uneven. It was like I'd forgotten how to glide, my hands missing the air, I fell straight down. The earth drawing nearer. I could smell it.

Just in time, somehow, that rush of sense came over me and I projected my soul into the air around me, tearing at my connections and forcing the air to bend to my commands. Forcing pressure under my belly, I diverted the ground, a bolt of Vasloka's teal quatra scarring the mud in my falling path.

I soared up in my arc, rising from the earth, right towards Talik's rear. I extended my palm, quatra oozing from it, watching for that perfect moment, for *contact*.

"Talik!" A voice yelled from behind me. The Suneva turned on his retreating step, helmet and slitted eye glancing at me, then lighting with shock. He pulled the rest of his body around to fight, but it was too late. My hand crammed into his neck and I fired my bolt of quatra. With too little room to reject the foreign energy, his armour shattered off his skin, raining like glass. Letting go, I blasted a kick of air off his body to fly for the stumpy tree.

Although the stumpy tree was already flying towards me – part of it anyway. What was that? It glimmered in the light, rising from the earth just as I had.

I was rocked with warmth I wasn't expecting. Transfixed, I missed the quatra bolt crying at my senses which had flown towards me. My armour was retreating before I realised what had even happened, and my senses drew dim.

Yet I was still soaring – thrown dumb through the air on my own blast.

Suddenly that mysterious flying object didn't seem so bad of a threat as it still hurtled towards me, because the ground looked *much* worse. Rigid roots, rocks, branches, all flying under me.

Or, it seemed worse until the mysterious object hit. It slammed into the bone of my left shoulder, some sharp bit of it grazing at my skin before flying away. I screamed, throwing my right hand to the bruise, flipping me around as I crashed into the ground. I impacted on the wound, a root cramming itself into the meat of my shoulder at the back, twisting the muscle, crushing my hand into it. I flopped across the floor in the centre of the fight, barely containing my agony. I moaned, knowing that this was shock, and it would only get worse from here.

An animal was running towards me, digging at the mud on all fours, pouncing with fury. I scrunched myself up into a ball, but my shoulder screamed in pain and I spread to the dirt again, whimpering.

Vasloka skidded to a halt beside me, coming off all fours. A bolt of quatra nailed her squarely in the face, but she didn't seem to mind as her armour shattered to the wind, revealing a blonde girl with a square face.

"Oh Omercronius, are you okay?" She spoke Liktan with a slavic tongue, holding my face, to examine my eyes. I tried to paw her away, but I didn't have the strength, and my left arm protested so violently that I thought I'd throw up.

"No," I said, "no, I'm not."

"I'm so sorry!" She blurted, and tried to wrap her hands around more of my body. I had no choice but to accept her movements, although I didn't want to, and I kicked away. "I'm taking you to safety," she said, although when I looked up, a tall man of similar features was jogging towards us. I could assume that he was Talik. He grabbed at my waist and together the two of them hauled me to my feet. Around us, the fighting Suneva stood awkwardly, not wanting to fire a bolt, or waiting for someone else to be the first, like dogs growling at a fence line. I stumbled with Vasloka and Talik away from the creek, into the woods, where I was laid by a tree.

"What are you sorry about?" I finally asked. "It's a fight. People get hurt."

"*People* don't get hurt," she asserted. "Suneva do. Hesslik teaches us better than this. How can I brush this aside, your whole arm is lame! I sent that thing for your body and almost killed you."

Was the arm lame? I certainly couldn't move it right now, but that was temporary…right?

"What does Hesslik teach, exactly?" I asked, looking out over the battle. It was now Fisira against Ferrad, Iva, *and* Zamelle, and she wasn't losing. Fisira rained a barrage of quatra on her enemies, a dance of redirection and quick firing which I had never seen. Zamelle cancelled many of the bolts, and Iva saw an opportunity to run for Boekidin. She sprinted towards the creek.

"He built his moral code from Kuvalik's – he just improved it," Talik said, also observing the battle.

"And Kuvalik got his moral code from the Vochduh," I recalled my earlier memory, of the Sunesca diplomat *Salak Nolver*. "What did Hesslik change?" I might not have needed to ask this question had I never lost my pamphlet from Hesslik last year.

Iva cleared the creek, and Fisira let a white bolt roar after her. The beam of destruction obliterated the trees in its path, setting the dense scrub to flames. Iva ducked and rolled, and Fisira, countering Zamelle's quatra into Ferrad's to create silence, fired a bolt after Iva which hit. Celeste emerged from the shattered armour, slumping to her knees. She cried a frustrated scream.

"You've asked the right Suneva," Talik chuffed. "Vasloka has been studying Suneva morals for years."

"Hesslik has eight rules," Vasloka said. "The first is that one cannot use quatra and quatra abilities against a person."

Ferrad tried shifting the dirt under Fisira's feet again, anything to throw her off balance. She kept firm footing against it, dropping to keep a palm on the ground.

"The second is that if met with a threat, you must only retaliate with power equal to the threat."

Zamelle fired on the Daemonic Witch, but even against Ferrad's disruption of her solid ground, she could not be bested. No bolt made it to Fisira, they were each cancelled in a volley of small explosions.

"The third is that one must only present a fair fight. To outnumber an opponent by even one Suneva is dishonourable."

Ferrad growled and tossed a boulder at the Witch. She ducked away, and he took the chance to run. The witch shrieked her departed howl, one strong and shocking enough to force Ferrad to stumble, me to lose my breath, and Vasloka to stutter her words. Fisira laid a barrage of fire into the boy as he ran, and Zamelle fired on each bolt, cancelling them masterfully.

"The fourth, is that quatra is a gift of knowledge and meaning. It is to be used for self-improvement and innovation before warfare."

Ferrad heaved into the ground and forced a column of rock to cross the creek. Fisira changed her focus, shrieking and firing two huge, white bolts at Zamelle in a succession so quick that I didn't believe it. Zamelle leaped away, crawling under the fire, and Fisira was able to fire her indigo bolts on Ferrad.

"The fifth is that quatra must be controlled. The energy of souls has the power to *destroy* souls, and must be treated with respect."

Fisira's bolts missed, slamming into a wall of mud Ferrad erected. He ran now on Boekidin's tree, clearly sensing the raven-man's location. Fisira charged on her feet after him, absorbing Zamelle's bolts as they came and redirecting them towards the running Suneva of earth.

"The sixth is that quatra must not be used with ill intent for personal advantage."

Ferrad unfurled the chain from his back, whipping it around the tree to where I couldn't see. He yanked the line into the clearing, and in the metal links Boekidin was snagged. Ferrad grinned with his victory, the mind-vacant Shiverman limp in his grasp.

Either trusting the sensation of Zamelle's bolts flying towards him, or simply not thinking past lining up his own shot on a restrained Boekidin, Ferrad did not dodge the redirected bolts which came his way. They slammed into his side, downing him by surprise as his armour slipped away. The bird awakened before hitting the ground – and I felt him leave my head to do so. He stumbled back behind the tree, and my mind was heavy again.

"The seventh is the reverse of the sixth – quatra can't be used with ill intent to disadvantage somebody else."

Chad joined Celeste by the rut of the creek, crawling low to avoid fire. The two witches now stood like cowboys, weapons drawn, waiting on the other's fire. Even without my Suneva connections, I could feel the oppression of thick quatra hanging in the air.

"The eighth is that quatra must not be used to harm or kill people. It can only be used to defend from the harm of people."

Zamelle fired first, finally. Fisira roared, unleashing a white bolt to meet Zamelle's orange, obliterating it and crashing towards the witch of water. Zamelle leaped from its path, firing two or her own bolts as she rose. Fisira met those with two white bolts, two fired in quick succession, which once again ripped through Zamelle's, charting roaring paths towards her.

Zamelle was like the water. Where white quatra came, she whipped herself from its wake, moving like fluid, dancing through the mud. She twisted and turned, avoiding the white lights of godly death. In the theatre behind her, trees were set ablaze into gas and plasma. The forest fell, broad spruce by broad spruce.

But Zamelle held her ground. Some of her shots cleared the field of blinding, heavenly white, forcing Fisira to take them in to redirect. It was when the Daemonic Witch was redirecting that Zamelle fired faster and harder. Fisira became flustered, dodging from the fire, and it only enraged her. She pounced across the gap between them.

384

Zamelle had nowhere to go. She turned to run, searching for a tree behind which to hide, but they'd all been destroyed. When Zamelle pivoted back to face the Daemonic Witch Fisira, there was already a white bolt flying for her helmet. Zamelle planted her foot to face the energy, but her foot snagged on a root. She stumbled, right at a fatal moment, fear building in her slit-eye. The white raced towards her.

It collided with her helmeted face.

Zamelle's head was encompassed in a blinding white glow, and the ground at her feet exploded into molten, flying debris of leaves, sticks, and gaseous mud. What was left of her body slumped into the hot pit, fizzling. Smoke rose from the crater.

"Fucking hell, Natalie!" I screamed, leaping up and running to the clearing. I fell as I rose, not running so much as stumbling to my knees. My shoulder cried at me, and I found myself crying. Natalie was dead. Her corpse smoked in the strange silence.

"You're kidding!" Chad yelled from across the creek. "How could you do that?" And he clambered onto his mud-bridge, eyes blazing with hate. "You killed her, your crazy demon! You killed her!"

Fisira dropped her weapon, stumbling away from it. She peered over to Boekidin's tree, but her master was dormant. There was a struggle in her eyes, the humanity in there trying to rest its roots, to take hold, but it couldn't control her. There was nothing there.

But then a limb rose.

Zamelle's blue armoured hand clasped at the crater's edge. She dragged herself up to a squat, then rose slowly, unsure of her feet. The slit of her helmet did not glow. It was stained grey, smoking, as if her soul was extinguished. Zamelle eyed Fisira, and sighed.

Her slit glowed white.

Blinding white, whiter than any white quatra I'd seen. It was an impossible hue, the light of truth and knowledge itself. Some manifestation of that which nobody could understand. It radiated over the darkening forest, the twilight kicked back from the clearing of scorched, obliterated trees.

"I can save you," Zamelle said finally, and raised a twin-sword. From it projected a radiant bolt of pure white quatra. Fisira lunged for her staff. Holding it in uncertain hands, she fired back on the bolt with white fire of her own, and the two collided.

I was stunned by the shockwave. Worse than lightning next to my face was the meeting of two pure souls.

Fisira fired again, and Zamelle lunged into it. Taking the bolt through one twin sword, she channelled it across her body, and projected it from the other arm at twice its size. A toxicated white bolt of quatra.

"Impossible," Vasloka awed.

Fisira awed as well. She tried to move, but the energy came too fast, and was too large. She stumbled from its path, but the bolt nailed her in the arm, and then it was over. The Daemonic Witch sparked white before blowing into a cloud of black dust and molten debris. A body lay in the dirt of the explosion. It was lifeless.

Zamelle then turned to the tree behind which Boekidin sat. Without another step, she threw a bolt of white quatra at it, and the whole, hulking redwood puffed to black gas. Boekidin was revealed now, and Zamelle held her sword out to him, but turned to face me.

"It's over Boekidin. Come into your body now."

His midnight black figure seemed to stand, and then run. Zamelle fired a bolt of orange into his path, and he seemed to accept his fate, taking the hit in his stride as his armour shattered like glass. He ran to Fisira.

"You're alive, Zamelle," I gawked, limping over to her. Chad and Celeste met my movements, and we closed in on the witch.

"That didn't kill you," I said again, still not believing it.

"I can't see," she admitted, letting her armour slip away. Behind the helmet, Natalie's eyes were pale. Their prominent, deep blue had leaked away to grey. "It blinded me. My life is over."

"Well…that's not true, it's not *over*." Chad tried to cheer her.

"*Your* life is over?" Boekidin snarled at Natalie's remark. I could see him now, a slender, tall Polynesian man. "Look at what you've done to her!" He held Fisira's body in its crater.

"She was already dead, Boekidin," Natalie frowned. "Destiny had decided it would take her soul a long time ago. She was never given a chance."

"Oh can-it with the spiritual shit!" He ordered. "I mean that you've *really* almost killed her. You want to be a good Suneva? Get over here and do something quickly! She's fading."

"Do what?" Natalie growled, flinging her body to face his voice. Her golden locket bounced about her neck. "Do I look like a doctor or a necromancer to you?"

Despite Natalie's protest, I ran over to the downed Daemonic Witch. As I ran, my senses were flooded, and for the now countless time today, my Suneva abilities had been restored. The air was vibrant at my fingers' tips, and I could feel it *just* wading about the unconscious girl's lungs.

"Magical CPR!" I yelled to Natalie. "Get over here. I do the breath, you do the blood." And I turned to Talik, who now squatted beside me. "You have to start the heart, or zap the brain, or something, anything!"

"I can't move," Natalie said, and now she sounded scared. "I can feel where you are, but I can't feel the ground. I don't want to trip."

"I've got you," Chad said, and squatted under her, hoisting Natalie onto his shoulders and running her over to the scene. He dropped her down just as Boekidin and I heaved Fisira's body onto its back, revealing the girl's face.

They were Natalie's cousin Christina, the girl with a greyed-out eye.

"Oh my God, Natalie, it's your cousin Christina," I gawked.

"Christina!" She shrieked, and panic swept her face. "Oh *Amasos*, you failed her. Oh no…she can't die."

"Good, good, use that," Boekidin encouraged. "Save her."

I was already working at the lungs, using throws of my hand to balloon the things full of air. The body resisted, and realising my mistake, I handled her head and tilted it back, opening the windpipe. Natalie joined, rubbing at the girl's limbs, circulating her hands about. Talik crossed his palms over the heart, thrusting into their chest until the whole body shook.

"Yes, that's it," Boekidin said, crazed. "I can feel her coming back."

Tilting the head did naught for me, I realised. My arm was screaming at me, and maybe I'd never notice it, but my right hand had never connected to the air as well as my left had. With only one operating arm, it was hard work, and I was sweating.

Natalie worked at her element, pumping the blood, drawing it from the heart. Talik had flopped into the dirt, desperately shocking the girl's chest.

A raindrop wet my hair, and then another. Around us the dark forest set into cold rain.

"Come on, you're almost there!" Boekidin strained.

Talik flopped, emotionally drained, his chest brimming into the mud. He placed a lazy hand on Fisira's forehead and eyed me for support. I could see that he'd never done this before, and he nodded his guilt to me. Perhaps an admission that this could be the end. He applied a shock to her brain.

Christina woke. She spluttered back into existence, her dumb eye rolling weakly in her head. When she saw Natalie, the girl started to cry, and reached out to hold her. Natalie had no idea what was happening, but accepted the embrace, falling onto the mud on her arse. Her locket, which had only been loosely straddling her neck, was flung away. I dove to catch it, forgetting my arm as I slammed it into the ground. The shock was wearing off now, and the pain was intense. I yelped, but held the piece of golden jewellery tightly.

Christina appeared even less human now than she had at the lunch in Sparta. Gone from her eyes was any glint of something living. The grey eye was no longer creepy, it was just *dull*. There was no aura to the girl, and she did not even attempt to speak.

"Her thread is gone," Natalie said, sensing my discomfort. "She might recover, now." Natalie searched her neck for her locket, and panicked when she couldn't find it. I placed the item in her palms, only to be met with a look of abject suspicion. "We saved her," Natalie continued the previous thought.

"Yes…" Boekidin finally caught himself. "You did." And he stood, his expression now sullen as he faced Chad, Celeste and I without his raven façade. He didn't know where to look.

"You found what you were after?" Chad asked.

"Only just," Boekidin nodded. "Fisira is a good guard. Or, she was…" And he turned to the girl. "Her skills will be missed."

"She's better without them," Natalie stood, hauling Christina up.

"I suppose she is," Boekidin agreed. "Hesslik won't be happy though…"

"So, what happens now?" Celeste asked. "Everybody has their connection back…"

"Nothing," Boekidin said, wiping rainwater from his eyes. "We're not savages, plus you've got us beat by numbers. We operate on a code of honour, and don't have a feud anymore. Not until you find something else valuable to us."

"So why did you keep attacking? Why didn't you call Fisira off before she got obliterated?" Natalie jumped at Boekidin, attempting to point a finger at him but missing dreadfully.

"Because I didn't find the information until the final blow."

"Dishonourable," Natalie scorned. "Putting Hesslik's wants above the life of a fellow Suneva."

"And you put her life at risk by continuing to attack," Boekidin remarked.

"To protect a young man who doesn't need to be found out," she snapped.

Boekidin frowned and conceded, "thank you then, Natalie, James, Celeste and Chad."

"For what?" Celeste asked.

"For saving this girl's life. You're right, Natalie, I put her at risk. She was a friend of mine and I was foolish. Saving her means a lot."

"A friend of all of us," Talik spoke up. His voice was deep and demanding. "I don't think I could have taken her death – even if she never said much, she was kind and generous. She saved my life more times than I can count…"

"It's alright," Natalie said, standing tall and wiping the rain from her face. I couldn't help but stare at her glassy, grey eyes. Those eyes used to hold so much for me – I'd fallen into visions when lost in them, but now they were voids. "Although for her case, maybe death would have been more peaceful." She turned from her cousin and towards the setting sun. The rain continued to come down over us. "You will help her get better, won't you?" She asked into the expansive forest. "You won't abandon her, will you?"

"It's the honourable thing, as friends, to do," Vasloka said.

"Boekidin?" Celeste asked. "You will look after her?"

"Yes. Of course," he nodded.

"Good," Chad remarked. "Now, I think we've long ignored one thing here – Natalie, are you okay?" He stepped over to her and grabbed her face with his meaty mitts. "You've been blinded – maybe we should go to a hospital."

"It's the best outcome of white quatra to the face, *really*," she huffed. "Plus, with the way they treat Suneva around here, I'd rather not try a hospital."

"Quatra can heal you," Boekidin suggested from afar. "Let it into your body, but not too much…"

"…or it will consume you," Natalie finished the sentence. "I'm aware. Christina, unfortunately, was not."

Boekidin fell silent, and nobody filled the void he left, allowing rain to drown our thoughts. Behind us, a mighty creak groaned, and the charred top of a tree broke from its trunk, falling to the forest floor. A confused and frightened Christina flung herself into Talik's arms, where she stayed.

"Let's head off," Natalie said to Celeste, Chad and I. "We're done here."

"What about Christina?" Chad asked. "You'll leave her with Boekidin?"

"They're her friends," she said. "They just said they'll care for her. I can visit later, when there's time."

"Okay," Chad nodded. Natalie went over to hug her cousin, and pulled the girl away and into the near woods, out of earshot.

"I guess we'll follow," I pointed awkwardly back the way towards the road. "It's been…good?" I shook my head. "It's been *something* to meet you all."

"And what happens when you leave?" Talik asked, his face was tense. "You're just going to go back out and keep building on your plan to destroy Hesslik's empire." And He gripped with his hands, his legs twitching. "It's just not fair. I couldn't stop you if I wanted to. Why do you have to destroy the Suneva community? Why can't you just be good?" And he grumbled, like a sulking child. Arcs of charge bounced between his fingers, but he didn't dare use them.

"It *is* frustrating," Vasloka agreed. "Hesslik's plan to use thread removal is a form of policing Suneva abilities, it's meant to hold the community self-accountable for what we do. It will be a proper system. What can't you see in that?"

"I…don't have a problem with that…" I said, furrowing my brow.

"Don't speak for all of us," Celeste huffed. "I'd like to have a *little* more personal freedom than Hesslik is offering."

"Their problem isn't with thread removal as a concept," Boekidin interrupted, talking to his agents. "James saw in a vision that Hesslik was going to plug a thread remover into Vestas' long-range transmitter. He's worried about Suneva annihilation."

390

Vaslok and Talik turned pale, eyeing each other through ill faces.

"You saw that?" Talik asked me.

"I saw it in a vision. I've seen the place in the castle where the vision took place long after having it, too."

"Is there validity to it?" Vasloka asked Boekidin.

"I don't know," Boekidin frowned, and turned to me. "In James' mind, in my many adventures there, I have only found evidence of a dedicated, trustworthy, and honest young Suneva. I've doubted his claim for a long time, but maybe it's time to test it."

"Really?" I coughed, and the tall Maori gentleman only had a solemn nod for me.

"Your conviction is too strong, given the demeanour you've proved to me. I know you're not a badly-intentioned person," Boekidin said. "For my own sake – for the continuation of the Suneva – I should properly test your claims."

"Thanks," I found myself saying, "and what happens when you find that I'm right?"

"*If* you're right," Boekidin corrected. "I'll probably join you in finding the Legendaries and taking down Hesslik. If you're wrong, however, you will stand down, or I'll personally present your thread to Hesslik. Is that clear?"

He'd already grabbed my hand to shake it before I'd considered the deal. It was a closed contract. I gulped.

"Okay, that's enough ominous plans for one day," Chad said, pulling Celeste and myself aside. "Good meeting you, finally. We'd best be off."

"Goodbye," Boekidin bowed as I was dragged away. "I'll be sure to tell Nick – the Sheriff's son – that you sent us. I can't wait to hear what he says."

Chapter 39
Admissions

We packed our bags as soon as we'd reached the motel, not spending another moment in this town. We'd managed to coax the car home through the rain by having me focus my soul's connection on the bullet-punched tyre, using every last ounce of my energy to keep the air inside. The hole-ridden car waddled into our parking space, and we threw our bags in before we'd even asked Chad if he was done with this village. Chad's only reply to the question was a solid nod of the head as he stuffed in his suitcase full of the pointless crap he'd lugged along.

We changed the tyre with a spare from the motel staff, and cruised along the dark, wet road, coming to a stop one town over to rest for the night. The only room still available was a cramped affair, somehow even more claustrophobic and run-down than the first place. Orange wallpaper peeled and cracked at the edges. A double bed without spring sat sad in the centre of the dark space, with two fold-out singles rising from the stained-armed couches. There was no fancy deliberation of the beds here. I collapsed onto the first semi-comfy object I saw and fell into delirium. My arm screamed at my careless treatment of it, but my brain had no fight for it, shutting down into a fast sleep. I saw Celeste and Chad take the double bed, and Natalie slump onto the couch closest to the window. There wasn't even a 'goodnight' from a single soul, or any attempt at debrief. There was only sleep.

***

"Where's Natalie?" Celeste said, and stirred me in the morning. I was groggy, my mind still stretched out, stressed from the previous day's chase and roller coaster.

"Over by the window," I pointed lazily with a closed eye. Natalie had taken the couch. I tried to pry myself up to see for myself, but my left arm cried in pain and I could not force myself to rise.

"Would I be asking if she was there?" Celeste grumbled, tugging at my hand. She pulled me to sit up against my will, and my body threatened to topple down under its own weight. "I knew she slept on that couch, but the *blind girl* isn't in this room at all."

She's missing? My brain buzzed alive. "Oh *cheese*, where has she stumbled too?"

"She's not in the bathroom," Chad said, emerging from a toilet that I'd never noticed was behind my head.

"I'll check the bed," I said stupidly. Even from my perch, it was plain to see that the couch-bed was empty. Still, I forced my groggy body over to it, and I flipped back the rustled covers.

There was a note.

"A note…" I said out loud. It was in Natalie's handwriting alright – the neatest handwriting I'd ever seen produced.

"What does it say?" Celeste asked. I read it aloud.

"How did a blind person write a note so neatly?" Chad quizzed, and I really had no idea.

Dear Celeste, Chad and James,

I've had to come to terms with a lot recently – truths about myself and about those around me. You've all been very honest with me – at my insistence, but I may not have been so open with you all.

I am the White Witch. No, it was not that I defeated Christina, and so became the White Witch. I have been the White Witch since my Yamitse first sensed her successor, and I have known it from when we first found the code. Fisira was a Quatra Daemon, possessed by the black hole Amasos.

My Yamitsira told me what this future meant when we visited her in Sparta. Since then, I have been training to see the world through quatra, to identify auras, to channel the black hole directly through my body and control *these abilities. I now do not believe that control of these things* can *be learned.*

Quatra has been the root of many problems in my life. My mother left me when she knew what I would become. When I shrieked and howled through nightmares like her own mother used to, she couldn't deal with it. I am the rift in my family.

Recently I've struggled to justify why we should possess these abilities. Quatra is powerful, and for many of us too powerful to control, too powerful even to resist its temptations to control us instead. I can feel myself losing this battle now. Amasos is invading my soul, I can feel it every day. Who knows how many other Suneva are losing this fight, because nobody has taught us how to defend against it, and there isn't really a way to fight it without unwavering personal dedication and self-introspection.

And somehow my life has all led to this moment, anyway. Not only are we given more power than we can control, but this power makes us pawns to higher beings. Every nudge we've experienced in our lives was given by them, and led us here. They wanted my mother to leave me. They wanted me to kill my cousin, and it was my determination to fight their urges which saved her. They want me to possess abilities that I can't control, and be a symbol that I can't be.

So, I'm joining Hesslik. Hesslik has methods to control powerful threads, it was something that he told me in his castle. With him I can save Suneva from ourselves, from this world that contorts us to do dangerous, bad things, from these beings that want to possess us with power. Not everybody could make this step to support our destruction, and you might see it as foolish, but I see this as a very difficult, very brave decision.

I will be the White Witch to save the Suneva. Even if you may not suffer with thread control, many do, and it is dangerous to everybody, not just ourselves. I will break destiny to do all of this.

I'm sorry.

It's been lovely growing with you, but I can't continue in our journey.

Love,
Natalie Athanas.
Zamelle Menas – Na Ocras Quatrona

"Ah!" I shrieked, throwing the letter down.

"Oh no…" Chad grew stiff lipped. "This isn't good at all." And his fright turned quickly to a jittering frustration as he punched the head of the couch. "She was the *White* damned *Witch!* We were one step closer to stopping Hesslik without even knowing it!"

"And now he's got her," I mumbled. But surely this couldn't be it. "We've got to go and find her." I said.

"You think you can convince her against all of this emotional release?" Chad slapped the page where it lay. "No, man, she's gone. She decided this long before yesterday pushed her over the line."

"That's too defeatist," I tried to reconcile false hope. "We can't give up on her."

"She's made her mind," Celeste said, taking the paper and scrunching it in her fist. "Let's go on without her. Nothing said we needed her to find the last legendary. Nobody said we needed *her* to defeat Hesslik's plans."

"Celeste…Celeste…." Chad grumbled, rubbing the bridge of his nose. "That girl can redirect *white quatra*. She's already more powerful than Fisira, and that witch could have stopped us all singlehandedly. By her title, Zamelle Menas is *the* most powerful witch alive. If we face Hesslik, we face *her*, and that's just not possible."

"Don't be so dramatic," Celeste dismissed, stepping onto the bed. "Zamelle Menas is the *Ocras Quatrona*, but I'm still *Iva Argol*, and an *Ivaer* of the pink flame. I don't know who might be piloting the Argol forces *now*, but with my pink fire and claim to the family throne, we can control them and take on Hesslik."

"You want to take over the Argol gang?" I eeked.

"You want to march an army into bolts of white quatra?" Chad huffed. "Have respect for their lives, Celeste. Fisira took out redwoods with a single blast. Suneva *will* die."

"You guys think Natalie would kill?" I asked, but my question went ignored again.

"We fought Fisira just fine, Chad. Just four of us, none *dead*."

"Sure…"

"Look, James is right, you're being defeatist," Celeste said, and I cringed, having been used as an argument's pawn. "If you don't want to fight Hesslik, that's up to you, but I've spent too much of my life fighting for my rights as a Suneva to let that fat-headed, battery-fingered *bastard* take my identity away from me. I'm going to fight, Chad. It's all I've done my whole life, and frankly we're the only Suneva who can save us all. To hell with Hesslik, Zamelle, and anybody who wants to threaten our liberties. I'm a proud Suneva."

"You'll down *anybody* who disagrees with you?" I winced. "That sounds like a dangerous rhetoric."

"Oh, I might not be my father, but I've got his spirit to fight for what I'm worth. I'm no pushover, James." Celeste bore over me, still standing atop the bed. "I'd rather that society think I'm a menace than I would bow down backwards to please everybody like Hesslik would have us do. We have rights and I will fight for them, and one of those is the right to our Suneva identity. Hesslik will *not* take that. Are you with me?"

"I don't know," I said. "I don't want the Suneva to be destroyed, but…"

"And have you got a better plan, then?" Celeste snapped. "I'm offering something *useful*. I'm offering an army."

"We should find Natalie." I said. "That's my plan. I don't think she'll be convinced back to our side by fighting."

"Fine, then," Celeste huffed, jumping off the bed. She grabbed her bag and started to stuff it full. "Join me if you want, James, but I'm going to save the Suneva people."

"Cheese, Celeste," I growled, finally fed up. I zipped her bag and went to pick it up and throw it, but I'd forgotten about my shoulder. The muscle screamed at me and I slumped on top of the luggage instead. "Can't you calm down for a second and be reasonable? You're just going to run away and leave Natalie on a whim too?"

"James, I'm *never* running again," She eyed me off, coming close to my face. "What exactly am I running from? We have to stop Hesslik, and my family is my plan. To hell with finding or convincing Natalie or anything to do with her. I am tackling my responsibilities head on this time. If you or Chad don't join me, then you're the ones running away."

I took a step back from her intimidating gaze. "I'm sorry," I said, "but a war isn't the answer here. A war won't unite the Suneva against Hesslik or stop his ideologies. We need Natalie. We need to follow the code."

"Why?" Celeste asked. "She's the one who lied to us the whole time, but demonised us for keeping secrets. Screw her if she wants to be the biggest hypocrite Suneva to walk the Earth. Plus, the Legendaries have been nothing but useless. I've got a real plan to save the threads."

"And I'm sorry," I retorted, "but if the code has taught me anything, it's that conflict can only be beaten with internal peace, not with further conflict. There are better ways to resolve this."

"Then you're running, James," she said. "You can't keep following this code and expecting different results. It's time to make a better plan."

"So it's just you and me then, Chad?" I looked to the man, who was now flopped over a bed, head stuck staring out of the window.

"No...no, James. It's just you now," he responded and sat up to face me.

"What, why?" I asked, and stood over him. "We'll get there, man, have hope. We'll win Natalie back, and we'll stop Hesslik."

"No, we won't," he looked up to me. "Zamelle's complaints are all legitimate. Quatra is dangerous, and destiny is dangerous. We're pawns, stuck in the flow of the river between this world and the void. We can't escape that truth. You want to convince her against the truth?"

"No," I defied him, "we'll find a way to fight the tide. There's got to be an answer out there."

"Find some cosmic, philosophical answer of those proportions in a few months? If *anybody* knew how to cheat destiny, everybody would know about it. We don't even have a plan James, let alone a hope. All we're doing right now is finding Legendaries. We've wasted half a year just to be told twice to fuck off by them. You can go waste time finding the last one – go get a badge for being the first guy to find all three, but I'm not wasting the effort. All they'll tell you is that they're not getting involved, just like the others. Winning Legendaries over won't fight destiny, it won't lower the lethality of quatra, and it won't win Natalie back. Maybe they're right James. Maybe it's better to not be involved."

"Shit, man. Come on," I strained to provide optimism. "If you don't stand then nobody will. The threads will all die. That's the end. I thought you considered me a friend. Stand by me."

"James, you are," he reached out and patted my arm. "But look, man, I don't want to fight anymore. I'm done. What I want to do with my *remaining time* is go back to the forest where this all started and connect with nature again, while I still can. Make yourself happy James. Do something with your remaining time."

"With my remaining time?" I coughed, backing away. "You can't be serious – is this real?" I looked around to my friends in panic. Chad kept his defeated yet peaceful grimace, and Celeste held her distain, now back to stuffing a bag full.

"It is," Chad said. "It's done James. You can come with me if you want. Come as my friend and connect to the forest. Or you can go with Celeste and tackle the issue head on."

"No, man," I said. "Thanks for the offer, but no." I stumbled towards the door. "And I'm not going with you either, Celeste. I'm sorry, but fighting Hesslik army-to-army isn't the solution to an *ideological* problem. You've all given up hope on Natalie, but I'm going to find the friend that walked into this crazy Suneva world with me."

I went to exit, but knocked my left shoulder into the doorframe. I yelped in pain and flopped through the portal, clutching the swinging door. Behind me, Celeste hadn't even looked up from her packing. Chad nodded a goodbye.

"We can track her through the woods!" I pleaded to Chad. "You can find her footprints, and I'll *smell* for her. I'm *sure* that's a *kiin* ability."

"It's not, James," Chad shook his head. "Find your peace in the time left."

"Well fuck you, too," I growled at him. "You have the power to find her and you're choosing to do nothing. I'm the one who'll have to face her family when I go home and tell them…what? That she just ran off? I'm finding her. I'm going to do *everything* that I can."

"Good luck," Chad nodded, and to this I slammed the door in his face. The defeatist *coward*. I *had* to bring her home, her issues with her Sunevahood could be solved after that.

I stumbled into the woods holding my right hand in the peace-sign pose. As always, the quatra field was dun to my hands – but I'd been getting better and sensing the *presences* within. Natalie was not here, but I already knew that much. *Had* she been this way, though?

Still, holding my hand before me, I had no sense of *anything*.

That's wrong. Surely not. I panicked. Looking around to check that I was alone, I summoned my *alis*. Maiki took my body, and suddenly there was no pain. My arm felt fine, regular even. Not a hint of pain to keep me awake – it was a magical reprieve, and I suddenly felt invigorated. I *could* save Natalie. I grappled at my connections, which now flooded towards my soul. Eddies and flows of the breeze rushed between the trees, all around was the thickness of carbon in objects, screaming to me in colour maps.

There had to be some clue of Natalie's path here, in the forest just steps from the motel door. The air would tell me nothing, but was carbon useful? I connected to the lumps of it around, the patches along the ground. One of those patches seemed a familiar shape, and suddenly it clicked. A *footprint*, and another. A whole set of them appeared, leading to the window of the motel.

I ran along the path, away from the room, into the forest. The armour of Maiki carried me, thrusting my determination. Natalie couldn't be too far, and I was on her trail. I could find her, and I could talk sense into her. She just needed a friend to understand her, one who had walked into this Suneva world with her.

I reached a road quickly, and the path stopped, no carbon of footsteps traversing the asphalt. I paused, sensing for more carbon left and right, up a tree, back the other way, but nothing appeared. Nothing but tyre marks were imprinted on this road.

She'd gotten in a car and left, that was the answer. I tried to sense her presence in the quatra field, clinging desperately to any extra feeling I could juice out of my dumb armour, but there was nothing to sense. I couldn't do this witchcraft, and now wasn't the time it'd magically work.

I kicked a tree, my frustration bubbling. I could run down the road after her, but I didn't know which way she'd gone, or where, or how long ago, or with whom, and I certainly couldn't do it in this religious countryside in the armour of Maiki. It hit me, suddenly, that I knew *nothing*, and I'd just dragged my pain-ridden, dumb body through the woods for nothing. Chasing her now was brash, but I had nothing else.

I did still have my friends though. Celeste and Chad – we might have just fought, but right now Natalie was gone, and we still had each other. We just had to work together instead of letting the situation drive us apart. We all needed each other.

That was the answer, and once again my swimming, jostling mind forced me to run back for them. Alone I was nothing, but Celeste, Chad and I were so strong together. I leaped and bounded between the trees, vaulting off their trunks now with gusts of air. Running at ground level, I was running for my last hope – the last hope for *Suneva*. Our unity.

In the distance the motel appeared, and I now sprinted for it. Coming near the building, I let my armour subside, and with it I was launched back into severe pain, my left arm drooping and screaming. The sudden shock of it all forced me to trip a step, ripping the lame arm about in its socket. Fumbling for a connection, I blasted air at the forest floor to vault myself up the small set of stairs, and I just barely made the landing of the weak push. I threw my weight into the door, and it wouldn't bulge. In my hand, even the knob slipped. With no time, I fashioned a diamond knife and jammed it into the door crack. It opened, and I fell into the small, decrepit room.

But it was empty, bar my belongings. My friends were gone.

They weren't in the airport either, I found after hitching rides there. With Celeste and Chad unfindable too, I had no choice but to head home. I needed rest to get better, and my sister was the only person left who could help me defeat Hesslik. I could still do it. I knew it.

But with my pain, my hope was fading.

Episode 7

A Precautionary Tale Against Getting Drugged Up On Quatra

Chapter 40
In Health and Happiness

Chad's last words to me rang through my head. I needed to spend my time wisely.

I had an emotional plane ride home. Alone, I was faced with the fact that not only could I not find my friends today, but I might never find Chad again. Gone into the woods somewhere between his hometown and Santa Fe, I'd never track him down without a considerably strong witch. If only I'd taken up his offer to live out my time as a Suneva in nature.

But that wasn't the way forward. Failure wasn't a future I could find peace in.

Celeste would be easier to find again – if only just. I'd been to her childhood home, I'd been to Naxaer Argol's head office. I could only assume she was going there, to show off the power of the pink flame and teach others about the secret to being an *Ivaer* through heat. She was hoping to gain control of the Argol throne, and I didn't doubt that she'd do it. I wondered what would have happened to Celeste and my brief romance. Would it continue in the future if we met again? It was almost funny that I'd stressed so much on her thoughts of me, only for it to never matter, now. We kissed, agreed to be casual, and now that was all wasted.

If only my last words to the two of them weren't a terrible argument. The whole situation reminded me of my last words to Dad, and mulling it over forced a tear from my eye.

I got home at midday after a flight paid for in diamonds and luck, the jetlag melting my brain. I stumbled in the door with my duffel bag over my good shoulder, my left arm riding my torso in a sling and my face dirty from hitchhiking and the fight in the forest. The number of things I'd experienced between showers was deplorable, and I was glad that the house seemed empty so that I wouldn't be asked about any of it. I sighed deeply, envisioning the bathroom and my eventual hygiene.

The door to the front room opened, and Simone peered her head to my disgusting mug hanging in the doorway. I yelped, flinging my bag down and trying to adopt an innocent smile. Simone's eyes were agape as she analysed me.

"James," she gawked. "What the hell happened to you?" And she grabbed at my chin, examining the marks on my face and neck.

"You know how I said that this mission was too dangerous for you to come on?"

"Yes."

"It was, in fact, too dangerous."

She grumbled, frowning. "But what *happened*? Wasn't this meant to be some sort of family-reunion, find-yourself-adventure for Chad? What went *this* wrong?"

"Boekidin found us," I said, then pointed to my arm. "I got taken out of the sky and slammed into a magnetically charged object, then the ground."

"You're in a bloody sling," she pointed to the rag holding me together. "You need to see a doctor. Have you seen how swollen your shoulder is?"

Ignorance truly was bliss. If I never clarified my physical situation, I'd never learn how much I *couldn't* do, and then I'd have no excuses getting in the way of finding Natalie and stopping Hesslik. "It's fine, no doctor required." I stuck to my logic.

"The whole thing looks broken," she gestured at my whole body.

"It'll heal," I insisted, keen to leave my body to its own devices. "Just needs time, that's all."

Simone grumbled, and poked my collarbone. The pain that shot through my being was agony, and I barely held my face together.

"Okay," I grimaced. "Maybe a doctor will do good."

"I'll take you myself," she nodded. "I don't understand your aversion to medical help. You're an idiot."

"Fine, I know," I said, slumping to pick up the bag. Simone was ahead of me though, grabbing it from the floor and walking it, and me, towards my room.

"Why was Boekidin so keen on a fight?" She asked.

"We found the Legendary of Time," I said.

"*What?*" She gawked. "A *second* Legendary?"

"And he refused to come with us."

We entered my room, and I lay myself carefully down on my bed. It was barely past midday and I was already hungry for sleep.

"That's still incredible, you'll make history already," Simone chuffed. "I can't believe that."

"It barely matters, though," I said, remembering my situation beyond having to visit a doctor. "Natalie turned out to be the White Witch, and got so scared of her powers that she left us to help Hesslik."

"Uh…" Simone hummed, frowning. "Excuse me, but cover that point again."

"She left us in the middle of the night, left nothing more than a note about how we can't handle our power and destiny is untrustworthy," I barely elaborated. "Chad got all hopeless and went to live the life of a forest hobo. Celeste went back home to try and rule the Argols."

"This isn't good," Simone coughed, slouching down onto the bed next to me.

"We've still got time," I said, rolling to face her. "Hesslik isn't gathering the Suneva till September, right? It's the nineteenth of Jan…"

"Twentieth."

"Twentieth?" I quizzed. "Cheese, I gained a whole day. Well, it's the twentieth of Jan now, so there's plenty of time to convince Natalie and save the Suneva, just you and me." I reached out with my good fist to tap her arm. "We just have to prove to her that destiny is either circumventable or trustworthy, and that Suneva *aren't* too powerful for their own good. There's time…" and I laughed, knowing that this task was well beyond anything I currently understood. I had been dredging my mind on the plane for an answer to either of these conundrums, and came up with nothing.

"This might be worse than you think," Simone coughed, and pulled me up. "Follow me."

Simone dragged me to her computer, setting me down onto the office chair in the room lit only by the blue buzz of the computer's tower. She handled its reigns, leading the squeaking, zipping beast to Hesslik's Empire's main news page. "It's here somewhere," she said, intently scrolling until she found what she was after. She clicked into the article, but I'd already seen the title.

Great Gathering of Suneva – 7th of May, 1999.

"Do I even need to read it," I coughed, choking on my fright.

"No," Simone shook her head.

"We've got…" and I counted the months on my hand, sounding them out. "…just over three months."

"We sure do."

"But…that can't be right." I closed the window on the computer, hands to my cheeks and head to my lap. "I was at Vestas' lab on New Year's Eve, it didn't sound like he was even *close* to getting the power transmitter right."

"He must have solved it," Simone shrugged, pulling me up. "We need a plan, then."

"Plan, right," I hummed, mind racing. I tried to think of things, but all my mind drew was a white sheet of paper. Around me were only events – Chad resigning to the forest, Celeste going to the Argols, Natalie leaving because of destiny and quatra, Hesslik shifting the date. These events each seemed like their own huge issues, and there were no strings to link them, no thing to solve first to save the rest. They were all important.

But one still seemed more important than the rest.

"Save Natalie," I said. "In…*Omercronius*, less than two months, really, we have to find out how to prove her wrong on destiny and the danger of quatra."

Simone nodded, her gaze shifting back to her computer. She flipped it back to the top of Hesslik's news feed, scanning the article there. "Have you got any ideas on where to start with that?"

"None," I whined. "Maybe Chad was right, maybe I should be using my time more wisely."

***

I waited in the doctor's office. My arm was killing me today – my first night of sleep in my own bed caused me to toss and turn over the inflamed thing, enraging it.

If my arm was broken, then – I theorised – it might be the end of the Suneva people. Simone was quick to point out that my conclusion was weirdly dramatic, but I stood by it. If I was the only person convinced to prove to the White Witch that destiny is bullshit, quatra is fine, and that the Suneva are worth saving, then I was the only person capable of saving us all. With my arm in pain, my ability to do *anything* with quatra had been squashed. I could barely connect to the air, or feel the fullness in carbon without my left arm. If this injury took more than a month to heal, the Suneva would be lost.

Time didn't move in doctor's waiting rooms, in fact, it seemed to have no meaning in these frighteningly *sanitised* places. Minutes were but a metric of mere humans, no quarrel for doctors. Fifteen minutes late was practically on time for a cosmic being who spent six years in university to look at the sick and broken all day – yet moving your appointment in any time under a day in advance was a blasphemy to their grace. When the doctor finally did come for me, I was met with a smug smile, a grin which did not apologise for the twenty wasted minutes I'd spent in the hellish white boredom-scape, and a grin which did not give grounds for the tardiness. I was sat in the pedestrian chair by the doctor's swivelling, black lounge on wheels. He regarded me with sterile happiness.

It was with an odd glee that he had me perform painful movements – all through which he took genuine joy in examining my grimaces. It was a dance in vain, too, for his conclusion was one of "bad bruising, likely to go down in a week or two", but his proclamation was "I can't see enough with my eyes to be sure, go and get an ultrasound and an X-ray."

This was a mission that sent me across town, on what was admittedly a sunny and vibrant summer afternoon, if only to spite my mood. The next office also had a waiting room, which managed to be whiter and even more sanitary than the doctor's, as if they dunked the building in bleach between guests. I wasn't sure what to make of the radiologist's drab and uninspired conduct as she lathered my bare shoulder in cold, strange goop, but I soon found that she just had distaste for her job, like all good people did.

"Lots of bruising," she mumbled, her eyes scanning a monitor which was hidden from my view. "Doesn't look like ligament damage here. Move your arm up like this...okay, there's something."

"What is it?" I asked, trying to peer around to see the monitor. She threw out a second palm to hold me steady.

"Minor tear," she said. "Do you feel it when I go over here?"

Pain shot all throughout my shoulder. My arm tensed and tingled. I gasped as my connection to the elements felt severed by the touch.

"I'd say that's a yes," she said. "I'd recommend you see a physio about it. It's not too serious, but you'd want to take care of it well."

"How long do you think it will hurt like this?" I asked.

"Wait for the bruising," she told me. "In about a week it should go down, and you'll know just how bad that tear is."

"Great," I sighed.

There was an X-ray after that, and to complete the day I had to return to my original doctor to view the results. I lugged myself back across town, the afternoon sun beating hot and in the eyes. The doctor, with his smug face and joy in the inhumane, was surprised to see me back so soon, but confirmed that there were no breaks. I would be okay.

"You're lucky," he told me. "Rest up, and spend your time wisely."

Spend my time wisely. Why were reminders of Chad's words hidden in everything? It was almost as if I could hear the sands of time ticking down the hourglass drain. No movement I could do was fast enough for the world. Now I was confined to *wait and see* how things turned out.

The next morning, spent at the physiotherapist, had me doing the same painful routine like a monkey for yet another expert. In each instance, the pain of this tear was excruiciating. It drowned my quatra sensations of the world, yet somehow yearned for the energy itself. Boekidin had mentioned using quatra to heal when he spoke to Natalie – maybe my body was trying to do that.

The physio showed me what to do, laying out about half-an-hours' worth of elastic-band work a day for the next week. It will take over a month to heal, he told me. I probably wouldn't move without *any* pain for a good three months.

The prospect broke me. At least three months of average connection of my soul to the surrounding world. That would be it for the Suneva, probably. Natalie and Hesslik would lead them to their demise, unless Simone and I could somehow bring the White Witch back without using any significant amount of quatra at all. It seemed lost.

I needed a solution, and so I went to see the most powerful witch I could reach – a witch who could have seen Natalie's gradual ideological demise and who might help me fight it; a witch who could help me use quatra to heal – if it could be done at all. I went to the house of Tess Floros – Natalie's Yamiste.

Natalie's father, Nick, answered the door, and the surprise on his face brought a realisation to mine.

He had no idea I was home.

"James," he quizzed, then stepped out of the door, peering past me. "You're all home."

I turned white, freezing on his doormat. My face melted off my skull, unsure of what to make itself. I hadn't prepared anything to say to this man.

"Yes, *I'm* home," I said.

"*You're* home?"

"Natalie is not," I squirmed, and the glance of confusion he gave me did not ease me in the slightest.

"What's going on?" He asked. "Where *is* Natalie?"

"Maybe we should take a seat inside," I suggested, gesturing towards the couch. Now his face turned white and his body red.

"She's not dead!" I blurted, catching his concern, then coughed. "If that's what you thought."

"It's one thing…" Nick caught himself, then gestured me in. "Sit. Tell me what's happened."

I followed his hand, coming to sit on a black leather couch by the front bay window. I lowered myself onto it, sinking far further into the couch than I'd have though possible. Nick took a seat across the coffee table from me, and Tess Floros next to him. She brought us coffees as she came to sit, but I couldn't bring myself to reach for it from the depths of the black leather.

"Just be honest with me, James," Nick instructed as he sipped the coffee. He read my pale face, my body an open book. "You won't get in trouble for anything you admit. I just want whatever truth you're too afraid to tell."

"Afraid isn't the right word, really," I stammered. "It's just…a lot." And all at once I lunged for the coffee, holding it in my hands and taking its warmth. I glanced to Tess – the old Lilawelle Menas. She put me at ease – my discussions of Suneva story aspects wouldn't go over her head, she could back me up.

"Natalie is a Suneva. Did you know that?" I squawked to mister Athanas, and he nodded.

"That's obvious by now," he said.

"Oh good," I sighed, "because I thought I was going to have to go through the whole story of what a Suneva was and my god that would take a lot of…" He was staring at me to hurry up, as was Tess. "…time." I gulped. "Look, to put a long story short, she's incredibly, incredibly powerful. She's the new White Witch, after your mother in law." He glanced at Tess then back to me. "And she didn't think she could handle the power, because she almost killed her cousin Christina with a white bolt of quatra..."

"Excuse me?" He asked, sitting further along the couch's edge, bearing over me.

"She didn't know it was Christina at the time... your daughter isn't crazy."

"Right."

"Anyway, Natalie had a crisis because apparently your ex-wife abandoned her when it was apparent Natalie was a powerful Suneva..."

Nick shot me a severe glance, his hand grasping at his coffee mug. I coughed under the stress of it. "Look, I know this sounds bad. She ran off. That's it. She got so scared of herself that she ran off to Mount Olympus to help a powerful Suneva get rid of all of the Suneva."

"She...okay." He placed the coffee cup down. He rubbed his face with his hands. "Did you...try to stop her?"

"I ran after her, but I couldn't stop her even if I found her. She's the most powerful Suneva in existence right now."

"My daughter?" He snuffed, then shook his head. "Right." Nick stood, coffee firmly in hand. He couldn't stop his head from shaking. His mouth grinned as if the whole thing was funny. "Jesus, now I know why Elenna didn't want this Suneva shit in the house. Now it's very clear." And he rounded the coffee table, refusing to look Tess or myself in the eye. "I'm going outside. I need a moment."

The back door was shut gently behind him, and I expected to hear a muffled scream, but there was only silence in the house. Slowly, I turned to Tess Floros. Her face was neither unimpressed nor disappointed.

"You knew she was the *Ocras Quatrona*, didn't you?" I asked her.

"Yes," Tess nodded. "I knew it before Natalie even knew she was a Suneva. What I didn't expect was how quickly she would gain power. Do you understand how many years of intense training and reflection it took me to produce a white bolt?"

"I have no idea," I shrugged. "Fisira seemed to do it quickly, too."

"Twenty years, James," Tess said. "Fisira was possessed, those bolts were directly from Amasos, that doesn't count."

"Twenty years?" I gawked, sinking into the couch. "Natalie's only been training for what, one year?"

"I have been worried for her soul," Tess said gravely, "to gain such power, it's not right."

"Natalie was worried too. It's why she ran. She was afraid of possession, of losing control to the cosmic force. She was afraid of destiny. To get her back, I have to solve those concerns, but I don't know how to do it."

"That's because it can't be done, James," Tess sighed, shaking her head. "If I was a young Suneva I'd be joining Hesslik too."

"You would?" I quizzed, confused. "With your whole life in retrospect, being so connected to the quatra field and so involved in Suneva politics, you'd have gotten rid of that identity entirely?"

"Yes," she said, and sipped a long drag from her mug. "It's frightening to possess such a powerful soul in one's body. Losing control of it feels like losing your humanity, and it's happened many times. I never feel safe, and I'd have long ago given up the power."

"I see," I gulped, but had a rebuttal. "But that can't be true. You taught Natalie to be a Suneva, but you had to have known what she'd become."

"I taught Natalie because *you* went and showed her a ghost who told her who she was."

"Oh…right…"

"It wasn't an easy decision to teach her, but it was better than letting her chase the answers herself and losing control of her humanity."

"I see the conundrum," I mumbled. "Surely, then, I could convince Natalie just to take her own thread? Then she could be happy, and we could face Hesslik."

Tess shook her head, leaning away from the conversation. "You won't stop Hesslik now," she said. "He has too much support. Other Suneva fear your group, they wouldn't follow you against Hesslik. Especially if the White Witch removes her thread."

"And what if we had the Legendaries?"

"Barely any Suneva believe they exist…"

"But Vectra showed up at Hesslik's New Year's party."

"Magnetism," Tess shrugged. "If you presented the three Legendaries together, people might believe you're glory seekers, or tyrants."

"What about the Code of Connections?" I grumbled, growing frustrated. "*You're* the one who said it might prove useful."

"It *is* useful, for self-introspection and understanding," Tess said. "It helped you find yourselves, and now you're stronger, wiser Suneva. Wiser *people*, too."

"But...but...I refuse to believe we just wasted the better part of a year chasing Legendaries."

If things hadn't already crumbled around me, I could feel them crumbling again. Our search, our protection of Nick and Amalie, my injury, the loss of my friends. We'd found ourselves, and we'd each found that we needed to be in a different place when our cohesion mattered most. It didn't even matter whether the Legendaries joined us: if they joined us, we were glory hunters and madmen, if they joined Hesslik, he was the destined ruler many believed he was.

"You've wasted nothing. There was progress," Tess snapped to my objection. "I'd spend your remaining time wisely."

And there it was again, that urge to join Chad and dance with the forest pixies. Three months of carefree Sunevahood before it all ended. That was too bleak to face.

"I did come here for something else, too," I spoke, and Tess' harshness seemed to shift, from disapproval to indifference.

"What do you want to know?"

"I injured myself while fighting Boekidin. He seemed to suggest to Natalie that quatra could be used to heal, but I'm not sure how to do it. Could you teach me?" She hummed, some consideration ticking in her mysterious mind. "I'll never get my 'time spent wisely' if I can't feel normal."

"Yes, that's true," she nodded, relaxing. "But it is dangerous to rely on quatra to heal."

"Why is that?" I asked, and Tess stood. She circled around the couch to come to my back, and I craned my head stupidly to follow her.

"Because you are vulnerable, and your body will like using the quatra to heal itself. If you do not control your quatra consumption when you are weak, you may open yourself to possession or control by the black hole."

411

I gulped, and the old lady mashed her palm into my left shoulder. I yelped in pain, biting my lip.

"It also teaches your pathways that it is okay to accept such high levels of quatra, and it will leave your soul susceptible to any future attacks Omercronius might make on it. Destiny might sway you severely."

"And the benefits?" I eeked, still reeling at she felt for some connection in the wound.

"You will get over an injury of this size quickly. I can feel the quatra pooling here already. If you draw the energy to the region yourself, you can meditate on, and *control*, this flow. I would recommend that."

"And how do I do that?" I asked. Tess raised an eyebrow – she'd clearly never had to spoon-feed a Suneva through such basic witchcraft.

"Draw quatra like you might usually, just to your pain instead of your hands or connections," she chuffed. "It's quite easy. But whatever you do, don't spend time in your *alis*. You can't heal whilst in that body."

"Thank you," I said, and finally she let go, allowing me to stand. I'd gotten my answers, I'd seen how grim my situation was with convincing Natalie to come back, I was keen to leave. "Thank you for your time."

"You're welcome," Tess said, and grabbed my arm to halt me. "My words today have been harsh truths. Take the path you see right, but heed my warnings."

"I will," I said, "but if you don't mind me asking; why did you help Kuvalik if you don't like being a Suneva?"

"I do like Suneva," she said. "Kuvalik wanted to spread information and teachings when the time was right. Ideally, I believe that Suneva should be taught properly how to control such power, and not be left to die. Ultimately, it's easier to have no Suneva than it is to teach them all how to respect great power."

"Well said," I noted. "Then why not join Hesslik yourself?"

"Because I'm too old, and between you and me…" She looked around, then whispered in my ear. "…He's not a good boy."

"No, he's not," I smiled, and journeyed towards the door. I wasn't sure of my options now – but there would be time to think in mediation. If Hesslik was unstoppable, the crowd unswayable, and Natalie stuck to the convictions of her grandmother, then any task I had ahead would be rough. I still had my conviction to bring Natalie home, but saving the Suneva was another task all together, and neither was going to be easy.

As I rounded the front gate, a hand pulled me around. Nick had me by the shoulder, and his eyes were pleading.

"Mr Athanas…" I coughed, shaken from my restless thought.

"How do I find her?" He asked. I frowned.

"I don't think you can convince her to come home," I said. "She thinks she's saving people."

Nick rolled his eyes. "Bloody, Suneva *shit*," he grumbled.

"I know," I agreed, "it's insane. It's a whole other world." I'd struck some chord, because he nodded along with me.

"I'll find her, and I'll convince her to come home," I said. "I think she got hit by too many truths at once. I'll get her back, I promise."

He frowned to my suggestion, "just give me an address of where she's gone to, mate. I'll get police on it."

"Or that…too." I laughed nervously. I wasn't sure how much the Police could do against the White Witch, but I humoured him, handing over an approximate address for the castle. No force could stop the powerful Zamelle Menas, only reason. I had to find that reason.

Chapter 41
The Visionary

"I don't get how you can avoid me for a whole day," Mum shook her head as I came through the door. It was true, although not by my own trying. I'd been out the previous day chasing doctors down around town, coming home when Mum had already left to head out for the night. This morning I'd gone early to the physiotherapist, and missed her before work. It was only now, in the afternoon as I prepared to meditate, that I'd caught her.

"It's just as bad as Simone said it was, holy hell James. What did you go and do this time?"

I wasn't prepared for this conversation, even though I should have been. I'd been so caught up thinking about healing and Natalie, that I'd forgotten the wrath of my mother.

"It's fine," was all I had to say, which turned the woman's face red.

"It's fine? *Mate*, you tore your shoulder, *funculo*. You promised me that you knew what you were doing. When you came home from Europe early, clearly disturbed by *something*, you told me to just trust you. How can I trust you now, James? Did you *intend* for this to happen?"

"It was an accident," I said, "but I knew what I was walking into when I left."

"Oh, you did?" Mum quizzed, standing tall over me as I shrunk into the couch. "So, you know something is dangerous enough to injure you, you weigh up that risk, and you go head first into it?"

"I didn't have a choice."

"I don't even want to *know* what the alternative was, then, if *this* was the only way out," she scorned, and I shrunk further. I didn't have grounds to stand on here. This whole situation seemed familiar, although now, more than ever, I needed to stand my ground.

"I don't know what to say, Mum," I said, "but I can't give up now. I'm going to need you to just trust that I can deal with this."

"No," she said. "I can't trust your judgement anymore."

"I'm sorry, then, but…"

"There is no *but*, not this time," she said, and the air in the room seemed to pause. "No more of this Suneva business. None of it."

"I…but…"

"No, I won't have it." Mum drove her point further. "You *don't* know what you're getting into, and if you *do*, then your sense of judgement is severely lacking, James. No more."

"But, I need to get Natalie back home!" I blurted, and Mum furrowed her face.

"Natalie ran off?"

"She found problems with destiny and control over her soul. Ran off to join the guy we've been working against. I have to at least go out and bring her home."

"Destiny, and the soul…" Mum chuffed, crossing her arms. "It's like you're speaking another language these days. Where did my James go?"

"I am. It's called Liktan," I folded my arms to follow.

"And where has she run off to?"

"Greece," I said.

"Oh, Greece again," Mum groaned, turning away, stalking off down the hall. "I didn't even *ask* what happened on that trip. I won't, and I won't ask about this one. I don't need to know, but James, there will be no more of it!"

"But Natalie…"

"There are authorities designed for that, James! Missing person's units, *police*, those with authority. You're not a hero, James. You're an idiot. Sit-down…" I was already sitting, practically all the way through the couch at this point, "shut up, and get a job. This is real life. If all of the Suneva threads go soon like you've claimed to me, you'll be better for it. Christ." And she plucked Errol off the front couch, producing the lead from the front door and dragging him out of the house. The air finally shifted, ruffling in its usual eddies, and I sat in my pain.

My heart was thumping, my adrenaline running. Every force around me was *yelling* the point that my last-effort plans would be fruitless, worthless, that I should not attempt anything but sitting down and idling by. But I could not do that. There was still a spark of my soul edging me on, despite the hopelessness.

Despite my mother's wishes.

That hurt. Was I ready to betray my mum? To keep adventuring, even though it truly *was* insane, even if the danger was now *beyond* what I knew? I'd be potentially facing Hesslik, his armies, and the White Witch as just the rag-tag team of myself and my sister. Did Mum even know that Simone was involved in this?

Whatever, I grumbled. I couldn't think about that yet, now I had to rest to get better.

"Mum wasn't happy about that," Simone said, and I jumped in surprise – I hadn't even realised she was home.

"*Cheese*, Simone…" I wheezed. "No, she's not."

"You're not deterred, are you?"

"A little," I admitted. Simone came to sit by me, but I didn't turn to look at her; moving still hurt. "Tess Floros won't join us – I didn't even bother asking. I *could* get assistance from LeGrand if I wanted, just to avoid leaving the house to keep Mum happy, but he'd have enough to deal with, what with Argol's loss of his thread. I don't think there's anything I *can* do right now. Tess told me to rest, and I guess that's what I need."

Simone huffed, but nodded. "That's fair," she said, "but annoying. You're the only Suneva right now who's convinced of Hesslik's plans and willing to do anything useful. I know we can't butter up Mum over that..."

"No, we cannot," I chuffed.

"But we've got to try. You've found two Legendaries, I trust that you can find almost anything you seek by now."

"Thanks," I smiled. These were strange words from Simone – the girl who under a month ago I could have sworn would tear out my eyes if she knew of my identity.

"How long will healing take?" She asked.

"I'm not sure. Hopefully no more than two weeks."

Simone frowned, serious. "Let's hope." And she got up, making her way into the study. "I'll see if I can find us anything useful. You focus on getting better."

"Thanks, dude," I called, and then readied myself on the couch. Any moment now, I'd be meditating. Any moment.

Any moment.

It had been so long since I'd mentally let go like this; and I'd never done it with a dull, throbbing ache tearing at my consciousness. I'd accumulated many memories of curling my leg's up on Kuvalik's floor, the ghost circling about me as I expanded my soul into its surrounds. I remembered the many frustrated sessions there with the old King, where I couldn't connect at all, and the frustration it caused me that Natalie was so advanced.

But I'd come a long way since then. Now I could throw myself from buildings and tear at the air flows on my body, gliding and soaring through the skies. I could kick myself high off jets of air, and form diamonds from the atmosphere. Simply using my power to manipulate my body was second nature. The quatra flowed through me not by my special demand, but by the fact that I now always let it flow, because I might need to use it so casually at any time.

I drew quatra to the wound, imagining the grips of my soul pooling there as thick slime. My connections grew as I did this, pushing themselves alongside the pain to the forefront of my mind. The quatra made warm my bruises, setting the tear alight. The pain was soothing, however, like the stretching of a sore muscle. It was the kind of pain which made you feel that achieving it was only helping.

"James," an old, wise voice pierced my concentration. I opened my eyes to see the black, sliming ghost of Kuvalik standing over me. I peered around, and saw that I was sitting on the floor of his bedroom.

"Kuvalik," I greeted, but my smile soured to his sight. The ghost's purple veins oozed like sludge under the black, transparent veil of his body, quatra erupting from the surface like volcanic pimples. His apparition wavered and whined as it tried to form an existence. I tried to say something more, but couldn't form any other emotion than horror and disgust.

"James," his voice said again. A pus-filled sore exploded onto my face. I slapped myself in the head desperately to claw the goo from my skull. "Don't lose hope James. You still have my memory…"

A sword cut cleanly through the figure – a machete through a black sheet. It *just* scraped past my nose to jam into the floorboards. The two halves of Kuvalik held at first, then comically came untwined, fluttering down to the ground peacefully like drifting paper. Red-hot blood spewed from the split, and my eyes followed the halves down as they fell. They drifted into a large, bottomless pit in the floor, on the other side of which the figure wielding the sword came into view.

The two black halves descended peacefully into the darkness.

Before me, across the steadily increasing gap in the floor, was a crazed Hesslik. His shoulders were broad, and over them hung a cape with the black sun symbol which fluttered in the wind. The quatra in his eyes was red instead of cyan, and he laughed with the squeal of a girl. Blood dripped off his sword and into the hole.

Behind Hesslik, from down the recognisable hallway, shone a bright, white light. Hesslik became a black silhouette in front of this holy glow, his massive shadow casting me in darkness. The blood on his sword glistened as the source of the light advanced. It was a brilliant white – pure and true, like the soul of the divine. As the light came closer, I could see the source in the shape of a T and an arrow – Zamelle. The White Witch pulled to a halt behind Hesslik, then pushed him aside to engulf the entire doorway.

Blinding white light was thrown into the room, so bright that I had to raise my hand and peek between closed fingers. I could just make out Zamelle's hand held to me, and her pearly glow drew me closer, it *begged* me to take her hand. I shuffled across the floor, the endless pit now gone as if it were never there, to grab

417

her long and wretched claw. Its fingers were drawn twice as long and sharp as normal. They were black too – just shadows against the glow of Amasos which shone through her eyes.

As I reached for her hand it turned on me. Her palm aimed towards my eyes.

"It's only destiny," she said to me, "it's nothing personal. I can't fight it."

A bolt of steaming hot, white quatra ejected from her hand and into my face, and the force of it threw my ragdoll body backwards. The waves of energy rushed over my body as I span – and I kept spinning, never hitting the floor behind me. Then my feet struck some ground – some grainy surface which I dug them into, gaining my balance. The slurry of quatra continued coursing over my face and head, but was now a constant pressure all around. I opened my eyes, and rather than being blinded, found that I stood in a sea. I pulled my feet from the bed of it, launching myself to the surface.

I drew a sharp, needed breath. All around me the water sloshed and churned, with no end in sight.

I heard a swell, and before I could even turn to see it in full, a ten-foot wave was crashing over my head. I plunged back into the water to dive under, but the churning force of it pulled and tossed me along.

I searched for the air to find an 'up', but there was no air for my soul to find. Panicked, I threw myself against gravity, and found myself at the surface once more. I held my head out of the angry sea, to see the backs of rolling waves as they crawled away.

And that only meant that another was coming from behind.

I felt its tug before I turned, but this time I was prepared. I kicked off quickly, diving through its centre, and emerging on the other side to face a great set of tidal breakers, all headed for me.

And beyond them, the shore. The waves, strangely, seemed to originate from the sands, rolling out past me and into the great ocean. The beach beyond the strange water was made of huge sand dunes, with rocky cliffs jutting from beyond the horizon. Cutting through the immediate landscape, capturing my attention, was a pyramid-like temple. A façade of sand and dust flew off its walls in the harsh sea wind. The sun was caught in the structure's dull, greenish stone.

I decided to swim towards the shore. The rips of coming waves would pull me in, and the force of their mass would push me back as I dove through them. I couldn't feel the ground, so I couldn't kick off to get any further. My arms quickly became tired and my legs couldn't keep their pace. I was moving nowhere – after each wave I dove through were the same amount to come, and the temple stayed just as far away, if not further. Swimming against the waves was the wrong approach, there had to be something else I could do.

But it was hard enough just to stay afloat. The sea had a vengeance, and I was trapped in its tumultuous grip. I was gasping and flailing for air with each dive, reaching for the shore-side temple. In its penthouse chamber I could make out a figure standing in the sun. They wore the blue and green robes of a Vochduh monk. I pushed down on the water to try and get a better view, but wash kept rolling into my eyes and mouth. I spluttered at the image of an ancient man.

"You cannot struggle with the tide," the monk said; his voice carrying clearly to me. "You're in too deep, Kuvalik. This is not your time."

"I am Maiki," I spluttered defiantly. "Kuvalik is dead!"

"Is he?" The monk chortled.

The sea churned. It bubbled and spat and roared as the waves grew taller, they turned tumultuous. The waves crashed and rolled around me on the wobbling ocean surface. I flailed for my life, but couldn't stay afloat as a monument of water crashed onto my head. I was sent spinning into the abyss. I could only feel water all around, not even a sense of gravity to find my way. I would drown.

I could not breath, and somewhere in my body a clock ticked. My vision was black, my ears were filled with the sound of violent, churning waters and bubbles racing past my face. I felt my own death impending, and wondered *what now?* My consciousness came to a close, the sensation of black imposing on every sense I had. All was silenced.

Then I took a breath.

I scrambled backwards on my couch, tearing at it with my clawing hands. My left arm throbbed as I realised it definitely should have. I tweaked the muscle by pulling myself up, which hurt, and I involuntarily grappled at it. The whole slab of my back was white hot and sweaty, the couch behind it wet. I could feel no immediate difference due to my meditation, but surely, I expected that. The region cooled down as I calmed myself and regained a footing in reality.

"Sweet *cheese*," I uttered to myself, still with too many questions. I glanced through the kitchen at the clock to see that three hours had passed. I jolted at the implication of that too. It's not like I had anywhere to be, but that amount of time did not seem like three hours.

I decided to call Tom and invite myself over to his house for a little while. I needed to get my mind off what I had just seen.

***

I'd only been a Suneva for a year, and so much had changed in that time. Hanging out with Tom, though, made it feel like maybe I could just go back to regular life if I wanted.

Sure, the dynamic between us was different now. I noticed it as soon as I walked into his house, that shift to his demeanour, the way he held himself more guarded. He was suspicious of me, but it didn't get in the way of our fun, and for the purpose of clearing my mind of visions, I didn't care.

We played snooker in his bunker room, chatting shit about life, girls, and dreams. Tom had made it into a prolific technical university, he'd go on this year to become an electrical engineer. I'd been so delayed by my running around as a Suneva that I didn't even *have* a future life vision beyond stopping Hesslik. What would I do with myself when this was over? That future, whichever way it went, was only a few months away.

Halfway through laughing my guts up at some comedy show Tom and I had put on whilst we ate, I came to a strange state of peace with inaction. I had a duty to Natalie, sure, but to the Suneva? It had only been my life for a year. My friendship to Natalie and to Celeste, only a year long. My friendship with Chad just less so. But Tom, my life, and my direction? These were things that had lasted much longer than a short phase. Maybe it was time to let go of my Suneva friends, of my Sunevahood. Although I was sure I'd want to find Celeste someday – there was a fling to continue, and she was hot.

If I never got better, and never stopped the Suneva thread-death, maybe life wouldn't be so bad after all. Mum might have been right.

***

420

I was struggling to sleep peacefully that night, as I had struggled on previous nights with my arm. It was impossible to get the lame thing into my favourite sleeping position, and when I did doze off, I'd roll onto it funny and jerk myself awake in pain. I just laid perfectly still, hoping for the best.

I heard a noise, a creak of some kind. The house was old, and always groaned and growled like that, but the sound came again, and it had more force than a restless home. Neither Mum nor Simone were home, and with Errol outside, my interest was piqued.

It banged again, rapidly, rhythmically, footsteps across the length of the house. I pulled the covers up to my cheeks, my eyes wide behind the linen armour. They came from the attic space. *Huge possums, that'll be it,* I nervously laughed to myself. They were followed then by the sound of fumbling metal, some kind of hook or latch, and finally a sound that I knew well.

The attic trapdoor clunked as it pressed out from its frame.

I paused, drawing a breath so sharp and full that I silenced the room. Not a speckle of carbon danced under my fingertips. I waited for any confirmation – I'd like to believe I'd imagined it, that…

BANG!

The stairs from the trapdoor crashed into the floor. Errol growled and howled from behind the back door of the house. I could barely hear him beyond the wild beating of my heart. I pulled the doona up further, as if I could force this to be a nightmare if I just slept through it, but everything was real – this was no vision. I waited for further footsteps – the foul groan of each dying rung of the ladder, but none came. A ceasefire had fallen.

Now I could be brave.

Slowly, I worked my way out of the bed, into the warm night with just my underwear on. I went to summon my staff, flicking my left wrist only to yelp in pain. The arm refused the movement, but weirder still, I couldn't draw my staff. It refused to come, even as I felt it under my skin. I hadn't tried to draw it since my fall, and maybe I couldn't until I got better. This was no time to discover this kind of pitfall, so I took my drastic action. I let the armour of Maiki course over my body, and as it finally locked into place and my pain subsided, I drew that staff for which I had been searching.

I palmed my door open, coming into the small hallway. I found the sliding door into the main hall slightly ajar, moonlight seeping through the crack. I reached for it, and paused with my fingers around it, searching for another noise, connecting to the air in the next room.

There was no sound, and I could sense no movement. I felt for carbon, too, and could not connect to any unexpected centres of it. I must have just been imagining noises – dreaming with quatra – but I still had to check it out. More confident now, I pushed the door aside and came into the main hallway.

The trapdoor was open, the ladder stretched from the floor to the attic. I was shocked frozen, staring, as if going back towards my room wasn't an option. I stared whilst my brain swam for an explanation.

There was another footstep. It rung out overhead, directly above where I stood, and the next came closer to the trapdoor. Dust tricked from the ceiling in the place of the bootprints as they fell, sauntering towards the open trapdoor.

I had swallowed my brain, not able to run, simply embracing my staff and grappling it with both hands. I held it ready to strike, when the last footfall approached the ladder.

And the first foot landed on it.

The creak from the rung was harrowing – loud and piercing. The foot on it was the pure black of a shadow. The second foot landed and creaked just the same. Although, in my frozen stare, I realised that I could see *through* the feet and legs to the rungs behind.

The black body descended, a sharp, pointed being emerging from the attic, the black silhouette of something else. And when it turned to face me, I locked my green eyes with its which glowed teal. There was a ghost in my attic.

I knew it! I would have celebrated, but I was too frightened to even move. The sensation of this ghost was so familiar. I could feel it through my palms, this connection I shared with its gaze. Every time I'd been alone in the attic, I'd felt it. But it was familiar from some other place, too. I couldn't pin it down.

The ghost flinched as it turned to face me, and backed into the ladder. I jumped back at its movement, baring my staff.

"A Suneva?" The ghost chuffed. "Who are you? Why are you in my house?"

422

"This is my house...ghost..." I stammered nervously. How pompously was one meant to address a ghost? All of my experience with the paranormal seemed to melt out of my brain, leaving me stranded and defenceless. "Who are you?"

"I am Muhrakiin," it boomed. "Why have you trespassed my house?"

"Muhrakiin?" I coughed. "Hesslik's dead right-hand man? You lived here?"

"*Kuvalik's* right hand man," the ghost grumbled. "I have little to say to Hesslik."

"Right, Kuvalik's man..." There was a nudge to my consciousness, some memory that couldn't break through. "Huh."

"Who are you?" The ghost boomed, breaking my ponder. "Who invades my house?"

"Maiki!" I stuttered quickly, grappling at my blade. *"Maikess Kiin."*

"Maiki?" The ghost quizzed, then its eyes grew wide. "Simone?"

"Simone?" I grumbled. "No, it's James, but how did you know that Simone was meant to be Maiki?"

"James..." the ghost stepped towards me. "What year is it? When are we?" and the compassion in the ghosts' voice, I knew it immediately. It had been so long, but I remembered this voice.

I fell to my knees, my armour fading away. "Dad?"

"Yes, of course it's me," he said. "Who else died here?"

"Any Suneva," I said, yelling. I had so many emotions, they all pushed for release, and my mouth couldn't handle to organise them. "Who the hell knew you were Muhrakiin, or a Suneva at all?" I lunged at the dark figure, following every compulsion to hug it back to life, but I fell through the shadow, smacking into the ladder with a crunch. My arm screamed in pain, but I ignored it.

"Don't think that works, mate," he chuckled, and I gagged a laugh through my tears.

"I love you," I said to him, the only thing to say. "I can't believe my last words to you were an argument. I can't believe I get the chance to make it right. I can't believe this. I let you die when I couldn't save you..."

"I love you too, James," the ghost glowed and emitted its love. I could feel it emanating through the quatra field, despite my injury and terrible connection.

"It's not your fault I passed, that much was inevitable and my fault, really. And I'm sorry I got mad over nothing that night, but you know how it is when you come home from work and there's shit all over the house, and…"

"I know, Dad," I said. "Why didn't you come back before this, if you can do it now?"

"I've been trapped in the between-place," Dad explained. "I don't know what it is, but the Vochduh used to write about it, and they called it the *Void*. I think I've been anchored here in the house, but I've been roaming that place looking for a way back. It's just a desert with a playback reel of every wrongdoing, every joy, every spark of destiny you've ever had, all bombarding you. I don't think I could deal with that for eternity."

"How'd you get out?"

"I found what I needed to do when I came back," he said. "I realised it was possible when I saw you in there with me. It was brief, but you were swimming, yelling to me."

Had I connected to Dad in a vision? I couldn't think of when, now. My brain was swimming instead.

"Now I'm back, and ready to do what I need to."

"What is it?" I asked. "Let me help you…"

"No, no, not just yet," he urged, and I calmed. "Although I fear that my time here is limited, I want to hear more about you, about Simone, and your mother.

"Okay," I sobbed. "Just…stay here forever. I have too much to ask."

"I'll try," he said.

"Mum and Simone will be home soon!" I remembered, bouncing to life. "If you stick around…"

"I'll try, I'll try, really," he smiled. "Tell me though, you're Maiki and not Simone, how did that happen?"

"How did you know Maiki was meant to be Simone?" I asked, and took a seat on the floor before the black figure, if only because my emotional state kept me from standing. Dad joined me, sitting upon the rung of the ladder behind him.

"Well, *Maiki* is a female Suneva name…"

"It *is*?"

"The Liktan masculine would be Maikiin."

"Great…"

"But Lilawelle told me. I don't know if you've ever met Tess Floros before, I'm very close with her, the White Witch."

"Her granddaughter is the new White Witch," I explained. "There's…there's a lot to the last year."

"How long have I been dead, again?" He asked.

"Two years, Dad. It's been just over two years."

"God, I made it through two years in that void?" He coughed.

"Anyway, Simone and Maiki?" I urged him on.

"Right, yes, time is of the essence," he hummed. "Lilawelle sensed Simone's destiny. How did you become Maiki?"

"Salak Kuul told me that I stole her thread when it hit," I said, and Dad's face soured to the demon's mention. My mind turned with his change, remembering my outrage at learning the truths behind my childhood haunting. I'd apologised to Dad and told him I loved him, but there were answers to come from him, answers that I hadn't realised I could now receive.

"You met with Salak Kuul?" He asked sheepishly.

"You sold me to a demon!" I accused, my past anger bubbling forth.

"I sold myself to a demon, James," Dad protested, although he sighed to keep restraint. "I let him take my energy, right up until I couldn't go on anymore."

"And you obeyed Kuvalik when he told you to let it feed on me."

"It was a hard decision to make, James," Dad pleaded. "There was a dangerous splinter of Argols on our doorstep when it started, the energy you gave Kuul helped us put them behind bars. They were going to kill our family, but you saved us."

"How did that blend into Kuvalik's plans?" I asked. "The torment lasted for years, not for an arrest."

"I was taking care of the Argols in those plans," Dad explained, "and I told the demon to stop after that single incident. I wasn't aware that he disobeyed me until you showed signs of depression. Finding out what he was continuing to do to you, that was my last straw, and I moved us away."

"Fine, fine." The answer was what it was – Dad had knowingly let Kuul into the family home. He had done it, and that couldn't be undone. "That's why I get it now, I just needed to hear your side."

425

"I'm sorry James," Dad sighed. "There were many things I had to risk, many hard decisions to make. I knew you would be strong enough – and that was beyond Kuvalik's reasoning to save Simone's image of the Suneva. You were *strong*, and you always have been the strongest young man I know."

The weight of the compliment slammed into me, and despite my disgust, and without being charmed by the excuse, I felt my heart beating faster.

"You did?" I asked.

"Why wouldn't I have?" He seemed confused.

"Because…well…" and it was hard to keep it down, the inadequacies I'd let fester for so long living in his bootsteps. I finally could discuss them with him, it was a dream. "Because I'm not like you, *at all*," I admitted. "I'm not tough like you were, I was never able to defend myself on my own, I never had to save my siblings from danger, I never could run the fastest, swim the longest, or work the hardest. I'm just so *nothing* of a man compared to you. I can't fill your shadow, and it's weighed on me since you left. I'm not a man…really." And straining to say the last words, holding myself together in front of my idol, I sobbed. The spirit of my father chuffed, rolling its ethereal eyes, and squatted down to me.

"Don't go on with that," he ordered, and I stared him in the eyes, I followed his authority. *An authority I don't possess.* "I'm not worth ideation, James."

"You are to me."

"Oh, really?" He hummed. "A man who kept multiple secret identities from family and friends to spy between Suneva groups, who sold his son to a demon, who's temper at the mundane could let him die with animosity towards his own son because of a slightly messy kitchen? I was a temperamental, brash man, James. I'm not the man to aspire to be."

"But the *heroics*," I urged. "You're tough, and wise, and caring."

"What heroics? What, me standing up for my sisters?"

I nodded to the suggestion.

Dad sighed, "I grew up in a tough suburb where every second kid's Dad was an alcoholic. I didn't want to be rough, but you had to be. It's not who I wanted to be." He sat next to me, crossing his ghostly legs. "I wish I could have grown up more like you, James. You've got this sense of justice that demands peace. You're always doing whatever you think is right and whatever makes you happy, no matter what others will think of it. You've carved yourself into only the person that *James Grey* could be, and you're so confident in doing it. I wish I could have been that."

I locked my starry eyes with his, and held back my tears to nod. I would have liked the embrace, but it wouldn't work. "Thank you, Dad," I said.

"You're welcome, James," he nodded, then looked to the sky, a brief panic striking him, before he turned back to me.

"So, you're Muhrakiin," I hummed. "You know that everybody talks about you as the last great *Kiin*?"

"I didn't know that," I chuffed, his chest puffing. "Great bloke and great *Kiin*, not a bad way to be remembered." And he leaned in to whisper closely. "Don't let everybody know this, but I was actually an awful *Kiin*. I was a great *lead* elemental, an okay translator and middleman, but air never caught on with me as well."

"*Lead*?" I asked. "What even is the Liktan word for that?"

"*Gahkess*, but it's not in my name," he tapped his temple, grinning. "Easy to mask your multiple identities when your Liktan name simply doesn't include your best connection. *Muhras* is the *Vochduh* word for lead, not that anybody else knows Vochduh. And the Liktan family name *Leukess* got mysteriously dropped as well. Couldn't have Simone connected to any of my legacies when she…or you now, I guess, found your powers."

"I have a Liktan last name?" I gawked.

"Yeah, of course. We're a *kess* family," Dad slapped the ladder. "The old *kess* line. Dedo controlled *Niskess* – that's silicon. You'd be *Maiki Leukess* if you took to the name. If you learned how to fly, you'd be the first *Leukess* since Dedo to do it."

"Shame I never really knew him," I frowned. "Now that he's living in the old-country, learning from him might be hard."

"Another excuse to travel," Dad laughed. "Take it, you should." He stared back towards the ceiling, momentarily straining as he had before.

"What's wrong?" I asked.

"I don't know I've got much more time," he said. "There is something though that I need to tell you, whilst I'm here."

"What, you mean you can't hold it?" I asked, my heart racing. "Simone and Mum could be home any minute."

427

"I know…" And he turned sharply to the door, before turning back to me. "I have something that could help you, something I meant to show Simone before I died, but it will be more useful to you."

"What is it?"

"You *should* travel to Dedo and Macedonia, because the Vochduh temples and libraries are in the hills near him, and they could help you to grow. I went travelling there when I was your age, and I translated the *Vatje na Vochduh*…"

"I've heard of that before, the *Vatje*," I recounted a vision from Kuvalik, the exchange in the garden between he and my dad.

"Good," Dad nodded. "The *Vatje* are the Vochduh moral rules, but there's more in those temples. In the void, I had some sense that I had to tell somebody about that library, that it had important information. I didn't get to translate much, but I know the other writings there will be useful."

"If the *Vatje* are the rules, then I've been wanting to see them recently," I said. "I could use them to help a friend." I thought of Natalie. Any information about *controlling* one's soul would be useful to her, and I was certain that the rules would contain that much.

"I shouldn't be surprised, but I knew you'd need them," Dad smiled tensely. "They're in your Baba's cookbook, in the back pages."

"The cookbook?" I exclaimed. "*Cheese*, we almost threw that out!"

"Well it's damn good you didn't, I might have never gotten back here otherwise," he chuffed, and stared gravely to the ceiling once more.

"Hang on longer," I urged him.

"I think this is it, James," Dad's eyes fell back to mine, and he rose to his feet. I followed.

"When will you be back?"

He shot me a guilty smile, shaking his head. "No, I mean this is *it*."

"Excuse me?" I coughed, then stared at the ceiling myself. A glowing orb was forming there, painted against the roof. It shimmered and swirled, growing larger by the blink. "No, no!"

"I got out what I needed to. That's my destiny done," he pursed his lips, and I could see the fear in the swirling quatra of his eyes.

"No, no it's not!" I said. "You've got a lot more to owe me than a cookbook and self-confidence!" I leaped onto the ladder, climbing it to the ceiling and blocking the orb with my hand. Instead, like a light shining from my dad's neck, it just drew itself on top of me. "No, no, no!"

There were footsteps coming towards the door. "Will James ever leave the light on for us? Damn it…" I heard my mum's muffled voice as she rose to the steps.

"I can't stop it," Dad said to me, drawing my attention back. "It's my final peace, I found it."

"No peace for you!" I ordered, scrambling for the front door. "What about your wife and daughter, you have to hang in for them."

"I love you, James," he said, and the light grew, casting his ethereal body in its glow. From under its lamp shade, his features turned teal – a painting of the man who had left us, standing under a streetlight, staring at the ceiling and talking to the Gods. "I can't hold on. Tell them the same as I told you. I love them, and will forever."

The light had fully engulfed him, illuminating his living image against the dark room. I threw myself at the door handle and whipped the front door open, casting teal light over Mum and Simone's faces. I fell to my ass in front of them.

Mum rose to her attitude. "James, why didn't you…"

"*Maria!*" Dad turned, awe striking his face, before his glowing apparition puffed to dust. The speckles floated, capturing the gaze of all, before flying into the light on the ceiling. The light collapsed with a rush of wind, and natural darkness returned.

Mum, her face blank, fell against the door frame. Simone stood in awe.

"I let him go again," I said, "but this time, he's really gone."

***

Mum begged no explanation from me. That night was never discussed again – a shared fever dream, something never to be mentioned.

When she left for work the next day, I explored the attic – trifling into Dad's old chest to uncover his mother's cookbook.

The attic was lighter on this day, no longer weighted by a thick atmosphere, and the constantly watching eyes. The new light was a strange disappointment – I wish I'd known that the imposition and strangle on this space was my dad's spirit. He was truly gone now, and I never realised he was here.

I pulled Baba's cookbook from the chest, splaying it over the floor. Simone had followed my commotion, rising into the attic and gathering around the book.

"It's different up here," she commented. "Less stuffy?"

"Dad's left," I said, flipping through the recipes. "It was him watching us up here."

"I wish I knew that earlier." She met my feeling, then examined the text. "Did his ghost tell you to cook?"

"No, there's more than cooking in here," I said, flipping through to the end of the book. "Dad translated ancient Vochduh texts in here. He said he has their moral codes written down, but there may be writings about the use of my abilities, too. It's important information."

"Moral codes?" Simone asked. "That sounds interesting."

"They're the basis for Hesslik's empire," I said. "Based on what got lost when Hesslik adopted them, they could be what we need to convince Natalie that Suneva can control themselves. It could also not be. I have no idea how I'll use the information."

"Let's find it first," Simone said. She watched on as I flipped through the pages.

Finally, we got to something interesting. Past the recipe for a lovely lentil soup was a page filled with Russian characters. It had a heading, which I wasn't sure that I could read, a body, which I wasn't sure that I could read, and countless other pages that I wasn't sure I could read.

"I thought you said he translated them?" Simone asked.

"I think this is *'translated'*," I said. "Translated from something we wouldn't understand into something else we wouldn't understand."

"That's useful," Simone sighed. She flipped through the book, turned it upside down, and shook it out.

"Hey!" I snuffed. "What are you…"

A smaller, thin book fell out of the protective cover. It was all but four pages folded over, stapled together, and bound in faux leather. This was the book which Dad usually kept in his work briefcase. Simone hurried to open it.

The pages were printed with Liktan characters. I recognised the title in a flash. *Na Vatje na Vochduh.*

"This still doesn't bloody help!" Simone whined. "What the hell language is this?"

"*Liktan*," I said, "the language of the Suneva."

"Why?" Simone slapped the book down.

"Maybe there's some concepts that just don't translate to English. You wouldn't lose much meaning from one Suneva language to another."

"Sure," Simone sighed. "I guess I'll leave this with you then."

"Look, let's just see if this leads anywhere," I said. "I don't know why Dad thought this would be useful to us, but we've only got a few months. Maybe we can do something with this, maybe we can't. I don't know that we can travel anywhere to share anything we find anyway. Let's give this a go."

"Sure," she agreed. "I hope it does help you with *something*. I, however, have my own idea to investigate." And she stood, making her way over to the ladder.

"Wait, you do?" I asked. "What is it? Why didn't you tell me?"

"Thought of it just this morning, when I was thinking about Dad's ghost..." she said, humming to ponder. "Natalie is afraid of destiny, but the Sunesca are all about freedom. Both being free, and having freedom from Gods. I might be able to help, but I have no idea how. I don't think freedom is something that can be transferred."

"That's very interesting," I noted. That train of thought seemed familiar, as if I'd had it before – but I couldn't have, or else I'd have started down it before now. "Where are you going?"

"I'm going to talk to Salak Kuul about it, see what he says."

"Alright, good luck," I said, waving Simone bye as she descended the ladder.

I pondered the text before me, writing it down into English with my arm whining in its dull pain. If this didn't reveal enough of what we needed to bring back Natalie and stop Hesslik, I wasn't sure where to turn. With my arm like it was, I didn't see myself travelling to Macedonia like Dad suggested, or fighting for further clues. Without Celeste, Chad and Natalie at my side, the world seemed so much larger. But Dad had given Simone and I hope, and I had to use what he'd given me.

Chapter 42
A Trip to the Bank

Boekidin walked confidently and briskly about Hesslik's castle. His claw-like feet tapped against the masonry and tilework which covered the main hallways of the impressive, restored structure. He had his hands to his side, discreetly testing the quatra field as he walked.

Boekidin felt the immediate and overwhelming spike in the field as he came closer to Hesslik's personal training dojo. The White Witch, Zamelle Menas, was in there, as was the *Fara*, Hesslik. He could sense their auras, their images dancing through the void of his mind's eye like neon serpents. Their quatra showed as ropes of vibrant colour swaying in a breeze, and reaching out to these apparitions in the field would allow him to feel the vibrations of their minds. This could allow Boekidin to speak with them, and hear their thoughts. In most cases, Boekidin did not need to enter an opponent's mind to glean the information he needed – people's intentions were often clear enough nearer the surface, even just in how they moved themselves.

"Maiki better be wrong," Boekidin hummed to himself.

Boekidin had claimed his fame as the Shiverman through his quatra abilities. There was a strange duality that he found between pure witchcraft and the abilities of a kidin. Witchcraft was the ability to manipulate one's own soul energy and read the soul energy of others. The soul and the mind were connected in all Suneva, and Boekidin knew that there could be no mastery of person-reading without understanding this.

Most Kidin needed to see their opponent to enter their mind. They had to reach out with their hand and grasp at the skull of their enemy, grabbing at space and spirituality and pulling their soul into the other's brain. It was an archaic, ancient process that few understood, but all kidin could do. Alternatively, they could broadcast their thoughts and receive the thoughts of an opponent, in a way which was equally inexplicable but easily achieved by manipulating their own soul.

Boekidin, however, had studied ancient texts and made up his own way of doing things. He savoured the image of Hesslik's aura in his vision, like a strange taste on his palette. He kept it on his tongue as he made his way back to his room.

Barricading himself within his own space, Boekidin sat to meditate upon his bed, and channelled himself through posed hands back into the quatra field. Connecting to the field all throughout the castle was simple, as Vestas had coated the wall linings with a substance designed to amplify quatra signals.

Boekidin followed the taste of Hesslik's aura through the winding field, and using his quatra to extend the influence of his soul, latched onto the vibrant serpent of Hesslik's spirit. His soul plummeted into the vast dancing colour, surfing through its body, through a tunnel of dazzling lights. He rode towards a distant blackness, a destination growing closer, and *closer*, until...

Darkness engulfed him, and Boekidin stood, opening his soul's eyes. He stood in a stone circle surrounded by a dense and green forest, somewhere deep in Hesslik's *slip*. Stone circles like these, often marked in runes, marked the entry and exit points for mind teleportation. The scenery here was admirable, a great green landscape of thickly growing forests surrounding him, a product of Hesslik's strong spirituality and introspectiveness. Hesslik had a developed soul, it appeared.

Boekidin extended his wings, letting the black, plated plumage grow to cast a shadow. In a single flap, he threw himself to the canopy and away from the stone circle, coming to perch high in the treetops. From here, the *Kidin* could see a clearing in the forest nearby, and beyond that, a metropolis encased within. The city skyline painted itself against the blue day.

Setting the direction of the settlement in his mind, Boekidin dropped to the floor and ran towards it. There was care to be taken in running not to disturb anything too greatly – the host could feel the ripples in their soul if they were attentive, and Hesslik appeared to be very connected to this spiritual forest.

Finally clearing the short stretch of scrub, Boekidin arrived in the clearing, the great city of Hesslik's mind sprawling before him, just across a no-man's land. The metropolis had high, defensible city walls – nothing as impenetrable as the minds of the Argol girls, he noted, but a formidable challenge none-the-less, designed to keep ordinary Kidin out.

Crossing the wall posed the greatest risk, and Boekidin could turn around now, if he chose. Permeating this great barrier, if done poorly, would give Hesslik the sensation of water in his ear, the fullness of the mind. Boekidin had spent his many years training to reduce the impact of the crossing, but he knew that no matter how skilfully he breached Hesslik's walls, he would start the countdown.

Once he was inside the city, Boekidin would have to sprint for the information he required, because Hesslik *would* know the feeling of a Kidin intrusion if he'd set up such strong boundaries, and he *would* come for Boekidin.

And Boekidin didn't want to know what might transpire then.

The bird-man gulped. If Hesslik was being honest, then Hesslik had nothing to fear from this intrusion. Boekidin needed to prove that his loyalty was well spent – I had dislodged his trust with my honest belief in my mad theories. Boekidin set aside his anxiety, and analysed the wall before him.

Touching it would notify Hesslik immediately of an invasion, but Boekidin couldn't scale the wall anyway – it rose to project a shimmering blue dome over the city, some sort of sensory forcefield. Generators, rising like merlons on a castle wall, pumped out the liquidous field, and below them the wall slanted back inwards, making it not only a stupid idea to climb it, but an impossibility. No guards stood sentry on it either, and Boekidin took a sigh of relief. He had no idea how Iva Argol did it, but she had guards on her walls, which were also twice as high as this and covered in smooth, unbreakable stone. Boekidin was perplexed by that girl's mental fortitude. *Daddy issues*, he had ruled it down to.

Boekidin squatted to the earth, and pawed at it. He connected to the ground at his feet, sensing for substructures which he could crawl through for entry. There was a risk that Hesslik might notice a disturbance in his city's service tunnels – the realm which simulated the subconscious, but it would be a foreign sensation to that of any ordinary Kidin. It was a promising route.

There was a single service tunnel nearby, but Boekidin wouldn't take this one – this tunnel pointing straight to the stone circle entrance point might have been a trap. Instead, he picked up his feet, and dodged between the trees of the forest ring, moving clockwise around the great city.

He squatted down again, palm to the earth, and felt for spaces therein. This was the second advantage Boekidin had above other Kidin which forced his rise as the Shiverman – Boekidin had expanded his possibilities.

The world of the *slip*, that realm containing the mind and the soul, did not follow the rules of the regular. Things here were not made of earth, air, water, or elements as we knew them, and one's ability to change the world was not limited as such. If you believed you could do it, and thought of how you could do it, then it could be done. Boekidin had spent his rise to power studying not *kidin* arts, but all quatra arts, and had found that he could emulate them in the slips of all Suneva.

It made him a fierce battle opponent, but an even fiercer invader of minds.

Boekidin had located the tunnel, just below the outermost edge of the wall, ending where the barrier receded towards the city. Connecting to the air around him, he puffed plumes of it from his feet, and toed lightly across the median strip and towards the breach point.

The first extra-quatran skill Boekidin had used in the slip was *ivaer*, and for a long time, he thought that it might be the only power available to him these realms. He soon after discovered *kiin* when gliding on his wings, and *liktas* when redirecting a mind-city's power to shut it down. It felt that in leaving the realm of the physical, his soul was open to the complete quatra experience. He had drawn no conclusions on the use of these powers as he studied them, except that perhaps we didn't know as much about quatra and the *slip* as we purported to – that maybe things were not black and white.

This was confirmed when he first produced an *ivaer* flame in the real world.

Boekidin stood above the service tunnel, the outward leaning great wall bearing over him. He would have to dig to reach the entrance, which insofar as ability wasn't an issue, but such a severe disruption to Hesslik's soul would struggle to go unnoticed. He stood, pondering, staring back into the forest and towards the stone circle.

You need your answers. He steeled himself. *The Suneva might suffer, and you're the only one who can confirm it.*

The dumb courage surged through him – Boekidin might be noticed, but he might not. Either way, a countdown would start as soon as he breached that wall, he could count on it, no matter how stealthy and careful he was. He grappled at the earth of the slip through his soul, all the way down to the service tunnel, and he *pushed.*

The fertile soil of Hesslik's soul compacted under his feet, rocking downwards. Boekidin shoved at the column again, and soon came to an open, metal pipe. It was dry, teeming with stale, hot air. Wearily, Boekidin stepped inside, and hauled at the column behind him, raising it to the ground.

It was pitch-black inside the pipe. Boekidin clicked the fingers of his claw, and a yellow fire burst to life in his palm, illuminating the long, narrow cave. He could see a ladder ahead, and a dark opening above it. He straddled the pipe carefully towards it, somehow fitting his extensive body within it. Boekidin climbed the ladder with ease, and found no lock on the manhole cover which capped it. He raised the cover slowly, peeking from underneath, to see little human activity in this area of the city. Sighing relief, he emerged from the hole, and raced towards the mind-city's centre.

Coming towards the middle, the commotion grew denser. This city populated itself with the faces Hesslik had seen in their life. No matter how important, they lived and breathed on the streets of this insulated, island state. There was no room for suburbs, or languished ghettos within these walls – Hesslik was a smart man, and his mind-city showed it. Right up to the border, skyscrapers rocketed towards the blue-shimmering limit of the forcefield.

Just like the brain, which ordered itself into regions that controlled certain tasks, so did the city of the mind, and each mind city shared a similar layout. Boekidin knew that he now walked through Hesslik's science and logic centre, a grid of buildings more futuristic than they were modern, stretching high to the dome's roof and filled with workers in suits who rushed about. It spoke to Hesslik's love of the sciences, and extensive knowledge thereof. Boekidin headed through this section to the city's centre, as just past the centre of town would be the banking sector, where the memory banks were staged.

Boekidin was careful as he walked briskly through the more crowded streets. The people here were sentries for Hesslik's subconscious. If they noticed an abnormality, their blabbering commotion and disgust for it would quickly run like fire through the whole metropolis and give him away. There was one major risk for Boekidin, and that was running into himself.

Still, he managed to avoid his alternate double, bumping into many familiar faces as they brushed past him. He noted in particular Vestas, the Suneva dressed in a suit over his armour, walking at an insane pace with an eye stuck to his watch. In his tail, the unarmoured version of the same man – the scrawny Englishman – jogged to catch up. This was a feature of only some Suneva minds – the total separation of *alis* and self. Boekidin wandered who's mind this was then, *Hesslik's*, or his human counterpart's?

Boekidin reached the city centre, a six-way intersection painted in moving billboards rising from between the highrise buildings. This was the sensory square, built high with screens which displayed what the mind's bearer saw, and speakers that blasted what they heard. Several of the city's people sat and watched here, distracted in the middle of their tasks.

Boekidin peered up to the screen too, between scanning the street options before him. To his right, just diagonally, he could see the Greek columns of a central bank towering over a thick sidewalk. On the screen though, he could see nothing of concern. Hesslik trained with Zamelle Menas, he was teaching her some meditation technique, circling around the girl with the white, glowing eye.

Boekidin waded on, through the crowd. It was easier to move quickly now, where the commotion was high and the people distracted, so he jogged. If he was being cautious, he would have gone into one of the storefronts of the sensory square and tried to determine if Hesslik's head felt strange – because even pain and touch were represented in this dimension – but he feared the answer, so he did not.

The sweeping steps of the bank came soon to Boekidin, rising out of the sidewalk and up to a set of grand, wooden doors, inset under an awning held by marble columns. This was the Central Episodic Memory Bank – it said so in an inscription on the stone awning. In this district were grand banks for sensory memories, semantic memories, and procedural memories, and in addition to these, many short-term memory banks dotted the city, but all committed memories would be brought to this street to be stored.

Boekidin climbed the steps, noting from this height the set of tubes through which memory orbs whizzed into the rear of each bank. Hesslik's memory infrastructure appeared to be one of the strongest he had seen – Hesslik must have had sharp retention.

Pushing through the doors, Boekidin found himself in a sparsely populated grand lobby, lit from sunlight streaming through a crystal domed roof. A small group formed a line before two tellers, sitting busy behind their high, marble desks. A large vault sat inset between them, and one of the tellers moved to enter it with a memory orb. The orbs themselves were the size of large fists, and appeared as cloudy glass spheres of swimming colours.

Boekidin eyed the vault, he'd need a way in that was discrete. With such advanced infrastructure on the bank's exterior, a break-in from the rear wouldn't be possible. He'd need to create a distraction here to slip in through the door. It was time to run one of his many routines.

A stumpy man brushed past him in that moment, pushing for the queue forming before the teller, but catching his suit on the Boekidin's claw. Acting quickly, Boekidin connected to his liktas abilities, and grabbing the coat to free the man, instead charged them full of electricity.

The man fell faster than an anvil, splatting on the marble lobby floor. Boekidin gasped for effect, then knelt to the body, shouting for a doctor. Soon, the crowd of the bank rushed over, a particularly concerned woman coming to brush against Boekidin.

He shocked her too, knocking her out.

As she fell, Boekidin feigned his own demise, stumbling past the crowd and falling down elsewhere. From there, he checked on the clerks to see that they still diligently manned their desks. Boekidin was getting nervous now, his time ticked away, and even though the crowd of the bank was distracted, he would have to conduct a risky move to gain access to the vault.

He pulled himself up, refusing a man's help, and stumbled towards the clerks.

"Are there doctors coming?" He asked.

"For what?" The clerk raised an eyebrow, not bothering to look from the computer screen. Boekidin peered to the second teller, to see that they had also not raised their eyes, remaining completely oblivious.

"For this, I guess." Boekidin shrugged, and grabbed the man's shoulder, zapping them too and felling them face first into the keyboard. From there, he ducked low and behind the desk, sneaking towards the vault out of the eyes of the concerned crowd.

The second teller, directly in front of him, examined an orb which they held in their hands. Begrudgingly, the woman sighed, and pulled herself from her stool. She came towards the vault, and Boekidin gasped, throwing himself into the foot space under an unoccupied desk. The woman barely looked at him anyway, instead coming towards the vault and placing her hand on a scanner.

The door clicked and chuffed pneumatically, its metal bolts shifting as the thing creaked open just slightly. The woman faxed herself into the gap, leaving Boekidin just an inch of space and a millisecond with which to follow her through.

He leapt from his haunches, throwing a claw to the door and holding it open, finally shifting his body through it.

This room was a vast, white warehouse, stretching endlessly, defying the size of the building in which it sat. Rows of filing cabinets stretched storeys from floor to ceiling, in a blinding white array.

"Who are you?" The woman turned, immediately thrown by his intrusion. Her eyes locked on a control panel nearby.

"A friend," Boekidin said, sending a claw to her face and an arc of electricity through it. She fell too, now, dropping her orb, and the Shiverman finally had Hesslik's memory vault to himself.

Boekidin decided first to investigate the dropped orb. It swam with reds and greens, but could not play its memory for an observer. Orbs instead carried their own aura, and touching them would imbue you with the *idea* of their memory.

This made sense to Boekidin, as memories were never exact playbacks of experiences. A memory of your mother handing you an icecream on your beach holiday, for example, would not contain every lump and bump on the icecream, the exact jewellery your mother wore, her perfectly rendered face, nor even the gender of the server unless they were important, nor a perfect recreation of the flavour you experienced. Instead, when you thought back on it, you would remember the feeling which invokes the *idea* of your mother. You would think of everything she represents to you, what the word 'Mum' means, probably her hair colour, the love you have for her. You would think of the enjoyment of tasting the ice cream, not the exact flavours. The cashier, unless pertinent to the point of the memory, would probably just be a faceless blob with a hand, not rendered by the brain and simply imbued with the idea of 'server'. In this way, memories stored representations of ideas and feelings, rather than exact details. The auras which surrounded the orbs told Boekidin what Hesslik felt because of their memory, and tapping into the orb would let Boekidin experience it.

This memory he held was so clouded that it held only one idea – comfort. This was likely a first memory, so often recalled that it lost any semblance to its event. Boekidin set it aside, careful not to rob Hesslik of this experience by losing it, and raced towards the right-hand side of the room.

Memory vaults were arranged chronologically, starting from the earliest memories in the bottom space of the leftmost aisle, and filling up to capacity as the person aged. There were only limited spots in the vault, and so old memories were discarded to allow the new ones to stay.

Boekidin knew roughly when I'd had my vision, around March or February of last year. He ran to that section, somewhere along the right-hand side of the room. Passing drawers as he sprinted the aisle, many of the memories contained therein reached for him, forcing their auras on him. In them he felt all emotions encroaching, but one set more than others.

Glory and joy.

Then he came to it, a column of drawers labelled as the first quarter of nineteen ninety-eight – or, roughly anyway. Some memories were misallocated when retrieved and delivered back to the bank. He tore the first drawer open, palming at the many orbs which bustled within.

He dug in the box of them, not sure what he was looking for. Most of these experiences seemed benign, things Boekidin would expect any Suneva to forget. The timing pressed on him – at least five minutes had passed since his intrusion, the bank tellers were down, the semantic memory bank was in shock. It was a smooth operation comparatively, but Hesslik was an advanced mind, and would have noticed by now. Boekidin didn't have time, he had to find this memory *now*.

He slammed open the next drawer, but didn't have to palm the orbs before noticing the strange one. Where many orbs here sang their glory, this one glowed with rainbow coloured clouds. It was mystifying in its difference, and it screamed noisily with its aura. Every emotion possible shone off it. The experience he sensed emanating from it shone of guilt overshadowed by righteousness. It sang of victory, power, and pride, yet shame and loss within.

Boekidin grabbed it, and he had to suck in a powerful breath to keep his mind straight. An onslaught eroded his perception, trapping Boekidin in a vivid reality. In it, he was Hesslik, and he had the idea that he was standing over a Suneva bearing the qualities of Vestas. They were represented by loyalty, trust, and friendship, but now muddled by something else – Vestas had become unclear within Hesslik's mind. Hesslik felt proud, yet guilt in his pride. Vestas was passed out now, as Hesslik had used his mind controlling abilities on the scientist. Hesslik didn't like that he did it, but it was the right thing to do. Vestas had today not been loyal, and Hesslik needed Vestas to see that his way was the *right* way forward.

Boekidin dug through the feelings and ideas of the moment. The dark room, the weird smell, the sense of pride in the machine just created, its proven use, the tingle in the air of his electricity having graced it. There was an idea of discomfort though, discomfort in the triumph and peace he'd attained. Hesslik finally knew how to help his people, Boekidin sensed, but the price was grave, and it was hard, and it was the only way.

No Suneva would mean no problems for the Suneva in this world.

Hesslik was going to eliminate all of the threads.

Boekidin dropped the memory. It bounced on the floor, flopping its wispy, insubstantial form around like jelly. He tried to comprehend what this meant for him, which subsequently meant that he couldn't even comprehend moving.

He felt only… disappointment. It swayed in his stomach for a moment, then settled deeply towards *betrayal*, even. *This* was Boekidin's whole life – he'd risen through every rank of current Suneva society, he'd aggressively fought human establishments who sought to bring him down, and he'd even had to argue tooth and nail against other Suneva to rise as a prominent member of Hesslik's council, his kidin powers marking him as an untrustworthy risk. All of that effort into image, the dedication to his identity, the tactical manipulation and moral unrest, the signing of his life away for the very *chance* at becoming a free kidin in society and carving the path for others to come, and it was for nothing. Hesslik had signed away his destiny, had *squashed* Boekidin's hard work, as if it never mattered.

Boekidin wasn't just disappointed, he was angry. He was enraged beyond all belief. He wanted to grab every memory orb in this goddamn hall and crush them all. He wanted to wipe Hesslik's memory clean – really fuck him up. It wasn't even something Boekidin could do, he knew he couldn't physically alter Hesslik's mind in here, this was just a viewing platform. Surely there was a way though, with all the advancements he'd made so far.

No, he couldn't do that. Hesslik was playing him… Hesslik was playing everybody, and in the end, if you wanted to get shit done, Hesslik had proven that you'd have to play somebody to get it. Boekidin would get out of Hesslik's mind and pretend nothing had happened. He could undermine and overthrow the disloyal, ungrateful Liktas. How *dare* Hesslik be given these powers and not fight for them, when so many others would fight for their rights and so many more would fight to have them – that Iva girl being one of them.

How *dare* Hesslik determine Boekidin's destiny. The black holes wouldn't allow this, or else Hesslik becomes the ultimate controller of destiny and becomes more powerful than any of the Gods. Amasos gave meaning to Hesslik, and Amasos would not let this happen.

Boekidin ran. He burst through the vault door and sprinted out into the street. He blasted off the floor in a burst of *kiin* controlled air and leaped off the skyscrapers adjacent the banks. He zipped between buildings, extending his wings and gliding on them through the city streets. He reached the sensory square, with all of its billboards and speakers showing exactly what Hesslik was seeing around him. Boekidin glanced out of curiosity, but was stopped in his tracks.

Boekidin froze, almost choking on his tongue. If he could have vomited in that moment, he would have – instead, he found himself falling out of the sky, rolling across the asphalt with a thud and grind. Boekidin had no care for scratched or dinted armour, because on the main screen glowed a truth which truly frightened him beyond anything he had ever seen.

Hesslik was standing over Boekidins body, their lightning sword directed at the *Kidin's* chest. Boekidin's body jerked from the shock its soul was experiencing, and he realised that he had never seen a *Kidin* flinch as such before.

Although he had the immediate sense that Hesslik *had*, and Boekidin knew he was fucked.

"Did you find your answers, Boekidin?" Hesslik asked, his voice booming around the quiet square. Boekidin gulped, his bubbling rage smothered for anxiety. Was Hesslik bluffing?

"I know where you are," Hesslik said, calmly.

Boekidin knew better than to give Hesslik any information – the Suneva was a master of the bluff, and gained most of his upper hand through directed questions like these. Boekidin pursed his lips behind his armour, staying perfectly still.

"You've just been to my memory banks. You're now in my sensory square. I can hear you breathing in my head."

Boekidin became aware of the sound of his breath, which he was never aware of before. Nobody else ever noticed it. How was Hesslik this perceptive?

"Now, I know you can hear me anyway, wherever you are, through your body's ears. So, if I'm wrong, you've got thirty seconds to get back to your body. If I'm right…you'll never make it."

Boekidin could feel the earth tremble beneath his feet. Through his connection to it, he felt giant structures tearing at the ground. It was all around him, something was *forming* deep under the city. There was the sound of a massive laser ignition. A second dome of light force field grew over the original one. It was so thick, and pink, that almost all outside light became obscured, casting the city in shadows. Boekidin could feel that this dome was no dome, but a sphere, encapsulating the city from every direction. There was no escape now.

"Please, Hesslik. Don't do this," he begged.

"Ah," Hesslik smirked, "we have our traitor."

"With no due respect, Hesslik. You the traitor of all the people." Boekidin's rage surfaced once more, and with dying words, there was no point holding back. Boekidin didn't know what happened when you were killed whilst mind-running. Death seemed the only logical answer.

"I see you found your answers," Hesslik said.

"I found that Maiki was right," Boekidin hissed. "I gave my life to you, because you promised me that I could be truly free to be myself in this world. *My whole life…*"

"There is no freedom for Suneva," Hesslik said, "We are controlled. We're a danger to everything."

"There might not even be free will in this world for anybody, but at least there's the sense of it," Boekidin yelled. "Don't we at least deserve a chance to prove that we're not evil? Why would you subscribe to that self-incriminating bullshit?"

"Because it's true. Every Suneva has screwed up," Hesslik spat. "We are dangerous by our design. We can kill, and for it we will forever be cast aside."

"Innocent until proven guilty, mate," Boekidin rebutted. "Most nations follow it. We were on our way to a fair system."

"Plans change," Hesslik said, "and you wouldn't have stuck around for the new one. I couldn't afford to lose you."

"What, because the Shiverman is just another of your pawns?" Boekidin hissed.

443

"Because you're one of my closest friends," Hesslik said. Their whole voice shifted as they said it. The snarky, dominant, deep tones replaced by a lighter, less commanding voice. "I'm sorry that I have to do this. I'm so close to saving us all. I can't let you stop it."

Hesslik flicked his weapon. It sparked, and almost immediately formed a red rope of deadly, hot plasma from its tip. Boekidin's body glowed crimson in its reflection. Hesslik wound up his sword arm, then slashed the fat snake of red plasma across Boekidin's neck. The armour on his body crumpled and sublimated, erupting into the air like black dust. His human head rolled off the plasma tip and landed on the ground with a wet thud. Blood poured from every orifice except the neck, which was instantly cauterised by the attack.

Hesslik removed their armour, squatted down, and cried next to the body. It had to be done, they reasoned.

Chapter 43
An Unexpected Visitor

Simone and I sat in the study on a strangely cold and cloudy January day. Her eyes, lit by the computer's blue buzz, fought the internet lazily for some kind of useful information – although her search landed her more often in procrastination. I lay draped over the couch, reading the texts that I had translated from Dad's booklet. As I did this, I let quatra energy course through my veins, my shoulder throbbing with the devil's energy to heal. Liktan words seemed to leap from the page at me, and I translated them to Simone. There were six rules Dad had passed me.

"*One must control their quatra, and not let it control them.*"

"Makes sense," Simone nodded.

"*Quatra is the source of knowledge, but the taker of free will. One must understand the duality between self-sacrifice to the cosmos and the ability to understand said cosmos.*"

"And there's Natalie's conundrum," Simone hummed. "These Vochduh might be more useful than Dad knew."

"Destiny had it that he handed this to us, literally," I mulled it over. "The man's soul found peace when he had told me everything. I don't know whether that's a good thing or a bad thing, though. I'm not sure what to think."

"It's strange," Simone noted. "Destiny for the sake of curing Suneva of destiny? There's some trap in that logic."

"Totally," I agreed, and continued. *"quatra must not be used to kill or bring harm to those without it. It can be used to defend from harm, but only at a level equal to the threat.* That's like what Hesslik and Kuvalik teach," I noted. "You can see their influences already, from self control, to quatra as a knowledge source, to the protection of others."

"You said that Kuvalik based his rules from this, though, didn't you?"

"Yeah, that's the point," I said. "It's more interesting where they *deviate* than where they agree. The Vochduh seem to have placed a strong emphasis on the sacrifice of using quatra.

"Anyway, fourthly: *an honourable fight is fought between parties of equal number. One must only instigate an honourable fight, and may disgrace a Suneva who starts a dishonourable one."*

"Hesslik has that one too," Simone hummed. She still hadn't looked away from the computer this entire time – I was surprised she could pay attention to either I or it at all.

"Doesn't encourage disgracing others, though," I pointed out. "That's a strange one."

"Eh, honour systems keep people in place better than punishment systems." Simone waved her hand. "Next."

Throughout my endeavours, I'd forgotten that Simone was a sociologist by study. The foreground of her battles was centred on Suneva and physical power imbalance, so much so that I'd forgotten just how much she might have known about societies in general, and how much they interested her.

"Combat comes second to self-understanding. Altercations should be avoided."

"That's what, fifth?" She asked. "I feel like that should go higher if they're trying to be peaceful."

"A fight with another Suneva, no matter their prowess or quatran, is considered an honourable fight."

"Why the focus on fighting all of a sudden?" she asked, finally turning to face me.

"I think the Vochduh were a warrior type city-state. The old '*enslave and conquer*' style of people," I said, closing the book. "I was shown a memory from

445

Kuvalik once that…well…gave me the idea that that was true. I never actually saw it…"

Simone wasn't sure what to say about these phantom memories, and winced away, changing the topic. "So, what are the differences then, if they're the important parts?"

"Well, Hesslik and Kuvalik put much more emphasis on banning ill-intentional quatra use," I said, thinking back to what I'd noted of Vasloka's words. *If* I'd remembered them correctly. "They both seem to discourage financial and physical exploitation of abilities, the only thing seen here is the *fair fight*."

"These Vochduh guys do seem to like a fight."

"Well, they've found a way to justify dominance over other Suneva, by the looks of it," I pointed to the sixth rule and turned the book to Simone, only then realising that she couldn't read it. "But they still seem adamant not to use these powers against regular people, which is consistent with Kuvalik."

"They probably saw themselves as superior, but *separate*, from regular people," Simone said, stroking her chin. "Like humans weren't worth their time."

"Maybe," I said, leaning into the speculation. "Still, the most jarring difference is attitudes towards destiny. Modern Suneva culture is *Liktan* culture, the kind that Kuvalik promoted hundreds of years ago. All modern Suneva praise destiny, it's a blessing. I always treated it that way too, why wouldn't you? Destiny is purpose – the Gods looking out for you."

Simone had a sly frown to this remark.

"But the Vochduh are allied with the Sunesca here, they see it as a curse, clearly. Their rules are warning against it as a trade-off to power. They seem more scared of their abilities than modern Suneva."

"It's a humility that shouldn't be lost," Simone noted. "Suneva *are* dangerous. I just wonder what the Vochduh thought of the Sunesca then."

"They interacted – Kuvalik's memory showed me that much. Sunesca appear in these texts, too." I said, and pulled over Baba's cookbook from the couch-side table. Dad had made his original rubbings of the Vochduh tablets on the paper stored therein, and I pulled these out to show Simone evidence of Sunesca in their writings.

The rest of Dad's writings, which I had read thoroughly prior to sharing the translations with Simone, had limited use to us. They were the liktan transcriptions of a number of tablet rubbings, which talked about the use of flight for ceremony, none of which elaborated on *how* to fly. One of the tablets described the proper way for a *Kiin* to enter the great Voochduh city, the *Vochduhgrad*. The familiarity of flight which these monks described, and their flippant attitude towards it as a feat, turned my face hot, and I was quick to never examine those texts again after reading them once.

I regarded the next page that I pulled out. It had the Vochduh scripture rubbed into it, and I was sure that its first half covered the first four rules – I'd seen this stone somewhere before, and maybe I'd opened this book when I was younger unknowingly. Past the fifth sentence, the rubbing was new to me. Two words did strike me though, and I pointed them out to Simone.

"See here," I pointed to the page, "this one is *Zondeca*, for the Suneva. The word near it…here…is *Zalach*, which means Salak, or Sunesca. They were clearly aware of them."

"How did you know those words?" She asked.

"Dad translated them," I scoffed. "It's all in Liktan."

"Yeah, James, I'm not stupid," Simone threw back my attitude. "But where did you learn to pronounce those letters?"

"I…uh…" I turned the rubbing towards me, and then it hit me: I'd never learned to read this script – which appeared as a mix of Liktan and Cyrillic symbols. It didn't make sense that I'd picked out the two words, even after having read a translation, but with my arm pumping full of quatra they just seemed to *pop* at me. "It's complicated," I said. "I just know that those are the words."

"*Right*," Simone tapped at her mouse. I examined the charcoal-coated page again, and another word screamed from the paper. The symbols were recognisable, but nonsensical to me. This word said *Vochduh* – and I'd read it on another tablet before, where the link had seemed more obvious. *Where was that tablet?*

I flipped through the pages, looking for the word. It was common, as were *Zalach* and *Zondeca*, but none of these were *the* place where I'd learned what the word looked like. I hummed, and I could firm a picture of the engraving in my head, that first time I'd seen it. It was clear, straight from the rock, shining in the light of the Vochduh Library.

Yes, that was it. I'd been to the Vochduh library – the Vochduhvlad had shown it to me as he greeted me into his kingdom.

I stood in his temple, having just scaled its cliff face for our meeting. Before me, its marble columns rose like legs of giants, supporting a ceiling of bored domes to the mountaintop, from which pools of light stretched to the tiled floor. My Salak robe blew in the gust, and there was nobody to greet me.

"Monk," I turned to the man I had met just before, and he was once again pulled from meditation.

"Yes, *Zalach*?"

"Where is the Vochduhvlad?" I was having a meeting with their king after all, and I had been left little for instructions.

"Head to the library," the monk said, and pointed towards the end of the temple's lobby. Past the columns and scattered, studying monks, were two embossed archways, carved into the cavern's rock. "It is the right-hand door. He will meet you in there."

"I see, thank you," I nodded, and left him, traversing the grand columns towards the lobby's rear. The monks who I passed would pause to observe me, many of their faces in awe, but all of them bowing as I passed. This was not a respect to me as the Liktan leader, but as a *Zalach*, a holy being for these monks and a focus of their studies.

I came through the archway, entering a dual-levelled cylindrical room, its walls cut into shelves and racks the whole way around, housing books and old tablets. I stood on a mezzanine which encircled the room, hanging above the library's pit which housed a lectern. Above me the room was carved into a sky-seeking dome, cut at its centre to bathe the central lectern in the sun's light. Before me, on a separate podium, stood a preserved stone tablet.

This contained the original rules of the *Vochduh* people, scribed hundreds of years ago. The rules of current use had evolved from these, and were only marginally altered.

I read and examined the handwriting of the first few rules before shuffling feet interrupted me. I turned to the entrance, to see the spectacularly robed *Vochduhvlad*. He was an impressively tall, green armoured Suneva wearing royal robes of silver, blue, and white atop his armour. His *alis* donned a wide and predatory helmet, and was comprised of thick, bulky armour, unlike the sleek *Vochduh* armies I'd seen invade my homeland. His fat fingers clutched a long, golden staff with a prong-end.

"*Zalach Nolver*," he greeted me, his voice as commanding as it was deep.

"Your learned-highness," I responded in return.

"I'm glad that you chose to join my study, Zalach Nolver," he said, stepping his broad feet towards mine. "Your *freedom* is interesting to my people. We want to understand it."

"We might be political enemies, *Skenios*, but I need your help, so I will help you in turn."

And the Vochduhvlad nodded, his smirk nothing but grateful. "There is much to learn from you, Zalach Nolver."

The memory contained nothing more right now. I found myself staring blankly past the characters on the page.

"Kuvalik could read it," I said, peering back to Simone who was now staring at a scrolling screen. "He has memories of meeting with the old Air King. There's a whole library of these texts somewhere."

"A whole library?" She turned back with intrigue. "Well, it could be useless unless you can remember the whole language from him."

I grumbled, looking back to the scribed pages. It was still only those few words which popped out at me, but two words and four sentences were more than *nothing*. "You're right, though. There's not much time, and we're talking about learning and reading a whole *language*."

"Let alone finding it," Simone pointed out, turning back to her trawl of the internet.

"Something tells me that's the easier task of the two..."

I closed the book, huffing. Out there was a library of secrets, shelves of tablets with Vochduh learnings on the Sunesca. Raking it, I might just have the *chance* to find some way to bypass destiny, but there was a lot of risk in that plan. If we committed the time to finding it and learning this ancient language, if it was even possible to do so, there was still the likelihood that it would lead to nothing – months of lost time that we didn't have. There was a difficult decision to make now, and hard work to do quickly.

I put the book aside, ready to stand, when the air shimmered between Simone and I. It cracked, as if that was possible, and from the crack in the centre of space drew ten, huge fingers. They sprang like a spider from crevasse, grappling at the crack and tearing it apart.

449

"What the *cheese!*" I yelled, pointing. I blasted air to throw myself against the back wall, and the armour of Maiki joined me there, strengthening my arm. Simone turned, and by the time she'd registered what was going on, the crack had expanded with the hands forming it, opening as an anulus to spew out a whole Suneva from its boundaries. Simone screamed and threw herself away as the Suneva fumbled onto the floor of our study, the tear closing behind them and the world restoring.

Their white and bronze armour, covered in gnarly spikes, glistened in the computer's blue haze. Their helmet was adorned by deer antlers, and their hands three times the size of a regular Suneva's and just as sharp. Noticing our cries, they joined in, yelling and pinning themselves to the far wall. They – or *she* as it appeared from their scream – tore at the wall with her metal mitt, ripping at the world just *before* the plaster, and tearing another crack through reality, and alternate world shining through the tiny hole.

"Who are you?" I yelled, but she had already committed to ripping open space and thrusting herself through it. I flicked my staff down, blasting air to the floor and shooting my body towards this mystery Suneva and their tear in space. Seeing my speed, they hastened their leap through the hole, and I landed at their foot just as the crack closed around it. I desperately grabbed at the boundary, trying to stop it consuming them, to feel that it was *tangible*, and malleable. Still, their foot flew away from me, and as I expanded the tear in the world, it swallowed me without my doing, wrapping my whole body before I could escape.

I flew through a void, like a tunnel through the universe. The world raced past me, but cross sections of it, as if everything had a column bored through it that ripped it inside out and the wrong way around. Objects which came towards me split into lasers and slivers, joining again past my belly and flying off into three directions at once. It was a nonsensical, beautiful lightshow, with things buzzing by in incomprehensible directions, indeterminable by the human brain.

The tunnel ended in a bright light, and I was spat out of it with force.

Missing my feet, I was thrown to the grass of my front yard atop my golden, armoured wrists. I went to pry myself up, but a weight fell on me, crushing me into the dirt. The Suneva atop of me rolled off hurriedly and pulled me to my feet.

"Now that is how I like to travel, Kuvalik," the strong, female Suneva said to me as she brushed off my armour. I stood tall and importantly as she did so, looking up to the sun. It was years since anybody had looked at me like the great leader I once was, but it was important to maintain the image. She chuckled at my attempt to restore my glory, so I dropped the act.

"Maybe a bit too hard on my old armour and bones now," I laughed, "but definitely worth the ride."

A fresh wind smacked me in the face, tearing me from the daydream, as I found *my* body, that of Maiki, being ejected from a sphincter in space and across a grassy field. The white and bronze Suneva was just getting to their feet as I bowled into them helplessly. Closing my eyes and protecting my face, I threw them to the dirt with a crash.

I felt their huge, spiked claw crush into my armoured neck, and I finally opened my eyes again to see them bearing over me before a sun-rise yellow sky. Their pink, radiant eyes were mean, and glowed with intent quatra.

"How did you do that?" They demanded. Their harsh accent broke their Liktan, and I'd barely registered what they'd said before their claw pressed further into my neck.

"I just followed you," I groaned. "How did *you* do that?"

The Suneva hummed, their sneer growing. "Who are you?"

There was one correct answer here, although I shouldn't have felt inclined to give it. I didn't know this Suneva or their affiliations to Hesslik, and there was no reason to trust anybody with their giant, space-ripping claw to my neck. Still, I felt compelled to be truthful. Omercronius pushed me to do it.

But should I trust destiny still?

Their sharp fingers tightened around my neck.

"Maiki!" I blurted. "I'm Maiki Luekess."

The Suneva atop me immediately changed their mind about my fate. They released me, leaping off to stand a few feet away, their gaze scuttling about the landscape.

"You're *the* Maiki," she asked.

"Yes," I replied, standing myself. They didn't try to stop me from getting to my feet.

"I've been looking for you," she said. "You and your friends."

"Ha!" I laughed, and her face dropped behind the big, pink quatra eyes. "Sorry, it's just that everybody left. Just me and Salak Nera, now."

"What, they all left?" She asked me, backing into the tall grass of the field. Peering about, I wasn't sure where I was, or *when*. Dawn was breaking overhead. "I can't be too late…do you know how long I've been looking for you? I need to help you fight Hesslik. It's my destiny."

"I think the fight's over," I mused. "If you want a fight, find Iva and join the Argols. I need help, but I'm not facing Hesslik just yet. Salak Nera and I are trying to toy with destiny so we can win back the White Witch. This is a battle of ideologies, not fists."

The Suneva gulped, but nodded. "I still want a part in it."

"Sure," I took their word, but I was still puzzled. "Who even are you?"

"I am Annikida," they said, taking a knee and stabbing their gauntleted fist into the earth. "The one living *Kida*. The Legendary of Teleportation."

End of Volume II: Code of Connections